S0-ASI-346

"Elegant . . . The book opens with a boy, lost and then found again, but truly that is the course of the whole book—what we give up, what we have taken from us, and the price such actions exact. Brown . . . draws from a careful sense of detail, used here to transform time and place, and fuel the intricate flashbacks that permeate Arthur's many lives. By the novel's end these flashbacks have imbued each small action with terrific weight. Arthur's last gestures towards Agatha are full of sweet, sad, absolute truth, and perfect balance." —*The Westchester County (NY) Journal*

"Stirring characterizations and a vivid setting drive Carrie Brown's latest novel, *Confinement*. Brown constructs a remote, cold setting that reflects the somber tone of the novel and supports each character's feelings of alienation and confinement. Adept at her craft, Brown communicates the power of the past on a person's perception of the present . . . Moving moments of hope and growth. The resolution brings promise for more than one of the characters." —*Newport News (VA) Daily Press*

"[A] piercing, unusual novel set in the suburban northeast in the years after WWII . . . The edge in the plot comes from Henning's teenage son, Toby, who wants to see his father break away from the dysfunctional Duvall family and carve out a new life of his own . . . Haunting and memorable." —*Publishers Weekly*

"It's hard not to care about these likable characters." —*Library Journal*

"The interplay between love and loss—major themes in Brown's fiction—is handled masterfully here . . . Most of the events in this novel are apparent early on, but the how and why that matter most are revealed gradually through seamlessly woven flashbacks . . . With its luminous language and an ending more sweet than bitter, this poignant, richly layered novel is something exceptional."

—*Booklist*

continued . . .

TITLES BY CARRIE BROWN

Novels

Rose's Garden

Lamb in Love

The Hatbox Baby

Confinement

Stories

The House on Belle Isle

CARRIE BROWN

Confinement

BERKLEY BOOKS, NEW YORK

THE BERKLEY PUBLISHING GROUP
Published by the Penguin Group
Penguin Group (USA) Inc.
375 Hudson Street, New York, New York 10014, USA
Penguin Group (Canada), 10 Alcorn Avenue, Toronto, Ontario M4V 3B2, Canada
(a division of Pearson Penguin Canada Inc.)
Penguin Books Ltd., 80 Strand, London WC2R 0RL, England
Penguin Group Ireland, 25 St. Stephen's Green, Dublin 2, Ireland (a division of Penguin Books Ltd.)
Penguin Group (Australia), 250 Camberwell Road, Camberwell, Victoria 3124, Australia
(a division of Pearson Australia Group Pty. Ltd.)
Penguin Books India Pvt. Ltd., 11 Community Centre, Panchsheel Park, New Delhi—110 017, India
Penguin Group (NZ), Cnr. Airborne and Rosedale Roads, Albany, Auckland 1310, New Zealand
(a division of Pearson New Zealand Ltd.)
Penguin Books (South Africa) (Pty.) Ltd., 24 Sturdee Avenue, Rosebank, Johannesburg 2196,
South Africa

Penguin Books Ltd., Registered Offices: 80 Strand, London WC2R 0RL, England

This is a work of fiction. Names, characters, places, and incidents either are the product of the author's imagination or are used fictitiously, and any resemblance to actual persons, living or dead, business establishments, events, or locales is entirely coincidental.

PRINTING HISTORY
Algonquin Books hardcover edition / March 2004
Berkley trade paperback edition / March 2005

Library of Congress Cataloging-in-Publication Data

Brown, Carrie, 1959-
    Confinement / Carrie Brown.
        p. cm.
    ISBN 0-425-20027-2
    1. Illegitimate children—Fiction.   2. Children of the rich—Fiction.   3. Teenage pregnancy—
Fiction.   4. Fathers and sons—Fiction.   5. Refugees, Jewish—Fiction.   6. New York (N.Y.)—
Fiction.   7. Chauffeurs—Fiction.   8. Adoption—Fiction.   I. Title.

PS3522.R68529C66 2005
813'.54—dc22   2004062393

PRINTED IN THE UNITED STATES OF AMERICA

10   9   8   7   6   5   4   3   2   1

For John,
as always

And for Olivia, who came to Vienna

It was only when He saw that justice by itself would undermine the world that He associated mercy with justice, and made them to rule jointly. Thus, from the beginning of all things prevailed Divine goodness, without which nothing could have continued to exist.

—LOUIS GINZBERG, *The Legends of the Jews*

You'll race through the uninhabited park,
a shadow facing more shadows.
You'll think of someone who's no more
and of someone else living so fully
that her life at its edges changes
to love. Light, more light
gathers in the room. No sleep, not tonight.

—ADAM ZAGAJEWSKI, "Lullaby"

Confinement

ONE

THE AFTERNOON THAT ARTHUR came upon
the child again, he had not been looking for him. It was not
that he had forgotten him—never. Every year on September
15, the boy's birthday, Arthur had put a notch—at roughly the
height he imagined the boy to be—in the bark of the beech
tree that stood at the highest point on the Duvalls' property.
Just this year, according to these calculations, the boy had
reached Arthur's lowest rib. Laying his hand on the trunk of the
beech tree and looking out over the fields and forest that spread
away endlessly into the distance like a deep, moving ocean,
Arthur had imagined he could feel the boy there, just below his
heart.

For a year the family who had taken the child had lived at
the same address, the double house in Wappingers Falls with
the divided front porch. Eight years ago, Arthur had watched the
front door of the house open and the couple disappear inside,
the young woman carrying the baby, the man following her, his

hand at the small of her back, the screen door falling closed behind them. Someone had tied a garland of white ribbon to the porch railing.

That fall, the willow oaks lining the street had flamed gold. Arthur had kept watch the next spring as the trees let down a soft blanket of catkins and through the summer as they spread a rippling coverlet of shade over the street. By the time fall returned, the child's family—he must call them that, for what kind of a family had he himself been to the boy?—had moved away, and Arthur lost the boy, the grandchild he had loved from street corners and from behind the steering wheel of Mr. Duvall's car, from behind newspapers and sunglasses and foolish, inadequate disguises.

Eight years passed. Then, late on a Thursday afternoon in January 1963, when the air was full of a bleak winter haze and a foot of new snow lay on the ground, Arthur found him again.

HE HAD BEEN to Creston that day, running errands. In the backseat of the car was the box of groceries for Peggy, who stubbornly maintained a full kitchen for the Duvalls despite the fact that Mr. Duvall was rarely at home anymore. After leaving the grocery store, where he had bought two net bags of oranges and grapefruit, a box of Wheaties, and a sack of rye flour, Arthur had stopped at the dry goods store to pick up the crimson velvet that he had ordered for a dress for one of Peggy's friends. When he got back into the car, the windshield was coated again with light snow. The steering wheel felt like ice.

At the intersection ahead, a snowplow had stopped. A car, its nose deep into a dirty drift at the curb, blocked the side street where Arthur usually turned to head home. Two women in galoshes stood helplessly in the road. The driver of the plow descended wearily from the cab, a snow shovel in hand. He waved Arthur past with an impatient gesture. Arthur hesitated— should he get out and help? But the man waved him away again, and so Arthur drove on for another block and took the next turn instead.

Creston was a small town. Over the seventeen years he had been in America, the seventeen years he'd been driving the Duvalls, Arthur had found a reason to travel down practically every one of its streets. He slowed now to turn the corner. He knew these neatly kept, modest houses. Children played here, pedaling bicycles up and down the sidewalks under the trees in the summer. On warm afternoons, an ice cream truck idled at the corner.

He was halfway down the street, past a little fir tree strung crookedly with colored Christmas lights that glowed in the half dark of the late afternoon, when he saw him.

At the sight of the boy crouched in the snow, his fair head shining in the bleak winter light, Arthur panicked, disbelieving. Even as he stepped on the brakes, he knew he shouldn't have; the car slid heavily on the icy street, slipping sideways toward the boy's small front yard, the insignificant picket fence, the snowman hunched by the mailbox, a plaid scarf wound like a turban about its empty face. In the backseat of the car, the box containing the groceries tipped over. Oranges tumbled across the car floor; suddenly the air was full of the smell of them. Arthur spun the wheel frantically, though everything he had learned about driving in snow in America told him this was the wrong thing to do; and then finally, just a few feet shy of the mailbox, the car gently righted itself, bumping up against the curb like an ocean liner pulling into its berth. Arthur, breathing hard, brought it to a stop.

He looked up. A white curtain moved in a window of the house; Arthur thought he saw the woman's face peer out from behind the glass. He held his breath, expecting the door to open. But nothing happened. The snowfall of the night before, twelve inches and higher in the drifts, made everything unusually quiet. The muffled stop and start of traffic at the intersection behind him, the noise of someone scraping a windshield a few driveways away, the whine of tires spinning in the snow— all these sounds came to Arthur as if from a faraway place.

Arthur watched. The boy had not looked up at the sharp squeal of Arthur's brakes, or at his thudding collision with the curb. Not even a glance. He was busy heaping snow onto the battlements of a fort, patting it with his mittened hands. His nose and cheeks were bright from the cold. His fair hair ruffled in the wind.

Sparkling, Arthur thought. He sparkles.

This time Arthur knew he was right. There could be no mistake. He had not seen him for almost eight years, but the child looked exactly as his father had looked at that age—he had Toby's white gold hair, Toby's expressive mouth and chin; even the intensity of the boy's posture looked like Toby's. For a moment Arthur wavered in a sickening confusion of time. Everything he had lost—his son, his grandson—came roaring up out of the past in a dark wind that clamped its palms over Arthur's eyes.

What was he seeing?

The little boy was consumed with his play. A car in clanking snow chains came down the street and passed Arthur. Two enormous black crows flapped onto the snow a few feet away from the boy, working their wings and restlessly hunching their shoulders. Big mottled gulls, lured inland from the icy floes on the nearby Hudson River to the dirty parking lots and Dumpsters of Creston's grocery store and lunch counter, careened and circled in the sky overhead, calling in their melancholy voices. Across the street, a car's engine started up suddenly and backfired once with a loud report. But the boy knelt undisturbed in the snow within the circling walls of his ice castle, his head bowed, his hands busy, the weak light of the ending day in his pale hair. He had left little booted footprints in the snow.

The child's physical likeness to Toby was astonishing. And yet it was more than that: his posture, as he stood up suddenly and prepared to leap over the lowest wall of his snowy fortress, mimicked that of Toby's in a photograph Arthur had saved, taken of Toby at roughly the same age as the child was today—eight, Arthur calculated. Eight years and four months. Though it was faded now and curled at the edges, Arthur had kept the old photograph of Toby tucked into the mirror on the dresser in his bedroom. The picture had been taken on a day of rare sunshine seventeen years before, the first winter after the war

ended, when Arthur and Toby had come to the Duvalls'. Toby
had climbed into one of the apple trees at the end of the rear
kitchen garden, the raised beds like mounded graves under the
glittering white snow. Toby held in his hand an apple, incongruously red and ripe, which had been given to him by Peggy in
the kitchen a few moments before. His face wore a defiant
expression, as though he had been caught at something and
snared in the bare branches of the apple tree while in flight
from his pursuers. He balanced on a lower branch, one arm
hooked around the tree trunk, his free hand holding the apple,
one leg resting in midair as if aiming for an invisible stair step
that would take him higher. Behind him, the bare twigs of the
tree embroidered curving shapes on his shoulders like the trans-
parent, veined wings of dragonflies. Arthur always thought of
Icarus, the boy who flew too near the sun, when he looked at
that picture.

But that is not what happened to Toby. Arthur felt the Duvalls'
failure in the matter—never Agatha's and never Toby's. But
mostly he was aware of his own cowardice, lurking like something frightful that crouched in the shadows and leaped out
with fangs and talons, causing Toby to beat his wings in fear
and horror and escape.

Toby, wherever he was, would be twenty-six now. But he had
left the Duvalls'—left Arthur, left Agatha, left the newborn son
he had never seen—and had never come back, never written.

In his worst moments, Arthur assumed Toby was dead.

• • •

LONG BEFORE, IN VIENNA, a crowd of men with their Nazi armbands had beaten a man in the street outside Arthur's uncle's shop.

Arthur had known the man only by sight. Dr. Ornstein had been a customer at the shop, and Arthur had once delivered a suit to his grand top-floor apartment and surgery on the Türkenschanzplatz near the park; a maid had come to the door in her carpet slippers and soiled apron that day. Arthur had never spoken to Dr. Ornstein himself. Yet it was Dr. Ornstein, a virtual stranger, who often appeared in Arthur's memories of Vienna, as if his own past had fallen away into a chasm. There was only Dr. Ornstein and his bloody face and hands, every moment of his beating on the street as clear to Arthur as if it had taken place only the day before.

It was a March evening in 1938 when Austria gave way to Hitler. Arthur and his uncle Julius had been in the shop, hunched over the radio, listening to Chancellor Schuschnigg's farewell to his people. At the sudden sound of trucks roaring in the plaza outside, they had looked up, alarmed. Truck after truck full of screaming men, swastika flags fluttering over their heads, rolled into the square.

Dr. Ornstein's children attended a fencing school near the shop. He sometimes came to fetch his son and daughter after their five o'clock lesson, and Arthur, on an errand for Julius in the street, would raise a hand in greeting to the doctor where he sat waiting in the coffeehouse across from the shop, enjoying a *Kapuziner* and reading the newspaper at one of the tables by the window. When the trucks roared into the square, people on the street scattered in terror. But Dr. Ornstein only stood up from his table, a copy of the *Neue Freie Presse* in his hand, his coffee and whipped cream unfinished, and stepped outside.

A Jew, Arthur thought. A Jew, and he thought those hysterical, murderous madmen in the trucks would not touch him.

How could none of them have seen it coming?

Only much later did it occur to him that Dr. Ornstein had been worried about his children, that he had gone out into the street, despite his own fear, to try to find them, two beautiful young people, freshly showered after their fencing lesson and hoping for pancakes or curd cheese dumplings with sugar at the coffeehouse if their father was still at his table.

A policeman, a swastika brassard already over the sleeve of his green Austrian uniform, descended on Dr. Ornstein in the furious crowd that spilled from the trucks.

Arthur's uncle hurried to bolt the door and turn off the lights, pulling Arthur away from the window, but not before Arthur saw Dr. Ornstein fall to the street on his knees in his striped trousers, his hands over his head, his fallen newspaper fanned out around him on the pavement.

No one could come to his aid until the troopers had moved on, leaving behind them a wreckage of broken glass, including the windows of Arthur's uncle's shop. When Arthur and Julius helped him to his feet at last, Dr. Ornstein, blood running down his nose and mouth, his trousers torn and bloodied, silently held out his precious surgeon's hands.

His fingers had been broken.

WAS IT THEN that Arthur's own childish belief in God, the unexamined assumption that had passed for faith, had been shaken? Dr. Ornstein was a Jew. Arthur's uncle was a Jew. Arthur and his wife and newborn son, Toby, were Jews. But what did that mean to him? Arthur had been to the Stadttempel on Seitenstettengasse with his uncle Julius as a child, though they'd stopped going after Arthur was separated from the Gentiles with the other Jews at the *Volksschule* he attended until he was fourteen, where a crucifix hung in a prominent place on the wall in the classroom. But they were not observant Jews; they'd also been to Christmas celebrations at the homes of well-to-do Jewish friends whom Julius courted and whose social position he envied, all of them standing around the tree singing "Silent Night." The difficulty of this—what Arthur had only later recognized as difficulty—had not troubled him at the time. He was young, and he knew too little about being a Jew to recognize either his uncle's dissembling, or his sense of loss, or his desperation to be successful, to be accepted, to be safe.

But the war changed everything. What had passed for Arthur's faith, the flickering, unformed thing that he had unconsciously counted as his faith, was extinguished in the face of the war. He was a Jew who knew scarcely anything about how to be a Jew, but he listened to the radio reunions of survivors broadcast on WNYC. He read the accounts in the newspapers of what they found in the camps. He made himself consider how Dr. Ornstein, surely, had died: gassed, or burned in an oven, or shot. He stood in the synagogue with the Lehmans, in the early years of his immigration to America, or, later, in the Duvalls' little white Episcopal church in Creston at Christmas or Easter, looking over the bare heads of the husbands and the heads of the wives in their perch hats with scraps of netting and bunches of artificial berries, or in their neat Lilly Dache cloches, with his doubt and his disbelief and his sorrow seeping out of him, running down his arms and out his sleeves to fill his palms with an invisible weight.

Still, after everything that had happened, with no experience or example or evidence of God's existence, Arthur talked to God. He did it, he sometimes thought, out of loneliness, the way a child speaks to an imaginary friend when there are no real friends to be had, when that child finds himself in a place where no one is familiar, when the language being spoken by all those who surround him is foreign or strange. He talked to God, and he talked to Dr. Ornstein, turning back and forth between them as if one might contradict the other, as if between them, man and his Maker, the inscrutable darkness might be swept away and truth come forward to take its place.

God never spoke back, but if anything proved his existence, Arthur thought, it was the terrible precision of His wrath against Arthur: it had taken exactly the shape of Toby's absence.

THERE WAS SOMETHING else in that old photograph of Toby that looked like today, looked like the peaceful, quiet square of front yard in Creston, pristine and white, its single child busy on his hands and knees in the snow, the air filling with the smoky haze of winter twilight: in the photograph, you saw the same sad ending of the day's light, the sun falling toward the western horizon and the ragged shoulder of Wallace Mountain, in whose shadow the Duvalls' property lay and whose gloomy bulk fell early on winter afternoons, submerging the fields below in its shadow. On certain freezing nights, from Wallace Mountain's rocky slopes and bare tree line and cold eastern hollows, Arthur had heard the screams of bobcats, and he knew that thickets of hickory and ash and twisted laurel hid caves whose walls glittered with mica, where bears and wolves wintered. In the photograph of Toby in the apple tree, you could see Wallace Mountain in the distance and, in the foreground, a fraction of Agatha's eight-year-old cheek, just the edge of her fur-trimmed hood, the slightest suggestion of her face tilted up toward Toby, watching him fly away.

Arthur closed his eyes briefly. If he were Aggie, would he want to know what had happened to the child?

Over the years since the child's disappearance, Arthur had been spared that question's barb. What he had to tell Aggie— that he had followed the couple who had adopted the baby, that he had tried to keep sight of him for a year—became without consequence once the family had moved away. What good would it have done to tell her then, when he knew so little, when the child had vanished? But now, with the boy's miraculous reappearance, Arthur felt the question emerge with an urgency that had not been there before. If the boy could vanish once, he could vanish again. How long did Arthur have?

Idling at the curb, his excitement so great that it set up a

sickness in him like a chill, Arthur marveled at the likeness between child and father. It was shameless, his pleasure at the
boy's beauty. Toby, too, had been a beautiful child, beloved in
England and America alike even by strangers whose antipathy
toward the refugees was often melted by the plight of children.
Once again, strangers had come to his aid after Anna and the
baby girl born in London and Arthur's uncle Ivo had been killed
in the bombing, a whole terrace of houses in London's Gold-
ers Green destroyed one night by a series of bombs, the humped
Anderson shelters in the back gardens collapsed in on themselves, steel death traps.

An angel, they said of Toby. What an angel.

THE BOY'S NEW HOUSE—though who knew how long
the family had lived there now—was a step up from the duplex
they'd lived in before. It had a steep, black-shingled roof with a
single dormer, a red front door. Small shrubs under the front
windows were bound up with burlap and rope against the winter's snow and ice, making them look like the victims of a kid-
napping. The boy knelt in the shallow front yard. His gray snow
jacket was unzipped, his head bare. A hand-knit muffler of blue
wool with a white fringe was wound around his neck. He worked
alone in the late afternoon light while two squirrels ran back
and forth overhead along the snow-covered branch of a tree.

Had the family been here all the time, ever since leaving the
house in Wappingers Falls? Arthur had driven down this street
before, past this house. There was an Esso station that he used

sometimes at the corner, and on the other corner a liquor store with a silent man who wore a black patch over one eye and helped him load into the trunk of the car the cases of wine Mr. Duvall ordered. Countless times over the years, as if his hope had refused to be extinguished, Arthur had imagined he'd found the boy again. Once, early on, he had seen a stroller parked in front of the drugstore in Creston, a yellow balloon tied to the stroller's handle. A woman, her back to Arthur, one slim foot up on the brick stoop of the drugstore, had been turned away to exchange greetings with a passerby, an old man in a hat who leaned down, smiling, to offer a bent finger to the child in the stroller. Coming down the sidewalk behind her, Arthur had stopped, stared, and then moved slowly forward, recognizing the woman's red curls, recognizing—he thought— the child's dimpled wrist, his hair the shade of apricots, two feet in white socks waving playfully in the air. The woman's face was a blur reflected in the glass of the drugstore window, her hair tossed by the wind and bright as a penny among the apothecary jars and pyramids of soap and potted geraniums. But then she turned around, and she was a stranger. Inside the stroller, the child's face was too young, impossibly unfamiliar, a betrayal. How could he have mistaken them?

It was because he had wanted it so much.

ONE DAY THAT first year after the child was born, after months of Arthur's surveillance, there had been boxes on the porch of the old duplex in Wappingers Falls, and a car with its trunk open. Arthur, who had managed to drive by at least once or twice a month since the couple had brought the baby home, had stayed as long as he dared that day, though he was late picking up Mr. Duvall in the city that evening and Mr. Duvall was annoyed. By the time he could return to the house, two days later, he had known it would be too late.

The old woman who lived in the other half of the house came to the door when he knocked. She talked to him through a crack, the chain on the door still latched.

"If they wanted you to know where they'd gone, they would have told you, wouldn't they?" she had said craftily. He'd realized it was his accent: Years after the war, people were still afraid of a German accent, and they could not distinguish the Austrian from the Berliner, of course, or the Jew from the Nazi. All Germans had become Nazis after the war. People thought first of the Nazis when they heard a German voice; later, sometimes, they would remember that some Jews spoke German as well.

"They're good people. You leave them alone," she had cried after him as he left, walking heavily down the porch steps and across the sidewalk to the car. The terrifying sight of it, the long black Lincoln Mr. Duvall favored, brought the woman's door slamming shut and a final silence. In the past, Arthur had left the car at the gas station a few blocks away, asking them to change the oil for him.

He had been lucky enough to see the boy up close only once; who could blame him, he thought later, that he had lingered then, wanting to fill himself up with the sight of the child?

Turning the corner one mild summer evening that first year, he had seen the baby carriage parked alone on the porch of the house. Arthur had waited a moment on the sidewalk, but no one had come out to frighten him away, so he had quietly climbed the steps. In the carriage, the baby had looked up at him. His hair was fine and light, an almost pure white. In his little hands he clutched a stuffed animal, a monkey. He slowly raised it to his mouth as Arthur watched, biting down on one ear, staring back at Arthur. Arthur's gaze had traveled over the child's round cheeks, the delicate curve of his ears, the tempting, familiar flesh of his knees. Arthur had wanted to take the boy in his arms, wanted to lay just one palm on the child's head, touch him just once. But then he had heard the sound of footsteps approaching from inside the house, a woman's heels, and he had hurried off the porch and down the sidewalk. Pausing to lift his watch from his pocket and pretending to inspect its face, he had turned enough to see the young woman, a scarf tied over her bright hair, reach down to pick up the child. For a moment, as she stood there with the baby in her arms, she had looked at Arthur. But he had turned his face away and continued walking.

Then today, just as he had found him again, he was gone.

The side door of the house opened as Arthur sat there in his car at the curb. The woman came out, pulling a sweater around her, her boots unlaced at the tops. She'd had her hair cut short since Arthur had seen her last. Trimmed to a thick, shining bob around her head, it moved in the wind. She came across the snow toward the child and stopped to squat beside him, putting out her hand to touch the walls of the castle, touch the boy's head, smiling down at him. The boy glanced up at her, returning her smile. After a moment the woman stood, and the child stood as well. She bent down to brush snow from his knees, zip up his coat, tug the muffler close around his throat, still smiling down into his face. And then she turned with him, her hand on his head, back toward the house. She had not spoken a word.

Arthur, his heart wild in his chest, took note of all that had happened. Not a word had been exchanged between them—he'd noticed that. There was quiet then, he thought, in this house. That was good. No one shouted or raised a hand in this little white house with its one dormer and its green shutters. They loved this boy, and he was glad to run inside to the warm kitchen beside the woman who had become his mother.

Arthur sat still in the car for a moment. Then he reached awkwardly into the backseat and picked up the spilled oranges, replacing them in the box. One had split open on the floor mat, and it came up wet and sweet-smelling in his hand, with the scent of rot. Arthur started the car and drove away, turning toward the Duvalls'.

That would be enough to tell Agatha, he thought. The people who had taken him loved him.

Two

Snow had fallen heavily in the winter of 1946, and the open countryside beyond New York City lay white and glittering in the late afternoon light. Fence wire between nearly buried posts flashed past, skimming the unbroken surface of the snow. Here and there, fir trees climbed the slopes, verging to black in the defiles between hills, dark resting-places for the eyes.

Arthur sat in the backseat of the car, Toby beside him, the sewing machine and their two suitcases in the trunk. Blinded by the blazing light off the snowfields, they squinted out the windows in a mutual silence that Arthur feared weighed upon the Lehmans, who wanted them to be happy and deserved to expect it, having already gone to so much trouble on their behalf, this afternoon's drive being the least of it. Arthur had wanted to feel confidence about the trip, pointing to things, drawing Toby's attention to various sights. He was aware of trying to disguise his own trepidation and aware of failing. A child should feel excitement at this journey; he wanted Toby to feel pleased—here they were, in America at last, on their way to their new home—but his own voice sounded unnatural to him.

"We can go sleighing, yes?" he asked heartily, loud enough for the Lehmans to hear, his hand on Toby's small knee. "So much snow?"

There was nothing outside the car windows but the weary beauty of whiteness and more whiteness, the occasional crumpled outcropping of rock close by the road and bearded with yellowing cataracts of ice.

What kind of God would make a place like this, so forbidding and empty?

God was often in Arthur's thoughts, and yet he had never known how to arrange God's expression in his mind. God's face was shifting and vaporous. Sometimes he was the small God who walked in the Garden of Eden and addressed Adam and Eve face-to-face ("Can a house hide itself from an architect?"); this was the God Anna imagined, she'd told Arthur, a God who comes from between the trees to ask his questions and make his accusations. But sometimes he was the God of unimaginable proportions, the God who flooded the world and then caused a wind to make the floodwaters dry up, the God who stood by and let a terrible war happen, let all the Jews be murdered. Regardless, Arthur thought, Anna had always known the words to say to God; she had known *how* to pray. She had blessings for this and that, for peace, for forgiveness, for redemption, for after meals, for before meals, and Arthur heard her prayers with a feeling of pride and pleasure: he had married a woman who could talk to God properly. Arthur's own conversations with God, his own prayers, drifted like a river without banks to guide it. He could only speak to God as he would speak to anyone, and he did not know, now, whether even Anna would have been able to pray to a God who could fail to rise up against such evil as the world had seen.

You hurried here, he thought now, watching out the car window and assessing God's performance in this new place that was America. You rushed.

Arthur cupped his hand to the glass and bent his face close to the window; the snowy folds of the fields and hills appeared to have been gathered up recklessly by a large hand. Seams of forest ran through the whiteness like heavy black stitches. If there was comfort or beauty to be found here, it might be in summer, Arthur sensed, when green would soften the countryside and hide its crude edges. America was a new place, he reminded himself, a wilderness. He did not think it majestic, though that was the word people used when describing America for those who had never seen it, a place of canyons and deserts and mountains and plateaus and raging rivers, at every coast a new ocean. But this place now, this countryside just beyond New York City, seemed instead close and complicated, hard to look at and take in, as if after a recent upheaval. It was a place where you could easily lose your way, baffled by the roads' twists and turns.

They drove past a house, smoke from its chimney streaming away into the wind, white against the sky. A lonely figure by the side of the road, so bundled up that it was impossible to tell if the person was a man or a woman, turned around to watch them drive past. Arthur reached over and pulled Toby close.

AT LAST THE DAY began to fade into evening, and the glare from the snow-covered fields dimmed. The long blue shadows of bare trees fell over the fields and arched across the road. When Arthur craned his neck and looked up, he could see a few stars low in the deep blue of the eastern sky. Leaning over, he pointed them out to Toby, who nodded gravely and leaned back again against Arthur, his eyes sad and watchful.

"It will be an adventure," Arthur had told Toby in London when he was informed that he and Toby had been sponsored to come to America. "Everyone wants to go there. We are very lucky."

"I want to go home," Toby had said, but Arthur knew he didn't really mean that. He could remember nothing of Vienna; he was less than a year old when they had escaped after Hitler's triumphant march into Austria, when Jews were dragged out of their homes to scrub the pavements by hysterical mobs shouting, "*Ju-de ver-recke!* Perish, Jew! At last the Jews are working! Thanks to our fürher!"

During the Anschluss the windows of the shops owned by Jews had been smashed and their contents looted; men had been dragged away from their wives and children by SS officers in the middle of the night. Sometimes, later, there were photographs of these men in the SS newspaper *Das Schwarze*

Corps (The Black Corps), looking ill and unshaved: the Gestapo refused to allow the prisoners to shave, as if to confirm the anti-Semitic notion that all Jews were filthy. Most of these men had been killed then or later in Theresienstadt or Auschwitz or Bergen-Belsen, names of places where the extent of human atrocity and suffering was only still beginning to be known to the world.

Toby could remember nothing of that, for which Arthur was grateful.

Sometimes, though, he would surprise Arthur by the fierceness of what he claimed were memories: the mottled gray-and-white branches of the trees along the Kärntnerstrasse; the shop of the one-eyed clockmaker Farkas and the beautiful watches in his window; the silken spaniel who lay at the feet of the old men who played chess in the park; the pan of ice in the larder; the night porter at the hotel by the streetcar stop who sang "Erlkönig" or "An die Musik" on the sidewalk under the hotel's awning. How could he remember such things, a child who was only six months old when they escaped for the relative safety of England? Anna had told him these things, Arthur knew, whispering to him when they sat crouched in London's bomb shelters or in the Tube, describing it all for him so that he would know his home if he ever saw it again.

"It will be an adventure," Arthur had insisted in England, rubbing Toby's back after his bath one night; his thin back, his delicate arms and legs, were pink and flushed. "In America there is freedom. In America you can grow rich and wise."

"I want a dog," Toby had said suddenly, turning within the embrace of the towel to look at him.

"Yes. OK. A dog," Arthur had said, grateful. "We'll have a dog."

THEY HAD HOPED to arrive at the Duvalls' earlier in the day, in time for dinner perhaps, or at least before nightfall, but there had been trouble about borrowing the car, Mr. Lehman had explained, apologizing, and then the roads were difficult because of the snow. At half past four it grew dark, and Mrs. Lehman passed a packet of sandwiches to them in the backseat, and a chocolate bar for Toby. A little later she turned around to offer Arthur a cup of sweetened coffee poured from a thermos; it spilled onto his cuff when he leaned forward to take it from her, and he folded back his sleeve so as not to have the cold wetness next to his skin. In the front seat, Mr. Lehman fussed over the heater. It was cold, and the heat in the car didn't seem to work very well.

Arthur shared the coffee in sips with Toby and tore the sandwiches into bits that he fed to him as if he were a baby; about the chocolate, Toby shook his head. He wanted to save it.

Toby had been storing things in the cloth pocket of the suitcase he had been given when they left England two weeks before on the army transport ship—food, scraps of paper, even the mittens Mrs. Lehman had made for him. Worried, Arthur had ventured to speak of it to Mrs. Lehman, hoping also to soften her dismay about the mittens, which Toby had never worn despite having received them politely; Mrs. Lehman could be touchy, he sensed, as very generous people sometimes were. But she had seemed to understand when he tried to explain it, and he was glad he had made the effort. It would pass when they were settled, she said. She had seen such things before, children who refused to speak or eat, children who never cried. Hadn't it been hard on everyone, but especially on the poor children?

The next day, Arthur caught her hand lingering gently on Toby's head when he came to the table and sat quietly to eat. Another kind of crossing had been safely accomplished, Arthur thought. Now it was just—what was the expression?—one foot before the other.

LONG AFTER THE EARLY winter darkness had fallen and he and Toby had been jostled together in and out of sleep so often that Arthur had lost all sense of time, Mr. Lehman turned the car off the empty road. The quiet of the snow-filled night deepened as they passed slowly between the high banks of a long lane; even the trunks of the trees were flocked with snow caught in the rough bark, and Arthur had the impression of crossing into a place of deeper, more permanent cold. Overhead, swiftly moving clouds slid away to reveal the moon and a piece of black sky bristling with stars. Alerted by the change in light—he could see far away down the fields now, over their endless frozen sameness—he craned his neck to look behind them. The fields on either side of the lane shone coldly under the lamp of the moon, beautiful and forlorn.

Ahead of them, the house's long, low shape was defined by glowing windows under snug dormers. It nestled like a remote hostel in a depression between two low hills, smooth and flawlessly white, that rose away into the darkness. The wind had driven deep drifts into the little valley, piling snow high against stone walls that ran away from the house in uncertain dark lines and then disappeared into whiteness.

They proceeded slowly, the tires spinning here and there when they encountered deep snow that had fallen over the road since a plow had last been through. Arthur's gaze traveled from the steady lights of the house, which grew brighter as they approached, out across the immaculate surface of the snow-covered fields, faintly blue in the moonlight, and back to the house again. Towering oak trees, their heavy bare limbs each carrying a shadow weight of snow, leaned close around the house. Boughs of evergreen banked the lowest windowsills, and yellow light shone behind the windows' glass.

The front door of the house opened as the car crunched to a halt. The solid shape of someone moved against the light, withdrew, and returned, shrugging into a coat.

"They're still awake," Arthur heard Mr. Lehman murmur to his wife in the front seat.

"Will they ask us to stay, do you think?"

From the backseat, Arthur watched Mrs. Lehman's head disappear as she bent to gather up her belongings, the knitting she was able to do even in the dark. Every immigrant was given a pair of mittens.

"I hope so." Mr. Lehman passed a handkerchief over his forehead.

"I brought a bag. Just in case."

Mr. Lehman turned around. Arthur saw his bald head glistening and felt a moment's shame: he had been brought all this way without any effort on his own part, as if he were a helpless child. A man older than he, almost old enough to be his grandfather, had done all the work, finding their way, steering through the snow, holding the car over icy stretches of road.

Mr. Lehman looked down at Toby, smiling. "He's asleep."

Arthur shifted his shoulder where Toby had slumped against him and patted Toby's warm cheek to wake him.

Mrs. Lehman turned around and glanced at Toby, who was struggling sleepily to bury his face against Arthur's coat. "It's a shame to have to wake him now," she said. "Still, he'll see it all tomorrow." She turned around again and gazed vaguely into the darkness. "A boy's paradise, this."

More figures had appeared at the front door, crowded against the light, looking out. Arthur thought a child was among them, a girl in a nightgown. He didn't know they had a child, too. No one had said anything about a child.

Mrs. Lehman cracked open her car door as the man came up alongside them, a compact, dark shape in a heavy coat.

"You found your way," Arthur heard him say. "The roads were bad?"

Arthur watched as Mrs. Lehman climbed out, awkward in

her long wool coat and rubber boots. The man took her arm to help her.

"It's deep, but he took it slow," she said. "We've kept you waiting."

"Not at all. We were only just beginning to worry that perhaps you had turned back if the roads were very bad. Come in, come in. What can I help you with?"

The back door of the car was pulled open abruptly. A cold dryness, crossed by the tang of woodsmoke, entered the car, along with a glare from the snow, illuminated by the light falling from the open door. Toby burrowed against Arthur.

"You're Arthur." The man leaned inside, extending a hand. "Welcome."

SOMEHOW THEY WERE helped to the door up the snowy path, Arthur holding Toby in his arms, Mr. Lehman and Mr. Duvall carrying the bags and the sewing machine between them.

In the front hall, with its low ceiling and a staircase that vanished up toward a dark landing, the women backed away from the door to let them in. Snow from the travelers' boots fell onto the rugs. The little girl Arthur had seen in the doorway scurried up the stairs a few steps and sat down, staring at them, pulling her nightgown over her knees and her feet, on which she wore a pair of red slippers with pointed toes, like an elf's.

"You must be Arthur." One of the women—she must be Mrs. Duvall, Arthur thought—came forward, a wineglass in her hand. She was small and slim, her blond hair held off her face with a black ribbon. She wore gray slacks and a white shirt of soft material tucked into the waistband. She was lovely, yet she seemed in her exquisiteness not quite real to Arthur, like a statue made of gold that had come troublingly to life one day. She reminded him of no woman he had ever known, certainly not his Anna with her friendly, consoling imperfections, the sprinkling of raised moles across her shoulders, the surprised exposure of gum above her top teeth when she laughed, the asterisks of broken blood vessels at the backs of her knees.

Mrs. Duvall put her hand on his arm and then briefly on Toby's head where it rested against his father's shoulder, his face averted from the light and so many strangers.

"I'm Nina Duvall," she said, smiling, looking up into Arthur's face. "Welcome. And here's Peggy, and Kitty." She held out a graceful hand with a formal, slightly comic grandness. One of the women she indicated, the younger of the two—though the woman was approaching fifty or so, Arthur thought—was extraordinarily tall, over six feet, with coarse black hair cut short like a man's and bristling away from her face where it grew low on her temples. She made Arthur think of a big dog—the heavy jowls, the wide mouth, the lack of guile in her expression. She grinned at him and nodded her head in greeting. The older woman was gray haired and heavyset, mother to the giantess, perhaps. He saw something alike in their faces, besides the familiar, entrenched expression of servants: a broad forehead, fat like folds of turtle skin at the chin and neck. The older woman was missing two fingers on one hand, which she had entwined closely with the other over an apron. He wondered if the women were, like him, refugees who had been taken in to work for the Duvalls.

"I've made coffee, Mrs. D.," the giantess said. " I'll go and get the pot." Her voice was loud, her accent American. Arthur felt a pang of disappointment.

The mother followed her daughter at a shuffle through a swinging door, giving Arthur a sly smile as she went, as if they had a secret together. Her slippers were broken-down at the back and her cracked heels sat unevenly in them. Arthur heard the women's voices pick up in rapid conversation as the door closed.

"Don't unpack, beyond what you'll need tonight, Arthur." Mr. Duvall moved past them, heading up the stairs with Arthur's bags. "Aggie, you're in the way."

The little girl made herself small against the banister to avoid the suitcase swinging by her ear and looked down at Arthur. She had large gray eyes set in a compact face like her father's, the even features gathered together neatly. Like her father's, her face gave the impression of efficient balance, of boyish pertness, rather than beauty, but her eyes redeemed her from being plain. Her brown hair was untidy around her head, as if she'd woken up at the noise of the visitors' arrival and had hurried downstairs straight from her pillow.

Mr. Duvall's voice came down to them in the hall as he reached the turn at the landing. "You'll stay here tonight," he called down. "It's too late to walk over to the cottage now. Not in all this snow."

Mr. Duvall's feet and Arthur's bag disappeared from sight at the turn in the stairs.

There was nothing rude in his way of speaking; he was used to giving orders—that was all. But his manner could create a smallness in other people, Arthur sensed, as if they had no voice in what happened to them. Arthur was sensitive to that now, the superior tone of people who had survived the war intact, their homes and their possessions and their family members untouched. Mr. Duvall wouldn't necessarily care about that, though; he did not have time to talk about things that could not be changed. He himself did not linger over matters, Arthur guessed.

Arthur saw Mr. and Mrs. Lehman exchange a glance—were they being blamed for arriving so late? Arthur felt a spasm of worry: if the Duvalls were annoyed with the Lehmans, it was his fault. But Mr. Lehman lifted Arthur's other suitcase and the sewing machine in its battered black box and began to climb the stairs after Mr. Duvall, hesitating on the step by the little girl and then hoisting the bag high to avoid her as she crouched low against the banisters.

"Agatha." Mrs. Duvall moved forward. "Come down and say hello properly to Arthur. You're in the way there."

The little girl hesitated and then, without another glance at them, flew up the stairs instead behind Mr. Lehman, her white nightgown billowing.

Nina Duvall turned back to Arthur with a smile that seemed to ignore the fact that her daughter—he supposed she was their daughter—had run away upstairs and refused to be polite.

Arthur felt himself take note of the lapse, storing it up against something he could not yet identify.

They were not perfect, these Duvalls.

"You must be so tired." Mrs. Duvall's sympathetic smile broadened to include Mrs. Lehman, who stood by the front door still, her big purse held in her hands, her coat dusted with snow, her eyes bright and watchful. "Please come in and sit down. Would you like coffee?"

"Maybe they'd like something stronger after that drive," said Mr. Duvall, returning down the stairs. Mr. Lehman followed him, relieved of Arthur's suitcase and the sewing machine but sweating now worse than before.

"What can I get you, gentlemen?" Mr. Duvall asked, smiling at Arthur as he passed him. "Whiskey? Glass of wine?"

"I'll have something small, darling." Mrs. Duvall moved across the hall. "Let me take your things," she said, helping Mrs. Lehman out of her coat, a brown tweed with big buttons like blackberries and a cloth collar. "You *will* stay, of course." She hesitated. "You're *not* planning to drive back to the city tonight?"

Arthur heard Mrs. Lehman demur; then she said they'd be grateful, if it wasn't any trouble. The roads had been awfully icy. She didn't relish a drive back tonight in the dark with all that snow.

They moved toward a room just off the hall, a small, dimly lit, L-shaped room with green-and-white patterned curtains at the windows. A low yellow sofa and worn leather chairs were grouped around a fireplace in which bright flames hissed and settled. Several old Chinese porcelain urns stood on the mantel, and the bookcases to either side of the hearth were crowded with books and photographs. A small oil painting in an ornate frame—a conventional still life of grapes and a cracked gray pitcher on a red cloth—hung on one wall over a cluttered desk on which a small brass-shaded lamp illuminated scattered papers. Arthur wondered briefly at the painting's being, obviously, the work of an amateur. There were others on the walls that were very good, probably valuable. In the corner stood a small Christmas tree hung with golden walnuts and popcorn balls wrapped in brightly colored cellophane. Cranberry chains and a string of bright electric candles wound through the tree's branches. Arthur was surprised. He had supposed the Duvalls were Jewish, though no one had actually said so. Mrs. Duvall didn't look Jewish. With Mr. Duvall, it was harder to tell. She was much younger than he, in any case—he guessed that she was only in her early thirties, younger than Arthur himself, perhaps, while Mr. Duvall must have been fifty, at least.

He felt Mr. Duvall's hand on his back briefly as they entered the room.

"That boy needs a bed, I'd say," Mr. Duvall said. "Peggy will take him up, if you like."

Arthur felt Toby stiffen slightly in his arms. He was nine, too old to be carried and held like this, but he was small for his age; the Duvalls might excuse such babyishness tonight.

"It's all so new . . ." Arthur made an apologetic face, embarrassed.

There was a moment's pause, and then Nina Duvall said,

"Well, of course. He must stay." She had taken a seat on one of the sofas, her legs folded up beneath her. She reached for a small pillow and propped it up against the back of the sofa, patting the seat beside her. "He can sit right here with us in front of the fire. Wouldn't he like some cocoa? Some hot milk?"

"No, thank you. He needs nothing, thank you," Arthur murmured. The sofa was very small. Toby held on tightly, his arms around his father's neck. Arthur had to disengage one of the boy's legs from his waist in order to sit down himself; Toby was stiff as a stick of wood.

"Toby, please," he said quietly into the boy's ear.

"*Toby*. That's right. I'd forgotten for a moment." Mrs. Duvall leaned forward, her hands clasped around her elbows, and tried to see into Toby's face. "You're nine, aren't you, Toby? That's a year older than Agatha. I'm afraid she wasn't very polite tonight. She's sometimes not very polite. It's one of her little faults." She gave a laugh. But Toby only pushed his face deeper into Arthur's collar. Mrs. Duvall laid a smooth white hand, not much bigger than Toby's own, against his back briefly and then turned her gaze to Arthur. "We're so terribly sorry," she said, looking directly into Arthur's face, "—about your wife. They told us. You've had a dreadful time, all of you." She glanced around at the Lehmans, including them in her sympathy; the Lehmans had been in America for years, but perhaps she didn't know that, Arthur thought. She didn't say anything about the baby.

"We hope this will be a brand-new start for you, here in America, a new life. Mr. Duvall and I hope you will be very happy here."

Arthur lost control of his face momentarily. A hot flush crept up his neck. He had been doing that often since they arrived in America four days ago, breaking down the way he had after Anna and the baby were killed in London during the bombing, along with his uncle Ivo and the people in the house three doors away, two very old ladies and a grown son, who was weak in the head, and an elderly Indian caretaker. The houses between Ivo's and the two old sisters' had been empty, their occupants having already fled London for the countryside. Arthur remembered the rubble in the street after the first bombs had fallen nearby, the English policemen standing at the door of the old ladies' house, arguing gently with them, trying to persuade them to go away to the country. The policemen had come to Arthur's uncle's house, too, hoping to enlist his help in getting the old women safely out of the city. His uncle had said he would do what he could, but he had come back after a visit there, shaking his head.

"They won't leave," Ivo had told Arthur. "They're too old to be persuaded, I'm afraid. I don't know as I blame them. I think they feel they'd like to choose a familiar coffin, thank you very much." He'd paused, taking off his glasses and polishing them on his shirt. "We need to think about getting you out as well, though," he'd told Arthur. "Anna and the children, at least, as soon as Anna is well enough."

But they had lingered; Anna had been very weak after the baby's birth. They had not gone in time.

"It is very kind of you and Mr. Duvall, all the families," he said now, when he thought his voice was steady. There were vast numbers of people looking for sponsorships to America, he knew, people distributed with a terrible temporariness into countries that had taken them in provisionally during the war and were now anxious to get rid of them. A friend of Ivo's in London had helped Arthur make an application to the Hebrew Aid Society after the war. The Duvalls had volunteered early on, offering both work and a small cottage on their estate. They hadn't minded that he had a child. He was to be the family's driver, he had been told, and help out on the property with gardening and maintenance. "Tailor," he had written on the many forms he had filled out, but no one had said anything about that when he was notified. Still, he had held on to his sewing machine, the one possession he'd been able to save.

"You are very kind. Thank you," he repeated to Mrs. Duvall. He wanted nothing more, at that moment, than to be everything the Duvalls hoped he would be.

Mrs. Duvall glanced up. Mr. Duvall stood at her elbow, holding a glass. She reached up for it. "Chin-chin, darling," she said brightly, looking up and meeting her husband's eyes. She raised the tumbler to him, smiling.

"Whiskey?" Mr. Duvall held out another glass to Arthur.

"Thank you." He had never had American whiskey before. It was strong and sweet and burned his throat on the way down.

The giantess came in with a tray holding a tall silver coffeepot, cream and sugar, a plate of cake. Arthur saw that she had taken off her apron and exchanged her shoes for slippers like her mother's. It must be later than he had thought, perhaps past midnight. They had kept the servants up waiting for them, he realized, and felt another pang.

"A little sugar, please. A little milk, yes. Thank you," Mrs. Lehman said, sitting upright in her chair by the fire and accepting a cup from Mrs. Duvall. She was tired, Arthur saw, rousing himself. Her cheeks had turned pink from the heat of the fire. Her white hair, carefully combed into a large knot at the back of her head, had flattened a little on one side. The Lehman's apartment in New York was just three small rooms, one behind the other, and crowded with heavy furniture—wall benches and mahogany dressers and carpet-upholstered chairs, an incongruously magnificent Italian majolica mirror. It was filled with the sound and smell of hissing radiators, which reminded Arthur, with an ache of longing and familiarity, of the singed smell of starch on an iron, the smell of Julius's shop in Vienna. A round table of dark wood draped with a baize cover, in the middle of the center room in the Lehmans' apartment, had been piled with papers and a typewriter in a black box; the Lehmans had helped to resettle any number of people in America through the Hebrew Aid Society and were working on several more. Mrs. Lehman had patted the papers, showing him, and sighed over the work to be done.

Mr. Lehman and Mr. Duvall stood by the fire, their backs to it. They spoke back and forth, Mrs. Duvall offering a comment or asking a question from time to time, and though Arthur knew he ought to try, fatigue overcame him, and his attention wavered. After a while, his eyes growing heavy, he lost the thread of what they were saying, the foreign accents and phrases fading to undifferentiated sound. He sat beside Mrs. Duvall in a kind of stupor, the glass in his hand, Toby pressed against his chest.

ONCE, HE HAD BEEN a more talkative person, prone to saying too much, sometimes, out of nervousness or excitement. Anna had put her fingers to his lips, shushing him. But now Arthur looked back on himself with a penetrating sense of unease. It was as if the young man he remembered was someone who had died, a young man at the periphery of their social group, a boy no one would remember unless he *did* die, for to remain alive made one forgettable; and then his friends would recall all the heartbreaking ways in which he had been, they had *all* been, so foolish. A group of them, young people who were his and Anna's friends, had sat together in the coffee-houses and cafés in the evenings sometimes. They talked about Germany, yes; they speculated about the future. They knew about Hitler's anti-Semitic tirades, of course—who could ignore the swastikas painted on the walls? (Though there were just as many crutched crosses, the symbol of the Fatherland Front.) They'd experienced the boycott of Jewish shops, the Nuremberg Laws. But they were surprisingly free of real worry; some of them, even some Jews, donned the uniform of the Nazis, the high white socks and the black raincoats and Tyrolean hats, with what later seemed a sickening innocence. Their attachments to Austria, to Vienna, were as sentimental and deeply felt as those of their Catholic or Lutheran friends and neighbors, their expulsion from it unthinkable. They did not worry nearly as much as one would think, knowing what the world was to discover in the wake of the war. It was Julius's brother, Arthur's uncle Ivo, who had immigrated to London years before and had a tailor's shop there, who held out the hand that allowed Arthur and Anna and baby Toby to escape finally.

The story of how they had come to London always began with Churchill, for that was how his uncle had been moved to act so quickly. Ivo Henning had a reputation among the MPs for thorough and fast work, and though he had not sewn for Churchill before, when the great man's wife summoned him to their London address one day—this was in January of 1938, just two months before the Anschluss, twenty months before Britain would declare itself at war with Germany—asking in the most pleasant way if he would please come and do them a very great favor, he had hurried, eager to be of service. Given directions to Churchill's London address, Ivo had been admitted by Lady Churchill herself, who had shaken his hand at the door and smiled apologetically as she led him upstairs.

"You won't find him the most patient model, I'm afraid, Mr. Henning," she said over her shoulder as they climbed the stairs, her mouth betraying wry amusement. "He looks very fierce, but don't let him frighten you, will you?"

Churchill himself had been pacing up and down in a high-ceilinged drawing room with yellow walls. Four tall front windows with long blue drapes looked out onto the street and the weak afternoon light. Another woman, with cropped dark hair and a pale, heart-shaped face, was seated on a small chair in the light by one of the windows, taking dictation on a pad on her knee, a teacup and linen napkin on a table nearby. A large tea tray sat on a round table in the center of the room beside an enormous pink geranium whose blossoms had been disturbed and were now scattered over the plate of cake.

"Here he is, Winston," Lady Churchill had said cheerfully, opening the door wide and ushering Arthur's uncle into the room. "Here is Mr. Henning, come to perform miracles on your trousers and run you up a new suit in record time."

Churchill scowled but took his place obligingly in the center of the room, standing there as if he were making a speech, a cigar in one hand. He did not stop dictating to the woman writing furiously on her notepad. Lady Churchill removed the cigar from his hand gently. "Don't drop cigar ash on Mr. Henning's head, Winston," she said, smiling, when he paused. "He's doing you a great favor today."

"Lost my train of thought. Blast." Churchill gave up his cigar and nodded to the woman with the notepad. "Have another cup of tea, Mary. Refresh yourself." He stood still, his gaze focused outside the window, while Ivo knelt and began taking measurements, setting in pins here and there. Mrs. Churchill withdrew to the tea table. "Will you have a cup of tea now, Mr. Henning? Or would you rather wait until you've finished?"

"Thank you, madam." Arthur's uncle glanced up at her. "No, thank you. I've had my tea."

Churchill looked down at the top of Ivo's head. "Always take two teas, if I can get them."

Lady Churchill laughed. "Hence the new suit, I'm afraid."

Churchill gave her a benign smile. "Where are you from, Mr. Henning?" he asked, regarding the top of Ivo's head as he knelt at Churchill's feet.

"Austria, sir. Vienna. Many years ago."

Lady Churchill put a slice of Dundee cake on a plate and brought it to a nearby table, placing a fork carefully on the rim.

Churchill was silent. "Jewish?" he asked after a minute.

Arthur's uncle took a pin from his mouth. He did not look up from Churchill's shoes. "Yes, sir."

Churchill shifted slightly. "Have you family still? In Vienna?"

"A brother. A nephew."

There was a pause. Ivo said later that he became aware of the silence in the room, the steady ticking of a clock on the mantel, the sound of a telephone ringing suddenly in a nearby room, a spoon meeting the fragile edge of a teacup, a gentle darkening at the window as the afternoon clouds closed in.

"I'll get it." The pale young woman with the notepad got up quickly and left the room. The ringing of the phone ceased abruptly, but she did not return to the room.

"I should get them out, if I were you, Mr. Henning," Churchill said after a long moment. He cleared his throat. "If you have any means at all. If you can."

Arthur's uncle had dared to glance up then. "Yes, sir," he had said.

Arthur's own parents had died when Arthur was young; he did not remember them. He had been raised by his father's bachelor brother, Julius. Anna's parents were in the countryside, too aged to contemplate leaving Austria. When the urgent letter had come from Ivo Henning to his brother Julius a few weeks later, just days following the Anschluss and the terrifying changes it had wrought in the streets of Vienna, it had contained money and the promise of visas to be held for them in Berlin. It had been Anna who had wanted to waste no time, who had packed their clothes, who had pushed Arthur before her as if he were a sleepwalker. Julius, his face gray and drawn, had wanted to wait until he could arrange to have the contents of the shop shipped to Ivo in England, the sewing machines, the irons and presses, the supplies —nothing at all really, Arthur thought later, just handfuls of buttons and pins. And Julius had some money in the bank; he wanted to have it transferred to Ivo in London. It had all seemed like so much to lose. After the Anschluss, they no longer believed that what was rightfully theirs would remain theirs. But if they left—this was all the Germans truly wanted—perhaps they would be allowed to take something with them.

Anna argued with Julius, her instincts aroused, perhaps, by fear for her new child. Arthur argued with him. But in the end they left without him, with his promises to join them as soon as he had made his arrangements. Julius had sewn some money into the satin hem of Toby's blankets, pressed his lips to Anna's forehead, held Arthur against him in a fierce gesture that betrayed his fear.

They never saw him again.

Anna and Arthur took the night express train to Berlin in July, procured the visas that were waiting for them at the British Embassy (arranged for Ivo by a sympathetic Jewish customer who had useful political ties), and caught the train to Riga. From there, a boat took them down the Baltic Sea and eventually to Dover.

Their escape had been almost without drama or urgency, apart from some intimidation from a Nazi official on the train who had taken their passports and visas and disappeared with them for a long time at a stop a few hours east of Berlin. When he had come back, he had returned the papers to Arthur, but not before turning his face aside to spit violently on the floor of the compartment at Anna's feet.

Arthur did not know what had happened to any of his friends from Vienna. He assumed they were all dead. Julius died in Auschwitz.

Most people, Arthur thought, seemed to have died.

"ARTHUR NEEDS TO go to bed."

He jerked awake at the sound of his name. Someone had switched off the lamp between the chairs, and the only light now came from the fire and the brass lamp on the desk in the far corner of the room. Mr. Duvall's face was lit from one side by the firelight; Arthur noticed that he wore a hearing aid in one ear.

"Our travelers have had a long day of it," Mr. Duvall said, smiling at him from out of the shadows.

"Excuse me . . ." Arthur tried to shift his weight to sit straighter.

Beside him, Mrs. Duvall set down her drink. "It was terrible of us to keep you up. You're still exhausted from your journey, of course. From everything . . . I'll just ask Peggy if you've got towels and things upstairs." She rose, smiling down at Arthur, and left the room. Arthur caught the scent of her as she moved past him, a pleasant perfume.

Mrs. Lehman stood up unsteadily. "Excuse me, please . . . ," she began.

Her husband rose from his chair opposite, as did Mr. Duvall.

"Of course," Mr. Duvall said, and though he got to his feet, he made no move to leave the room with them. Mr. Lehman came over to his wife and took her arm. Arthur struggled to his feet; Toby made a noise against his neck and burrowed closer. Arthur's arms ached.

"Well. Good night, then." Mr. Lehman turned around and held out his hand to Mr. Duvall. "Thank you."

"I may miss you in the morning. You were good to come out and bring Arthur." Mr. Duvall took his hand. "We'll stay in touch, yes?"

The Lehmans and Arthur moved toward the door as Mrs. Duvall reappeared. "Everything's ready upstairs," she said, smiling. "I'll take you up."

"Arthur." Mr. Duvall spoke from behind them, and Arthur turned around. "Welcome to America."

Mr. Duvall was waiting by his desk, his face in shadow, the light on his hands resting on the blotter, his fingertips poised as if itching to touch the papers beneath them, to return to work.

Arthur had the feeling that he would be staying downstairs rather than coming up to bed. He wondered if he did that often. He had a great deal of money, the Lehmans had said, but they had been unsure about what exactly he did; he was in banking.

"You must consider yourself at home here," Mr. Duvall said quietly. "I hope you will."

Arthur dipped his head in a nod of thanks, awkward because of Toby. "You're very kind," he said again. He waited uncertainly, but Mr. Duvall said nothing further, and Arthur turned away and left the room with the sense that he had been dismissed. Behind him he could hear the legs of the chair scrape the floor as Mr. Duvall pulled it out to take his seat at the desk.

"Peggy's put an extra blanket on your beds," Mrs. Duvall said as she led them up the stairs. "It's awfully cold tonight. I hope you'll sleep well."

They stopped at an open door just off the landing. Mrs. Duvall didn't linger, only opening the door for the Lehmans a little wider.

"Good night," she said to them. "The bath's just through there. Come down for breakfast in the morning whenever you're up."

Arthur glanced in the room as they passed it; twin beds were tucked under the eaves in an alcove. A low upholstered chair and round wood table, its surface gleaming, had been drawn up in front of a fire, and a soft-looking blue rug was spread beside the glowing brass fender. A lamp with a yellow shade on a table between the beds cast light over the pillows, high and white and starched. Someone had set Mrs. Lehman's little cloth overnight bag on a folding luggage stand at the foot of one of the beds.

Mrs. Duvall faced Arthur at the next door, down a turn in the hall. "Tomorrow we'll talk everything over. Have you everything you need for tonight?"

"Yes. Yes, everything."

"There's a basin in the room, but the bath's just across the hall. Do sleep well."

They could not shake hands, as Arthur still held Toby in his arms, but she laid her palm on Toby's head briefly, smiling, and then moved away back down the hall. Arthur heard her descending the stairs.

He turned into the room and with an aching back set Toby down on the bed, where he immediately curled up into a ball. "Use the toilet first," Arthur whispered. He caught him up under his arms and walked him to the bathroom across the way, where the boy let a little weak spray into the toilet and yawned wide, his breath sour. Arthur filled a glass of water from the tap and made him rinse his mouth. Back in the room, he ignored the little daybed under the window, neatly made up with fresh sheets and striped woolen blankets and an eiderdown, and pulled back the heavy coverlet to help Toby into the big bed. Toby shivered. "Cold," he said indistinctly as he lay down and curled into a tight ball.

Arthur's bags had been set down on the floor near a small desk. He was glad they had not been opened. Some people managed to have so much, he thought, leaning down to open the smaller of the two suitcases and retrieve a clean undershirt.

There was no sense to the world that way. Of course, it was best never to think in those terms, but the comforts of the Duvalls' house, the sense that they and their things had always been there, safe and undisturbed, made it hard not to reckon the balance of his own possessions. Still, tomorrow he would have a house of his own, and work, and then he could begin to make a new life for himself and Toby.

In the bathroom the floor was like ice under his bare feet. He splashed water on his face, running just a trickle into the basin so as not to make any noise. A dish filled with little soaps in the shape of scallop shells sat on a glass shelf. He brought one to his nose to smell it but replaced it in the dish, careful not to get it wet. Then he worried that perhaps it was better to have used it; if anyone noticed that it had been untouched, they might think he was unclean, so he cupped one in his hand and ran a little water over it and then rubbed it between his fingers before replacing it in the dish. It smelled sweet. From a bag that held his razor he took a little vial full of coarse salt, extracted a pinch, and scrubbed his teeth with his fingers and the salt, spitting into the basin, his face close. He would have to shave in the morning, he thought, staring at himself in the mirror. Once, he'd had the smallest bit of vanity about how he looked, another of Anna's gifts to him—she'd rubbed her hand over his receding hair and told him he had a lovely brow, lovely eyes. He looked like an old man now, he thought. Gray skin. Gray eyes. Hair, whatever was left of it, going prematurely gray.

He lay in bed between the cold white sheets. Toby was warming up, and Arthur moved close to him, pulling up his knees and gathering Toby to his chest. It was better to keep the boy close in bed beside him, in case Toby should wake and be frightened, not knowing where he was or how he had come to be there. But he was a comfort to Arthur as well.

The window held the brightness of the snow outside, a strange false night. Anna had wanted to go to America; she had found the English cold and indifferent. In London, Arthur had read to her from a German children's book lent to him by a teacher at the school where Arthur worked at night; in addition to his work in Ivo's tailor shop, he kept the school's furnace running and carted coal and mopped the wide hallways that smelled of polish and sour potatoes. He had brought the book home to the bedroom he and Toby and Anna shared in Ivo's house, and they had lain in bed together, Arthur reading aloud about moose and elk and snowshoe hares and buffalo and ermine, animals that roamed the wilderness of America. Arthur remembered those evenings as a time of melancholy sweetness; his wife and son lay beside him, safe and unharmed, and the troubles in the world, the threat of the Nazis moving across Europe, receded a little to become distant, almost impossible events taking place far away across the hazy sea. Only Julius's devastating disappearance from Vienna a few weeks after Arthur and Anna's departure—this news conveyed by another refugee from Vienna who passed through London on his way to Ireland and brought the story of Julius's arrest, though thirdhand by then, to Arthur and Ivo—remained with him at all times, a permanent tightening of fear in his chest.

But less than two years after their arrival in England, in the spring of 1940, Arthur and his uncle, though Ivo Henning had been in England for nearly thirty years by then, had been rounded up with all the other "enemy aliens" and interned on the Isle of Man. Anna, who had been five and a half months pregnant, had been spared and allowed to remain in London.

Arthur had been certain that he would never see either Anna or Toby again, though Ivo, frightened and angry and bewildered, as they all were, by their treatment at the hands of the British government, by the sinking of the boats that summer carrying deportees to Australia, kept assuring him that they would all be let go; it was impossible that England would send them away. Finally, in late October, Arthur and his uncle were released. Arthur was sent to a factory at Enfield, on the outskirts of London, where he sewed buttons on uniforms. Ivo returned to London and his failing business—no one thought about their clothes anymore. The first mass bombing raids had begun striking London that fall and continued all through the winter and into the spring. Arthur made it back to Ivo's house from Enfield as often as he could. On the winter evening in 1941 when the bomb fell in Ivo's garden, killing Ivo and Anna and the baby girl—she had been born in early October, while Arthur and Ivo were still interned on the Isle of Man—Arthur had been out with Toby, who had been fussing at Anna all day and wearying her. Arthur, Toby in his arms, had taken refuge in the Tube when the sirens went off.

Hours later, when they finally arrived home, there was nothing left.

• • •

Tightening his arms around Toby, Arthur stared into the darkness over his son's head.

It was Anna who had told Arthur stories at night. God made more than one world, she said, sleepless beside him in London, whispering into the cold air above their heads; all God's trial worlds and heavens dangled from his fingers like yo-yos on strings. In one world, Anna said, the people had two heads and four arms and legs, and all their organs were doubled, and the two heads would quarrel and bicker with each other, especially if they were eating or drinking. In one of the heavens were stored all the troubles to be visited on earth, the storms and the hail and the poisonous dew and the sickening vapors. Even this world of theirs, Anna said to him as they lay awake together in the strange English darkness, Toby nestled between them, had not been so easy to arrange. When God commanded the waters to come together in one place and form the oceans, the waters refused at first, like disobedient children. Even the earth itself resisted God when he was trying to scrape up a bit of it to make a man; "I am destined to be a curse," it said, and wriggled away from his fingers. But God snatched it up. God was too quick for it.

Sometimes at night now, when he was trying to fall asleep, Arthur heard Anna whispering to him. She had talked at night, those early months in London, like a possessed person. During the day she was the Anna he knew and loved, calm and even cheerful, rejoicing over their safety, sure that they would make friends, that they would be happy, eager to make Ivo glad that he had taken them in. But at night sometimes, especially after the baby was born and she and the baby were so weak and sickly, she was someone he did not know, feverish and irritable and frightened. He had stroked her hair to quiet her.

"No, listen," she had said, catching his hand roughly. "Please listen to me."

And so he had listened.

"Angels are fashioned from fire, Arthur," she said, their cheeks pressed close together as they stared up at the ceiling with its fearsome crack across the plaster. "When they come to earth, they are disguised as the wind and they take on the faces of men."

Arthur had stroked her hand, pressed it to his lips.

"When you die," she said, "the same angel who pulled you into the world, crying and protesting, comes back for you. 'Now it is time to give account of yourself,' he says, and you must give account. You must tell him how you have spent your life."

Sometimes she would pause as if exhausted at last, and Arthur would hope to calm her, running his hands up under her nightgown to take her heavy breasts in his hands, stroking her soft skin. Her stories both repelled and intrigued him, but he was mostly frightened by Anna's tone, the dead weight of her voice. She had pushed his hands away, distracted. "What if Germany wins?" she whispered to him in the darkness.

"They won't win," Arthur told her, though he had no idea if this was true. Uncle Ivo had said it would never happen. "They've never made it beyond the Marne," he'd said confidently.

"I am afraid," Anna had whispered. "What will I say to the angel when he comes for me?"

Arthur got up now and crossed the room to the window. A radiator hissed suddenly in the darkness, startling him. Arthur opened the window to let in the night air, wincing at the sound the wood made moving in the track. The room filled suddenly with the cold smell of the snow; he eased the sash back down until it was only a quarter inch from the sill and breathed in fresh air against the sick feeling in his head. For a moment he stayed like that, crouched at the windowsill, his legs trembling with the cold. Then he climbed back into bed and gathered Toby against him again, burying his face in Toby's hair.

Anna's voice seemed to have gone away. It was terrible, wanting to hear her but not wanting to, not wanting to remember those nights when she had kept them both awake with her talking. He pressed his face deeper into Toby, breathed in the smell of him.

When his eyes closed at last, the fields around the Duvalls' house filled in a dream with a swarm of lithe, low animals, white weasels that darted over the crust of the snow, blue in the moonlight. They ran from tree to tree with the start and stop of feral creatures, their shadows fishtailing over the snow behind them, tatters of old sod caught in their claws from digging in the snow for a hiding place. Then there was a hunter—a man in a black coat, the barrel of his gun visible from behind a stone wall—and an explosion. A flower of red burst open in the snow.

Arthur woke with a pain in his chest. The light outside the window was unchanged, the ghostly, magical blue of a snow-filled night; he had slept for only a moment. He closed his eyes again, breathed in the smell of the cold air streaming through the crack in the window. He spent two or three or four hours awake this way almost every night, sometimes failing to fall asleep again until close to dawn.

But what of it? He shifted impatiently in bed, pressed his face against Toby's hair, closed his eyes. His life had been disturbed by the events of the world and its war, and so his sleepless hours were often filled now with evil thoughts, with the consequences of that disturbance, especially Dr. Ornstein. Why did Arthur remember him so clearly? Though *remember* was not perhaps the right word for what he saw at night: the pages of Dr. Ornstein's newspaper fallen to the street, Dr. Ornstein and his ruined surgeon's hands, Dr. Ornstein's children (whom Arthur had seen, in fact, just once, and then only fleetingly, the girl unspeakably, mysteriously lovely). At night, though, in Arthur's dreams, they knelt weeping over their father's body, kissing his hands. This perplexing, endless tallying of injuries inflicted upon a man he hardly knew, Arthur placed before God night after night, bewildered even as he did so by the strange indirectness of his sense of injury.

He turned away inside himself from Anna's death, the death of the baby girl who might have been at Anna's breast even as the German bombs fell, but Dr. Ornstein stood frowning before him night after night, blood on his shirtfront.

He himself was alive, he thought. Toby was alive. Wasn't that enough?

I'm not blaming you, he said to God now. If you have hidden your face, as Anna said you have, then maybe you have a good reason.

SOMETIMES HE COULD make himself fall back to sleep by taking apart a man's suit in his head, stitch by arduous stitch, and reshaping it for someone twenty pounds lighter, the seams shredded and slit, the fabric stretched and pressed and recut. On rare occasions he took a pill from the dwindling supply given to him by a Viennese doctor he had met at the internment camp on the Isle of Man, a refugee like him, who had a store of hoarded medicines that he shared with his countrymen. The pill was to relax you before a surgical procedure, useful during a war when anesthesia was unavailable, and it had the effect of sending Arthur almost instantly into deep sleep. Putting the packet into Arthur's hand, the doctor had acknowledged, with his eyes and with the pressure of his fingers as he closed his hand over Arthur's, the dangerous temptation of oblivion.

He could not afford to be so exhausted tomorrow. The Duvalls would think him unfit. He had hardly slept for nights now, ever since leaving England on the boat. He got up again, shivering against the cold in the room. Rummaging in his bag, he found the pills. He took one, weighing the remaining capsules in his palm, and then climbed back into bed beside Toby. There would be wool in his head in the morning, but he needed to sleep tonight. Toby would wake him.

He did not like to think about what would happen when he ran out of these precious pills, but in a few minutes he was asleep, and then, at least, he did not have to think anymore.

THREE

DRIVING HOME FROM Creston on the January afternoon that he rediscovered the boy, Arthur found himself hoping that Peggy would be asleep when he got to the house; she often took a nap in the late afternoon if Mr. Duvall was staying in the city and not expected home for dinner. Arthur did not want to face Peggy until his mind was composed. Surely it must be apparent on his face, this enormous thing that had happened today. It was a miracle.

But it was often hard to come home to the Duvalls' these days, regardless. Arthur steered Mr. Duvall's car slowly through late afternoon traffic in Creston. What did it feel like, he wondered, having servants who looked after your house and property for you while you stayed away, week after week? Did Mr. Duvall miss his home? It was impossible to say; Arthur only knew what it felt like to be the caretaker. He swept the dust from around teepees of kindling arranged in fireplaces that remained cold for weeks at a time. He sat at the kitchen table to help Peggy polish silver so rarely used that the pieces had no opportunity to tarnish, resting in darkness in their felt-lined boxes. He replaced flowers on the dining room table, or in the crystal bowl on Mr. Duvall's immaculate desk, or in the bud vase on the bureau in his dressing room, the arrangements wilting before anyone had ever enjoyed them.

Sometimes he opened the door on the undisturbed darkness of the living room, the last room redecorated by Mrs. Duvall before she died: gray-and-rose silk upholstery on the love seats and sofas, long, tasseled drapes the color of pewter brushing the floor. Old, speckled mirrors reflected the room in a mist of cool dampness. When he remembered, Arthur wound the old ship's clocks on the mantelpiece; he adjusted with a fingertip the arrangement of Oriental snuffboxes, picked up a petit point pillow from a chair and tapped it gently free of dust. But he didn't like the room; its impenetrable, silvery silence—like a beehive in winter—made the hair rise on the back of his neck.

He knew what it felt like to shovel a path from a front door that was never opened, to push the vacuum cleaner obediently over carpets across which no foot had trod, to turn waste-baskets upside down into which no scrap of paper had fallen. The house was often cold, especially in the winter, and dark, but it had to be ready to come to life at any moment, because Mr. Duvall might suddenly decide to come home. It was like keeping house for a phantom. In the winter, Arthur helped Peggy with the inside work when there was less to do outside, and they were both discouraged, he thought, by the pointlessness of their days, the cleaning and the polishing, all for nothing. Aggie herself lived mostly in the kitchen with Peggy, or up at Arthur's cottage, as if she, too, were afraid to venture into the other rooms of the big house. Working outside, Arthur felt that at least he was caring for living things, that without his care they might suffer. Spring and summer were always easier.

Mrs. Duvall had died in 1959, four years before, while Aggie was at college. Hers had been an alcoholic's predictable end— unstoppable bleeding in the stomach and esophagus, details for which Peggy had a grim relish. Summoned to the big house by Peggy one morning in May of that year to find Mrs. Duvall unconscious on the floor of the bathroom, Arthur had driven Mrs. Duvall to the hospital's emergency room. Peggy, her body averted in grim disgust, sat stiffly in the backseat beside Mrs. Duvall, who lay passed out across the leather cushions, a monogrammed towel under her head. Mr. Duvall had been in the city and had told Arthur over the phone that he could not get away from the office; later, Arthur wondered whether Mr. Duvall would have come if he had known his wife would die that day. Probably not, Arthur decided. By the time Arthur and Peggy had been able to reach Aggie, Nina Duvall was dead. Aggie had come home that evening on the train, but she had not wanted to go to the big house at all. She had spent the night with Arthur at the cottage, the two of them sitting outside until late at night watching the Eta Aquarids meteor shower (Arthur had read about it in the newspaper), though she had suffered through the funeral two days later at her father's side.

Since then, Mr. Duvall had been coming home only on the weekends, and then only once or sometimes twice a month. On those occasions, Arthur carried Mr. Duvall's case to the foot of the stairs and watched him take off his gloves in the front hall, dropping them on the copper plate on the hall table and disappearing into his study, the little room into which Arthur had been ushered on his first night. The discarded gloves and the light burning late at night over his desk were sometimes the only signs that he'd returned home. Every now and then he used the house for entertaining, but he seemed at those times as much a stranger to the place as his guests. Could he be immune to the charms of his house? Arthur wondered. The towering oaks that inclined their graceful branches low over the roof, the way the sunlight fell in slanting golden rays across the lawn on summer afternoons, the drowsy loveliness of the orchard—Arthur had recognized the beauty of the Duvalls' property slowly over the years, as if he were gradually coming awake, and his pleasure at its beauty held within it his triumph at having come to love a place so different from anything he had ever known, as if he were capable, after all, of more than he generally gave himself credit for. Agatha loved it, too, of course; he knew that. And Mrs. Lehman had been right that first evening so long ago: it was—it had been—a boy's paradise.

Arthur took the back lane onto the property now, the rough gravel road that curved past the barn and his cottage, and approached the house from the east between the stone wall of the kitchen garden and the garage, past the stand of Norway spruces whose cones Aggie and Toby had collected one year and fashioned with wire and glue into a striding figure, almost life-size, that stood slowly crumbling into dust now in the shadows of the barn. As Arthur rounded the corner by the trees, the tires spinning in the snow on the slope of the hill, Arthur saw that a light was on in the kitchen. Sometimes Peggy went round and turned on a few lights in the house in the late afternoon—just to make the place look a little lived in, as she said—but the rest of the house was dark now. She must still be asleep.

Arthur parked the car by the kitchen entrance and collected the box from the backseat. He did not want to face Peggy yet. He had never told anyone—not Peggy, not Mr. Duvall, not Agatha herself—that he knew where the child had been taken, that he had followed the couple who had taken the baby home from the hospital. He had discovered, too late, how wrong it had been to let the boy go in the first place. But to tell Aggie now, now that he had found him again? To tell Peggy? To produce him like a rabbit out of a hat, to say, Look, here he is, our lost boy?

How could he do that?

How could he not?

The autumn day eight years before when he'd had to tell Peggy about Toby, when he'd had to explain that Toby was the baby's father, Peggy had clapped her hands over her mouth and stared at him over her big fingers. Kitty had been there, too, home from the hospital after the strokes that had aged her so profoundly earlier that summer. She'd sat mutely in her chair in the kitchen as Arthur spoke, as she had done for most of the summer. She'd looked away from him finally, as if she'd lost interest in what he was saying, or as if she could not bear to hear any more. He had never been sure which it was.

It had been pouring that afternoon; he remembered that. He had stood in the kitchen of the big house, water dripping off his coat onto the floor, and made his sorry explanations. Lightning had flared outside the open window as he spoke, and thunder crawled over the sky, low and remonstrative. The kitchen had been stifling. Peggy had been boiling September apples on the stove for applesauce.

How can you bear it? he'd read in her eyes, full of pity. But there had been accusation there, too: How could you have let him go? How could you have let them *both* go?

In the chilly, tiled back passage off the kitchen he stopped now to knock the snow from his boots onto the mat. Peggy's coat had slipped to the floor from the peg on the wall; Arthur stooped to replace it, hanging up his hat beside it. He picked up the grocery box again and made his way down the passage.

The big, low-ceilinged kitchen was empty when he came in. The hanging lamp was on over the long table, but otherwise the room was full of deep, late-afternoon shadows. Peggy's sweater, an old one of Mr. Duvall's that she wore in the kitchen, lay discarded over the arm of her empty armchair by the fire, which had burned down to weak embers. One of the tailless cats dozed on the pile cushion of the chair that had been Kitty's.

Arthur put away the flour, left the cereal on the counter, heaped the grapefruit and oranges into bins in the cold pantry. Then he went outside again for wood to fill the box inside the back door.

All the while, the knowledge of the little boy, the image of him kneeling silently in the snow, stayed with him.

"She didn't want him," Arthur had tried to explain to Peggy. Neither Peggy nor Kitty had invited him to sit that afternoon, but Arthur, succumbing to his own exhaustion and the defeat of their silence, had shakily pulled out one of the chairs at the long table and sat down anyway, still in his wet coat. He'd taken off his hat, placed it carefully on the table. "She didn't even want to know which it was," he said finally to the floor, "girl or boy."

Peggy had thrown her apron up over her head and wept beneath it.

Finally Arthur had stood up uncertainly. "What was I to do? Tell me!" he had shouted at last as Peggy continued to weep. "I did not know what to do."

At his outburst, Kitty had looked up at him from her chair, her head swinging around laboriously to take him in. She had lifted her hand, a gesture he had taken to mean that he should be quiet, that he was hurting her, hurting them all.

"Sorry," he had said, breathing hard. "Sorry." He had bowed slightly and left the room.

He was still ashamed of having raised his voice.

Neither Peggy nor Kitty had offered him much comfort that day. That had come later, proof of their friendship to him.

His shame over what had happened to the child, how he had let him slip away, and also over what had happened to Agatha and Toby, revived at next to nothing. A breath, a whisper of a memory, blew it into a conflagration, the familiar burning of his

guilt, the sour stomach, the sleeplessness, the almost unbearable anxiousness: Where *was* the boy? Was he all right? Was he
cared for, loved, held? Arthur had repeated nightmares of a
child crying desperately in a park like the Prater in Vienna, a
child Arthur could never find among the trees and the amuse-
ments and the stalls and the fiacres with their burnished horses
and carriages. At those moments, as he lay wide-eyed in his
bed, the nearly twenty years of his life in America seemed to
him a sorry, shabby thing. He had tried, he had been forced, to
reinvent himself—no, he had been given the opportunity, the
privilege, had been plucked up out of the path of disaster time
and time again and set down at a safe distance—and he had
failed to make himself worthy. The hands that moved at the end
of his wrists, the mouth from which words came, the legs that
bore him along—to whom did they belong? What kind of man
had he become?

What kind of man stands by and sees his grandchild given
away?

Yet now, today, alongside the old companion of his shame,
there was this, this thrilling sensation in his chest: he had
found the child again.

Was it too much to hope that somehow some part of this
might be mended?

He carried an armload of wood inside, kicked off his boots,
came to kneel by the fire, laying on new logs, stirring up the
coals.

Might he, in the end, make it right?

• • •

CLOSING THE BACK door to the big house and pulling his hat down over his ears again, Arthur began the struggle up the hill to his cottage through the snow that had fallen the night before. He'd shoveled part of the route that morning before heading into Creston on the errands for Peggy, but he didn't have as much stamina for the work anymore. Half a day of shoveling snow and he was done for, these days.

The drifts were deep but dry. Powder kicked up ahead of his boots as he trudged into the swells of snow in the orchard. This had been a hard winter, but not as brutal as his first at the Duvalls', seventeen years before. The snow had been so deep that year that he'd waded out a few feet into shoulder-high drifts in the fields and stood there, feeling his blood freeze in his veins. The days had been almost electrically cold; Toby's fine hair had stood straight up on end when they came inside, and Arthur's own breath caught sharply in his lungs first thing in the morning when he went out to shovel the walks or start Mr. Duvall's car. All winter that year the sky had held forth, gray and close, bulging darkly, the sun breaking through only on rare days to fall through the clouds in weak rays that left Arthur's heart aching.

For two weeks after his arrival, the roads had been impassable, ice storms followed by snow followed by ice again; the Lehmans made it back to New York after delivering Arthur—the hour-and-a-half trip, even in heavy traffic, had taken them nearly seven hours that day, almost as long as their drive the evening before—just before the worst of it began. Even Mr. Duvall had stayed at home those early weeks instead of traveling into the city. He'd worked from his office in the big house, tying up the telephone for hours, when it worked. Nor had the children gone to school. A bridge near Creston had collapsed under the weight of the ice, and at the public school where Toby began that winter, the pipes had burst early in January, just after the Christmas vacation. The building had not opened its doors to students again until February. Aggie, whom Arthur drove in to the private school, Green Lakes Country Day, in nearby Sparta, had been sick with asthma much of that first winter and had hardly gone to school at all. During those first few weeks, they were all held inside like prisoners, Arthur remembered, strangers who developed for one another the cold, curious avoidances of those who are thrown together without choice, the habit of passing one another without greeting, eyes averted. Sometimes Arthur saw Mr. Duvall trudging out into the fields on snowshoes in his long black overcoat with the velvet collar; he would pass Arthur, who was always shoveling snow somewhere, on his way out or in, but without acknowledgment. Arthur had the sense—something about the ferocity of Mr. Duvall's struggle through the snow, the way he seemed to attack it—that the walks had to do with keeping his temper in check.

Without Peggy and Kitty, Arthur sometimes thought later, he might not have lasted that first winter. One afternoon, a week after Arthur's arrival, he had come down to the kitchen entrance of the big house with Toby, bringing wood for the fireplaces. He was shy during those early days and did not walk in without being invited. But Kitty heard them at the door and came hurrying down the cold passage in her slippers, smiling and nodding and beckoning them inside.

In the kitchen, Arthur had taken off his hat, holding it in his hands, and pulled off Toby's, too, passing it to him silently. The warmth of the room had made Toby stagger beside him; it had been bitterly cold all day, and Toby, who had begun the morning outside with Arthur, playing in the snow, had complained and wept and held on to Arthur's sleeve, his voice querulous. Arthur, sweating fiercely under his coat and exhausted by the labor of shoveling snow that fell faster than he could clear it away, had at last sent Toby inside on his own, where he sat looking out the window, anxiously watching Arthur work to clear the entrance to the barn. Arthur, desperate to finish the work, would stop from time to time and lift an arm to wave, his heart thudding violently in his chest from his exertions, but Toby had refused to wave back, staring mutely out the window instead, fixing Arthur with accusing eyes. When the snow shovel broke after a few hours, the handle snapping in Arthur's hands and gouging his palm through the heavy wool of his glove, Arthur had cursed at the pain and thrown the broken piece violently away from him into the snow.

Peggy had been at the stove when Kitty ushered Arthur and Toby in ahead of her that afternoon. She turned around to boom a greeting as Kitty herded them toward the armchairs and the rush-seated bench with its tattered cushions before the fire. The deep windowsills at either side of the fireplace were crowded with plants in various containers, a painted wooden shoe, a leather-covered ice bucket with a broken handle, and a mug in the shape of a man's face, a corncob pipe stem clenched between his teeth. Toby stopped to stare. The window glass was steamed over in rounded hills and etched outside with frost, wondrous miniature landscapes in each pane, to which Kitty, her hand on his shoulder, directed Toby's attention as if she were showing him something magical. Agatha, blue shadows of illness and fatigue under her eyes, was curled up in one of the chairs, engulfed by its high back and arms and wearing a pair of striped pajamas and a knitted hat finished with a velvety tassel that fell over one shoulder.

"Sit. Sit," Kitty had said to Arthur.

Agatha drew her feet beneath her, smiling shyly. Peggy came forward with a tray of mugs of cocoa that she set on the round table in front of the bench, elbowing aside a knitting bag, a stack of colored papers and scattered crayons, a paper crown decorated with gold stars and curlicues of glitter.

They had been reading to Agatha, Peggy explained; talking too much made her cough, and the asthma had been very bad. Peggy showed Arthur the book.

"*The Wind in the Willows*," Arthur pronounced, looking at the cover and then handing it back to her.

"Aggie and I like that Toad character." Peggy sat down heavily in one of the chairs. She spooned whipped cream and a marshmallow into a mug for Toby and handed it to him.

He took it from her, his nose over the melting marshmallow—another marvel.

Kitty leaned forward and dropped another marshmallow from the bowl on the tray into Toby's mug, nodding and winking at him. Arthur watched Toby's eyes slide toward Agatha. Did she always get this sort of treatment? he was asking silently. Was there always a fire and cocoa and stories? Agatha glanced back at Toby over her mug, but her eyes fled away before lingering too long. She coughed and bent her face over her mug.

"You can read English?" Peggy handed Arthur a mug.

"I can read it," Arthur said, returning his attention to Peggy. "Yes. Simple things are easiest, of course. Some books"—he waved his hand—"they are too hard."

"How about you read the rest of this chapter we're on? Would you?" Peggy held the book out again. "I've got dinner to get started, and my mother doesn't see too well to read. Stay for a little and warm up." She smiled in Toby's direction. He had his tongue out, testing the surface of the marshmallow. His nose and ears were pink.

Kitty smiled all around and nodded in agreement. Her eyes darted back and forth between Arthur and Toby. She reached over to pat Arthur's hand in an encouraging way.

Arthur took the book. He didn't like the idea of an audience, but he read aloud to Toby often. It was mostly his accent that worried him, not whether he might know the words. He reached for his glasses in his shirt pocket and fit them over his ears. He cleared his throat.

"Here's where we are." Peggy leaned over and pointed to a spot on the page. But she didn't stand up to go attend to dinner.

Arthur cleared his throat again. "'Very long ago,'" he began at last, after a nervous glance at Aggie, whose gray eyes rested on him, " 'on the spot where the Wild Wood waves now, before

ever it had planted itself and grown up to what it now is . . .' "
He paused, struggling with the syntax. " 'There was a city—a
city of people, you know. Here, where we are standing, they
lived, and walked, and talked, and slept, and carried on their
business. Here they stabled their horses and feasted, from here
they rode out to fight or drove out to trade. They were a powerful people, and rich, and great builders. They built to last, for
they thought their city would last for ever.' "

Arthur stopped. Peggy had not left her chair. Kitty's eyes
rested on the fire, but Agatha held him quietly, gravely, in her
gaze. Arthur heard the hiss and snap of the fire. He thought he
could tell what was coming to these people in this city in the
story, these rich, powerful people who thought they would last
forever. People did not last forever, of course. That was a reck-
less foolishness. Even the Nazis—look what had happened to
them, despite their having behaved as if they would rule the
world. And all the Jews, all the people who had expected to
have a future—there was almost nothing left of them. Virtually
everyone Arthur knew had disappeared in the war. Julius had
died, and Ivo and Anna and the baby; Anna's parents would not
have lasted a day in the camps, if they even made it that far. He
had tried to discover what had happened to them; he had written from England to another family he had known in their village. His letter had gone unanswered. And his friends, his and
Anna's? It was as if an enormous drawer had opened up; people had marched toward it, fallen into it, been pushed by those
coming from behind. When it snapped shut, there was nothing

left but darkness and an empty plain, an unimaginable nothingness.

The fire gave a snap; a log collapsed. Arthur collected himself. He adjusted his glasses and read on. "'But what has become of them all?' asked the Mole," he continued. "'Who can tell?' said the Badger. 'People come—they stay for a while, they flourish, they build—and they go.'"

Peggy never moved to take up preparations for dinner. Kitty's head fell to her chest; she snored gently. The light from the window dimmed as night fell and then brightened again as snow began to drift downward once more. Every now and then, Arthur glanced up from the page to find Aggie's eyes on him, her regard steady. Toby, marshmallow on his upper lip, his mouth open, listened quietly, his face rapt. Finally, when the clock struck once at five-thirty, Arthur stopped and looked up. He had reached the end of the next chapter. He cleared his throat and read the last sentence.

"But it was good to think he had this to come back to, this place which was all his own, these things which were so glad to see him again and could always be counted upon for the same simple welcome."

Arthur closed the book and looked down at its cover. The words of the story, this story meant for children, had moved him.

"Well!" Peggy put her hands on her knees and pushed herself to her feet. "Well. Time for a bath," she said, looking at Agatha. "I got so caught up I haven't done a thing for dinner. Thank you, Arthur. Say thank you to Mr. Arthur, Aggie."

Arthur stood up, too. "Thank you for inviting us."

Kitty reached up a hand and caught his arm. "Come back and read to us again?" She smiled at Toby, reaching out with her other hand to stroke his arm gently. Arthur noticed that Toby did not pull away from her, as he usually did from strangers. It was something childlike in Kitty's own demeanor, he thought.

"Tomorrow?" Peggy reached down to pick up Agatha and held her for a moment, Aggie's legs wrapped round her waist, before setting her back on the floor. She pulled off the girl's hat and rubbed her head with her heavy fingers, loosening the thick, shiny hair. Agatha blinked up at Arthur from under her dark brows and lashes. She gave him a quick smile.

"Yes. All right," Arthur said. "Tomorrow."

HE AND TOBY had gone down to the big house every afternoon that first winter until Toby's new school opened and Agatha's asthma had abated and she, too, had returned to class. By then, Mr. Duvall had gone back to work in the city; Arthur had had to make arrangements with Peggy and Kitty to keep Toby for him in the mornings from six o'clock until he could get back from the city at quarter to nine or so, in time to drive the children to school, and then again in the afternoons, after he'd dropped them at home and sped back into the city to fetch Mr. Duvall. They finished *The Wind in the Willows* and *Alice in Wonderland* and *Treasure Island* and *Heidi*, a book Arthur found so sad he could scarcely read it aloud. He had read them

"A Child's Christmas in Wales," which tested his English, and "Jabberwocky," which also tested it, and *Hiawatha*, which he and Toby had loved.

There seemed to be an endless supply of books in the Duvalls' house. One day early that March, when the children were at school and Arthur had come down to clean the fireplaces and brush the chimneys—a "Monday" task, Mrs. Duvall had written in her neat, schoolgirl handwriting—Peggy took him into the library. Apart from his first evening, and then his regular visits to the kitchen, Arthur had seen nothing else of the big house.

The library was the most wonderful room, he thought when he saw it, a long room lined floor-to-ceiling with bookshelves and tall windows, a bay window and a cushioned seat piled with silk pillows at one end. Tufted leather chairs in a rich shade of mahogany were set at angles before the fireplace, along with an Oriental table painted a beautiful deep red and decorated with intricate darting figures in gold and black, which Arthur peered down to inspect, unfolding his glasses and fitting them on his nose for a closer look. A folding wooden bar with a tray top and shiny brass fixtures stood beneath one window, lined with neat rows of glasses and decanters that wore little silver tags on chains. Running the length of the room between the shelves was a long embroidered rug; on it was worked the arching back of an enormous gray whale, its pearly baleen plates bared, bursting from a curling froth of green-and-blue seafoam. Whaling boats manned with tiny sailors in black oilskins, their harpoons raised, had been stitched into the whitecaps alongside the whale's bulk. The humped back of a green island was sewn into the end of the rug, the welcome port of a harbor village crowned with fir trees.

"Don't they like funny things?" Peggy had whispered when she'd opened the doors for him. "Why would you want that under your feet?"

When he finished with the chimney and was cleaning up, Arthur took off his shoes to wipe them down, afraid of tracking soot across the floor, and paced off the length of the whale in his socks, staring up at the spines of the books, slowly saying aloud the words of the titles.

"You can take books from that room?" he asked Peggy later, when he was in the kitchen and she had brought him a cup of coffee and a square of coffee cake.

"Aggie gets books," she said. "He's never said not to. He's never said anything at all about the library—whether we could read what we wanted from it or not." She took away Arthur's plate and put it in the sink. "We're not much in the way of readers," she said. "Mother likes magazines. I like the books Aggie brings, though." She'd grinned at him from the sink, where she was running water into a pan.

Arthur had thought that one day he would like to have a room like that library. "Mrs. Duvall—does she allow the books?" he asked after a minute.

Peggy turned off the tap and opened the oven door. The delicious smell of roasting meat filled the room, along with the spatter and crack of fat. "Oh, she doesn't pay any attention." She poked at the roast with a long fork, squinting against the

heat. She turned around and looked at Arthur; she mimed tip-
ping a glass toward her mouth. "Bit of a tippler, you know."

The word meant nothing to Arthur, and for a moment he
was baffled. Then he understood the gesture. Many times over
the years to follow, summoned by Peggy or sometimes even
Aggie, he would be conscripted to carry Mrs. Duvall to bed when
she passed out downstairs. He was not an especially tall or
strong man, but Mrs. Duvall weighed hardly anything, he noted
on those occasions, her head lolling over his arm, her neck exposed in an ugly way, like an unnatural muscle. Usually Peggy
volunteered to sit by Mrs. Duvall while she slept, afraid she
would choke to death on her own vomit, though her distaste for
the job was clear. It was Arthur's task to take Aggie away at
those times, for Peggy wanted her out of the house then. When
she was very young, he carried her up to the cottage, sometimes in the middle of the night, her matchstick legs wrapped
around his waist, her head on his shoulder. When she was a little older, she brought her homework and walked silently beside
him through the orchard, her books held in her arms across her
chest. Arthur had never known what to say to her at those
times. Instead, he made her costumes and taught her to sew —
a princess's long organza gown, fairy's wings of rippling silk that
attached to her wrists and shoulders with satin ribbons, a
fringed green tunic and peaked cap like Peter Pan's. Her favorite had been the billowing, yellow silk trousers that gathered
at the ankles, and the blue velvet vest edged in sequins, a Gypsy
costume. She ran among the trees in the orchard in this garb,
a wand with long satin streamers in her hand, and Toby ran

with her, shirtless and beautiful, turning cartwheels, her Gypsy brother.

ARTHUR'S DAYS IN those early years, those early winters, had been busy, busier than they were now. There was always wood to be chopped—Mrs. Duvall liked the look of fires burning in the fireplaces, even if no one was in the room. There were endless paths to shovel from his cottage to the barn and down to the big house, the walls of snow growing higher every day until they reached over his shoulders and then finally over his head. It was also his job to sweep the gutters free of snow so that they didn't tear free of the house and fall from the snow's weight—an awkward and unsteady job conducted perilously at the top of a ladder. He worked in the greenhouse, too, bringing in flowers for Peggy or Kitty to arrange in the rooms in the big house, carrying heavy plants up the steep path from the big house to the greenhouse when they got too leggy or pale, replacing them with others. He could manage the cyclamen and the Christmas cactuses and geraniums, which weren't much trouble, but most of the orchids died under Arthur's inexpert care: he had no idea what to do with them. He had brought the first dead ones to Mrs. Duvall early that spring, mortified and apologetic. Ushered into the little sitting room off Mrs. Duvall's bedroom one afternoon, he had held the pot with its brown, brittle specimen in his hands and tried to explain that he was not familiar with orchids (or with any of the exotic plants Mrs. Duvall liked, for that matter). He was very sorry, he said. She must take it out of his pay.

Looking up from a chaise longue by the window, where she sat with the telephone on her lap, a cigarette burning in the ashtray, and a glass of wine, Mrs. Duvall had laughed. "Oh, Arthur," she said. "You're so *serious!* Of course they die. They're from the tropics. Just throw them away. Burn them or something."

That first winter, Mrs. Duvall had impulsively ordered ornamental lemon and orange trees, miniature ones that she wanted in the dining room on the sideboard for a dinner party. Arthur had to go and pick them up at the post office in town when the notice came that they'd arrived. The old man behind the counter at the post office, wearing stained trousers flecked with dried glue and ink, and a brace on one leg, had helped Arthur carry the trees, in heavy, wobbly crates stuffed with torn paper packing, to the truck Arthur used for farm business.

"You'll have to put them in the cab with you. They won't take the cold and wind in the bed," the old man said when they got them outside. They surveyed the truck. "You can't get but one in at a time, can you?" he added sympathetically.

Together they'd struggled to get one of the crates into the cab.

"She's not going to be able to eat these, right?" The man stooped to pick up a thumb-size lemon, green and hard, that had fallen to the gravel lot out of one of the boxes. "What are they for, then?"

"It's for pleasure," Arthur said, wedging a blanket around the crate so as not to have it tip over on him. "To look at with the eyes."

The man had shaken his head and smiled helplessly at Arthur when Arthur backed out of the cab and stood upright again. Arthur smiled back, his first moment of solidarity with an American other than Peggy.

"Ridiculous," Arthur had said. "Yes, I know."

The man had laughed and clapped him on the back and shaken his head again. "You got someone to help you with this thing once you get it where it's going, sport?"

"Oh, yes. No problem." Arthur had climbed into the truck and waved gaily, feeling elated.

"I'll help you load this other one when you get back," the man called.

Arthur had barely been able to see around the crate to drive home. And of course there was no one to help him once he got there. He'd sprained his back getting the trees into the house, but he had to admit that they looked beautiful—glossy-leafed and exotic—in the Chinese pots Mrs. Duvall had chosen for them.

So his days were busy in those early years, if not always purposeful. He moved furniture in the house for Mrs. Duvall, who never seemed satisfied with the way things were arranged. He picked up packages for her in Creston or in New York. He noticed how often she had a highball glass in her hand, or a wineglass, how often her breath smelled of liquor. He drove Mr. Duvall in and out of the city, drove the children to and from school. By nightfall, he should have been exhausted. He was exhausted. But he couldn't sleep.

He sat up by the window night after night that first winter, staring out at the unending whiteness, watching the deer, mysteriously weightless creatures on their delicate legs, slowly crossing the fields below the house in the moonlight. The Duvalls' dog, a skittish sheepdog named Byrne, was sometimes let out of the kitchen briefly before Peggy and Kitty went to bed; he bounded out after the deer, his baying carrying over the stillness of the night up to Arthur, lying sleepless in the cottage, Toby beside him.

All that first winter, snow fell as if there would be no end to it. It drifted down to earth, day after day, night after night, in impenetrable curtains. Arthur lay in bed at night, longing for Anna, mourning the baby daughter he had lost, mourning Julius and Ivo and everyone he had known.

Bundled up in a long overcoat and thick scarf and galoshes, Peggy had made repeated trips up to the house with boxes of books and old puzzles for Toby: an impossible one of Niagara Falls, another of a phalanx of colorfully attired American Indians on horseback, the horses' manes flowing dramatically in the breeze. But mostly those first few weeks, when he was shut inside alone so much with Toby, Arthur had held his son close with the sense that this first winter in America was their own private epilogue to the war, a final, quiet chapter in which nothing happened and every loss was felt all over again. It was the last winter he would be able to remember Anna's face clearly, as if the air of America, where she had never been, bore no trace of her, and so she faded away in his memory, nothing to hold her there.

His cottage was dark when he got to the top of the hill. Its emptiness made him reckon for a moment with the desire to drive back down into Creston, to park on the street in front of the boy's house. He could hope for a glimpse of him through the window. He could imagine, for the first time, his nearness. That would be something.

Sometimes Agatha came up to visit in the evenings and would wait inside if Arthur wasn't home yet, building him a fire, rummaging around in his cupboards for something to fix for supper. Those were evenings he cherished—the company, Aggie's company in particular, someone to play chess with, someone to talk to. But she clearly wasn't inside now. Arthur couldn't decide whether he was grateful that she wasn't there (he did not know what he would have said to her about the boy; they never mentioned him between them anymore, just as they never mentioned Toby) or disappointed. Despite all the ways in which Arthur worried about Aggie's happiness, despite the territory of subjects that went unremarked between them, despite his uncertainty now about what to do about the boy's rediscovery, he would rather have had her company than anyone else's. This was a truth he had admitted to himself long ago. He had always loved her—the worst, most impossible kind of love.

He let himself in through the back door of the cottage, stepping out of his boots to leave them draining onto the newspapers left there for that purpose. Walking into the sitting room in his socks, he unwrapped the bolt of velvet he had bought that afternoon and held it up to the weak light of the west window. It shone in his hands. It would make a lovely dress; if there was enough left over, he could make something for Aggie, too, a vest or a stole, lined with silk. He had plenty of scraps of silk. He turned to his dressmaker's dummy; it stood silently by the window, its stained, mottled brown covering draped now with the pieces of a tweed coat he was making.

That first winter in America, he had sat up at night when he could not sleep and taken his place at the sewing machine, the treadle cold beneath his foot. Under his hands appeared shirts for himself and for Toby, cut from worn-out sheets Peggy saved for him from the big house, trousers with their cuffs unfolded and let down to accommodate Toby's extraordinary growth that winter. He had offered his services to Kitty and Peggy—bringing them as a gift that first winter matching aprons in green checked gingham with big pockets on the front—and then to their acquaintances. He had sewn countless coats and dresses and skirts and aprons over the years, cutting, basting, lining, pressing, ordering patterns through the Sears Roebuck Company. Peggy spread the word about his talents, and all that first year and in the years to follow she pushed friends ahead of her up the curving flagstone path to Arthur's cottage, where the women stepped modestly out of their dresses and stood in their slips behind a screen, while Peggy, her big mouth full of pins, pinched and measured according to his directions. Sometimes the women came alone; Arthur had tried always to be courteous.

Some of them had been old enough to be his mother; they were married, all of them, and full of heavy longing, and he slept with a few of them. One woman, a perfect, tiny blond, almost distantly small, had come half a dozen times while being fitted for a dress and a matching traveling coat in pale pink linen, and they had made love in his bed every time she visited, beams of midday sun swarming with dust slanting in through the window, both of them surprised at themselves and each other, sweating hard under the close eaves of his bedroom, flies buzzing at the screen. And then the dress and coat—clothes so perfectly small that they had seemed unreal to Arthur as he put the final stitches in their seams—were finished, and she had stopped coming. He never heard from her again. Peggy told him the woman's husband had taken a new job somewhere else, and his wife, of course, had gone along with him.

He wandered into the kitchen, but he had no appetite for supper. What was the little boy eating tonight? Applesauce and a pork chop? Spaghetti? Toby had loved spaghetti, sucking the long noodles into his mouth between pursed lips. Arthur looked out the window, restless. It wasn't completely dark outside yet. If he hurried, he could get down to the lake to skate for twenty minutes before night fell completely. He took his skates from the peg in the back hall, retrieved his coat and boots, and hurried off back down the hill. The exercise would do him good.

He had taught Toby and Agatha to skate that first winter at the Duvalls', Toby in an old pair of Mr. Duvall's skates—the toes stuffed with socks—that Peggy had found for him in the attic of the big house. Agatha had a tiny white pair of her own with double blades and pink wool balls at the ends of the laces. He had taken the children out often in the afternoons after school before driving into the city to fetch Mr. Duvall; they would sit down at the edge of the lake on a fallen tree branch and lace up their skates, listening to the murmuring of the ice, watching the flight of birds across a lead-colored sky. Sometimes they skated almost until dark, and Arthur lit the lantern he had brought with him and called for the children to come back. From the far bank, from the complicated folds of the shoreline with its secret hidden inlets, where there were beaver dams and the frozen paths of streams curling away into the snowy woods, the children returned to him, Toby first, Agatha behind him, the more uncertain of the two, at first. Arthur helped Agatha unlace her skates and then he and Toby saw her to the kitchen door of the big house, where Peggy or Kitty would come shivering into the back passage with something for Arthur to take up to the cottage, a meat loaf or half a roasted chicken wrapped in silver foil.

At the lake's edge now, the ice was black, with ghostly bubbles trapped in the depths here and there. He sat down on the rough bench he'd made a few years before and laced on his skates. He crunched through the frozen reeds at the edge of the lake and pushed off. It would be dark soon, but the snow on the ground filled the air with a hazy luminosity.

He saw Aggie when he was halfway down the lake and just beginning to warm up from the exertion of the exercise. She was skating alone with her hands held behind her back, describing a wide figure eight, her head bowed. She wore her long black coat and a high Russian fur hat that had belonged to one of her grandmothers. In the growing dark he could make out red mittens on her hands. Arthur slowed.

Was this the time to tell her? But he had not expected to find her here . . . and he needed time to think.

Aggie had never grown taller than slightly over five feet. She was not slim, as her mother had been. She had her father's solid build; her face, too, like her father's, was square-jawed and straight-nosed, with fine, dark brows. She kept her hair cut in the same blunt pageboy, trimmed neatly around her face, that she'd worn since Arthur had first known her. Somehow it had managed to suit her, year after year.

After graduating from Barnard three years before, Aggie had come home and gone immediately to work. She was the recreation director at a nearby retirement home, a shabby Italianate villa known as Tivoli, overlooking the Hudson River; she ran the bridge group, taught ballroom dance classes, organized birthday parties and a music series, managed the small lending library, and led the book discussion circle, which mostly amounted to Aggie reading aloud in the afternoons before the five o'clock dinner hour to a number of the residents, who seemed happy to listen to the Russian novels she favored—Tolstoy and Turgenev. Arthur had heard her read. Standing inside the French doors that opened out onto the shabby, grand, tiled sunroom with its empty fountain and chipped mosaics and shrouded, fraying chandeliers, where Tivoli's residents gathered before meals, he had listened as Aggie, sitting in a straight-backed chair with both feet planted on the floor and the book raised in her hands, read with what seemed to him thrilling authority. When the dinner gong had sounded, Aggie closed the book and held it against her chest, smiling. Several people clapped. The episode had only deepened Arthur's pity for Aggie, the nagging worry he felt on her behalf. She looked so impossibly young surrounded by all those old, bent-backed people. She looked like a child herself. What was she doing, spending all her time there?

Aggie taught the dancing lessons in the same room; she dressed for the occasion, and together she and Arthur had sewn all of her costumes—velvets and brocades, dresses with tulle or sweeping silk skirts. She brought him pictures in books and magazines and lay on the floor while he sewed, reading aloud to him in front of the fire. Sometimes she wore a tiara in her hair for the lessons, and Arthur thought then she had the stoic air of a banished princess. She never appeared to be leading, whether she danced with a man or a woman, even if she was practically holding them upright. Somehow she always made it look as if it were she who was being led, as if she had no will at all.

Aggie didn't need to work; she could have amused herself as carelessly and fatally as her mother had, drinking herself to death when she was just past forty years old. Arthur did not understand what had made Aggie turn her life over to the old people at Tivoli, why she sat beside them and held their hands, or why she read the newspaper to them or listened to their complaints. He did not understand how this child of an extraordinarily selfish man and a hopeless, petulant, spoiled drunk of a mother could have turned into someone of so much honor and dignity. She ought to have been a monster.

He told himself, when he was lying sleepless in his bed at night, that it wasn't just Aggie—he had always loved women, always been a connoisseur of the female form: a flattering hat, though women wore them so rarely now; the drape of good fabric; the shimmer of stockings on a pretty leg, though no one wore stockings anymore, either. Now they wore those hose that looked to him like skin poisoning, a sickly orange color; Aggie told him it was supposed to look like a suntan. To sew well, Arthur thought, you needed to be able to imagine the body inside the clothes, the exposed shoulders, the narrow waist, the downy underside of an arm within a sleeve.

But sometimes he wondered what Toby would think of Agatha now, how he would feel about the woman she had become, whether he would notice what Arthur himself noticed—her waist, her ankles, her wrists, all the places where she was held together. He wondered whether Toby would love her, whether he had ever loved her. Theirs had been the love of children, hadn't it? Two surprised children, each exiles in their own way, who had discovered each other in the inevitable way of men and women, under the tree with the serpent's forked tongue flickering among the leaves. For weeks after Toby had disappeared and Aggie had returned home, Arthur had wandered vaguely around the Duvalls' property, imagining—trying not to imagine—how it had happened, where it had happened, where his son had slept with the master's daughter.

IN HIS DIARY from his first year at the Duvalls', Arthur had recorded each of the storms that kept him busy with the shovels and the Duvalls' plow day in and day out that winter. The last of the snow had not melted away until late in April, revealing sodden, brimming meadows, pools of crocus and snowdrops and early narcissus under the trees. One day that first spring, at the height of the daffodil season, he walked some of the property with Mrs. Duvall, and she showed him—extending her wineglass first in this direction and then in that—where she wanted the fall bulbs planted, where a drift of the white daffodils should be extended, where another thousand narcissus ought to bloom, where a carpet of crocus could be laid or an empty curve along the stone wall edged with hyacinths. After their walk, he had gone back to his house and drawn out a plan of what she wanted, afraid he would forget or get it wrong. He still had that plan, tucked away in his diary.

He recorded Toby's case of croup late that winter, his own bout of bronchitis, the daily temperature, emotionless entries that disguised the sense of panic he had felt at each mishap, every sickness, every moment of weakening. He had been terrified that he would make a mistake, that he and Toby would be turned away. He had breathed on the window in the mornings, then rubbed the glass with his sleeve to look at the thermometer mounted on the shutter outside and diligently record its reading. For nearly three months the temperature rose above freezing only twice.

He recorded Mr. Duvall's fall on the ice late in February, the harrowing trip to the hospital, the subsequent trips over the course of the year for the surgeries required to repair his hip and knee, though he would never walk again without a cane. His diary made no mention of Mr. Duvall's bad temper during the weeks of his recovery that winter, when he was a virtual prisoner in the house, but Arthur remembered it, remembered Nina Duvall, a highball glass in her hand, standing outside on the snow-covered terrace in her long sheepskin coat, staring out over the lake, exhaling clouds of cigarette smoke into the frigid air.

Despite the intimacy of their afternoon sessions in the kitchen over the books that winter, Agatha had followed Arthur and Toby around warily those first weeks, trudging through the snow up to the cottage, hiding behind trees and spying on them. Watching the bright patch of her red wool coat dart from tree to tree, Toby would follow her progress toward them, looking up from the woodpile where he and Arthur were working, Toby tying the smaller sticks into the neat bundles of kindling Mrs. Duvall liked to have waiting in the rush basket by the terrace door.

"Does she think we don't see her?" he asked his father, bewildered by Aggie's indirectness.

"It's a game," Arthur told him. "Because she is too shy to come and speak." Straightening his back, he had turned to smile at the sight of the little figure. He raised a hand and waved; she ducked back behind the tree.

She made him smile, always—something about her, he thought. You just wanted to smile at that child.

• • •

WHEN AGATHA'S PREGNANCY was discovered in the spring of 1955, when she was seventeen years old, Arthur was summoned to the big house and given his instructions. He had been with the Duvalls for nine years by then. It was a Friday morning in early June, clear and cool and lovely.

He was admitted to the dining room by Peggy, who gave him a frightened, tight-lipped look of warning at the door but could offer him no other help. Arthur was used to being summoned by Mr. Duvall. Though he regularly drove him into New York every weekday morning and then returned to fetch him most evenings, except when Mr. Duvall elected to stay in the city at his hotel, Arthur was often called for at the spur of the moment for other driving duties—trips to the houses of the Duvalls' friends or business associates, trips to the airport, trips to various shops where Arthur would be directed to go in and fetch a package of something Mrs. Duvall had ordered. Even before Nina Duvall died, Arthur had often driven Mr. Duvall to an address in the city that he assumed was that of Mr. Duvall's mistress, though he had seen her only once, an attractive dark-haired woman with a chignon beneath a broad-brimmed hat, wearing bright lipstick and, on that occasion at least, a suit that Arthur could tell was expensively made, even from a distance.

Mr. Duvall sat at the end of the table that Friday morning, one leg crossed over the other, the newspaper spread out in front of him. The table could seat twenty-four. Alone in a chair at the end, Mr. Duvall looked both ridiculous and tyrannical. The little dictator, Arthur called him to himself.

Yet he did not actively dislike Mr. Duvall.

Mr. Duvall was never—or rarely—rude, and his obligation to Arthur had never faltered; Arthur had been paid faithfully, with steady increases over the years and bonuses at Christmas. Mr. Duvall had appointed someone at the bank—where it was assumed that Arthur would keep his money—to look after Arthur's modest investments; all these decisions were made for Arthur by Mr. Duvall. The cottage was his to live in; he could take all his meals in the kitchen of the big house if he chose. Other than meeting Toby's expenses and his own, Arthur had few financial obligations. He gave money each year to the Lehmans for their work in assisting other refugees hoping to leave Europe for America or Palestine, and he made contributions to every charity he was asked to support— the library in Creston, the firemen's fund, the orphanage in Sparta, the meal service for elderly people, the animal rescue league, the radio reading service for blind people. For all this, for even his own generosity, he thought, he had Mr. Duvall to thank.

Yet Arthur also understood that Mr. Duvall knew no more about Arthur after nine years than he had read from the brief history the Lehmans had supplied him with when he had agreed to sponsor a young Jewish refugee from Austria who had spent the war years in Great Britain, losing both his wife and an infant daughter to the German bombers who blitzed London from the fall of 1940 to the spring of 1941. It was Toby who had pointed this out to Arthur, more than once, frustration and resentment in his voice, though he had not needed to remind him of the limits of Mr. Duvall's friendship, if it could be called that; Arthur knew them already. Mr. Duvall was not interested in Arthur; he would never be interested in Arthur or in Toby, whom he sometimes appeared not to recognize when their paths crossed, which was rarely.

The remains of breakfast—though it appeared that no one had been down to eat other than Mr. Duvall himself—lay on the sideboard in the sun, a chafing dish of scrambled eggs, another of bacon and broiled tomatoes, more than enough food for three people, let alone the one person who seemed to be enjoying it. Arthur could smell the polish on the table's gleaming surface where the hot sun lay; dust swam lazily in the light. It was a Friday, and Mr. Duvall was dressed in a suit as usual, his shoes immaculate. There were two dozen yellow and white roses in an arrangement in the center of the table. Peggy came in with the coffeepot.

"Bring Arthur a cup, Peggy." Mr. Duvall uncrossed his legs, lifting his weak leg with both hands and setting his foot down on the floor. He folded the newspaper and rested it beside his place. Peggy brought Arthur a cup and filled it and then left the room, the swinging door shutting behind her with a hiss. She had not looked at Arthur.

Arrangements had been made, Mr. Duvall began, explaining nothing, speaking to some point in the air over Arthur's shoulder. They would leave the next day, early in the morning. Arthur was to drive Aggie into Dutchess and then Ulster County, through Greene County, and on through Schoharie; he was to follow the directions on the map he was given—a map was sent sliding down the shining surface of the table—and take her to

Breakabeen, where there was a place for girls like Agatha, where their difficulties would be managed.

It was early in June 1955. Agatha was nearly six months along.

She would be back by September, Mr. Duvall said, just the length of the three-month summer holiday.

"It is unfortunate," he said at one point, as if Arthur had expressed his sympathy. "It cannot be helped. It is too late." Later in the conversation, though Arthur had not questioned him, he said, "We have no alternative."

Agatha would say later to Arthur that it was very American, this business of sending away pregnant girls who might shame their family. She understood her father perfectly. She knew a girl at school, she told him later, who had an incorrigible cousin sent away not once but twice to a home in Ottawa where they made the girls wash bedclothes in lye for the Catholic hospital next door; they were really just a laundry service. In college, years later, she met a girl who had run away from a home called the Cradle of Little Sisters, known as a seclusion sanatorium, where the girls wore uniforms of aprons and starched caps and were made to pray for hours every day, the one concession to their condition being that they did not have to kneel, as their legs swelled so terribly. (She'd been caught and returned to the home; a month later, her baby had been born eight weeks early and had died in a day.) Most of these places, Aggie told him, were dreadful. There was a whole chain of such homes, called the Door of Hope, run by a matron who wore a pin engraved with the initials PBF on her lapel.

"Guess what that stood for?" Aggie asked Arthur.

He had shaken his head, bewildered.

"Past—buried and forgotten."

"No!" Arthur was horrified. *"Buried?"*

"Isn't that awful?" By then, Aggie had been able to laugh.

It was characteristic of Mr. Duvall, however, despite what he must have known about the reputation of such places, to have acted quickly, once he discovered Agatha's condition, and to have made the arrangements in clear and emphatic terms. There was to be no conversation, no bargaining, no escape. How he knew about the house in Breakabeen, Arthur never found out. Other rich men, presumably, had discovered their daughters knocked up—Arthur learned the expression—and had seen fit to deal with the situation in similar fashion. Mrs. Duvall was going to Florida for the summer, Mr. Duvall told him; people would be told Aggie was with her and traveling with friends. Mr. Duvall himself would stay at home, though he would spend weeknights, at least, in the city. Arthur would remain as he was, to look after the property.

At no time did Mr. Duvall explain what had occurred, how they had come to understand what had happened to Agatha, what she had done, what had been done to her. At no point was the pregnancy mentioned, nor the baby. Arthur sat in his chair, a heavy sweat breaking out on his forehead as he listened to Mr. Duvall.

No one mentioned Toby, of course. If Arthur thought of him then, he realized later—and he is sure he did think of him—it was the way you thought about a bird colliding with the glass of a window, the sudden sound of its concussion, its startled, sickening, uneven swerve up and away from the ground, where it had fallen for a moment, stunned. You thought it, and then you forgot it, a little death delayed.

There was only this. As Arthur rose to leave the table that morning, dismissed, Mr. Duvall looked up at him. "I assume your discretion, Arthur, of course."

Arthur nodded his head, clutching his hat.

Mr. Duvall reached up toward his ear, the curve of his hearing aid. His fingers found it, felt tentatively over its surface. "She won't tell me who it is," he said.

Arthur waited.

"Not that it matters." His hand dropped into his lap. "It doesn't matter, does it?"

Arthur said nothing, uncertain. He felt stunned with regret and horror.

Mr. Duvall reached into his breast pocket then and withdrew an envelope that he held out to Arthur. "Give this to them," he said. "Their . . . fee. In your assessment, Arthur, if there is anything that she needs . . . there is plenty there." He reached for his stick, the silver-topped cane he used to help him.

"By the way," he said, rising from his chair, his eyes meeting Arthur's at last, "I don't want to know anything."

THE NEXT MORNING, Arthur had dressed quietly and fixed himself coffee in the cottage kitchen. Toby was still asleep in his bedroom upstairs under the eaves. Arthur had said nothing to him the day before; Toby had been gone when Arthur came back from his meeting with Mr. Duvall in the big house, anyway. He worked at one of the apple orchards near Kent Furnace in the summers; another boy gave him a ride, and they went out with a crowd sometimes in the evenings afterward. He had stuck his head in Arthur's door around one in the morning to say he was home.

"Yes, all right. Everything all right?" Arthur had said, pretending he had just woken.

"Everything's OK. Go back to sleep, Dad," Toby had said.

Arthur opened the back door; the breeze, as it came in the kitchen window and fluttered the paper pattern pinned to the dressmaker's dummy in the next room (Arthur was making a trousseau suit of cream-colored silk for one of Peggy's friends, who was getting married) was already warm.

He had slept hardly at all the night before, his mind occupied with Agatha, with what had happened to her, and with the terrible fact that she had said nothing to him, had not trusted him. He had seen very little of her that spring, in fact —now he understood why. Lying sleepless in his bed, he concluded that she had been avoiding him. But then he hardly saw Toby, either. In the evenings he mostly sat alone in a lawn chair outside and read until it grew too dark to see; he tried to read everything Agatha and Toby were reading in school. He'd liked *The Sun Also Rises* and *The Grapes of Wrath,* the poems of Robert Frost and some of Shakespeare's plays. He had loved *The Bridge of San Luis Rey* by Thornton Wilder, finding in it an obscure comfort.

Standing at the back door that morning, knowing what lay ahead of him, considering what lay ahead of Aggie, he felt a first sudden surge of anger toward Mr. Duvall, his rage like a stone being heaved up out of his chest.

"You do all his dirty work, Dad," Toby had argued with him one day earlier that spring. Toby wanted Arthur to move into New York—there were other Jews there, Toby argued, and Arthur would find friends, despite the fact that Arthur almost never went in to the synagogue. For years the Lehmans had invited Arthur and Toby in for the holidays, until Mr. Lehman grew too ill for company and then finally passed away. Without the excuse of visiting them, Arthur's attendance at temple dwindled to nothing. Years went by and he observed no seder, no prayers, nothing. If Anna had lived, it might have been different, but without her? He took no comfort from it. He felt as much a stranger there as he did at Saint Barnabas, the Duvalls' Episcopal church.

"Why do you stay here, Dad?" Toby had argued. "Why don't you get a place of your own? You can afford it."

Arthur had been distracted from the question by its implicit reminder that Toby would be leaving for college in the fall. Whatever future Arthur had—at the Duvalls', at a place of his own, maybe with his own business as a tailor, for certainly he had thought of this—it would not include Toby anymore. Arthur understood this, of course, but it was hard for him to dwell on it.

"I live very inexpensively here," he had protested from his chair by the cold fireplace, his hands between his knees, his head down. "I have been able to save money for you," he'd added pointedly—and he'd been ashamed of it later—looking up at Toby, as if reminding him of all that Arthur had done for him would distract him, put him off. But what he had been unable to say aloud, what he had been unable to explain to Toby, was how he had come to care for this place he now knew so well, that he had cared for so devotedly. And he loved Aggie, too—though he did not yet understand just how much, nor how difficult it would have been to speak to Toby of such things.

Of course he knew that some German Jews, a few, had inexplicably gone back to Germany despite what had happened there. Austrians had gone back to Vienna, Czechs and Poles had gone back to Prague and Warsaw. These were men and women who seemed unable to survive in America, who had been gasping for breath the whole time of their exile. Yet he had never wanted to go back. Vienna felt full of nightmares to him, of Dr. Ornstein and his bloody hands, his broken watch, his thinning hair so disarranged—nightmares and absences.

In England, while staying with Ivo, he had been given a brochure produced by the German Jewish Aid Committee: *While You Are in England: Helpful Information and Guidance for Every Refugee*. Arthur had read it carefully.

"Refrain from speaking German in the streets and in public conveyances and in public places such as restaurants," began the instructions. "Talk halting English rather than fluent German . . . Do not speak of how much better this or that is done in Germany. It may be true in some matters, but it weighs as nothing against the sympathy and freedom and liberty of England which are now given to you . . . Do not make yourself conspicuous by speaking loudly, nor by your manner or dress . . . The Englishman attatches very great importance to modesty, understatement in speech rather than overstatement, and quietness of dress and manner . . . Do not spread the poison of 'It's bound to come in your country.' The British Jew greatly objects to the planting of this craven thought . . . Above all, please realize that the Jewish Community is relying on you—on each and every one of you—to uphold in this country the highest Jewish qualities, to maintain dignity, and to help and serve others."

Arthur had kept his copy of this brochure, though he did not need to refer to it to recall its exact words. He had followed its advice. He had become a citizen of this new country. Yet he had always been afraid to step out from behind the perimeter of the Duvalls' shadow. He had always been afraid to leave the place.

His last words to his son, just a few weeks later, were an echo of Mr. Duvall's, an exact echo, as if over the years he had become so thoroughly the servant of the master that he had ceased to be himself at all.

"I don't want to know," Arthur had shouted, his hands over his ears, turning his back on Toby and his terrible confession. "Please. Don't tell me. Don't tell me."

AGATHA HAD SEEN HIM, and Arthur watched her skate toward him through the growing darkness. A few snowflakes fell sideways, drifting on the cold wind.

"What time is it?" she called to him.

Arthur thought. "Five," he called back. "Half past. I'm not sure."

"Oh, I'll be late!" She skated toward him, stopped with a flourish on the ice, and then began to circle him, skating backward. There was bright color in her cheeks.

"Where are you going?" he asked, turning around, trying to keep her in sight.

"Is it really that late already?" She circled him again, skating hard, blowing clouds of her breath into the cold night air.

"I think so." Arthur waited a moment. "Where are you going?" he asked again. He felt disappointed that she would not be home. Loneliness made him pitiful, he thought. But he couldn't stop himself. "You want me to drive you somewhere? The roads are pretty bad."

Agatha never let him drive her anywhere. He didn't know why he'd asked.

"I'm only going back to Tivoli. We're having a party tonight; I'm the DJ. You want to come?" Agatha had her own car, which Arthur thought too decrepit to be safe, a Ford Falcon that she'd bought used from someone in Creston. She had refused to get in the car with him as the chauffeur once she had her own license, though she liked driving *him*. He had taught both Agatha and Toby to drive. Arthur had discovered in America that he liked driving. He liked listening to the radio in the car. He also liked the mindless quiet of it. In the summer, he drove with his arm out the window, his shirtsleeve billowing, and felt powerful and proprietary. Mr. Duvall always had an expensive car—a big Cadillac or Studebaker—and Arthur was not above imagining that people assumed the car was his and then enjoying their mistake. That he had known nothing about cars when he arrived—certainly not how to drive one—had dawned on Arthur and the Duvalls at the same awkward moment; Mr. Duvall had uncovered this fact to both his and Arthur's simultaneous dismay and Mr. Duvall's barely concealed annoyance on one of his rare meetings with Arthur early on, when they were all still snowbound at the house. He and Arthur had stared at each other for a long minute, Arthur's horror clutching at his heart and making it hard to breathe. They would send him away. They would send him and Toby away.

"Of course," Mr. Duvall had said quietly at last. "Why the hell would you know how to drive? No, no, it can be fixed," he went on. "We'll just get you lessons." A policeman had been summarily hired to give Arthur cursory instructions in the parking lot of the grocery store in Creston and then to sit beside him in silence while he negotiated the roads for the first few times. Arthur had wanted to die of shame. He'd been hired as a *driver*, he'd thought in anguish. Of course they expected that he would know how to drive. Why had he never even *thought* of this?

"Tailor," he had written on the forms. *Tailor*.

Garment workers, Mrs. Lehman had said that first day in America, when Arthur had ventured a question about his alternatives. What if things didn't work out with the Duvalls? "You don't want to do that, Arthur," she had said, dismissing his questions with a judgment and apparent familiarity with the consequences that had cowed him. "That's a dreadful business. You make things work out with the Duvalls. You won't find a better place than that, I assure you." She had gone on to describe for him the cellars in New York where Jews worked as cleaners, places she had seen as a young girl when she had first come to New York, forty, fifty years before. God forgive them, those old men in their yarmulkes, they took in dirty clothes and washed them with benzene and dyed them with brushes and pressed them with hot irons. Fires started in the tenements when pails of kerosene were knocked over. Whole families, whole communities, were incinerated in those blazes.

There had been a warning in her voice that had stayed with him all these years; the alternative to his position at the Duvalls' was unthinkable.

"I'm going in to see Dad tomorrow night," Aggie said. She stopped on the ice and stood before Arthur, breathing hard. Overhead, the light of the first stars trembled on the wind in the dark sky.

She turned and Arthur began to skate with her back toward the top of the lake.

"I'm going to try and wrest my inheritance from him," Aggie said, still breathing hard.

Arthur glanced at her, puzzled.

"*Wrest*. To seize. To take by force." Her habit of translating for him, amplifying his vocabulary, was ingrained in them both. Aggie tugged off her hat and held it in one hand while she skated. They reached the bank. Aggie clambered over the snow and sat down on the bench to unlace her skates. "I'm meeting him at a restaurant in the city for dinner. What do I have to wear that won't offend him?"

Arthur bent down to untie the laces of his skates. "Suit," he said. He liked the look of women in trim suits, like the ones poor Jackie Kennedy wore, though they weren't Aggie's style, exactly. She was more of an untidy tomboy, or like a child playing dress-up. "I made you a brown suit two years ago," he said. "Fur collar. Same time as we made the cape."

Aggie stuffed her feet into her boots. "Oh, yes." She sounded distracted.

"He's coming home next weekend, yes?" Arthur wondered why Aggie was going in to the city to see her father. They hardly spoke to each other. "He's having a meeting here. Big dinner party, board of directors. Peggy's already cooking."

"I know." Agatha stood up and waited for Arthur. "Peggy told me. She's fattening the calf." They began to walk up the hill together. "But I want to be gone by then."

They had come to a shallow patch of woods, not more than thirty feet across, the same distance deep. In the spring, it was filled with snowdrops and dog violets. Agatha and Toby had liked to play there when they were young, the trees—birch and aspen and fir—forming a shady roof above their heads. The path wound through the wood. Arthur stopped. Agatha moved into the engulfing darkness ahead of him. She turned around after a minute, as if aware that he was no longer beside her. A silence spread between them, like a shadow. Arthur's heart had begun to beat hard in his chest. He was fifty-six years old. Men had heart attacks at that age. Mr. Duvall had had one himself at fifty-six, a mild one, four years after Arthur and Toby had come to America.

"That wasn't the way to tell you." Aggie waited, several yards away, indistinct in the shadows. "I'm sorry, Arthur."

Arthur had no voice. What did she mean? A little trip someplace, with a friend?

"I've got a week's vacation from Tivoli." Agatha did not come any nearer to him. "I'm not going to take it, but I've told them I'm leaving."

Arthur stood rooted. He said nothing at first. "What will they do without you?" he asked finally. It wasn't what he meant. What about your son? he wanted to cry out. You should see him, Aggie! He's so beautiful.

"I'm going to be late," she said. "Come on, Arthur. Please. I'll tell you about it. I'm sorry."

But Arthur didn't move. The image of the little boy in the snow, the woman's hand on the child's head, touching his hair, her hand on his shoulder as they went inside—all this flashed through his head. Now she would be giving him a bath, maybe. He remembered bathing Toby, his narrow little back bent over, the sponge sliding down his spine, soap in his tiny, perfect ears.

"Arthur." Aggie dropped her skates from her shoulder, letting them bang into the snow, hanging on to the knotted laces. "You're going to make me die of guilt here. I just have to. I *have* to."

Arthur said nothing.

"It's not like Toby, I promise. I'll come back."

Arthur flinched at the sound of Toby's name.

"I should have gone a long time ago," Aggie went on. "I'm twenty-four years old, Arthur. I should have had the courage. You know that. I shouldn't have let him keep me here. I shouldn't have stayed . . . for all kinds of reasons." She hesitated. "But it was complicated, wasn't it?"

"Complicated." Arthur repeated her words.

She made a sound of impatience. "Look at me, Arthur," she said. "I don't have any friends, I—"

Arthur felt anger rise in him, reproachable, foolish anger. "No? No friends? What am I, if not a friend?" He flung his arm out as if to indicate masses of people, legions of Aggie's friends, all standing around her, wounded by her accusation.

Aggie walked back to him and put her arms around him. The top of her head fit four inches beneath his chin, her cheek right against his heart. Her hair smelled of the cold and the wind, of the ice and the scent of pine, too. He put his arms around her, inclined his cheek to the crown of her head, and closed his eyes. Don't leave, he thought. Don't leave.

"You remember Loretta?" Aggie pulled away and leaned back to look up into Arthur's face.

"Loretta Jolly," Arthur said. They had all, even Loretta, laughed at her name when they had met at Breakabeen. Her baby had been due at the same time as Agatha's, but she had ended up keeping hers despite her parents' pleas and tantrums and ultimatums. Finally she had worn them down. She had said from the beginning, confiding in Aggie and Arthur, that she would not give up the baby; never, no matter what. She'd fight for it. "Molly Jolly," Loretta had joked when asked what she would name the baby, the enormous hill of her pregnancy shaking with laughter. She had a wide, freckled forehead and a fluff of red hair, a narrow nose with a bump in the middle of it, pale skin that was chapped around her chin and nose and would flush a hot pink when she laughed or cried. "Holly Jolly. Polly Jolly. Rolly Jolly."

"Jolly's folly!" Arthur had shouted, triumphant, and they had all screamed with laughter and surprise, Aggie clapping him on the back. "A joke in *English*, Arthur!" Aggie had cried, delighted. "Your first joke!"

They had laughed until they had wept, all of them, Arthur just like one of the girls. How could he have been so happy?

"She's asked me to come and stay. She's married now; she lives out in California. She has another baby coming, after two miscarriages, and her husband's been drafted. I'm going to go give her a hand. And find a job, something to do. Maybe I'll go back to school out there."

Arthur said nothing. He did not trust himself to speak.

"Do you remember what she called the baby?"

Arthur shook his head. He did not remember; it troubled him that he could not remember, but that lapse seemed like a distraction now. He didn't want to think about it.

"Lawrence. Larry." Agatha smiled up at him. "He's eight now, Arthur. And guess what her husband's name is?" She went on without waiting for him. "Parry. And he wanted to adopt the baby, so now he's Larry Parry." She laughed. "Isn't that funny? After all that worrying about Jolly?"

"*Aggie*." Arthur looked down into her face. "You're leaving me." He brought his hands up and put them over her ears. The little boy—he had not seen it at first this afternoon, because he was so struck by the child's resemblance to Toby, their coloring, like Arthur's own, a lemony pink that would verge to ginger as he grew older. But he remembered it now: the small, straight nose, the eyebrows like fine brushstrokes. Those were Aggie's. Snow began to fall, settling on Aggie's hair lightly, on her eyelashes. Arthur stared down at her. What welled up inside him at that moment was familiar, forbidden: he wanted to kiss her. He could never kiss her.

She put her mittens up to cover his hands and brought them down to hold them between her own. "I won't make it out of here by next weekend, anyway," she said. "I've got too much to do. I've got a plan—" She stopped. "I'll tell you about it." She looked up at him. "But I've *got* to go, Arthur. You understand that."

He pulled his hands away from hers, fastened the top button of her coat with trembling fingers.

"Now I'm *really* going to be late. Don't you want to come with me? I'm playing rock 'n' roll for them—Elvis. They *love* Elvis."

"No." He tried to smile at her. "I'm a little bit tired, I think."

Arthur looked away from her eyes. Peggy must have woken up, because here and there a few lights had been turned on in the house. They winked through the trees.

"Oh, you sound like an old man." Aggie took his arm, and he allowed himself to be pulled up the hill.

Four

SENDING AGATHA AWAY to have her baby had seemed to Arthur a bewilderingly cold measure, even for the Duvalls, but it had not occurred to him that he might be able to change the course of events laid out for her. At six o'clock on the Saturday morning he was to drive her to Breakabeen, while Toby slept on in his bedroom upstairs, the spring breeze gently filling the curtains in his room, Arthur dutifully brought the car down to the big house as he had been instructed by Mr. Duvall the day before. He wore a clean shirt and a tie; the occasion seemed to call for formality. The night before, he had pressed his trousers and hung them in the kitchen.

He'd had nine years of taking orders from the Duvalls by then. Later, during the nights he lay awake after Toby had gone, he understood that doing what he was told had become something greater than habit. Over the years, doing what the Duvalls told him to do had become inseparable from his own character, his own will. Too late, he understood that the obscure pain he had felt for so long was connected to this abdication, and when it finally left him at last, he experienced a sensation he recognized from descriptions of torture: the release that was like bones breaking at last after prolonged stress, the pain of submission replacing the pain of resistance. Yet by then it didn't matter. Toby was gone. The baby was gone. Arthur believed himself broken, a man who had lost everything, a man who stood empty-handed.

On the morning of Agatha's departure, he did nothing to betray his own unhappiness at the situation, the sorrow he felt on Aggie's behalf, on behalf of her unborn child. Yet the thought of her carrying a child, let alone engaged in the act that created that child, troubled him in every way. She was a child herself, he thought as he started Mr. Duvall's car that morning.

He turned down the long hill that swept from the barn toward the big house. Surely someone had taken advantage of her, he concluded—of her tolerance, her kindness, her humor, the decency that stood in her character, Arthur thought, like a vivid and upright flower in the woods, something unmistakably worthy and lovely.

Yet he did not think of Toby as a child anymore. At eighteen, Toby was over six feet tall (six inches taller than Arthur himself) and his life had become, in the last year, dizzyingly separate from Arthur's own. So why did Arthur persist in seeing Agatha as a child? he asked himself. It was partly her size, he thought, though he knew that was a foolish measurement. Agatha had the air of something that was beautiful because it was small and precise, like the face of a watch. Still, everything he knew about her contradicted the notion that she had been a victim. It was not so surprising to him, in the end, that she had made love with a boy. In fact, he was able to picture it more clearly than he would have liked—those smooth arms around someone's neck, the neat sweep of her neck and jaw and ear, the smiling curve of her mouth.

He parked the car in front of the house, edging it gently over the gravel so as to make as little noise as possible, and sat behind the steering wheel a moment. An unpleasant jealousy that he tried to push away kept veering back toward him like a magnet.

It was probably true, he thought, that Aggie had chosen to give herself to someone—willingly, enthusiastically, lovingly. Though unlike her parents in almost every other way, Aggie shared her father's air of certainty; if she had decided to bestow her love and her body, Arthur realized, she would not have been troubled by the impropriety of that choice. It was not that she was a rebel—her defiance of custom (she shared none of her parents' social habits, for instance, nor what Arthur had come to recognize as their insincerity) was conducted instead with an unassailable calm. She had her own standards.

That past winter, Mrs. Duvall had wanted Aggie presented to society at a ball in New York. Aggie had refused.

"The whole idea of it makes me feel sick," she had said to Arthur and Toby one evening when she'd come over to the cottage, snow fringing the hood of her coat. "But they can't *make* me go." She sat down on the footstool, pulling off her boots and depositing them by the fireplace. "I'll just go limp, like a fish."

She flopped backward dramatically against the sofa, as though her bones had dissolved. Toby, watching her from the table where he was doing his homework, had laughed.

Aggie sat up and folded her arms over the back of the sofa to smile at him.

Toby rolled his pencil over the table with one hand. He crumpled up a piece of paper and threw it at her.

Arthur, looking up from where he knelt on the floor, laying out the pieces of the suit he was making for Toby, noticed that Aggie's hair, which had deepened to auburn over the years, shone with a remarkable range of color in the firelight. "They had such dancing in Vienna, very fast waltzes," he said abruptly. "In the Konzerthaus, during Carnival. All kind of balls, yes. *Alles walzer!* Everybody dances. What happens at these balls, here? How is it done, the presenting?" He looked away from Aggie, took a pin out of his mouth, and set it into the paper of the pattern. How old he had become, he thought.

"They get drunk." Aggie turned around on the sofa and stretched out her toes toward the fire. "And then they throw up in hotel rooms."

The three of them said nothing for a moment. Arthur exchanged a glance with Toby; he knew they were all thinking of Nina Duvall. She'd been sent away somewhere twice—to dry out, Peggy said to Arthur, who had appreciated the deftness of the expression—but whatever reforms she had managed there lasted less than a month once she was home again.

"Maybe I could go in costume." Aggie looked over at Arthur,

who was sitting back on his heels on the floor. "Could you make a mermaid costume, Arthur?"

"Certainly," he said automatically. "Yes, anything. In silver lamé." He thought of Aggie's body in close-fitting silver, flickering through the waves.

"Well, maybe that's worth it." She turned around to look at Toby. "Want to come with me? As a merman? With a trident?"

Toby laughed again. "And we'd come home in a pumpkin?"

Arthur looked up from the floor, watching them.

Aggie smiled, but there was sadness in her face. The Duvalls would never allow Aggie to attend a dance with Toby, Arthur thought. If you were the daughter of Lee and Nina Duvall, you were no stranger to disappointment.

Aggie did not go to the ball. In the end, for her defiance, she had been slapped by her mother.

"Should have slapped her back," Peggy reported to Arthur in a hushed tone one morning later that week, when he came down to take Mr. Duvall to work and stopped in the kitchen for coffee. Peggy's voice had blazed through her whisper. "All over a stupid dance. I'd leave if it wasn't for Aggie, you know that, Arthur? We're all she's got."

But they were *not* all that Agatha had, Arthur thought. People liked Aggie. Perhaps they sensed how ready she was to like them in return, and after all, she had her mother's gracefulness and charm, her father's clever mind, and her own instinctive generosity of spirit. Aggie usually behaved as if the baffles that had been erected around her—her mother's addiction to drink, her father's coldness—presented no impediment to her happiness; she could break through them as if through air. Yet of course it was not so easy as she made it look. Arthur had seen her wounded by her parents too many times to suppose she did not feel their failures. But she was never self-pitying, and that she had known what she wanted in some boy's embrace, that she had found such love tempting and marvelous, that she had found it a consolation—this did not surprise him.

It was the fact that she had become pregnant that made Arthur reckon with the extent of Agatha's vulnerability.

Experienced women did not get themselves pregnant.

Yet for all that, it did not occur to Arthur to ask Agatha herself, until much later, whether she wanted to keep the baby, despite what her parents had decided. And at no time that morning did it occur to him that he had any role to play in the events as they unfolded, that he could have stopped things, or changed them, or altered their course in any way. Aggie was a child. What could she feel about this that would be effectual, that could make a difference? This time, she would have to do as her parents wished.

And he was a servant. What he thought mattered not at all.

As he brought her father's car down to the big house that morning, he felt so far away from Aggie that he could never have imagined how they had already become twined together in a way that would have appalled him, that did appall him when he learned it at last. And when he understood exactly how he and Aggie had been joined together, blood of his blood taking substance in her through Toby, the worst in him rose up to protest.

Later, years later, trying to comfort him, Agatha had said, "What could you have done, Arthur? Taken me to a motel for three months? And then what? What choice did we have? Anyway," she'd added, as if he might have forgotten, "I was *seventeen years old*." She'd put her head in her hands during that conversation, a rare gesture of defeat for her. "Don't make me think about it, Arthur," she said. "I don't want to think about it."

Yet Arthur had known himself better by then.

He should have saved them, he thought, too late.

He should at least have tried.

THAT MORNING—A MILD June morning, sunlight gleaming on new leaves, sweet-smelling steam rising from the fields—he parked the car before the front door and went around to the kitchen entrance of the big house.

Peggy was alone at the stove, her hair standing up in the back from sleep. She wore a creased green housedress Arthur had made for her years before. Arthur had sewn her several identical dresses over the years; once Peggy found a pattern and a color she liked—this dress had a wide pocket like a trough running across the waist—she lost interest in anything else. Over her shoulders she'd draped a tweedy old cardigan that had belonged to Mr. Duvall. She served at the table dressed like that sometimes; Arthur wondered if the Duvalls minded.

As he pulled open the screen door, one of the bobtail cats for which Peggy had a weakness shot out past his ankles. There were usually a few of these cats in the kitchen, suspicious, feral creatures that had been given sanctuary in the back passages. Several litters had been born in the cold pantry, in a box lined with old monogrammed towels. The kittens that didn't survive were given to Arthur to bury. He'd lost count of how many he had fitted in beside the stone wall that formed the north shelter for the vegetable garden.

"You do bury them, Arthur, don't you?" Peggy had asked him once, clutching a shoebox with another dead kitten in it, and he had felt sorry for her worry. It had never occurred to him not to do as she asked.

He stopped now at the door, wiping his feet. He could smell burned toast.

Peggy glanced around at him from the stove, where she was turning eggs in the pan. "She's having her breakfast. She's not ready yet. Have you eaten?"

Arthur shook his head.

"Go on and sit down. I'll bring you some eggs."

Arthur slid onto a chair at the long kitchen table, taking off his hat and putting it on the chair beside him. The table's oilcloth smelled unpleasantly sour, its surface crowded with newspapers and magazines, pill bottles and a chipped sugar bowl, a pair of Kitty's glasses mended with tape. Peggy brought him a plate. Arthur took a fork from a mug filled with silverware in the middle of the table.

Peggy left the room with a plate for Agatha and came back a moment later. She sat down across from him. "Bad business," she said.

Arthur glanced up at her and then down at his plate.

Peggy got up and poured them both coffee. She carried the cups back to the table. "I would have had her eat in here with me this morning." She heaped sugar into her cup. "He got up with her, though. Seeing her off, I guess he calls it."

Aggie preferred to eat in the kitchen with Peggy and Kitty; Arthur knew that she would never have had Peggy wait on her alone in the big dining room. She never ate in the dining room at all, if she could help it, and she liked to cook. Kitty had taught her how to make chicken and dumplings and chicken paprikash and stuffed cabbage and Lady Baltimore cake. Aggie sometimes made dinner for herself and for Peggy and Kitty, as her parents were so seldom at home. Sometimes they called up to Arthur's when she was cooking and asked him and Toby to come down to the big house to eat. Arthur felt sure the Duvalls didn't know about these occasions, when the family servants and the daughter of the house ate together at the long table in the kitchen as if it were a celebration, a pitcher of milk on the table, thick slices of cake for all. He wasn't sure whether they would approve or not, but there was so little of family feeling among the Duvalls that he guessed they either didn't know what took place in their absence or didn't care.

"How can he live with himself?" Peggy said. "*She's* never come down at all. Sleeping off a hangover, as usual." She swept some crumbs from the table into her hand. "You don't see half of what we see down here, Arthur."

Mrs. Duvall wasn't home much, which was a good thing, as far as Arthur was concerned; over the years, she stayed for longer and longer periods in Palm Beach, where the Duvalls had a second house, especially for much of the winters. Arthur ran the property well enough on his own by then, anyway; the era of his daily instructions from her, when he had appeared in the dining room or in Mrs. Duvall's sitting room, sometimes while she was dressed in only a robe and slippers, had ended years before. When she was home she liked to walk around the gardens, though, a glass in her hand; she would wander outside sometimes while he was working and make conversation with him. He had wondered what she did with herself all day.

"She doesn't show much." Peggy pushed her coffee cup to one side to press her fingertip to the tablecloth and lift away spilled sugar. "I can see it now, of course, now that I know. I should have seen it before . . . You didn't guess, did you?"

Arthur didn't answer her immediately, and she sent him a sharp look. "Arthur, did you *know?*"

Arthur shook his head and looked down at his plate. He didn't know how to tell Peggy that Aggie had been avoiding him for weeks. He was too hurt by it.

"What's the matter with you this morning?" Peggy said, irritation in her voice. "Cat got your tongue?"

Arthur looked up quickly. He knew the expression—Aggie had explained it to him before, along with some others: frog in the throat, dog-tired, smelling fishy—but he was surprised at Peggy's sharp tone. He looked away again, embarrassed.

"Arthur. I'm sorry." She reached across the table and put a hand on his arm. "I don't have to drive her there, do I?" She put her hands up in front of her face and slumped into them. "What makes these people so mean?" she said after a minute from behind her fingers. "They could take in a baby here, give it everything a child could ever want." She looked up and met Arthur's eyes. "Their own *grandchild*."

Arthur stared miserably at his plate. He put his silverware down. "What kind of place is this, where they are sending her?" he asked after a minute.

"Well, if it's costing him a lot of money, and I bet it is, it'll be better than most of them, I hope."

"They are bad places?"

"Well, you don't get sent there because you've won a prize, do you? No, they're terrible, most of them. It's the shame of it, you see."

Arthur nodded his head.

"When I was a girl, there was a lady down the street from us," Peggy went on. "She took in girls who'd gotten themselves in trouble. She did it for the money, you know. But she was a good woman. She had candy pulls and popcorn parties for the girls. We weren't supposed to talk to them, but she gave them pennies to go to the park and feed the ducks, and we'd see them there, a little group of them together with their big bellies, all over shame and humiliation. They were just like any other girls, though. They came back to visit her sometimes, after it was all over, you know. She was good to them."

"And . . . the babies? . . ."

Peggy looked at him. "They're given away. Adopted, you know. Or they get sent to the orphanage if no one wants them."

The extent of the trouble Aggie was in had not been entirely clear to him at first, Arthur saw, but now he understood. The thought of Aggie's baby abandoned in an orphanage was as terrible as anything he could imagine. "But *why* will they not keep the baby?" he said. "I don't understand this."

"It's an embarrassment! They couldn't have that happen to them, their daughter knocked up, bun in the oven, and only seventeen years old. No one would touch her after that, don't you see?" Peggy sounded angry. "They'll get rid of that baby so quick you'd miss it if you blinked. And none of us better say a word to anybody. Anyway, there's plenty of people who want a baby and can't have one. You know that." She lowered her voice, leaned toward Arthur over the table. "Who could it have been, Arthur? Who did this to our Aggie?"

The buzzer from the dining room sounded. Mr. Duvall wanted something. Arthur stood up quickly and took his hat. "I'll wait outside," he said.

"She's got her suitcase in the hall." Peggy got to her feet. "You'd better get it out to the car. And there's a bag there, by the door, with some sandwiches and things. Take some apples from the pantry on your way out. There's coffee in the thermos there. You take that, too."

Arthur went outside and came around to the front door. A suitcase was in the hall at the foot of the stairs. He stopped for a minute and listened, but he heard no voices. Arthur looked through the screen door, and then he opened it and stepped inside. He picked up the bag and took it out to the car, opening the trunk and lifting the bag inside. Then he opened the back door and swept the seats with his hand. With his sleeve, he polished the side mirror.

When he heard the screen door bang closed, he hesitated for a moment before turning around. Aggie was coming alone down the walk. She was wearing loafers and a navy skirt, and over that a boy's white button-down shirt—probably one Toby had outgrown—untucked and rolled up at the sleeves. Her hair was still damp from the shower, dark at the ends. She looked smaller to Arthur, somehow, not larger.

This, he thought, would be the worst moment—having to face her and know that she understood he knew what had happened to her.

"Hi, Arthur," she said.

She stopped in front of him, and he put his hands on her shoulders. It reassured him, to touch her. When she was a child, he had picked her up and carried her, he had lifted her up into trees and down from stone walls, he had held her hand, he had pushed her feet into boots and shoes, he had bandaged cuts, he had comforted her after falls and scrapes, just as he had with Toby.

Arthur found it difficult to speak. "Your father," he said at last, "he is coming out?"

"He said his good-byes inside."

Arthur turned away, embarrassed. He could not explain how it was that the Duvalls' failures as parents should have made him feel ashamed, but they did. They always had. He bent down to pick up the small bag Aggie had carried out with her.

"I'm sorry my father made you his henchman," she said.

Arthur stopped, concerned. He did not know this word.

"Faithful follower," she said. "Maybe it means executioner,

too. Hired gun. You know—" She made a slicing motion with her hand across her throat. She didn't move.

Arthur looked down. He felt himself blushing.

"It doesn't matter," she said quickly. "Of course you had to. What choice did you have?" She walked around to the other side of the car and got in the front seat. Arthur glanced back at the house. There was no sign of Mr. or Mrs. Duvall. He got in beside Agatha.

"You saw Peggy? Kitty came down?"

"I went up." Agatha held up a little package wrapped in Christmas paper. "She gave me a present. She looks so old, lying in bed like that. She'll probably die while I'm gone."

Arthur shook his head. "She is all right, Aggie," he said. "Don't say things like that." There was silence between them. "So," he said finally, quietly, "there is nothing else."

Aggie turned her head—a slight movement, barely perceptible—to look out the window over the fields, toward the flagstone path that wound through the orchard and up to Arthur's cottage.

"No," she said.

Arthur started the engine, backed up the car, and turned to head down the lane. In a moment they were moving under the trees, away from the house. Birds crossed the lane in front of them, dipping and rising, swerving away into the sunlit fields. White and pink peonies drooped their luxurious heads over the banks of the drive as the car went past; Arthur caught the scent of them through the open window.

Aggie began to untie the ribbon around Kitty's package.

Arthur stopped at the end of the lane and leaned forward to check for cars before turning onto the road. Aggie had grown still, her head bowed over the paper and ribbon in her lap. Arthur could not see the thing her hands held. It was too small.

After a moment, Aggie picked up her head and looked out the window.

"Look what Kitty made me," she said after a minute, opening her hand. It was a handkerchief, embroidered with her name.

Five minutes later, without speaking a word, Aggie crawled over into the backseat and curled up on her side, her elbow crooked under her cheek. Arthur glanced at her in the rearview mirror. Her eyes were closed.

"Want to play twenty questions, Arthur?" she asked after a few minutes, her voice sounding small and muffled.

"OK."

"You think of something, OK?"

"OK."

But Arthur could not think of anything. His mind was trying to pull forward and back at the same time, ricocheting between Agatha as the child he had known—the girl in the red dress on the swing, the soles of her feet dirty—and the reality of her in the backseat now, seventeen years old and almost six months pregnant.

"Aggie? You are all right?" he asked instead, aware of how the question fell hopelessly short of conveying what he wanted her to understand, how sorry he was. He wanted to pour his solicitude over her, the way he had once poured water from a jug over Anna's plump, rounded back in the bath, Toby swelling in her belly. He wanted to put his fingertips to Aggie's temples and feel what was inside her head at that moment, take it into his own hands. He wanted to pull her onto his lap and comfort her. All these things—how he would treat a woman carrying the precious burden of a child, how he would treat this woman who was a child herself—warred with one another. He did not know how to say any of what he felt. He did not know what he felt. Horrified. Sad. Reverent. In an awful way, aroused.

"In what way do you mean that?" Her voice sounded tired.

He cast about helplessly. "You are . . . hungry?"

"I just ate breakfast, Arthur."

"Yes. But I mean, you feel well?"

She waited a moment. At last she said, "Are you asking me how I feel being pregnant?"

He heard her shift in the seat behind him and glanced at her again in the rearview mirror; she lay on her back now, her knees up. Of course it was what he meant. Delicacy, the strangeness of the situation, his embarrassment, had made it impossible for him to state the question deliberately.

"I feel . . ." She paused. "I'm sleepy a lot."

He nodded.

"That's normal, right?"

"Yes, yes. Normal." He nodded again, harder, glancing into the rearview mirror. He could not see her face. Anna had been sleepy, too; only, with the second baby, the one who had been sick, it had been a different kind of fatigue. The war made it so, perhaps. She had been drawn in the face, sick to her stomach, faint-headed. Arthur and Ivo, interned on the Isle of Man, had not been there to help her for most of the pregnancy, so Anna had struggled along alone with just Toby for company. At the end, her legs and feet had swollen so badly that they had taken her to the hospital and delivered the baby early, afraid for Anna's life. Her English had never gotten very good. Toby, just a toddler, spoke better English than she did.

"What do you think the others will be like—the other girls?" Aggie asked suddenly.

Arthur had no idea what sort of girl was sent to a place like this—girls with wealthy families like Agatha's, he supposed, who could afford to pay to hide their daughters away somewhere for months at a time, families who could afford to keep a secret.

"We're like the mad wives in the attic," Aggie went on. "Except, of course, none of us is married."

Arthur glanced into the rearview mirror again. This time, Aggie sat up and met his eyes. "Toby never read *Jane Eyre*, did he?"

"*Jane* . . . no."

"Mr. Rochester—he's the hero. He has a mad wife." Aggie folded her arms over the back of the front seat and turned her face to look out the window, her cheek on her arm.

Arthur watched her in the mirror.

"She had to be kept locked up in an attic room. She was completely crazy. She tried to kill him."

Arthur slowed down to turn onto the entrance ramp to the parkway.

"I guess I've been a bad girl," Aggie said. "But I don't really feel like a bad girl, Arthur. That's the thing."

Arthur felt his throat tighten. He reached back awkwardly to pat her arm. "No," he said. "No, Aggie. Of course not."

Aggie waited a moment. "There's no point in asking me who it was, Arthur," she said quietly. "Not that you would ask. I don't think you would, would you? But I wouldn't tell you, anyway."

Arthur struggled. He did want to know who it was, he thought. But he also wanted to be sure of something. "It was not . . . you were not . . . you were not hurt, though? It was not . . . forced?"

Aggie lay down again. "I don't want to embarrass you, Arthur," she said. "But it was the most wonderful moment of my life."

When she started to cry, he reached down to the seat beside him and passed her back the handkerchief Kitty had made. He clenched his jaw so tight he almost felt his teeth crack.

"You really stink at twenty questions, Arthur," she said, blowing her nose.

"Yes. Sorry," he said. "Aggie, I'm sorry."

A few minutes later, he could tell by the sound of her breathing that she had fallen asleep. She always fell asleep in the car.

He unfolded the map Mr. Duvall had given him on the seat beside him. He felt like a monster.

BREAKABEEN TURNED OUT to be both the name of the house where Aggie was to spend the next three months and the name of the town, though there was no town to speak of—just one sloping, ramshackle street ending in a sorry, abandoned-looking park at the edge of a long lake, trees mirrored in its surface at the edge.

Agatha woke up when Arthur pulled into an Esso station in the early afternoon. Slate-colored clouds had filled the sky as they'd driven northwest, and Arthur could feel a cool dampness on his skin when he got out to clean the windshield. His back ached. A painfully thin boy in a stained uniform shirt with a name tag that read HOWARD pumped the gas for him, hurrying out from the station with a dirty rag in his hands when Arthur stopped the car. He seemed to be the only one there. He stared in at Aggie, who had sat up in the backseat.

"I'm kind of hungry," Aggie said when Arthur got back in the car. "We're not there, are we?"

"This is the town." He hesitated. "Not much to see, I think." He drove down the street, past a luncheonette that looked dark—odd that it was closed on Saturday afternoons, Arthur thought—a hardware store, some nondescript storefront offices, a drugstore with a dark neon pharmacy sign, a tiny market with a tattered awning that read GREEN'S PRODUCE. Empty banana crates stood on the sidewalk. There was a small movie theater, also dark, with an empty marquee, another restaurant, its dirty, heavily curtained window crowded with philodendrons, a storefront with a barbershop pole and a painted sign that read WIGS in fancy, faded lettering.

In the backseat, Aggie was silent.

A park at the end of the street overlooked a marshy inlet of the lake, which continued for some distance, as far as Arthur could see, finally curving out of sight among the fir trees far away.

"Lake Sack-o-net," Arthur said slowly, putting on his glasses and consulting the map after he had pulled into one of the three parking spaces. "Shall we have the picnic here?"

Aggie smiled at him.

And he thought about it then, when she smiled; he knew he did. There it was, the fleeting possibility contained in her eyes, in her smile, that he could make her happy, that he could be father and husband and companion and lover to her, all at once. He loved her—he knew he did. He loved her for being so beautiful. He loved her for her generosity to him, for the friendship she had offered, even as a child, when he and Toby had first come to America. He loved her for appearing at his door, for sitting at his table, for walking with him in the evenings when he and Toby set out with the dog. He loved her for reading by his fire, for asking him questions, for explaining words, for understanding in an instinctive way his loneliness, his horror and shame over the war, his sorrow and anger over all the people who had been killed. He loved her for liking him despite the sadness of a history both personal and collective that he felt ran down the center of his being like a black stripe. He loved her for wanting his company, for seeking him out—and Toby—day after day, year after year, until it seemed they had never been without her, until he could not imagine life without her. He did not want to imagine life without her. He wanted to be able to see her every day, and when he could not see her, the world seemed flat and colorless, a penance of boredom.

I would never let any harm come to her, he thought. I would be so good to her. Please.

He realized that it was the first time he had spoken to God in a long time. But was it a prayer if you were trying to bargain with God: Give her to me, and I will make her happy?

In any case, he would not get an answer from God. But Dr. Ornstein glanced up, a busy man still living in the bliss of his ignorance of the awful things that lay ahead, the violent beating in the street, his lost children, the whole of the war, his own death. From the safety of the past, from his table in the coffeehouse, from behind his newspaper, Dr. Ornstein looked at Arthur over his glasses.

Why do you bother me with this question? Dr. Ornstein said, impatient, even a little cross.

Sometimes Arthur wondered how it was that God and Dr. Ornstein had come so close together in his mind over the years, like two men shoulder to shoulder, or two brothers in a faded portrait. A blind man touching them with his fingertips might have guessed they were related. Was that a blasphemy?

It's a simple matter, Dr. Ornstein said, uncrossing his legs and touching his mouth with the corner of a handkerchief, white as snow. You cannot change how you feel. You love her. You know that you love her. I can tell you that you will always love her.

But what do I do? Arthur wanted to ask.

And then there was the sound of running feet in the street outside and suddenly the coffeehouse was empty. The newspaper went up again before Dr. Ornstein's alarmed face, and then his two hands were gone and then his white, starched cuffs and shirtsleeves, and then the newspaper itself was gone and the lights went out in the coffeehouse and the dust of years gathered on every surface, in the bowl of every spoon balancing on every glass in the row in front of the long, beveled mirror. On the floor, a chaos of dirty footprints ran amok.

Aggie opened the car door. She picked up the bag of sandwiches and the thermos. "Are you coming, Arthur?" she said.

He blinked. "Yes. Yes, OK."

There was a parking meter, but when Arthur fit a penny into the slot, it jammed. He cast about; maybe he should move the car. In Creston they were very strict about parking meters, and a meter maid in a jaunty hat rode down the main street on a scooter, checking the meters and writing tickets, which she stuck under the cars' windshield wipers. He'd never gotten a ticket. He kept a purse of pennies in the glove compartment for the meters.

But Aggie had glanced at the meter and moved on, heading toward a picnic table near the water under some pine trees. "It's OK, Arthur," she called back to him. "I'll tell them you tried, if they come to arrest you."

Aggie ate two turkey sandwiches and a piece of lemon cake Peggy had packed, and drank a thermos of milk. Arthur had no appetite. The scent of the pine trees was powerfully, nauseatingly aromatic. He tried a sandwich, but it tasted like paper in his mouth. He poured some coffee from the thermos.

"You're not eating," Aggie said.

Arthur looked out over the lake. A breeze was lifting its black surface into tiny waves; it looked like broken glass. "Does he know?" he asked. "The boy? . . ."

Aggie looked back down at the wax paper that had held the slice of cake. She pressed her finger to the paper, picking up cake crumbs. "No."

Arthur looked briefly at her bowed head and then back over the lake. Whoever he was, he ought to be told, Arthur felt. Maybe he ought to marry her.

"I'm too young to get married," Aggie said, as if reading his mind. "It would be ridiculous."

Arthur stiffened. He'd heard a touch of Mrs. Duvall in her voice just then, its irony, its sarcastic lightness.

"I know," he said, defensive. "I know it."

Aggie folded her hands together and looked out over the water with him. "It's pretty here, in a kind of sad way," she said.

And then he saw her face change. Arthur glanced over his shoulder. Coming toward them over the grass was a policeman in a gray uniform. He had parked his car at an angle in the small lot so that it blocked Mr. Duvall's big Lincoln. Arthur felt his stomach lurch. A few drops of rain suddenly spattered hard onto the surface of the picnic table, making Arthur jump. He turned back to Aggie, who met his eyes. Arthur had had no dealings with the police in America. Every time he saw one, he felt his heart begin to pound. In Vienna he had seen policemen he knew—men with whom he had waited in line at the shops, men who gave passersby polite salutes, men who had greeted Julius and even Arthur by name—transformed suddenly into people he did not recognize, their truncheons raised, moving in a blur of fury, the swastika brassards already on the sleeves of their dark green uniforms, clubbing men who writhed beneath them on the pavement of the Nussdorferstrasse. That was what had happened to Dr. Ornstein.

"That your car, folks?" The policeman approached the table, but he stayed behind Arthur.

Arthur had to turn around awkwardly on the bench seat of the picnic table in order to face him. "It is my employer's." He tried to stand up, but the policeman held out his hand, palm toward Arthur's chest. He was a heavily built man, perhaps in his late fifties; his graying hair was cut so close to the scalp that Arthur could see the whiteness of his skin through it. His trousers were shiny, crisply pressed.

"Driver's license," he said. He glanced from Arthur to Aggie to what remained of the food on the table.

Arthur tugged his wallet from his back pocket and gave the policeman his license. He had begun to sweat. His stomach felt upset.

"Your employer know you got his nice big car this far from home?"

"Yes, yes. Of course." Arthur began to reach into his pocket for his handkerchief, but the policeman looked up sharply and tapped the gun at his belt with a finger. "I'd like to see both those hands, Mr. . . . Henning. That a Kraut name, you don't mind me asking, or a Jew name?"

Arthur felt his face blanch.

"Miss?" The policeman looked at Aggie. "You got some ID on you?"

Aggie feigned an idiot's delight. "My driver's license. I just got it a few months ago," she said. "But I'm afraid it's in my father's car up there. In my suitcase."

The policeman looked displeased.

"I'm on my way to a home for unwed mothers," Aggie went on. "It's called Breakabeen. Maybe you know it?"

The policeman's jaw unhinged with surprise; the shape of his face changed, the cheeks sinking.

"This is my father's chauffeur," Aggie went on. "He's driving me there because my father's too much of a shit to do it himself." As she spoke, she stood up and smiled and pressed her hands down over the front of her shirt to display the gentle rise of her belly. "Six months along," she said. "I'm Agatha Duvall. Would you like me to get my license for you?"

The policeman made a noise of disgust through his nose. He looked back and forth between Arthur and Agatha for a moment, and then he flipped Arthur's license toward him. Arthur tried to catch it and missed. It fell into the pine needles and grass. Arthur sat perfectly still, not looking at it, his heart pounding.

The policeman jerked his chin toward Agatha's stomach.

"What kind of baby you got in there, missy?" he asked. His mouth worked as if he would spit. "Chauffeur Jew baby?" He touched his belt hesitantly for a few moments and then put two fingers to his eyebrow in a mock salute and turned away.

It had begun to rain, a light rain that smelled like pine. The policeman strode up to his car. He drove off while Agatha, who had remained standing, watched him.

When the police car was out of sight, Arthur struggled out of the bench seat and bent over to retrieve his license from the grass. He cleaned it off on his trousers and fitted it back inside his wallet and then began hurriedly gathering up their picnic things. His skin felt chilled, as though he'd been wrapped in ice.

"He was a jerk, Arthur," Aggie said. She stood on the other side of the picnic table, the rain darkening her hair and running down her face. "Arthur. Look at me."

Arthur stopped, his hands full of wax paper wrappings and the cloth Peggy had sent. He could not bring himself to look at her. The fear he had shown, his humiliation, the man's sickening insult; that Aggie had thought it necessary to rescue him; that she *had* rescued him—it was shameful.

"*Arthur.*"

Finally he looked up.

"On behalf of my fellow Americans," she said quietly, "I apologize."

"I am an American now, too," Arthur said quietly. He busied himself with shaking out the picnic cloth.

"Yes, I *know,*" Aggie said. "I know you are."

He shook his head. "I am sorry you had to do that," he said. His face burned with embarrassment. "I am sorry he said such things in front of you."

"It doesn't matter. Arthur, it doesn't matter."

"He is no gentleman," Arthur said. He folded up the cloth and put it in the basket.

"I know," Aggie said. "You're right. He is not a gentleman."

Arthur took the thermos from her.

"Welcome to Breakabeen," Aggie said.

THE HOUSE ITSELF was set a distance back from the street, beyond a ragged lawn littered with broken branches and two crumbling gateposts faced in cracked cement. It stood too far from the buckled sidewalk outside the decorative iron fence for anyone to have looked in the windows, too far to make out clearly the faces of people who might have stepped outside the door or to overhear whatever words they might have exchanged as they came and went. Along the fence, weedy volunteer saplings with flapping, overlarge leaves had sprung up, further obscuring the view from the street. Yet the size of the gateposts, Arthur thought, the glimpse of the distant house's dramatic proportions, made you want to stop and peer down the drive.

There was no one out on the street, though they had passed several well-kept but smaller houses. The sidewalk that ran for several blocks in either direction up and down the street, suggesting evening strolls in the half-light and neighborly exchanges, was empty of passersby. It was as though everyone in the whole town, except for its policeman and the silent boy at the filling station, had been called away on urgent business, their doors left unlatched, their windows open, half-filled baskets of clothes on the grass beneath the line, letters unfinished on the desk. The whole town, Arthur realized, had the look of a place that had flourished once, a long time ago, but whose manners and customs had passed on with its oldest residents, and no others had ever come to take their place.

Arthur turned between the gateposts and then paused at the bottom of the drive. "This is it," he said. Aggie said nothing. They sat silently staring up at the house through the windshield of the car. It must have been grand, once. A pair of two-story wings of painted white stucco, peeling in some places, extended off to each side of a large center section with a flat-roofed portico, under which an old black car was parked. A circular window was centered above the portico. The roof was gray slate, almost exactly the shade of that afternoon's sky and punctuated by a series of third-story dormers. Scanning the front of the house, Arthur counted thirty windows to either side of the portico, not including the matched pairs of French doors that gave onto a flagstone terrace—its rail decorated with empty stone urns—that ran the length of the front of the house. It was the windows that gave the place its institutional character, Arthur realized; each looked exactly the same, the same curtains in each window half-drawn as if someone had adjusted them that way exactly. Otherwise, the only suggestion of habitation was the air of determined cleaning; the walls had been cleared of ivy, leaving rust-colored trails on the stucco, the empty terrace stripped of weeds, the stone urns left bare. The house was formal, heavy, beautiful in an austere way. Arthur was struck by the thought that it must have a history of some minor but perhaps embarrassing note—disastrous political decisions might have been made here, or ruinous business contracts signed. Thick woods full of dark spaces closed in around it.

There was nothing else to suggest the house's institutional purpose now: no sign, no marked parking spaces. There was nothing—except the car—to suggest that anyone lived there at all.

"Arthur? Is *been* the Irish word for baby?" Agatha sat up straight as Arthur pulled the car up the driveway and stopped in the circle of gravel outside the portico. "Break-a-*been*, like 'break a baby'?"

Arthur turned to look at her, stricken.

"I'm not kidding," she said.

"It can't be," he said. "No." He cracked open the door of the car, longing for fresh air, but the afternoon had grown still and heavy after the brief rain, full of a sour humidity and promising more rain to come. "It's just a name of a place, Aggie," he said. "It means nothing."

"Wait," Aggie said suddenly. "Don't get out, Arthur."

Arthur held on to the door handle. He felt an enormous wave of homesickness wash over him. It was ridiculous—it was Aggie who was being forced from her home, not him. But he recognized the feeling from the occasional nights he had to wait in New York for Mr. Duvall. Sometimes he was able to park in the garage two blocks from Mr. Duvall's office. He sat in the car those nights in the stifling, close darkness of the garage and read the newspaper or one of Toby's books by flashlight, eating a sandwich. But sometimes he had to let Mr. Duvall off at a different address and then wait for him for several hours, circling the block, hoping for a parking space or looking for a nearby garage. It was those evenings that felt most lonely to him, when he most clearly felt himself a foreigner, despite all the years he had been in America. Sometimes, sitting alone in the dark car, idling its engine on a dark street, he sensed that Dr. Ornstein had come to sit quietly in the seat behind him, his chin in his bandaged hand, waiting with him. With his long face and tapering goatee and watery brown eyes, Dr. Ornstein remained always just behind the wall, through the trees, over the hill, artful and elusive and melancholy as a ghost. Those crushed hands—how terrible that had been, a little death to precede his real death. For he had been a pianist as well as a surgeon, hadn't he? There had been a piano in the apartment on the Türkenschanzplatz—a Bosendorfer, Arthur remembered, with the name in beautiful gold script on the side. He'd stared at it, splendid as an ebony elephant, from the arched doorway between the apartment's first two parlors, where the maid had made him wait that day so long ago, the doctor's new suit in Arthur's arms. It had been a beautiful piano, a strong, surprising, beautiful thing.

Aggie interrupted his thoughts. "Arthur? What is going to happen here?"

Arthur, turning to look at her pale face, was struck by the fact that her question was exactly the same one he had asked Peggy earlier that morning.

"I mean . . ." Aggie began again, but then waved her hand impatiently as if acknowledging a stupid blunder. "I know about *adoption*." She said the word with a brave derision. "But . . . do they do abortions? I mean, that's what it sounds like. Break-a-*been*." She was silent a moment. "It must mean breaking something."

Arthur turned to her, his face aggrieved. "I know nothing of what happens in such places. I know nothing except what your father told me."

"You don't know what will happen to me here." She said it as a flat statement of fact, looking away from him. "I'll have the baby and then . . . do they just take it away right then?"

Arthur burned with shame; what kind of protector was he, to have found out so little of what would become of Aggie? He shook his head. "It will be OK—" he began, but Aggie interrupted him.

"I know. You're just doing what my father told you to do." Her tone was not accusatory, but he felt the indictment in it.

He shook his head again, a weak protest.

"I don't want to go in. I'm going to have to go in, and you're going to leave, aren't you?" Aggie wouldn't look at him.

"I won't leave." He surprised himself. "I will stay for a while. OK?"

She turned to him and met his eyes.

How much can a man love a woman? Arthur marveled, looking back at her. Is this what it was like, to fall in love after a lifetime? He was forty-nine years old, a wife, a war, a dead baby behind him, buried in his past. He had thought he loved Anna—no, he *had* loved Anna. But it had never contained so much pain as this. They had been happy, and then she had died. It had never been so sad, so impossible. And now he had

never wanted anything so much or been so aware of the truth
that he would never have it. He had never been so aware that
he was already too old, that the one thing that seemed to hold
out the promise of happiness was never to be his.

But some part of his mind, the part that pretended not to
know, struggled for hope. Rousing himself, he started the car's
engine, glanced behind him, and began to back up hurriedly.
He was not thinking beyond wanting to postpone this; he would
take Aggie away for a little longer. He wanted time.

But then the front door of the house opened and a man hurried out into the entry, waving his hand.

"Go," Agatha said urgently, turning from the man's swift approach back to Arthur. "Arthur, *go*."

The man jogged across the gravel toward them.

"Arthur! Go!"

But the man crossed behind the car, as if he could tell what
Arthur had in mind and sought to stop them. He waved his
arm, a warning, and Arthur, reluctant, let his foot off the gas.
He could not look at Aggie. He was breathing hard.

"You can leave your car," the man said, approaching Arthur's
window. "It's all right." He was small and slender, younger
than Arthur—in his midthirties, perhaps—with thick, honey-
colored hair that stood straight up from his forehead in a
brush. "I'm the only one who drives the sedan," he said. "I
drive it into town if we run out of something, or over to the
hospital. You won't be in the way if you leave your car there.
I'm Walter."

He put his hand in the open window. His gaze swept across

to Agatha. "Welcome to Breakabeen," he said. "What a lovely day. You must be the Duvalls."

Arthur slowly extended his hand. The clouds were a thin and ugly gray overhead, and a hard breeze blew. The air was full of yellow pollen. The branches of the trees bent and swayed and creaked as if disturbed. There was something odd about the man's manner.

"You got her luggage in the trunk?" Walter backed away from the window and opened the trunk. "OK, I can get this for you," he called around to them, as if he had sized up Agatha's bag and was relieved at its modest size. Perhaps he expected a trunk? Perhaps the girls usually brought more with them? No one had helped Aggie pack, Arthur thought. He glanced at her.

"What's the matter with him?" Aggie whispered. She seemed to have lost her panic, distracted by the man's behavior, his peculiar chatter.

Arthur shrugged and opened the car door. Walter had lifted Aggie's bag and was hoisting it in both arms. "Come on in," he said. "Let me show you around. They're having music hour."

He headed off toward the front door without waiting for them. Arthur went around to Aggie's side of the car. He leaned down to look in at her.

"He's missing a screw," Aggie said. But she got out and took Arthur's hand. "How interesting Breakabeen is," she said. "Anti-Semites, weirdos . . ."

Arthur squeezed her hand. She smiled at him. He smiled back.

The front hall, two stories high, was enormous and completely empty of furniture, not even a chair against the walls. A grace-ful curving staircase of cherry-colored wood on one side led to a balcony landing, a narrow gallery that ran the width of the far end of the room. The walls were paneled, painted white; the smell of fresh paint hung in the air. The floor was bare, a pol-ished expanse of wood. Light fell from the circular window over the front door. Walter stopped in the center of the hall, his hand raised. Arthur and Agatha stopped behind him. From a distant room, they could hear the sound of music.

That's a harp, Arthur thought, recognizing it. Someone was playing the harp.

Walter looked back at them over his shoulder. "Mrs. Lattimore," he whispered. "Our harpist." He listened for another moment, his hand cupped theatrically to his ear. "Saturdays it's the harp. Other days we play records on the phonograph. Some-times Mr. Vox plays the guitar. *Classical* guitar." He was silent again, an appreciative expression on his face. "I like the harp best," he whispered after a minute. "Saturdays are my favorite."

Agatha squeezed Arthur's hand. He didn't dare look at her. He was afraid he might laugh.

Abruptly, Walter began walking again, his tread quiet across the floor, echoing lightly in the empty space. "I'll give you the tour," he said, his voice still hushed. "We don't want to interrupt."

They passed through a door beneath the stairs at the back of the hall and into a long passage lined with cupboards and glass-fronted cabinets. Arthur caught the gleam of glassware and china. Everything seemed scrupulously clean.

"This way's the kitchen," Walter said. "Smell that? That's dinner."

Behind Walter's back, Aggie squeezed Arthur's hand again.

"Sunday's turkey. Monday's meat loaf. Tuesday's ham. Wednesday's fish—don't like fish. Thursday's chicken. Friday's soup—from leftovers. Saturday's pancakes—breakfast for dinner, that's the best."

Arthur heard Agatha stifle a laugh behind him, but Walter didn't seem to notice.

"We won't go in there," he said suddenly, veering away quickly from another door and heading down a different passage, this one tiled and lined with wooden pegs and sloping noticeably downhill. He was hurrying now. Arthur glanced at Aggie; she looked back at him, her eyebrows raised. But she was smiling. Walter was moving away ahead of them, almost at a run.

"Outside, outside," he was saying to himself, and Arthur thought he heard worry in his voice now. Then they rounded another bend, and Walter pulled open the door at the end of the corridor, letting it bang against the wall, and ran out onto a narrow terrace.

Arthur hurried to follow him outside.

Walter ran down the length of the flagstones. Gusts of wind followed him. The filmy green of new leaves shivered high overhead. Arthur could hear the sound of the harp more clearly now. Whoever was playing—Mrs. Lattimore—must be right above them with the windows open. A lawn spread out below them, ending in a scruffy wood. Walter disappeared down some steps, Agatha's bag bumping heavily against his leg as he ran.

Aggie came up alongside Arthur. Her expression had grown wary, grave.

And then they heard the sound of footsteps coming quickly down the tiled hallway behind them, heels clicking. A moment later a woman stepped out onto the terrace and caught sight of them, and her expression registered, very briefly, relief.

"I'm so sorry," she said, hurrying toward them. "You must be the Duvalls. That was Walter who met you, my son. He likes to be helpful to me."

"Mr. Duvall." She reached out and shook Arthur's hand. "I'm Ellen MacCauley. We have corresponded." Arthur had a moment of surprise, but before he could say anything, she had turned to Agatha; Arthur saw her take in Aggie's worried face. "Someday I'll tell you all about Walter," she said to Agatha in a kind voice, still holding on to Agatha's hand and smiling gently. "He's already told you what's for dinner tonight, I'm sure."

Agatha smiled. Mrs. MacCauley's face was long and narrow, like her son's, her hair the same blond shade but run through with silvery gray, parted in the center and drawn back into a low knot on her neck. Her eyes were very large and dark and heavy-lidded, her face still and peaceful, Arthur thought, like a nun's. She was the sort of woman about whom, if she *had* been a nun, a man might have briefly thought, What a pity, before turning away, for she gave no sign of longing or restlessness. There was nothing in her face to beckon you, though there was no hardness in her expression, or unkindness, only a profound reserve and carefulness.

She turned back to Arthur, still keeping hold of Agatha's hand. "I'm sorry I didn't hear your car. I only saw it when I came through the front hall. But you haven't been here very long, I know, because Walter only got you as far as the terrace. He wanted to show you the greenhouses. He's our resident gardener and very proud of his work. He grows all our flowers." She smiled. "Please come in."

She put an arm around Aggie and turned to steer her back inside. Overhead, the harp music suddenly stopped, and Arthur heard light applause and then silence.

"That's Mrs. Lattimore," Mrs. MacCauley said. "We have music in the afternoons, several times a week. Mr. Vox, our tutor, offers lessons on the flute and piano. Do you play, Agatha?"

Aggie shook her head.

"One of our girls is a very fine flutist." Mrs. MacCauley led them back up the passage, talking to them over her shoulder. "Breakabeen was a private home once, naturally. It was used as a hospital during the Civil War—for Union soldiers, of course. It was considered a rather important clinic at the time, especially for those whose sight had been injured and for victims of shell shock. There are fascinating records in the library. I hope you'll take a look at them one day. "

At the hallway ahead, she turned and opened a door into a room at the front of the house. Arthur saw, through the windows, a view down a thickly wooded hillside and below that, through the trees, the silent silver curve of the lake. A desk—a long wooden table stacked with books and lit by two lamps with tasseled silk shades—had been placed before the windows. Two small armchairs in a patterned blue material were drawn up in front of the desk. Along one wall stood a row of old file cabinets; the empty fireplace held a large copper bowl of dried magnolia leaves. A single painting, an abstract of gently curving shapes like slim fish, Chinese red and dark green and gray against a yellow background, hung over a small divan upholstered in a worn brown velvet. On the floor was an Oriental carpet in faded shades of blue and rose. The room's effect, Arthur thought, was of a spare but enlightened poverty, though it was hard to tell if the owner of these belongings had come down in the world or was struggling to rise up.

"Please." Mrs. MacCauley indicated the armchairs and moved around behind the desk to take a seat in a wooden swivel chair cushioned with a fur throw.

"You're planning to drive home this evening, Mr. Duvall?" Mrs. MacCauley turned her attention to Arthur. "It's rather a long drive for you, I'm afraid. Once the train stopped here, but the station has been closed for some years now."

Arthur's eyes searched the expanse of the windows behind her; it was late in the day now, and the sky had darkened even further, promising rain again. Against the gray, the trees' early leaves shone, phosphorescent in the darkness. Arthur thought of Toby. He would have assumed that Arthur had gone off somewhere on an errand for Mr. Duvall. Peggy, under the same restraining order as Arthur, would have to make something up if Toby came down to the big house after work to ask. But he was used to fending for himself. Peggy and Kitty had taught both Arthur and Toby to cook some simple things; Toby was a better cook than Arthur, in fact, and sometimes fixed supper for the two of them, setting aside a plate or a bowl for Arthur's late return from the city. Arthur had wanted to be sure that Toby could manage for himself—do his homework, keep the cottage tidy. He even ironed with some skill. He hardly seemed to need Arthur at all anymore, in fact.

The trees on the hillside outside swayed in the wind, filling the window with a blur of green. Arthur thought of the men who had lain in bed in this house during the Civil War, bandages over their eyes, their minds blank, the shadows of leaves shifting against the glass like phantom hands. How terrible, he thought, to lose your memory . . . Yet he had sometimes wished for his own past to be erased, even for Dr. Ornstein to fade away. He had wished for the streets of Vienna to shiver and break up like water fleeing through his fingers. He understood this, wanting to be free of what was in your past, what was terrible to remember. Yet suddenly, now, the thought of losing these things was dreadful. He closed his eyes: There was Dr. Ornstein, still sitting in the coffeehouse, a spoon balanced over a glass of water before him; he raised the newspaper before his face, leaned back in his chair, crossed his legs. And there was Julius and his carefully barbered mustache, nodding and smiling. There was the German State Railway travel office on the Opernring, with the immense portrait of Hitler on the wall. There was the retired colonel who walked every day in spurs and saber in the Prater, a maid in an apron at his elbow. There was the blue curtain that hung in the doorway of Julius's shop. There was the boy who had lived near Julius and Arthur and had one day ridden a beautiful girl on the *Pupperlhutschen,* the pillion of his motorbike, past young Arthur, who'd stared after him longingly; the girl had waved to Arthur; he saw her hand, small and white, disappearing. Julius's face contracted, sizzled like water spat onto an iron, vanished. Whole streets slid away from the center of the city and fell into the canal of the Danube as if in an earthquake.

Arthur opened his eyes.

"I am not the sort of man to abandon my child, Mrs. MacCauley," he said. He turned in his chair to face her, and Mr. Duvall's tone—the blunt definition, unequivocal and clear—came naturally to him, so easily that Arthur was aware of having to hold himself back. It was remarkable how easy it was. He remembered his accent, but without worry; his English would be perfect. He crossed his legs, leaned back in the chair as he had seen Mr. Duvall do. "I would like to see Agatha settled before I leave. There is a hotel in the area?"

Mrs. MacCauley's hands came to the desktop. "I'm afraid . . ." She hesitated. "There isn't anything nearby."

A troubled look had come into her eyes. Arthur pressed on. "I won't impose, I assure you," he said. He felt Aggie beside him, her gaze carefully averted. His heart was beating fast. Briefly, he regretted what he had begun. But there could be no harm in it, he thought, no harm. After all, she had made the initial mistake. And he did not want to leave Aggie here yet. He would have to, soon, but it could be postponed. He wanted time. Everything could be so easily lost, he thought. When it was possible, he saw, one ought to step forward and prevent things. Maybe you could become more of yourself, more of who you were, in mysterious ways.

And then he waited. He had learned that from Mr. Duvall, too. If you waited, people were made uncomfortable, eager to avoid awkwardness.

"Of course, we can give you a room for this evening." Mrs. MacCauley glanced at Agatha. She paused. "You'd prefer your father to stay?"

Arthur knew what Aggie would say. He had no worries about that. And he was pleased at what he sensed was protectiveness on Mrs. MacCauley's part. If people brought their unfortunate daughters here because they were ashamed of them, she would be used to sensing trouble between parents and their children, recrimination and blame and shame. Mrs. MacCauley's obligation, he sensed, though she might not say so, was to these girls, not to their parents. That was good.

"Please." Agatha could make good use of her manners, Arthur thought. She had said just enough.

Mrs. MacCauley hesitated for a moment. And then she stood up. "Mr. Duvall, I must say . . . ," she began. She paused. "These are girls who are very much in need of our support. I am glad to see that you recognize this."

Arthur nodded as if he had thought of this already.

Mrs. MacCauley took a breath. "Well. If you'll excuse me," she said, "I'll just go and see what we can arrange about a room this evening. Dinner's not for another hour or so; the girls generally have some quiet time on Saturday evenings to write letters and so forth. Will you . . . would you like some tea? Coffee?"

"Thank you," said Arthur. "Coffee would be welcome."

Mrs. MacCauley looked at him. Arthur willed himself to smile. That had been awkwardly put, he thought, a little flare of panic prickling his scalp. Too formal. He'd sounded silly.

"Excuse me then, won't you?" Mrs. MacCauley came around the desk and paused at Agatha's shoulder, smiling down at her. "And I'll see about retrieving your bag from Walter," she said, her composure regained.

Agatha turned to Arthur when the door had closed. "You sounded just like him," she said after a minute. "You almost scared me."

Arthur's heart was still beating wildly.

She reached over from her chair quickly, and he took her hand. "Good old Arthur," she said. "I'd never have guessed you could do that."

"I surprised myself," he admitted. He took out his handkerchief and pressed it to his forehead.

"I bet. You surprised *me*." She put her hand briefly over her stomach and then withdrew it. Her eyes shifted away for a moment and then came back to search his face. "She really thinks you're him, Arthur."

"I know."

"You did that for me."

"And for myself. Not all for you."

She smiled at him, squeezed his hand. "Now what?"

"I don't know, " he said. "I wanted . . . they shouldn't have sent you to this place, Aggie."

"I like her"—Aggie sat quietly, her hand cool in Arthur's—"Mrs. MacCauley." She looked around the room. "You have to go home, Arthur. What about Toby?"

"I will call him."

Aggie was quiet for a moment. "Does he know where you are now?"

"He was asleep when I left. I'll call him." Arthur was eager to reassure her.

"You'll have to tell him where you are."

Arthur shrugged his shoulders lightly.

"What will you say?"

Arthur rubbed her hand. "What would you like me to say? You want me to tell him where you are?"

Aggie looked down at the floor. "I don't know."

Arthur leaned toward her. "He will not judge you, Aggie. Is this what you are worrying about? You know him. He'll be sorry. He'll want to see you. You are such old friends."

"You could tell him I've gone to stay with Cornelia." Aggie's aunt, her father's sister, lived in Boston. Cornelia disliked Nina Duvall but loved Aggie; she didn't often come to New York, but Aggie had been to stay with her several times.

Arthur hesitated. "You don't want him to know. I understand. You are . . . ashamed—"

"It's *not* that," Aggie interrupted. "I mean, I *am* embarrassed . . . I'm embarrassed to be here . . ." She waved her hand around the room and then stopped.

Arthur tugged at her fingers. "You don't need to worry about what Toby will think. He is your friend!"

"I *know* he is," Aggie said, but her voice was miserable.

"I won't say anything, OK? You can write to him, tell him in your own way." Arthur wanted to soothe her. "You can have visitors here, I am sure. He could come and see you."

But Aggie looked stricken at this proposal. "Don't bring him here, Arthur. Please. Promise me."

Arthur faltered. "No, of course. I won't. But—"

"I really, really don't want Toby to know where I am," Agatha said.

"Yes. All right. You tell him in your own way."

Later, after he understood what had happened between Agatha and Toby, Arthur lay awake at night and went over this conversation in his head, marveling that he could have been so stupid, that he had been so blind all along. In every way that he had prolonged their words that afternoon while Mrs. MacCauley was off arranging for coffee to be brought to them, he had pained Aggie further, insisting on Toby's friendship to her, his support, his affection.

He would never forget the generosity of Aggie's initial silence, the extraordinary generosity of her impulse to protect both him and Toby. And she made the rules, in a way, once her father had sent her to Breakabeen. She said that this was civilization as she understood it. She said how it would be, how they were all to look at it . . . and for a short while, Arthur imagined it a kindness to pretend to believe it, though they all knew the truth eventually.

Kindness came into it, as well as fear. Even Toby's disappearance, Arthur sensed, was a type of kindness. And somehow, in the midst of all that kindness, first one child had been lost, and then another, until the big house was empty of everyone except Agatha herself, and on his hill a quarter mile away, through a grove of trees whose leaves whispered darkly in the night wind, there was Arthur, standing alone by the window late into the night, calculating the terrible cost of so much love.

Over the years, when he thought of Agatha and Toby together, he remembered only the more distant past, only the way in which they *both* seemed his children, both seemed to belong to him, their heads bowed together over supper or a book, or holding hands on the frozen lake, or pushing each other in the swing, or running through the barn, or playing with the kittens or the succession of dogs that Arthur had helped raise with Toby. Toby was the brother Agatha never had, and she his sister. Arthur had settled the squabbles that took place between them as between all siblings. Toby was unfailingly protective of Agatha, admiring, fond.

But of course, as Arthur learned, he had been something else, too.

Mrs. MacCauley returned with a tray set with the coffee things—a silver pot, two fine china cups, cream and sugar, a plate of plain biscuits, a glass of milk.

"Please help yourselves," she told them, setting the tray down on a small table by the divan. "You might like a glass of milk, Agatha? Do you drink milk? You ought to, you know. I've brought you one. I'll just go and see about your room, Mr. Duvall, and then we'll have a tour, shall we?" She took a deep breath, smiled, and left them again.

Aggie went over to the tray and poured coffee for the two of them, heaping sugar and cream into her own cup and taking a biscuit. She ignored the glass of milk. She brought Arthur his cup and then returned to sit down on the divan, where she watched Arthur. Suddenly she smiled at him. "I'm glad you're staying," she said. "But the other girls will think it's really strange."

"I will be charming," Arthur said expansively. He felt generous: he had filled Mr. Duvall's shoes, he had bought time. That was what money did for you, he thought. "I will charm them."

"I know you will," Aggie said.

ARTHUR FOUND IT interesting to sit at dinner that night with the occupants of Breakabeen, thirty pregnant girls, some of them very advanced, their big bellies concealed under maternity smocks and blouses with ribbons at the neck. He could not explain why he did not find it more uncomfortable than he did, except that the girls themselves did not seem unhappy. They looked well—well fed, well cared for. They chattered with one another just as girls everywhere seemed to. If you didn't notice their stomachs, you might think them a very charming group, he thought. The table was beautifully laid, with a white cloth and silver. The heavy mirrors on the wall, the only decoration, reflected the bright colors of the peonies and pink meadow roses—Arthur recognized the roses from the Duvalls' where they grew wild over the stone walls.

When Mrs. MacCauley came into the dining room with Arthur and Aggie, Walter was standing up and leaning over to tweak one of the arrangements, his untucked shirt falling onto his plate. He turned around when his mother came in, and hurried to pull out her chair for her at the end of the table. He made no sign that he recognized Arthur or Agatha.

Mrs. MacCauley introduced them, her hand on Aggie's shoulder.

"This is Agatha Duvall, girls," she said, "and her father, Mr. Duvall. He'll be staying with us this evening." The girls looked up from the table, murmuring hellos. Arthur saw a few of them exchange looks, but he took the seat Mrs. MacCauley indicated and smiled reassuringly at Aggie, across the table from him. Mrs. MacCauley sat down beside Walter and patted his arm. "The flowers look lovely."

"How do you do, Mr. Duvall?" The girl to his right smiled politely. She was sort of pretty, innocent-looking, Arthur thought—she didn't look much older than twelve—but her nose was unfortunate, turned up too much, like a pig's. Her blond hair was waved back carefully off her face and bobbed neatly at her shoulders. She wore a blue dress and a pink chiffon scarf at her neck. Arthur noticed, when he sat down, that she had slipped off her shoes beneath the table and that her feet were bare. Her toenails had been painted pink. It occurred to him that Aggie had nothing to wear for her pregnancy. She would need something other than Toby's old shirts.

"What kind of business are you in, sir?" The girl concentrated on her plate, cutting her pancakes into neat portions and heaping them into a pile. How old was this child? Arthur thought, suddenly troubled.

"I'm in banking," he said. "It's very dull, I promise you." He caught Aggie's gaze resting on him from across the table. She rolled her eyes at him and looked down at her plate. He looked away hurriedly. "And where are you from?" he said, turning his attention back to the girl beside him.

Mrs. MacCauley had been listening from a few seats away. "Sometimes the girls are not especially comfortable divulging information about themselves, Mr. Duvall," she said. "Those who choose to have even taken names that are not their own, but we have no way of knowing whether that is the case or not with any particular girl. They must weigh their own feelings in the matter."

Silence had fallen over the table. Arthur wondered what arrangements Mr. Duvall had actually made with Mrs. MacCauley. Did she believe their names to be a masquerade, too? No one looked up.

Mrs. MacCauley paused gently. "It is not a question of shame, you understand," she said, as if in explanation.

Arthur felt rebuffed somehow, but when Mrs. MacCauley turned away and conversation had resumed, the girl leaned toward Arthur and spoke quietly. "My name's Irene Milhouser," she said. "I don't care if you know where I'm from. I think it's really nice that you're here with your daughter. I guess you had to send her away, though, so people didn't find out? I'm from New Jersey. Patterson."

Arthur made an indeterminate noise, glancing at Aggie, and passed along a pitcher of maple syrup that had been handed to him. He was surprised by the girl's frankness.

"My parents won't let me marry my boyfriend right now, even though we're really in love," Irene said, helping herself to the fruit. "But he's going to wait for me. His name's Eddie."

Arthur smiled at her. Her disarming conversation cheered him. She *must* be older than she looked, he thought. "This is a nice place, this Breakabeen?" he asked her.

Irene ladled syrup onto her pancakes. She gave him a sidelong look and smiled ruefully. "Well, if you have to be someplace like this . . . I bet this is one of the nicer ones. There's a girl here"—with lowered eyes, Irene indicated a girl further down the table, her heavy dark hair piled into a bun on top of her head, her face round and placid—"she's been in this kind of trouble before, and her parents sent her to a different place, in Canada. It was called the Miséricorde, run by nuns. Isn't that awful? The Miséricorde. She said that place was terrible. They didn't have anything to do except clean and sneak cigarettes."

"And here? What do you do here?"

"Oh, there's no time to rest, practically. Mrs. MacCauley keeps us busy all day long. I mean, it's not always all that interesting . . ." She hesitated. "We have schoolwork, although not so much now that it's summer. Mr. Vox, he's our tutor. He's pretty nice. And there's music lessons and painting classes and cooking and health. And French discussion. We take turns helping with dinner, because Mrs. MacCauley says every woman ought to know how to cook. At night we watch films or listen to music. Or Mrs. MacCauley reads to us." She grimaced and made an apologetic face at Arthur. "It's mostly travel films," she whispered. "Of Mrs. MacCauley's travels, I think, some of them. Those are pretty dull. But she was beautiful when she was younger."

Arthur glanced down the table at Mrs. MacCauley, who had laid a light, restraining hand on Walter's arm and was listening attentively to the girl to her left. Then he let his eyes travel across the table to Agatha. She was eating, her eyes downcast. She wasn't speaking to anyone, and the girls on each side of her were either equally silent or engaged in conversation with the girl to their other side.

"You will be a friend to Agatha for me, Irene?" he asked quietly.

"Oh, sure," she said. "I know how she feels." She glanced over at Agatha and then lowered her voice again. "Are you giving up the baby, Mr. Duvall? I ask because most girls are, but some of them are pretty broken up about it. My baby's going into temporary foster care, until Eddie and I can get married and he has a job and everything. I mean, my parents want me just to give it up completely . . ." She paused uncertainly.

"Who would like to have a walk after dinner, if the rain holds off?" Mrs. MacCauley spoke from the end of the table, interrupting them. She spoke to Arthur. "We didn't go out after lunch, as usual, as it was so threatening. But it looks like it might be all right for a bit longer."

Several girls murmured agreement. Arthur glanced out the window. The sky was still gray, but a pink light shone behind the clouds in the west.

"Perhaps then we'll have coffee in the sitting room, before our film, and those lovely blueberry pies that Sarah and Eileen made," Mrs. MacCauley said.

After the meal, chairs were pushed back from the table. Four girls obediently began stacking plates and carrying them through the swinging door into the kitchen. A fifth girl brought a fine-bristled brush to the table and began sweeping crumbs from the tablecloth into a small dustpan. Arthur was struck by the order of the household, each girl with an assigned task, no one out of line. Several of the girls had hurried from the room, though, their heads together. He could not get over the strangeness of it, all these pregnant girls.

Irene waited beside Arthur as Aggie rose to her feet and came around to join them. "I'm Irene," she said, holding out her hand to Aggie. She leaned forward and whispered, "It's my real name."

Aggie smiled.

Another girl, in cat's-eye glasses, massively pregnant, her stomach rising up like a high shelf under a printed smock, came to join them.

"This is Loretta." Irene introduced them. She hooked Loretta's arm through her own and squeezed it, smiling. "We're bosom buddies. This is Agatha's father, Mr. Duvall," she said to Loretta. "He's in banking."

They turned to leave the room together. "Want to go for a walk?" Loretta asked, glancing at Agatha and Arthur.

Agatha looked at Arthur.

"Thank you," he said. "We'd love to."

They left Breakabeen by the front door and headed together down the long drive. White moths hovered over the tall grass of the lawn. The day's humidity had turned into mist that rose up from the cooling ground. Agatha, whose pregnancy was barely discernible under her big shirt, looked like an untidy urchin beside Loretta and Irene. Loretta's red hair was rolled into a fat sausage curl that threatened to fall over her forehead. Arthur took Agatha's arm. She put up her hand and squeezed his fingers.

"So, Mrs. MacCauley—she is good to you? She is a good person?" Arthur said as they passed through the gateposts and turned onto the sidewalk.

Loretta and Irene exchanged looks.

"Well, she is a *good* person, I guess." Loretta strode along. "You know Walter's her son?"

"Yes, she told us that."

"She's not really a missus, you know," Irene said over her shoulder. "There isn't any Mr. MacCauley."

"He has died?"

Loretta and Irene exchanged looks again.

"Well, that would be hard to say," Loretta said.

Arthur said nothing. There was something else here, he sensed, but he did not want to press the girls. He wanted to know, mostly, if Mrs. MacCauley would be kind to Aggie.

"Oh, yes," Loretta said. "She's kind." She reached over and picked up a stick that had fallen on the sidewalk and began swishing it in the air. "We have discussion circles, when we're invited to share our feelings about what's happening, if we want. She thinks it's good for us to talk about . . . well, you know . . ." Her voice trailed off.

"See, some girls are keeping their babies, but they can't bring them home because their parents don't want them to," Irene said. "So Mrs. MacCauley helps girls get jobs and helps them make arrangements about temporary care for their babies. That's what she's doing for me."

"But . . . their families . . ." Arthur began.

"Well, sometimes there's nothing she can do," Irene admitted. "But she talks to your parents, if that's what you want. She's talked to my mother, twice. My father won't speak to her."

Loretta brandished her stick. "She's very admirable, Mrs. MacCauley."

"I *really* admire her," Irene said. "She's very nice to Walter, and he's not especially lovable, is he? He kind of gives me the creeps."

"That's just because you're not his mother," Loretta said. She swiped at a weed.

"She's *very* dignified, though." Irene seemed eager to resurrect Mrs. MacCauley's image for Arthur and Aggie.

"Oh, *very*," said Loretta thoughtfully. "But not necessarily very happy."

"This house"—Arthur indicated behind them—"it is her house?"

"That's the romantic part," Irene said. "She was the housekeeper for the man who owned it. She took care of him for years and years. He must have really loved her, because he left the house to her when he died."

"But he was not Mr. MacCauley?" Arthur felt confused.

"No. He wasn't. I don't know that she likes men awfully much," Loretta said.

They passed in front of a house close by the sidewalk, a small, neat Victorian with blue trim and a garden dense with nodding white phlox and spires of Russian sage and pink and white peonies behind an immaculately painted picket fence. A trim, snowy-haired man had been standing on the porch in his shirtsleeves and suspenders, smoking a pipe, but he turned away abruptly and went inside when he saw the girls, the screen door banging shut behind him.

Loretta sighed. "We're the Typhoid Marys of Breakabeen," she said, running her hands over her stomach. "They practically evacuate the movie theater when we show up."

Agatha laughed. Loretta turned to her appreciatively, glancing between her and Arthur. "You two have a nice relationship, don't you?" she said. "That's pretty unusual for these circumstances, if you know what I mean."

Agatha glanced up at Arthur. "Actually," she said, "he's not my father."

Irene clapped her hand over her mouth. "He's not your *boyfriend?*"

Agatha squeezed Arthur's arm. "This is Arthur Henning," she said. "He works for my father. But he's like a real father to me. He's the one who takes care of me."

"Mrs. MacCauley doesn't know?" Loretta hooted. "You'd better be careful. She'll be livid if she finds out. She sets a great store by honesty."

Arthur felt a moment's guilt. "We do not mean to deceive her," he said. "But I didn't want to drop Agatha off, you know . . . like a bag of potatoes."

"That's what we are, all right," Loretta said. She laughed. "Bags of potatoes."

"It was sort of her mistake," Aggie said. "She thought he was my father."

Loretta looked them over, still smiling. "Well, you're lucky," she said to Aggie. "You're lucky to have a friend like that."

"I know," Aggie said, and when she looked up at Arthur, smiling, he felt his heart lift and fall, lift and fall.

It would always be like that, he thought.

IN THE SITTING ROOM later that evening, the warmest of the rooms in the house that he had seen so far, with groups of comfortable chairs and fringed pillows on the floor and a cream-colored rug, Arthur sat between Aggie and Loretta on a sofa and was helped to blueberry pie and coffee. Aggie, leaning over him to say something to Loretta, looked happy. She smiled up at him, put her head briefly on his shoulder. "Thanks, Arthur," she said quietly. "Thanks for staying."

From time to time, whenever anyone referred to him as Mr. Duvall, Loretta kicked him surreptitiously on the shin, suppressing a grin. Arthur, too, found that he was trying not to laugh, and he had trouble keeping a straight face. Once or twice he caught Mrs. MacCauley glancing over at him, but she was busy serving pie and chatting with the girls, and her gaze, polite but watchful, never lingered too long. At one point she looked around and, apparently failing to see two of the girls, excused herself to go and look for them.

"Have you seen Leona or Kate?" she asked Loretta on her way out.

"Uh-oh," Loretta said as Mrs. MacCauley left the room. "If she finds them smoking again, they'll be in trouble."

"We're not exactly prisoners," Irene volunteered, pulling her chair closer, "but she keeps pretty close watch."

"You know how mothers always say they've got eyes in the back of their head?" Loretta leaned over Arthur to address Aggie. "Well, Mrs. MacCauley just has one big third eye, like a scary Cyclops, under her hair. She sees everything. And she can smell smoke in the bathroom from down in her office." She glanced up at Arthur and then back at Aggie. "You'd better be careful," she repeated, and her face was serious. "I've gotten up in the middle of the night sometimes to use the bathroom," she said, putting her hand over her stomach, "—you know, it goes with the territory. And she's scared me to death, coming down the hall with a flashlight. She found a boy in here once, someone's boyfriend. She called the *police*."

When the girls turned off the lights and Mrs. MacCauley returned—without the two missing girls, Arthur noticed—to switch on the projector, Arthur allowed himself to appreciate, for a moment, the pleasant pressure of Agatha's shoulder against his side, the scent of Loretta's perfume, the sighs and rustlings and murmurs of the girls around him. It was wrong, he thought, to find himself happy here, wedged in among all these girls with their big bellies. They were, all of them, tragic, in a kind of trouble whose dimensions they could hardly be expected to understand, they who had not yet had children, who were too young to have children, who were children themselves. They did not know what they were losing.

He looked around the room at the profiles of the girls as they raised their faces toward the screen Mrs. MacCauley had set up in front of the fireplace with its carved mantel. They were so young, so innocent . . . yet it was a difficult innocence, an innocence that had been crossed by something adult, that had been compromised in a final way. One girl, big and ungainly as a horse, with a horse's long, nodding face and lower lip hanging stupidly like an open drawer, sat by herself in a corner, a balled-up handkerchief screwed up to her eyes. Arthur could hear her sniffling.

"Oh, no," Loretta whispered to him as the film began, leaning over to keep her voice soft, as a grainy image of several people in three-cornered hats and white leggings, standing in what looked like a colonial settlement, appeared on the screen. "It's Williamsburg again. I've already seen this one."

Arthur glanced at Agatha. She was watching the screen. Her face looked relaxed. Her hand had slid, unconsciously, to rest over her stomach. "I'm going to use the telephone," he said quietly.

She looked over at him, and their eyes met. "Don't worry," he whispered, and stood up.

He had seen a telephone in the hallway by the dining room.

He supposed it was the phone the girls were supposed to use; there was a small chair there with a needlepoint seat, and a little desk with a notepad asking for callers to record the number they dialed and the date of their call.

Toby did not answer the phone at the cottage. Arthur let it ring several times and then hung up and dialed the servants' line at the Duvalls'.

"How is she?" Peggy asked. "The place is nice? Why are you still there?"

"She's fine," Arthur told her, and tried to describe Breakabeen for her. "It's very large," he said. "Good food," he added, knowing that would comfort her.

"Well, that's something anyway. Toby came down. He said to tell you he's over at his friend's house, that tall boy . . ." Peggy had trouble remembering the names of Toby's friends. There were so many of them, she grumbled, and all so big. "They're working on his car over there. He said he left you a note. When are you coming back?"

Arthur thought. "Tomorrow," he said. "It was further than I thought."

"You want me to leave him a note up there?" Peggy hesitated a moment before going on. "I told him you were doing something for Mr. Duvall—fetching some papers. I'll leave him a note . . . He can come down here for breakfast if he wants."

"Thank you," Arthur said.

"Should I say anything to the Duvalls?"

"What is there to say?" Arthur felt some of his anger at Mr.

Duvall, from earlier that morning, returning. "She's here. I'll leave her tomorrow."

"You tell her everything's going to be OK," Peggy said. "You tell her she should call here whenever she wants, if she needs anything."

Arthur hung up the phone and sat at the little desk for a moment. He heard the sound of voices coming from the kitchen, laughter and the clatter of plates reaching his ears as the swinging door opened and then shut again. Then the house was utterly still. The film had no sound to it, and in any case he had closed the door softly behind him when he left the room. Mrs. MacCauley, her face so still and calm that she might have been a statue, was sitting on a folding chair by the projector, her hands in her lap. Arthur wondered what had happened to the two missing girls. Suddenly he became aware of someone watching him. He turned around.

Walter was standing in the darkened dining room, an armload of lilies in a trug on the dining room table. After a long moment he raised a pair of clippers in his hand. "I like flowers," he said. "I like them a lot."

Arthur stood up. "They are beautiful, your flowers."

Walter turned away abruptly and began replacing the flowers in the crystal bowls with fresh ones.

"You grow these yourself, Walter?" Arthur came to stand in the door of the dining room. It was so dark that he could not see Walter's face clearly, only the shine of his white shirt and his pale hands moving among the flowers.

"I grow them."

Arthur stood in the door, thinking of what Loretta and Irene had told him of Mrs. MacCauley's history. Something lay behind her mission here, he thought. He wondered what the circumstances of Walter's birth had been.

Suddenly Walter began to hum. The melody was wandering, tuneless, a haunting sound. Arthur felt the hair rise on his arms, though it was not fear he felt, more a piercing sadness.

Then Walter stopped abruptly. "Music while one works makes a glad heart," he said. He stood motionless. "A glad heart," he whispered. And then he gathered up the spent flowers and stuffed them into his basket and left the room.

Arthur waited in the door for a moment. A cold feeling had settled over him. He turned back to the telephone. He tried the number at the cottage again, even though Peggy had told him Toby was out. He let it ring so many times that he lost count, and then at last he replaced the receiver.

THAT NIGHT, HE could not sleep. He'd brought no clothes with him—foolishness, he reproved himself now—and so he slept in his shorts and undershirt. His shirt would be wrinkled in the morning. That had been a bad moment, when he'd had to confess to Mrs. MacCauley that he'd brought no overnight case with him. "The drive—it was longer than I expected," he had said lamely.

On the floors above and below him, in the rooms in the next wing, lay thirty pregnant girls, listening to the same noises

Arthur attended to now—the lonely nighttime warble of a whip-poor-will on the lake, the wind stirring in the leaves, the back-and-forth, irregular sawing of tree frogs. Or perhaps the girls were all asleep.

If they were lucky, Arthur thought, rolling over and staring wide-eyed into the dark, they were asleep.

For could they be thinking of anything happy, if they were still lying awake?

FIVE

ARTHUR MADE THE DRIVE from Creston to Breakabeen three times that June, leaving Friday evening and returning home late Sunday night. He found a motel called the Forty Winks—a phrase Aggie needed to explain to him—about an hour south of Breakabeen. Early Saturday morning, after a few hours' sleep at the Forty Winks, he would shower and change into clean clothes before driving the rest of the way. He returned to the motel each week late Saturday evening when Mrs. MacCauley put on her recordings of Beniamino Gigli singing "Panis Angelicus" and "Ave Maria," or the Lord's Prayer sung by John Charles Thomas. That was the signal that the girls, wherever they were in the house at that moment, whatever they were doing, were to conclude their activities and go to bed. Mrs. MacCauley, having carefully placed the needle on the phonograph, sat by herself in the dark in the big drawing room until the music ended. Walter would come to the door to say good night to his mother before heading off to his rooms above the garage, but he always waited until the last note had been played before disturbing her. "I don't like thinking about him, really," Loretta told Aggie and Arthur, "but I can't seem to help it. I hate seeing him waiting there at the door for her. Why *is* that?"

Arthur slept better during those few nights in his room at that motel, with its pine-paneled walls beaded with resin and its tiny corner sink and rusty shower, than he had at any time since the war. He stayed in the same room each time, the last at the end of the block of six rooms so low ceilinged that Arthur had to stoop to enter the door; once inside, his head was only inches from the light fixture. Each time he arrived, stiff and bleary-eyed from the long drive, he opened the window and hung his clean shirt on the curtain rod, where it billowed like a ghost in the night air.

He lay on his back on the bed in the darkness, smelling the unfamiliar smells of the strange room, his hands folded over his chest. The sounds of invisible tree frogs and wind in the pine trees came to him through the open window. He should have been ill at ease, he knew, but he fell asleep those nights almost instantly, with the unfamiliar certainty that he would sleep, that he would sleep all night long, and that he would wake, refreshed and calm, shortly after dawn, his shirt glowing at the window with pink light.

The crude simplicity of the Forty Winks reminded him of the internment camp on the Isle of Man, the seaside boarding-house he had shared with twenty other men. In that house there had been straw pallets on the beds and floor, only slightly less comfortable than the motel's mattress, and the same smell of damp.

But while he was completely alone at the Forty Winks, at the internment camp the men had lived on top of one another and could hardly scratch without bumping the fellows beside them. The men's washing hung on makeshift lines strung across the sitting room by the electric heater. The state of these lines—whether they were disturbed or crowded or whether items had been taken down before they were dry—was the subject of arguments and sometimes barely contained violence among the inmates. The weather was rainy and cold, even though it was summer, and dry clothes were highly prized. Also, those men who were tidy by nature—especially the older men—quarreled continuously with those who were not. Regardless, books and papers spread out on the rickety tables, and dishes and silverware cluttered the floor; the men ate on their laps, as there were too few places at the table, and set their dishes down by their feet when they were finished, distracted by the often passionate conversations taking place in the room.

To keep themselves busy and to maintain their spirits, the internees organized People's Universities, delivering lectures to one another on their respective disciplines—psychology, mathematics, biology, music—which spilled over into heated discussion after meals. Arthur shared neither his fellow internees' intellectual experience nor their confidence, but he listened to everything and made himself useful by helping to prepare and cook the food supplies that were dropped off at each house for the internees to fix for themselves. He and another man, an old

Jew from Poland who spoke surprisingly little English after a decade in London, where he'd worked at a relative's ribbon factory, listened through the open windows of the kitchen to the impromptu quartets that assembled on the porch to play Mozart through the mornings and long, cloudy afternoons of that first summer, moving inside once truly cold weather settled in to gather in the small sitting room. If Arthur had not been so worried about Anna and Toby and the baby on the way, he might almost have been happy then, peeling the ever present potatoes, chopping onions. He felt elevated by the discussions taking place around him, as though this were what had been awaiting him all the time, the better life his uncle had promised, the life Anna had believed in. How it could be that he felt these things while a prisoner, he could not understand, but he knew that he did feel them. His pleasure was that of the hidden child who listens without being required to speak and say what he knows. Arthur indeed felt childlike then—certainly as powerless as a child—though he was thirty-two the summer he and his uncle Ivo were surprised by British detectives who strode into the reading room of the public library on a Saturday afternoon, having barred all the exits, and rounded up every German and Austrian present in the building.

Many of the men taken away over the few days of that purge were already sick at heart. Jobless, without purpose, country, or identity, they had sought in their long hours in the libraries, in the distractions of the newspapers of the day and the hollow pretense of their engagement there, a little solace, refuge from the specter of their own uselessness, their own disenfranchisement. Most of the prisoners who ended up sharing the boardinghouse where Arthur was assigned were much older than he. Some were men of considerable experience and culture and industry. They were learned men, men of value, and Arthur, frightened as he was, especially of the Nazi sympathizers and Fascists who had been collected along with the others in the raids and brought an air of sullen violence to the boardinghouse communities, could not bring himself to believe that England would sacrifice them.

Yet the sense of timelessness he had felt on the Isle of Man —the days of boredom and isolation and fear spiked with impassioned discussion, the afternoons and evenings of music so beautiful, so heartbreaking, that many men wept for all they had lost, their hands covering their eyes—was not unlike what he felt those nights in the motel outside Breakabeen. It was as though the cords of his heart had been pulled tight, as though his heart had never been so large, so full of happiness and sorrow equally, two states that refused to reconcile. Before him now was the immediate happiness of his days alone with Aggie, or at least in her company with the other girls at Breakabeen— days when he felt inspired by his desire to take care of Aggie, to be as kind as possible to her, when he knew she was comforted by his presence. But ahead was something just as unknown and terrifying as what had lain offshore of the Isle of Man in the cold gray waters of the Irish Sea—as terrifying as the war and its unimaginable conclusion. As the weeks went by and Aggie grew noticeably larger, Arthur's love for her, along with his sense of helplessness, grew. The baby was due on Labor Day (Arthur knew what Labor Day was, but the coincidence of the holiday and Aggie's delivery date had to be explained to him by Aggie and Loretta), and every day Arthur had to fight against the knowledge of what would happen to the baby after it was born.

He began to feel that he was the only person who ever stayed at the Forty Winks, that the room had been waiting for him ever since his arrival in America. Sleep, usually so evasive, always began to overcome him on the last miles of the drive, as if in anticipation of the motel room's effect on him. Once, he left a handkerchief on the bedside table by mistake, and when he returned the following week it was still there, folded just as he had left it.

It was sometimes past two o'clock on Saturday morning by the time Arthur pulled wearily onto the grassy driveway of the Forty Winks. A heavyset old man with a shiny bald head and sagging purple pouches beneath his eyes came out in his suspenders and undershirt from a back room each time Arthur rang the bell at the motel office. Each time, the man took Arthur's money and silently handed him a key and a rough white towel. He never asked Arthur his business in the area, and he never seemed to have been woken by Arthur's late arrival. He appeared never to sleep at all, unless he slept by day. He was a warden of the night, Arthur thought, heading to his room, his towel under his arm; this man was the one who remained awake so Arthur himself could sleep, the one who took Arthur's nightmares and worries and love and loss of faith and held them patiently in his hands all night long, without thought or feeling, allowing Arthur the deepest, most restful sleep of his life.

We can carry someone else's burdens so much more easily than our own, Arthur thought, drying himself off after his cold shower in the mornings and knotting the tie he was careful to wear whenever he visited Breakabeen.

Mr. Duvall, he knew, always wore a tie.

TO PEGGY AND KITTY, Arthur told the truth—that he was going to visit Aggie—and they sent gifts of ladyfingers packed in one of Mr. Duvall's shirt boxes, pints of strawberries, loaves of the rye bread Aggie liked, jars of honey, tins of cookies. Kitty copied out verses in her wavering script from a volume of Walter de la Mare's poetry that Aggie had liked as a young child.

"You tell her I'd come with you to see her if I could," Peggy told Arthur as she put the packages into his arms.

As if Aggie's prediction that Kitty would die while she was gone would come horribly true, Kitty's health did in fact worsen that summer. The first week after Aggie left home, on Tuesday night, the household was distracted from its routine by the first of Kitty's three strokes, which were to be followed by a bout of pneumonia. Mr. Duvall, whom Arthur had taken into his office in the city as usual on Monday (Arthur having driven through the night from Breakabeen in order to be home in time), had elected to stay at his club in the city on the weekends, too, despite his original plan to come home on Friday nights; at least with both Aggie and her father gone, and Mrs. Duvall in Florida, Peggy was free to attend to Kitty. If Arthur was grateful for anything that week, he was grateful for that.

Arthur called Mr. Duvall in the city to tell him of Kitty's condition on Wednesday, and he was struck during the conversation that Mr. Duvall asked more questions about Kitty than he had about Aggie after Arthur's return from Breakabeen.

The Monday morning after Arthur had left Aggie at Breakabeen, Mr. Duvall slid into the backseat of the car as usual at six o'clock, pulling in his bad leg with one hand, and shook out the newspaper. "Morning, Arthur," he said.

Arthur, shocked, thought at first that Mr. Duvall would say nothing at all about Aggie. But at the end of the driveway, as if crossing that line would signal the point at which all domestic matters must be put aside until his return, Mr. Duvall had spoken at last.

"Everything go all right yesterday, Arthur?"

Arthur looked back at him in the rearview mirror. Mr. Duvall's eyes were fixed on the papers in his lap. He held a pen in his hand, poised over the page.

"Yesterday," Arthur repeated. "Yes. It was OK."

Mr. Duvall shifted in the backseat. He cleared his throat. "The place came well recommended," he said finally. "The woman in charge . . ." There was a question in his voice.

"Mrs. MacCauley."

"MacCauley. Yes. She is said to . . . run a tight ship."

Arthur said nothing. He thought of Aggie's face when he'd

left her the day before. She had hugged him good-bye in the driveway while Loretta waited discreetly under the portico. After a minute, Aggie had released him, her mouth wobbling with emotion, and had turned away, her eyes bright with tears. She'd raised her hand, a gesture of farewell, and also a plea. Arthur had known to say nothing more.

"You don't understand these things, Arthur," Mr. Duvall said from the backseat.

Arthur stared ahead through the windshield.

"All right," Mr. Duvall said after a minute. "What do you want to say? Let's have it."

Arthur glanced back at him again in the mirror. Mr. Duvall met his eyes, and Arthur thought: This is how it is with him. This is how he gets what he wants. He never backs down, even when he's in the wrong.

Arthur shrugged, knowing it was pointless. "She is very young," he said finally.

"Exactly."

But it wasn't what Arthur had meant. He had wanted to make Mr. Duvall see his daughter, see what Arthur himself had seen. "She is frightened," he said simply.

Mr. Duvall was silent. He turned his head to look out the car window. "You think we're monsters," he said at last.

Arthur said nothing. He noticed that Mr. Duvall had included his wife in this statement. To Arthur it felt like a shifting of blame, a diffusing of it. But perhaps, he thought later, it was also an acknowledgment.

"You'll see, Arthur," Mr. Duvall said. "One day you'll see that it was the only thing to be done." And then he had picked up his pen again and lowered his eyes.

Arthur sped up to pass the car in front of him. An hour later, having driven at breakneck speed into the city, he let Mr. Duvall out of the car at his office and drove away without looking back. They did not say good-bye.

FOLLOWING THE NEWS of Kitty's stroke, Mr. Duvall sent word to the hospital that she was to be shown every courtesy, an order that was apparently fulfilled, as later that day Kitty was moved to a private room and the nurses became very attentive. He also arranged to pay the hospital and doctor's bills, though he did not ask Peggy about this or inform her of his intention. His kindness, Arthur thought, was often like that; you couldn't fault him for his generosity, but he never mentioned the matter to Peggy one way or the other, and that made her uncomfortable and embarrassed. It wasn't the way to treat people, Arthur thought.

He also sent an extravagant arrangement of flowers that Peggy took apart and rearranged in cups and smaller vases borrowed from the nurses.

"Looks like a funeral in here," she muttered, taking her scissors to the lilies. But Arthur thought she was pleased at the attention, despite her anger at Mr. Duvall over Aggie. Mrs. Duvall, apparently contacted in Florida by her husband, sent a crate of oranges to Kitty at the hospital, a gesture that drew a shrug from Peggy. Her anger at Nina Duvall for being such a failure of a mother was deeper than her anger at Mr. Duvall, Arthur knew; a woman should have more heart, she said. Peggy cut away the fruit from the bitter white pith of the oranges and fed the dripping sections to Kitty with her fingers, but she would eat none of it herself.

Every morning that week, Arthur drove Peggy to the hospital and came up to hold the old woman's hand in his own; he would look down at her broad, pale, unresponsive face and untidy hair and try to smile and say something encouraging. But he was filled with pity for her and unnerved by what seemed to have been a premonition on Aggie's part about Kitty's health. If Kitty died, it would be very sad for them all, but especially for Aggie and Peggy. Smiling and nodding in her distracted way, Kitty had always been the one who somehow did the most to dispel the sickness the Duvalls seemed to spread in the house; in Kitty's kitchen, though it had become more and more Peggy's kitchen as Kitty aged, there was always the uncomplicated distraction of a crowded table and a good meal at the end of a long day. The afternoons Aggie had spent there, doing her homework at the table, sitting in front of the fire, helping Kitty ice cakes or chop vegetables or knead bread dough, had probably done her more good over the years than anything else. Kitty's spirits, despite how much work needed to be done, never seemed to waver from a steady cheerfulness. She seemed to need very little for herself, Arthur thought; perhaps that was the secret.

Kitty's illness was terrifying for Peggy, who hurried to her mother's side every morning when Arthur brought her up to

Kitty's hospital room. Peggy barely said good-bye to Arthur those mornings, and he often left after just a few minutes—it seemed wrong to watch, somehow, as Peggy sat red-eyed beside her mother, holding her hand. At four in the afternoon, after a day of mowing or weeding in the gardens or scraping the shutters at the big house in preparation for painting, Arthur returned for Peggy and brought her home, where she fixed supper for herself and Arthur and packed something to tempt Kitty and encourage her to eat. Then Arthur brought Peggy back for evening visiting hours at the hospital and waited for her in the nearly empty cafeteria, reading the newspaper.

He and Peggy agreed not to tell Aggie about Kitty, afraid of upsetting her. He didn't call as often as he would have liked that first week, worried that Aggie would become concerned when Kitty could never be brought to the phone, but the days when he didn't speak to her filled him with worry.

"You're all right?" he asked her on Friday morning when he called to tell her he would be there the next day to visit. "You're sure?"

"I'm fine, Arthur. Promise."

"What have you been doing?"

"Talking with Loretta. Making coffee cakes. Speaking French. Croquet."

"Croquet!" Arthur was fond of croquet.

"I thought you'd be pleased."

"How is Loretta?"

"Dutifully swallowing her cod-liver oil and planning her escape."

"What?" Arthur was alarmed. It had occurred to him that it was not beyond Aggie to do exactly that, to take matters into her own hands.

"She's not really going to escape. She just wants to keep the baby. And she's only got two weeks left, you know, so there isn't much time."

Arthur did know. He'd been keeping track. Aggie herself had twelve weeks left. But he did not want to ask, at least not over the telephone, what Aggie thought about her own baby. She had not volunteered her feelings about it, and Arthur had decided it was kinder not to mention it.

But each time he hung up the phone after talking with Aggie, he realized that he'd wanted her to tell the baby in her belly something from him, wanted her to lay her hand there and say aloud, "Arthur sends his love."

Standing there by the telephone in the hall of his cottage at night, he put his hand over his mouth, rubbing his jaw. He could not face what was coming. He knew he couldn't. But he would have to.

ON WEDNESDAY NIGHT, the day after Kitty's stroke, Arthur drove Peggy home from the hospital at nine o'clock, when visiting hours were over. Peggy was tearful and silent, and Arthur thought he ought to come in with her, but she waved him away at the door. "I'm going to pack up some things to take in to Mother tomorrow," she said. "Some little things to make her feel at home. You go on, Arthur. I'll call you if anything happens."

Arthur had been into Creston the day before to buy material for maternity clothes for Aggie. School was out, and Toby was now working full-time at Snyder's Orchard, coming home filthy and ravenous at the end of the day. Every evening that week, he'd gone down to the lake to swim before going out somewhere with his friends in the evenings. On Thursday, though, it rained all day and Toby came home earlier than usual. He stuck his head briefly in the door of the sitting room, where Arthur was working on a dress for Aggie; he was covered in mud. "Going to shower," he called as he headed upstairs.

Toby looked more like Anna than like Arthur; he had the coloring and build of some of the Russian Jews—curly blond hair darkening toward ginger and a heavy, handsome head and prominent chin and nose, which he had finally grown into in the last year. He looked older than eighteen; he'd started to grow a beard that summer, too, though Arthur disapproved. As Toby went upstairs, Arthur ran his hand over the material spread out on the table, feeling the smooth, cool finish of the brushed cotton he hoped Aggie would find comfortable. Toby did not look Jewish at all, Arthur thought, at least not the way people thought Jews ought to look. Anna herself had been only partly Jewish, and Anna's mother had been, like Anna and Toby, almost exotically Nordic in her coloring. But Toby was a good-looking boy, Arthur thought, and smart; he wanted to be an architect. The cottage was full of Toby's models, miniature houses mounted on plywood bases, built with scraps Arthur brought home from the lumberyard in Creston. Lately he'd been constructing models of big civic buildings—concert houses, government halls, schools, churches—carved out of Oasis and Styrofoam.

Toby came back downstairs and wandered into the sitting room, rubbing a towel through his hair. Arthur glanced over at him as he sat down in the chair by Arthur's dummy and reached out to touch the cloth.

"What are you making, Dad?" Toby said.

"It's a dress." Arthur busied himself at the table where he was unrolling the material for a smock to match the dress.

"I can see *that*. Who's it for? It's kind of a funny shape, isn't it?"

Arthur hesitated. "Friend of Peggy's," he said at last.

Toby got up, hooked the towel around his neck, and went into the kitchen. He came back a few minutes later with a glass of milk in one hand and a roll stuffed with cheese in the other. "Duvall's in the city?"

"At his club." Arthur frowned. He didn't like it when Toby referred to Mr. Duvall that way.

Toby sat down again, stretching his legs out in front of him. He scratched the whiskers on his chin.

"Why don't you shave away that thing?" Arthur pointed his scissors at Toby. "I could do it right now."

Toby ignored him. "You want me to take Peggy in to the hospital tonight? I thought I'd go in to see Kitty."

Arthur put his shears into their leather case and took off his glasses. He began to fold up the pieces for the smock. It was like Toby to want to see Kitty, and like him, as well, to offer to drive Peggy. Arthur looked over at his son, his heart doing a slide of forgiveness after his annoyance over the beard. "You're a good boy," he said.

Toby glanced up at Arthur over his shoulder. "She's OK?"

Arthur stretched his back and came to sit down in the chair on the other side of the hearth. "They say it will be OK," he said. "But she is pretty sick, I think. She doesn't look so good." He looked out the window. It wouldn't be dark for a few more hours. He'd had the windows open all day despite the gentle rain that had fallen throughout the afternoon until just a few minutes before, when the clouds had broken apart and a fresh wind had begun to blow. Arthur had spent the day in the barn with the doors opened to the rain, laying out the shutters from the big house on sawhorses and repairing the broken slats. Arthur had replaced almost nothing in his own cottage since his arrival nine years earlier. Mrs. Duvall had told him when he moved in that she herself had supervised redecorating it for him, but of course he was free to change it however he liked— at his own expense, she'd implied. For the sitting room she had chosen plain red curtains, well made and fully lined, with white panels inside. In the summer, Arthur pulled the heavy drapes aside with leftover ribbon from his sewing box and let the wind blow through the rooms, the sheer curtains flying nearly parallel to the floor when the breeze was strong enough. Arthur liked the wind. The month he liked least in America was August, when the breezes stopped and everything lay still and exhausted under the summer heat.

Now the curtains shifted gracefully, lifting high and then falling back. Toby reached up and batted one away with his hand. "Maybe Aggie wants to go to the hospital with me." He drained his glass of milk. "I haven't seen her all week. Where is she, anyway?"

Arthur stood up and moved back to the table, where he began rifling through his pattern box as if looking for something. He didn't like lying to Toby. He and Peggy had been instructed by Mr. Duvall to tell anyone who asked that Aggie was with her mother in Florida, but Toby would never believe that Aggie had consented to go with her. Still, Arthur had promised Aggie he wouldn't tell Toby where she was. He would speak to her about it again, when he saw her on Saturday; he would bring her around. Of course, Toby would understand about it all. It occurred to Arthur that Toby might know whom Aggie had been involved with, but he couldn't very well ask about it now. So there was not much help for it. He would have to tell Toby the lie about Florida.

"She's with her mother. In Florida."

"You're kidding." Toby turned around in his chair to look at Arthur. "What's she doing *there?*"

Arthur shrugged. "Holiday."

"She didn't say she was going to Florida." Toby sounded accusatory.

Arthur felt flustered. He hated doing this. "Maybe she brings a friend? Trip to the beach for some girls?"

Toby looked at Arthur for a minute and then turned back to the hearth. "Maybe," he said. "I don't know."

Arthur tried to change the subject. "So, how is Snyder's?"

"I'm just mowing this week. Tim mowed over a yellow jacket

nest. He got stung pretty badly." Toby sat still in his chair, gazing out the window. "I can't believe she went to Florida," he said after a minute. "When are they coming back?" He didn't wait for Arthur to answer, though. "It's strange," he went on, "because we talked about going up to Niagara Falls this weekend. We thought you might want to go, too."

Arthur had done very little traveling in America, though he had tried to hide from Toby his fear of straying too far from the Duvalls', his sense that something might happen, that he might somehow be prevented from returning home. He had nightmares, completely predictable nightmares, he thought, in which men who behaved like SS officers, although they were dressed like ordinary people, sometimes even people he recognized, ordered him away from the route he knew would return him home, threatening him, tearing up his papers, striking his face if he didn't obey. In the worst of those dreams, Toby was a young child again and was carried away from him, screaming, while Arthur was held back by his captors and then savagely beaten against the hood of Mr. Duvall's car, the dream blows falling with a kind of psychic pain that finally woke him, trembling and sick. Toby was always just a little boy in those dreams, his face a mask of terror.

Arthur didn't like New York City; he felt like an insect on its streets, with nowhere comfortable or familiar to rest, and he missed Vienna there in a way he did not like to think about. Toby went in often on the train, though; he and Aggie liked to go to the museums and to Central Park to ice-skate in the winter. Once, they'd taken Arthur in with them to go skating;

Arthur had enjoyed that, sitting with a cup of coffee afterward in the overheated little hut, watching the skaters go round and round. Toby had also taken up skiing a few years before, with Aggie's encouragement. Arthur had driven them up to the mountains in the winter, where he sat in the ski lodge and read and drank coffee and watched the skiers. Aggie and Toby had tried to get him on skis, but Arthur had resisted after their first effort. The one time he'd tried it, he'd hardly been able to stand up.

Toby had laughed at him. "What kind of Austrian can't ski?" he'd asked Arthur.

A poor one, Arthur had thought. A Jewish one. But he had said nothing.

Arthur had wanted Toby to have every opportunity, though. He had paid for the skiing lessons, and the swimming lessons when Toby had been younger, and the tennis lessons, too. Toby had never gotten very good at the game, but he was strong enough to give Aggie—who was a good player—a run on the clay court Arthur maintained at the Duvalls'. When they were younger, they had often played in the afternoons after school. Still, Arthur remembered having agreed once that he'd like to see Niagara Falls—one of America's most famous places, after all—and both Aggie and Toby had been enthusiastic.

Arthur wanted to comfort Toby now; it was clear that he was hurt by what he understood as Aggie's unannounced departure. Of course he would be hurt, Arthur thought. They were the oldest of friends. But almost anything he said now—that he was sure Aggie would be back soon, for instance—would be an extension of the lie he was already sorry he had told. And in any case Aggie wouldn't be back soon.

"You take Peggy in tonight and say hello to Kitty," he told Toby instead. "I will go back and get her later. You don't have to stay."

Arthur sometimes felt foolish around Toby. He seemed more like a grandfather to Toby than a father, he thought; he was older than most of Toby's friends' fathers, and his accent and his identity as an immigrant—and a Jew—set him apart. Toby, on the other hand, seemed as purely American as possible, and only Arthur—with his foreign looks and imperfect English and shyness—existed as a clue that Toby's background was not all it seemed. Toby had Anna's cheerful manner, too, and people seemed to like him readily, as they did Aggie. Arthur was bewildered in the face of Toby's ease in the world. Yet it was what he had wanted for Toby. He had tried to protect him from so much over the years, even from the knowledge of what had happened to the Jews during the war, though eventually, of course, Toby had asked about it. When Toby was younger, their conversations about the war had always gone the same way.

"How did we escape?" Toby had wanted to know.

"It wasn't really an escape," Arthur said. "You know the story. Ivo took us in."

"Why do people hate the Jews so much?"

Arthur had shrugged. "You cannot explain it. Why do the white people here hate the Negroes? It is senseless."

"Why don't we . . ." Toby had hesitated, searching for the

words. "Why don't we do anything Jewish? Why don't we go to a synagogue?"

Again, Arthur shrugged. "I don't know too much about it, how to be a Jew. Your mother—she knew more."

"Are you afraid?"

"No, no," Arthur had hastened to tell him. "This is why we came to America. It is safe here. You will always be safe here."

Later, when he was older, Toby had asked, "Doesn't it make you angry, Dad—what happened to all those people?"

And Arthur had thought of Dr. Ornstein—his newspaper, his striped trousers. Sometimes he remembered other details, too: Dr. Ornstein's glasses in the street, an emerald green fountain pen fallen from his pocket, a little brown-and-white dog running by, tail between its legs. But maybe he had made those things up. He couldn't be sure anymore.

"Is God real?" Toby had persisted. "How can there be a God? Why would God let all those people die?"

"Good question," Arthur had said. "Your mother would say—look, I remember this—she would say, 'O God, how can we know you?' It was a prayer. I remember that. So she had the same question as you. Smart boy."

And yet he was aware of how deeply he failed Toby in these conversations, aware of his own shying away from what he could not comprehend, what seemed too *hard* to comprehend—faith and atrocity equally, he thought, all the awful things he did not want to have to think about. He knew that the Lehmans were sorry he was not a better Jew. He himself was sorry. They had invited him to come into the city many times, to the synagogue, to the German-Jewish Club, where there were lectures on the American Constitution, on political life in America. The club had an arrangement with a restaurant in Yorkville: appetizer, soup, a main dish, vegetables, and coffee, for a dollar. But Arthur had made his excuses. It was not that he was ashamed, he told himself, or even that he was afraid. He was like that great big African bird, he thought, an ostrich that puts its head under the sand. He didn't want to see anything. "Yes, yes. All right, Arthur. I understand," Mr. Lehman had told him over the telephone when Arthur had declined yet another invitation to come in for services at the holidays. Mr. Lehman never passed judgment, Arthur thought. Or if he had, he had withheld his opinion from Arthur himself. "It is difficult for all of us, yes. You come when you're ready," he'd finished kindly. "Bring the boy."

Arthur had always felt ashamed of himself after these conversations.

Toby looked over at Arthur now. "You OK, Dad?"

"Yes. Yes. OK." Arthur struggled to his feet. He wanted to stand up suddenly, to go outside for some air. He wanted to take a walk. "So, OK. You will take Peggy to the hospital."

Toby picked up his milk glass. After a moment's hesitation, he asked, "She looks really bad, huh? Am I going to be shocked?"

"She's a little bit . . ." Arthur stopped and searched for the word. "Confused. A little bit lost. But the doctor told Peggy this is normal. She will recover. It was a mild stroke only."

Arthur passed by Toby and rested his hand briefly on his

son's head, smoothing his hair. It sprang back under his fingers, soft and sweet-smelling. Arthur allowed his hand to linger a moment; he did not touch Toby much anymore. But how many girls wanted to put their hands in Toby's curls? he thought. There didn't seem to be any special girl in his life. There was a crowd of boys and girls from Toby's school who seemed to do things together all the time, dances at the hall in Creston, swimming at the falls, movies. And surely Toby had kissed a girl already? Surely one had kissed him back? Maybe there'd been more than that? He didn't talk about it with Arthur.

Maybe he should say something to Toby, Arthur worried. A good father would tell his son some things about being a man. Ask if he had any questions. Dr. Ornstein—had he had time to speak to his own son about such things? A doctor would know what to say, wouldn't he? He wouldn't leave it until it was too late.

Toby looked up at Arthur. "Well, I guess I'll go down and tell Peggy, then. I can take her in whenever she's ready to go. She's not cooking tonight, is she?"

"Yes, yes. She wants to prepare something for Kitty. She said for us to come down."

"What's she making?"

"Ah. Your favorite. Frying chicken."

"*Fried* chicken," Toby said.

"Yes, yes. *Fried*. OK." Arthur waved away the correction. "*Fried* chickens."

• • •

THE NEXT MORNING, Arthur handed Toby a bowl of oatmeal and a bag of sandwiches when he came into the kitchen at seven o'clock, pulling on a T-shirt.

"I'm going away for the weekend," Arthur said, putting the milk on the table. He had lain awake for a long time the previous night. There was no question in his mind that he wanted to go back to Breakabeen and see Aggie—he had told her he was coming, and he and Peggy had agreed that he ought to go, despite Kitty's condition—but he could not tell Toby the truth yet about where he would be. He had worked out a story. "I am picking up Mr. Duvall in the city and taking him to Long Island. He has a meeting."

Toby sat down and poured sugar into his oatmeal. "You have to stay there?"

Arthur had thought of this. "Friday night he goes one place. Saturday night he goes another."

"Where are *you* staying?"

"At the house of his friends. There is a room for me."

"I bet." Toby got up and opened the icebox. "Downstairs with the butler."

"I like Long Island," Arthur said lightly. He could hear Toby's disapproval, and he wanted to head it off. "Sun. Sand. Ocean. I will get a tan."

"Yeah, Dad. Only you won't be lying on the sand getting a tan." Toby poured himself a glass of juice. "You'll be polishing the hubcaps."

"I never!" Arthur was offended. "The garage cleans the car."

Toby shrugged. "What a life," he said. "Having a *meeting* at the *beach*."

Arthur felt despair. He turned around to run water into the oatmeal pot. "It's a very important meeting."

Toby said nothing. He returned to the table with his glass.

Arthur shut off the water and went to put the empty milk bottles in the box outside. He hoped that would be the end of the discussion.

When he came back, Toby was lacing up his work boots. "So when are you leaving?" he asked.

"Late afternoon." Arthur picked up Toby's bowl and put it in the sink. "Peggy will be here. OK?"

Toby leaned back in his chair and looked at Arthur.

"Dad," he said, "Duvall is a complete jerk. And Nina Duvall is a lush. She's always drunk, and he drags you all over Long Island all weekend, or wherever he decides he wants to go. What are you supposed to do with yourself while he's having his *meeting?* Sit in the car and stare out the windshield? What about *your* life?"

Arthur felt flooded with dismay. He sometimes did just sit in the car and stare out the windshield. That was nothing to be ashamed of. What else was he supposed to do? Sometimes the driving made him sleepy.

He turned away, trying to control the fatigue that was creeping over him. He did not want to have this discussion with Toby again.

But Toby went on, his voice reasonable, earnest. "Why don't you leave here, Dad? Come on. You could open a store; you make beautiful stuff. I know you've got enough money to do that. And then you could . . ." He broke off, as if he couldn't imagine, suddenly, what his father might do if he were free of his obligation to the Duvalls. "I don't know, Dad. You could . . . have a hobby. Get a television. Go to a concert. Get *married*."

Arthur's head jerked up.

Toby stopped talking.

Arthur knew that Toby was thinking of his mother, that he was thinking he had stumbled into what he supposed was sacred territory for Arthur. Toby had no memory of Anna, he had told Arthur once many years before, a confession that had made Arthur weep later that evening, alone in his bed. Much as he wanted to have been a better man, Arthur had not honored Anna's memory in the way Toby had supposed. There had been the handful of women he had slept with over the years, his clients, as Peggy innocently called them.

But it was not Anna's face that Arthur saw at that moment. It was Aggie's. He felt himself flush.

"Look, I'm sorry." Toby stood up helplessly.

Arthur turned away. The shame of it, he thought, recognizing it again, letting it wash over him helplessly. The preposterous shame of it. How he wanted her, this girl he had watched grow into a woman, this grown child who was his son's friend, practically his sister.

This girl who was now carrying someone's baby.

Arthur wanted to be perfectly alone at that moment, to be staring out a windshield.

"I'm *sorry*," Toby said again. "*Dad*."

Arthur could feel Toby behind him, waiting. He put his hands on the countertop. "It is not right for you to speak to me that way," he said.

Toby was silent.

"You have no right." Arthur knew he should stop, but he didn't. "After all I have done for you. I have done it all here *because* of the Duvalls—because they made it possible. His *meetings*. His *money*. Now some of it *my* money. *Your* money."

He heard Toby move away toward the door. His footsteps stopped.

Arthur wanted to turn around, but he could not.

"OK, Dad," Toby said. "I just want you to be happy, OK? I'm sorry."

"I am happy," Arthur said. "What do you know about it? Yes, happy. I am happy."

ARTHUR TOOK THE front steps at Breakabeen two at a time on Saturday morning. He had woken at seven to brilliant sunshine, the kind of day that seemed to match and elevate even further his mood. He *was* happy, he'd thought as he showered. He would see Aggie, he would do what he could for her. How different it was, he thought, being useful for someone you loved. He had never minded, ever, doing things for Toby, or for Aggie. His work for Mr. and Mrs. Duvall had never held this happiness, the sense of purposefulness and power that came from making the choice himself, from *choosing* to be helpful. You had to love to be inspired to goodness, Arthur thought, knotting his tie and stooping to peer at his reflection in the tiny mirror over the sink. It was never the same thing as duty.

He breakfasted in the little restaurant on Breakabeen's main street, where he was regarded suspiciously by the man behind the counter. Arthur ordered black coffee and two boiled eggs and a Danish pastry. He cut up his pastry with his knife and fork and read the newspaper. He left a dollar bill folded neatly under the saucer of his coffee cup, hoping that would make the waitress more friendly the next time he came in. He planned to be there often, as often as he could make the trip until Aggie came home.

It was nearing nine by the time he arrived at the house, and though no one was in the hall when he opened the front door, he could hear the sounds of breakfast being taken in the dining room, the murmur of voices, the clinking of cups against saucers. The smells of coffee and bacon were in the air, and the hall smelled sweetly of floor wax and furniture polish. He noticed that a delicate round table with bowed legs and intricate inlay around its edge had been brought into the otherwise empty room and placed near the foot of the stairs by the newel post, like an object in a museum. An explosive arrangement of orange lilies stood in a tall vase on the table's surface.

He began to walk across the hall, but his steps slowed as he approached the door. A picture of himself breaking eagerly into the room and startling the girls at the table, not to mention Mrs. MacCauley, made him hesitate. Mr. Duvall would not make an entrance in that way, with the foolish enthusiasm of a lover. And it struck Arthur suddenly that Mr. Duvall would come bearing gifts of some kind. Arthur had seen how it was done. He had fetched such gifts himself for Mr. Duvall on many occasions—flowers or perfume for a hostess, bottles of wine or brandy for a host, sometimes porcelain boxes or crystal vases, cigars in boxes, or elaborately wrapped packages of chocolates. He brought chocolate cigarettes back from the theater, wrapped cleverly in white paper, with gold foil for the filters. Even for children, Mr. Duvall brought gifts—ducks and dogs and bears on clever tin bicycles that wound up with a key, cashmere scarves and fur muffs, charm bracelets for a little girl's tiny wrist, silver whistles on a cord for boys.

But Arthur had brought nothing with him today. Under the circumstances, would it have been proper to bring Mrs. MacCauley something? Or Aggie herself? He stopped uncertainly. How long did he think he could fool people into believing that he was Aggie's father, that he was a captain of industry, as Peggy called him, and not Arthur Henning, a poor Jew from Vienna? Someone, surely, would reveal the truth. Or Mr. Duvall himself would call while Arthur was there. Arthur had said nothing to Mr. Duvall about being away this weekend. What if he called the cottage, wanting something, and spoke with Toby? Arthur's stomach began to throb with a dull ache, and his ears buzzed. He glanced around furtively. Had Aggie told Mrs. MacCauley that he was coming? He had not asked her to do so. What would she say when she saw him? What would he say to her? How would he explain himself?

He backed away from the door. The double doors to the music room on his right were cracked open. Arthur hurried over to them and leaned through the opening. The curtains were drawn in the room against the bright light; a grand piano, covered with a white cloth, stood at the far end of the room under an enormous mirror in a gilt frame. Chairs stood here and there, scattered around the room as if an audience had risen from them suddenly. At the fireplace, two high-backed armchairs upholstered in faded rose-colored silk faced the empty hearth. Arthur stepped into the room and drew the doors closed quietly behind him. He sat down on one of the delicate wooden chairs near the door and removed his handkerchief from his pocket. Perhaps he could get back out to the car and drive away, call Aggie from a telephone some-where. Then she could tell Mrs. MacCauley that Arthur was on his way, that he was coming for a visit, and there would be no questions.

But before he could rise to his feet again, he heard a sound. Arthur froze, his feet and hands tingling with fear. And then a movement in the mirror at the far end of the room caught his attention. He looked up and in the mirror's surface saw what he had missed when he'd entered the room so stealthily, and in such haste, a moment before. Someone, her knees drawn up to her chest, was huddled in one of the large armchairs facing the fireplace, her face buried in her arms.

Arthur rose to his feet. "Aggie!"

Her head shot up, and their eyes met in the mirror. Her face was a mask of misery.

"Aggie!" he said.

She was as easy to pick up out of the chair as if she had been a child. She stood shakily and put her head against his chest, limp with grief.

He wanted to know then. He knew he did. He wanted to know who it had been. "Tell me, Aggie," he said urgently, his arms around her. "Tell me."

The room was quiet. Arthur looked over Aggie's head and saw himself in the mirror, holding her. Beyond him in the glass, beyond Aggie, beyond the serene, pearl-colored walls of Mrs. MacCauley's drawing room, was a darkness in which Dr. Ornstein raised his head from his newspaper and met Arthur's eyes. After a moment, Dr. Ornstein reached up and removed his glasses, withdrew a handkerchief from his vest pocket, and began polishing the lenses. He replaced the glasses on his nose and glanced up at Arthur again, but his eyes roved away over the coffeehouse as if he could not help it, could not accustom himself to the broken glass, the overturned tables, the smashed plates, the toppled cases that had held the *Apfelstrudel* and the Dobostorte, the florentines and napoleons, the Esterházy torte and *Punschkrapfen,* all that ephemera, melting on the tongue. "I had only a few months left," Dr. Ornstein said. "All of us. We had only a few weeks." His voice was a breath of steam in the chilly air of the dark room. The long black mirror of the coffeehouse, grimy and speckled with age like a brown egg, yawned behind him. He stood up, righted with difficulty one of the heavy marble-topped tables that had been knocked over. He rested his hands on the back of a chair, leaned over as if fatigued. "I can tell you how it went with me after that day," he said. Steam from his breath hung in the air a moment, dissolved. "I repaired all my quarrels with my wife. They seemed like nothing then, and when I lay beside her in our bed at night, and she held me, I knew she was truly my friend. I tried to get her out. I tried to get them all out. I wanted my mother-in-law to go to Ireland. The arrangements cost me a great deal of money, and even then I did not have complete faith in them. Also, it was not so easy to withdraw funds under those circumstances, I can tell you. But she refused to go. None of us could have imagined what would happen, of course, and her whole life had been spent here in Vienna. So." He sighed, his breath a cloud. "My wife refused to leave without her mother, and the children . . . well, finally, it was too late." He pulled out the chair and sat down in it. "In such circumstances, one understands what one did not fully believe before . . . that the worst may happen, that the worst *will* happen. One is like a newborn child, in that way, crashing into the world. Life will be all these things, you understand then: what is good and what is bad, the wife who forgives you, the man who shoots your son before your eyes. You cannot separate them, you see, they are linked together"—he made a brutal twisting motion with his hands—"like the spiral chain of atoms in a protein. One can see this under a microscope. It is all there." He reached up and took off his glasses again, rubbed his eyes with his hand. "How terrifying," he went on quietly, "those minutes in the birth canal. As if the life is being squeezed out of you. You do not know what you will find at the end, or if there even is an end.

And yet once we are here, in this terrible place that is the world, we want to stay here, isn't that so? I wanted to stay alive. Yes." He looked up at Arthur again, patted his chest. "Comfort her," he said. "It is all you can do."

Arthur stared at himself in the mirror, Aggie in his arms. He turned away finally from the bleakness of his own gaze, bowed his head, put his hand up to her hair.

"I can't tell you," she said. "I'm sorry."

"Don't worry," he said, his voice thick. "Don't worry."

She spoke, and he felt her voice against his chest. "Oh my God, Arthur," she said. "How can something so good turn out to be so sad?"

SIX

EARLY FRIDAY MORNING, the day after he had found the child again, Arthur parked Mr. Duvall's car across the street from the boy's house and put on his glasses to look at his watch. It was half past seven. Light snow had begun to fall, and the air was hazy as Arthur stared through the windshield. He didn't know whether he'd arrived early enough to see the child boarding the school bus, and he didn't know what he would do if he was in time, except catch another glimpse of him. It felt beyond him to determine what he wanted to do. He was aware only of moving forward helplessly from one thing to the next, from losing the child to finding him, to the news of Agatha's imminent departure, to what seemed to him his final chance, an offering that had come to him as cleanly as if God himself had divined the perfect, deadly lesson for him: Here is a second chance. Choose again.

Arthur sat in the car. He understood that he had a choice now in a way that he had not since the boy disappeared eight years before. He also understood that his longing had not diminished over the years but had spread under his skin until it lay everywhere against him like a pulse. And now the child had been recovered, and Arthur found that his longing was a hundred times stronger than it had been. It had lain inside him like something asleep all those years, and now, awakened, it staggered into the light after the long winter of Arthur's deprivation, ravenous and single-minded.

Arthur wanted to know this boy, this child who was his grandson—he wanted to know him and be known by him. He wanted all the foolish wants of an adult who loves a child. He wanted just to watch him, the impossible feast of standing still and looking at him minute after minute.

But the child had been given up, given away. The people who had taken him loved him, cared for him, considered him their own. What rights did Arthur—who had stood by once and watched him taken away—have now?

You have no rights, he argued with himself. The boy was given away by his mother. That is the end of the story.

All you have is your longing.

It was very cold in the car. The snow had stopped again, but the sky was gray, the air bleak. Arthur took off his glasses and put his hands in his pockets. He wondered if God was watching him now. Anna had thought of God as the voice of her conscience, but it made Arthur uneasy to imagine that God might be hovering overhead at this moment, waiting to see what Arthur would do. He could feel himself flinching against the thought of it, a godlike shape surging up out of the darkness.

Arthur could more easily imagine God as the far-off director of events staged for his own private, mysterious purpose than as a being so intimately connected with men that he could stand inside their souls, whispering. It was too complicated, too painful, to consider why God would allow such suffering to be visited on the heads of the innocent, anyway—Dr. Ornstein on the street on his knees, human arms sticking up out of the snow, the bones of little children scattered over the field. Look at the war, Arthur thought. Look at what had happened to all those people.

Still, Anna had believed that every life was shaped by God's hand, and he had wanted to feel persuaded by her. But if he believed as Anna had believed, God himself had driven Arthur from Austria; God himself had taken away Arthur's wife and newborn child; God himself had sent Arthur across the ocean to America, while the appalling fires of the Nazi camps poked their witches' fingers of black smoke into the skies on the continent behind them. Was Arthur to assume that God had purposely spared him? And that God had then spread out the richness of possibility—the lovely rise and fall of the land on the Duvalls' estate, the warmth and safety of the cottage, the gift of Toby's life, the privilege of Arthur's witness to that life? . . . That God had even given Aggie to them? And Arthur thought now that if it would have prevented what had happened to them all, he would have been content just to love her at a distance for the rest of his life, to love her in an absolutely pure way, full of patience and gratitude.

Dr. Ornstein glanced up from the table in the coffeehouse,

lowered his newspaper, looked at Arthur over the half-moons of his eyeglasses. What kind of man loves a woman at a distance all his life? his gaze said. What man could be content with such a state of affairs?

Arthur put his head down on the cold rim of the steering wheel. All right, he thought. Not content. I would not have been *content*. I *have* not been content.

And now here he was, sitting in the cold outside the house of the child he had lost and then found. Eight years of forever doing without the sight of him, and now the boy's proximity called to Arthur, a light that seeps through a crack in the door. Yet what kind of impossible forgiveness, what kind of impossible generosity, would have to be declared among them all for Arthur to have what he wanted? What would Aggie say if he showed her the child now? Did she want to see the baby she had given away, or would it break her heart? Would bringing them together be a kindness of the first order, or a cruelty? What would the people who had adopted the boy say if Arthur were to come to the door?

What would the boy himself say? Did he even know the truth of his life?

Years before, Arthur had taken Toby to school one Saturday, when it had been Toby's turn to feed and water the chicks that had been hatched in the school's biology lab incubator. The building had been quiet and chilly, and Arthur had accompanied Toby down the dark halls with the sense of being a trespasser. Here, Toby told him in the long, sloping hall near the auditorium, was where the children knelt against the walls with their hands over their heads, practicing for a bomb raid. Toby showed Arthur the place he was assigned for these drills. Its vacancy, as Arthur and Toby looked down at the empty spot on the tiles near the locked double doors of the auditorium, filled Arthur with an obscure dread.

In the windowless lab, Toby had felt along the wall for the lights. Under the red eye of the warming lamp, the chicks huddled together around one egg that had failed to hatch. Toby had lifted the egg out with his hand, and he and Arthur had held it up to the light as if they might see the curled shape of a chick inside the shell.

Arthur's life felt to him now like that infinitely mysterious egg: no one could say what it contained, death or life or something stalled midway between.

But he would not be self-pitying.

He bent his chin to his chest, closed his eyes. No matter what happened, he had been spared once—more than once, surely; none of the hundreds of bombs that fell on London touched even a hair on his head. He was alive. He could never forget the good fortune that sat on his chest, heavy as a mountain.

Yet as he sat there, he felt his will sink in him, a little death; pain fluttered in his chest.

Yes, he was alive . . . but what was to be done with all this *wanting?*

Tell me, he thought, and he knew he addressed God and Dr. Ornstein both; one of them, at least, ought to explain things to him. What is to be done with this longing, this longing for the door of the house to open and the child to run to me, to know me, to call me his old familiar?

His whole life, Arthur thought, he would want this, just as he wanted Aggie. He had been spared—if that was how one should see it—only to desire all his days what he could not have, as if desire itself were a curse. In another world, a world where Dr. Ornstein stood up smiling from his table at the coffeehouse to welcome his two children, a world where he helped them to pancakes and cream and heard the news of their day, a world that had lived once and breathed through the seasons and then died, the child would have run to Arthur. In another world, Arthur might have held him against his cold coat, felt the child's miraculous breath on his cheek. In another world, Dr. Ornstein's hands would still play over the keys of his beloved Bosendorfer, flying up and down the scales, while the housemaid tapped her foot in its carpet slipper and waltzed with herself in the kitchen.

It had grown fiercely cold in the car. The sky had darkened to the color of steel. The snow that had been so pure now had a leaden cast. Arthur sank down into the lapels of his coat. Pain beat behind his eyes. He was afraid to turn on the engine, though he longed for the heat. But a parked car with its motor running seemed more suspicious, somehow, than a car that might as well be unoccupied. If he slid far enough down into the seat, he might not even be noticed.

"It is my birthday tomorrow," he had said stupidly to Aggie the night before, when he left her at the kitchen door to the big house. It was all he could think of to say at the time, when she asked him what his plans were, proposing that they have dinner Saturday night, after her meeting with her father in the city on Friday.

"Oh, Arthur!" Aggie had said, upset. "Of course it is. I forgot."

"Yes. I forgot, too. Fifty-five, I will be. No, fifty-six. An old man." He gave a short laugh.

Aggie had stood waiting at the door. "Come inside, Arthur. Please. We can fix something quick to eat before I go over to Tivoli. I think Mary Anne's already come for Peggy." Mary Anne was Peggy's oldest friend; she worked in the dining room at the golf and tennis club to which the Duvalls belonged, but she sometimes worked private parties, too. That was how she and Peggy had met, years before, when Mary Anne had come out to the big house to help with a party. Once or twice a month, on Thursday nights, Mary Anne drove out to pick Peggy up and they would go to Mary Anne's mother's house and play cards.

Arthur knew that Aggie was worried about him, that she understood the blow her decision to leave had been. He didn't want to torment her. He himself had thought, all these years, that she must get away from her father, from Creston, from all the memories there. It was just that he was all tangled up with those memories; he could not bear the thought that she might want to escape him, too. And she did not even know about the child, the boy who was their lost baby, growing up. She did not know how close he was to them at this very minute, his head resting on the pillow, his little hands folded under his chin.

"I'm not hungry," he had said. "Thank you." He knew he sounded stiff, pathetic. He couldn't help it.

"You're not *old*," Aggie said, but there was a weariness in her voice that wounded Arthur, that made him persist, even though he wanted to stop, even though he wanted at that moment just to take her in his arms and hold her, knowing now, as he had always known, really, that he couldn't have her. Still, he wanted just to touch her. It was a punishment, it would always be his punishment. He ought to leave, he had thought, looking down at his feet. He ought to leave and go up to his own house. But he couldn't make himself move.

"I *feel* old," he had said, and realized it was the truth. He looked up and met her eyes, seeing in them the truth—that to Aggie he *was* old, had always been old. "I should have been better to you, to Toby," he said. He gestured with his chin. "Back then. I made a mistake."

"Arthur, don't do this. Please." Aggie closed her eyes, but she opened them again. She reached up and rested her hands on his shoulders. "You can come to California," she said. "You can come visit me. Loretta would love to see you. You'd like to see California, wouldn't you?"

Arthur had gazed down into her face, the thick, shining eyelashes, the white skin of her cheekbones, her small nose, reddened from the cold. How persuasive beauty was; one had reverence for such things, he thought, standing up taller in their presence, finer by proximity. Something inside him recovered for a moment, just long enough to allow him to let her go gracefully. "The giant redwoods of California," he said, as if reciting a lesson. He smiled. "I would like to see those, yes. So big a man can step inside and it is as if he is in a room all to himself."

And then he had leaned down and kissed her on both cheeks, holding himself back from pulling her to him. "You can wear the suit tomorrow night. OK? You can tell me everything when you get back."

A HANDFUL OF CHILDREN had begun to gather on the corner half a block up the street. The little girls huddled together in a circle; the boys, hatless, unzipped, scarves trailing, raced over the front lawn of the corner house, tossing fistfuls of snow at one another. Arthur peered over the steering wheel, trying to stay well down in his seat. Could he have missed the boy? A woman in a man's heavy jacket, her hair pushed up under a misshapen white wool hat, stood beside the girls, stamping her feet, her arms hugging her sides. She called something to the boys, returned her gaze to the street, searching for the school bus, Arthur supposed. It wasn't the child's mother, though. And he still didn't see his grandson.

When the school bus pulled up a few moments later, Arthur struggled upright in his seat. The children clambered aboard, the woman helping them up the steps and calling to the boys to hurry. She picked up a fallen mitten from the snowy sidewalk, stepped inside the bus briefly to hand it to the driver. She backed down the steps and waved as the bus pulled away. Arthur craned forward. He was sure he hadn't missed him. But where was he? The front door of the boy's house remained closed.

Alone, the woman returned down the sidewalk toward Arthur, her chin tucked down against the wind. Snow blew up from the drifts on the lawns, eddied in clouds across the sidewalk and the road. Arthur began to shiver. He slid down in the seat again as the woman passed him on the far side of the street, her head still down. She didn't even glance at the car. Arthur looked at the boy's house. There were lights on downstairs, and a car had left the garage that morning; he could see the tire tracks in the snow. But where was the boy? Why hadn't he gotten on the school bus along with the others?

Perhaps he was sick. Arthur remembered Toby's illnesses their first winter in America, the croup that had plagued Toby for several years until it mysteriously went away altogether. For nights at a stretch he had held Toby on his lap in the bathroom of the cottage, the hot water running full force from the showerhead into the old tub, the bamboo-patterned curtain pulled aside to release a torrent of steam into the small room. Toby, his eyes wide with fear, had leaned against Arthur, gasping and coughing, while Arthur murmured to him, hushed him, waited for the coughing to subside. When the bouts had passed, Arthur laid Toby, damp and exhausted, on the bathroom rug, covering him with a blanket while Arthur changed his pajamas for clean ones, applied Vaseline to his cracked lips, smoothed back his hair, offered sips of water. He would carry Toby in to the big bed for the rest of the night and lie awake beside him, listening to Toby breathe, jerking awake over and over again, waiting for the barking cough to begin again. In the morning, both of them would be shaky with exhaustion, Arthur sick with the anger that always replaced his fear once morning had arrived. On those mornings, he felt there were unseen enemies all around them, tormentors who were playing with him, torturing his son, before running off again. He felt such powerful anger he could hardly speak. It was good that Mr. Duvall didn't like to make small talk, because sometimes they drove all the way into the city without exchanging more than a brief greeting, Arthur brooding helplessly behind the steering wheel, savagely negotiating traffic. Arthur would have to leave Toby with Peggy and Kitty while he drove Mr. Duvall into the city, and all the way home he imagined Toby's death, the chalk white face, the blue lips.

Arthur gazed at the boy's house. Could such illnesses be passed down from father to son? Could it be that the boy suffered as Toby had suffered? Arthur studied the upstairs window; there was no way at all for him to help, to step forward and offer his reassurance, his sympathy, his experience.

Here and there along the street, cars pulled away noisily from the curb on their snow chains, or backed down driveways, slipping sometimes and spinning their tires in the snow as they drove off. The exhaust left a sour burning smell in the air. Somewhere a dog barked continuously, a series of short, maddening barks punctuated by brief intervals of silence before they would begin again. No one called out to hush the animal, though. Perhaps the mothers left at home were playing the radio while they made beds and washed the breakfast dishes. Arthur thought he understood the loneliness of those mothers, if they were lonely. He, too, liked the radio on while he was home alone. In his early years in America, the radio had been his tutor, his companion, the source of much that was mysterious and wonderful about the English language. He repeated phrases, dropped his chin and deepened his voice to imitate the cadence of announcers. The radio, and Burma-Shave advertisements, gave him many things to puzzle over. Aggie and Toby tried to explain.

"Doesn't kiss you like she useter?" Arthur had read aloud from the scrap of paper onto which he had copied down the phrase off a billboard he'd seen on his way into New York. "Perhaps she's seen a smoother rooster." He looked up, expectantly.

Aggie and Toby had been at the table, working on a puzzle together.

"It's to make the rhyme, Dad," Toby told him. "*Useter. Rooster.*"

"But it is not a proper word, *useter?*"

"No, Dad."

These phrases, and others, fascinated Arthur. "'The whale put Jonah down the hatch, but coughed him up because he scratched.' That's a good one, no?" Arthur had been delighted by the cleverness of these phrases. "OK. OK," he said, "here is another one. 'My job is keeping faces clean and nobody knows de stubble I've seen.'"

"It's a pun," Aggie explained.

"Ah, yes." Arthur looked down at the paper in his hand.

"*Stubble, trouble,*" Toby said. "Nobody knows the *trouble* I've seen."

Arthur had nodded slowly. "I see."

Aggie had exchanged looks with Toby. "He doesn't see."

"Yes, yes, I see," Arthur had protested. "I get it."

"Go ape, Dad." Toby said.

Arthur had looked up, mystified. Aggie had put her hands over her face, and Toby had laughed.

"It's a giant minefield," Aggie said.

That was happiness, Arthur thought now, staring at the house. That was happiness.

HE DECIDED TO go home; what else was there to do? He couldn't wait outside the house all day, and his fingers and toes were aching from the cold.

And then a small white bus turned onto the street. It pulled opposite Arthur's car, on the far side of the street, and stopped. The horn sounded twice. Arthur sat up. The bus had stopped between him and the boy's house. Hurriedly, Arthur pushed open the car door and stepped out into a snowbank heaped up by a plow. The snow came in over the top of one of his boots. Shaking his foot free, he clambered out of the drift and moved down the sidewalk where he could see around the front of the bus. Under the bare branches of a tree, he stopped. His breath made clouds of stream in the air as thick as if he were smoking a cigar. His bare hands throbbed with cold.

The front door to the house opened and the little boy and his mother appeared. She bent down to wrap a scarf more securely around his chin, pushed him out ahead of her, and hurried with him down the shoveled front walk. Her hair shone, bright as an ember in the gray morning. At the sidewalk, she stopped the boy and bent again to kiss him quickly, helped him up the step onto the bus. She wore no coat, only a man's gray cardigan, which she wrapped tightly around herself now as the door of the bus closed. She backed away from the curb, waving up at a window, at the face Arthur could not see, the little boy's face inclined to the glass and watching for his mother, his mittened hand raised.

The bus began to pull away; there was some writing on a panel on the side of the bus, but Arthur couldn't make it out. He fumbled in his pocket for his glasses, but the lenses had fogged over in the cold air.

He ran back to the car, clambered over the snowdrift, and got inside behind the wheel. He started the engine and put his foot on the accelerator, but the tires protested, grinding and spinning fruitlessly beneath him. The bus had reached the corner. Arthur jolted the car into reverse, snow flying, and then switched gears again. The car rocked forward over the ice and out into the street, just as the bus began to turn.

He saw the woman's face as he pulled even with her and then shot past. He did not want to look, but he had to, and their eyes met for an instant. She had taken a step closer to the street, watching Arthur's car. He saw her hand come up to her throat as he drove past.

Had she recognized him? How could she have recognized him?

He was no one, Arthur thought as he drove off, following the bus. He was only a ghost.

• • •

ARTHUR TRAILED THE BUS through Creston's morning traffic, barely managing to keep it in sight, and almost missed its turning onto a road that struck north. They quickly left the town in its close, rock-walled valley behind and moved out across the flat snowfields, the bus hurtling down the road that stretched out ahead, a gray streak in the whiteness. To the west, the hills rose, covered with stands of deep green firs that poured down to the edge of the fields like a crowd of silent spectators.

Arthur did not like to follow the bus too closely; certainly the boy would have no sense that he was being pursued, but the driver might have looked in his mirror and wondered about the big black car behind him. There was no one else on the road. Arthur could feel the silence of the fields blanketed under snow, the dense, green silence of the encroaching forest. Eight years before, he thought, he had performed this same chase, following the car that took the infant, now a grown boy, away from Mercy Hospital near Breakabeen. This recognition, that he was no closer now than he had been then, disoriented him.

Sometimes in his dreams Arthur tried to warn Dr. Ornstein. He came to the glass of the coffeehouse window and beckoned to him. Or he came directly into the coffeehouse and stood before Dr. Ornstein's table, his hat in his hands. "Please come with me, sir," he said, and tenderly took the doctor's elbow when he stood, bewildered, and allowed himself to be led away. In those dreams, Arthur helped Dr. Ornstein along the streets of Vienna, down into the gnarled rose gardens of the Hofburg, past the marble stallions rearing in the fountains, past the pacing tigers caged in the Schönbrunn garden, through the crowded stalls and umbrellas of the Naschmarkt, under windows in which heaps of folded bedding, set out to air, dried in the afternoon sun. They wandered like old companions into cafés, where they bent down beside the elephantine legs of the billiard tables to examine the dark space beneath. Arthur steered Dr. Ornstein past piles of dung from the horses that drew the carts, past the tubercular patients brought out on their beds into the sun by their white-coated attendants. Dr. Ornstein, asking for Arthur to wait with a touch on his arm, laid a hand on the patients' heads, took their wrists between his fingers, standing quietly. Or sometimes Arthur brought Dr. Ornstein directly into his own room above Julius's shop, where he helped Dr. Ornstein climb into the wardrobe, closed the doors, and then leaned back against them, confronting his own face reflected in the little mirror that hung on the far wall, his skin pale and sweating in the light of the gas lamp. But sometimes in these dreams Dr. Ornstein refused to come with Arthur, rustling the newspaper angrily before his face and leaning back in his chair as if he had not heard Arthur's pleas. He resisted, shaking away Arthur's grasp, making a noise of annoyance through his pursed lips, and then Arthur was in despair and wanted to shake him. Sometimes in these dreams Dr. Ornstein's face was split open by a man's boot, the bloody mass of his brains trampled underfoot; Arthur, finding him that way, sat down in the street when his own legs gave way, and put his head in his hands.

. . .

ARTHUR FELT THE TIRE under him explode at the same instant that he heard the sound, like a single gunshot. The car swerved hard to the right, and Arthur felt the wheels dig wildly into the drift on the side of the road. He veered away from the fence post, slid across the road into the left lane. By the time he brought the car to a stop, the bus was a quarter mile away, then a half. Then it vanished around a bend.

Arthur got out of the car on shaking legs. He looked out over the fields. The place was unfamiliar to him, a shadowless and flat gray; there was a percussive, ringing nothingness in the air in which he recognized how hard his heart was pounding. He found his handkerchief and put it to his eyes, which were watering in the cold wind. There was no telling how far it might be to a service station or a house where he could call a garage.

He walked around to the other side of the car and knelt down to look at the tire. It was shredded, the wheel rim packed with snow. What had caused the tire to explode like that? For all his years of driving, Arthur knew little about cars. He brought Mr. Duvall's cars to the garage to be repaired, and he understood very little of the car's workings beyond the simple mechanics of the engine. He was vaguely afraid of them.

Arthur got painfully to his feet again and turned around to look down the road the way he had come. There was nothing in either direction.

He was halfway through changing the tire, however, when a panel truck came toward him from the direction of Creston, its bed full of split wood. The truck slowed behind him and then stopped a few yards from the bumper. The driver's door opened and a man leaned out. "Plow's coming. Better get that out of the way."

Sweat dripped down Arthur's collar. He had opened his coat, and his hands were bare; the effort of jacking up the car had warmed him, but his hands were like ice. He looked up at the man for a moment, at his checkered jacket, his hat with fur flaps over the ears, his boots laced up to the knee. The man's eyebrows were spiked with gray, his face a dense purple as if it had been compacted.

The road was empty, as was the sky except for a pair of kestrels that circled high over the trees in the grayness.

"Need a hand?" the man said.

"No, thank you. It is all right." Arthur stood up stiffly to fetch the spare out of the trunk.

The man came over and inspected the car. He shook out a pack of cigarettes and extended it toward Arthur. Arthur glanced at the pack for a second before looking away and shaking his head. "Thank you. No."

"Maybe the plow turned off," the man said.

Arthur looked down the road over his shoulder. It was still empty.

"Where you from?" the man said.

Arthur knew what he meant. It was the accent again. But he chose to sidestep the man's implied meaning. "Outside Creston," he said again.

The man blew a cloud of smoke into the air, then hunched down beside Arthur to inspect the tire. "Nice car," he said. He ran a hand along the side of the car. "You come over after the war?"

Arthur felt the hair rise on the back of his neck. He did not like to talk about the war. He did not like telling people he was a Jew; you never knew what they thought. And they sometimes seemed strangely disappointed if he had to confess that he had not been one of the prisoners in the concentration camps; it was as if he had attended an important event but had carelessly kept his back turned the whole while. He had nothing to say about the war. He did not like to think about it. "Yes. After," he said.

He thought of the bus speeding away, the boy—his boy— sitting back quietly in his seat, watching the fields flash past.

"Guess the plow turned off," the man said, smoking and looking off over the fields.

Arthur stowed the jack in the trunk when he was finished, and walked across the road to pick up some pieces of the blown tire. He put those in the trunk, as well. The man watched him. Arthur felt exhausted. He buttoned his coat again, took his hat from the top of the car, and put it on his head. He could feel the lining slide unpleasantly against the sweat on his forehead.

"Well, you've done all right for yourself here, looks like," the man said kindly. "Nice car and all." He seemed in no hurry to go. "Hard for you fellows," he added. He took off his hat and scratched his head, replaced it.

Arthur wanted to be gone. There was no hope of catching the bus now.

"Just thought you might want to get out of the way of the plow," the man said.

"Yes," said Arthur. "Thank you."

"Nice to see you made a success of it over here. Great country," the man called to him as Arthur walked around to the driver's side and opened the door.

"Freedom," the man said. "That's the main thing. Nobody tells you what to do."

Arthur got into the car. "Good morning," he said as politely as he could.

"You can be your own boss here. You've found that out, I guess." The man backed away from the car and held up a hand to wave good-bye, exactly as if he were a host saying farewell to a guest.

Arthur lifted his hand and pulled away. He would never learn to be comfortable here in America, he thought. Never.

A mile down the road, Arthur came to a crossroads and was able to turn around. There was a thicket of signs at the corner, their posts leaning in the drift where the last plow to come through had churned up a shoulder-high heap of dirty snow: BEVERLY EPISCOPAL CHURCH, ONE MILE. STANDARD'S GROCERY. ROCK HALL FARM SCHOOL FOR THE DEAF. FIREWOOD FOR SALE— OAK. These signs whirled past as Arthur backed up and turned around to return home.

He would have to go by the tire store so he could get another tire. He could not drive Mr. Duvall without a spare tire. Mr. Duvall did not like to be surprised by anything.

Arthur glanced down at his hands. They were filthy.

• • •

LATER THAT AFTERNOON he sat with his sleeves rolled up at the kitchen table with Peggy and helped her polish the silver in preparation for the dinner meeting Mr. Duvall planned to host at the house the next weekend.

Peggy had been chattering to him about her friend Mary Anne, and about Mary Anne's mother, who had turned ninety the week before. Birthday cards had lined the dining room table in her apartment, and her friends—though they were mostly Mary Anne's friends, as there weren't too many of her mother's alive anymore, Peggy said—had chipped in to buy her a television set.

Peggy sponged silver polish into the crevices of a salt dish with a blue glass insert and laid it on the newspaper by Arthur's elbow. It was Arthur's job to rub the pieces dry.

"We watched that show, that western, but every time a gun went off, I thought my head would explode," Peggy was complaining. "They have to keep it turned up loud so she can hear it."

Arthur stopped. And he saw it then, saw the whole collection of signs planted in the snowdrift, remembered each one as clearly as if he had been stood to face them, a gun at his neck, and forced to memorize them: BEVERLY EPISCOPAL CHURCH. STANDARD'S GROCERY.

ROCK HALL FARM SCHOOL FOR THE DEAF.

Slowly he put down the rag he had been using.

Peggy glanced over at him. "What's the matter?"

Arthur stood up and crossed the room to look out the window. He put his hand on the back of the chair that had been

Kitty's, fingered the worn nap of the fabric there. Outside, the clouds had thinned as the day had worn on, and the sky was mottled now. The wind had picked up, sending gusts of dry, light snow over the hillsides and into the air like puffs of smoke. The temperature had been dropping all day. He could hear the trees cracking, even from inside.

"Do you think about the baby sometimes?" he said. "Where he is?" He did not turn around.

Was it possible? Was the boy *deaf*? Yesterday afternoon, the woman coming outside to bring the child indoors had said nothing to him. She had put her hand on his head. Had she said *anything*? Wasn't it odd that she had said nothing at all?

"What made you think of that right now?" Peggy said. "After all this time."

Arthur turned around. He still held the polishing rag in his hands. "Do you think about it?" he asked again. "If he is OK? If he is happy? If everything is all right with him?"

"Sometimes. I think about it, yes." She did not look at him. "Of course I do."

Arthur turned away again. A sheet of heavy snow slid suddenly off the roof and crashed into the boxwood bush below, splintering the careful cage of stakes and burlap that Arthur had built to protect it. Arthur noted dispassionately that the shrub would need to be cut back in spring. "She doesn't want to talk about it," he said. "She won't talk about it."

Peggy sighed with impatience. She was often impatient with him these days, Arthur thought, as if his failure to change, to do anything except what he had done all along, was irritating.

Of course, she had not changed either, he thought. She was still keeping house for a man who was never there. They were like a brother and sister who had lived together side by side for too long. Maybe they were sick of each other.

"It hurts her, Arthur. Don't you be bringing it up with her. You leave it alone. What's done is done. It's too late for any of that now."

Arthur turned back and came to the table. He sat down. "Now she is going away."

Peggy didn't look at him.

He searched her face. "You know about this already," he said, accusing.

Peggy put a carving fork in front of him, picked up a handful of spoons. She still didn't look at him. "She told me she wants to go. She told me about her friend in California."

Arthur said nothing. He was not really surprised that Aggie had confided in Peggy, but it hurt him, all the same, that she thought him too fragile to bear the news, that she had not known how to break it to him.

"She should have gone a long time ago," Peggy said.

Arthur put his hand over the silverware. "I know. I know it."

Peggy reached over and laid her hand on his arm, patting it briskly. "Don't you be thinking about all this now—the baby, and Toby. What's done is done. We can't mend these things."

Arthur looked down at the table. Anna had told him the story of Abraham, abandoned in the cave by his mother, Emtelai, who, to save her son, defied Nimrod's order that all pregnant women in his kingdom be imprisoned and took herself off in the throes of birth to deliver in safety in the desert. She abandoned the baby but returned, distraught, twenty days later to look for him and was confronted with her son, walking and talking, a strange baby-man whom she did not recognize. Abraham asked her, "What kind of woman, what kind of mother, would forsake her newborn son in the desert and then come back to look for him after twenty days?"

Arthur closed his eyes. He remembered Anna's voice. He thought he understood in the story now the fear that so disconcerted Emtelai, and also the love that had drawn her back to the cave. He understood that, in the story anyway, she had been forgiven by God and by her son.

What did God mean by putting the boy back within his reach now, just as Aggie declared her intention to leave? Was it a consolation, God offering him a second chance now to reclaim what had been lost, what he, Arthur, had given away, had let go so easily, had abandoned in the desert? Sometimes, Arthur knew, God did not speak in his own voice to those he wanted to hear him. When Moses was just beginning to be a prophet, Anna had said, God addressed him not in his own voice but in the voice of Moses' father, understanding that God's voice, to one unaccustomed to its tones, would be terrifying. Better to choose something more familiar, more persuasive, less alarming.

But was God speaking to him now? How did one know if one was being addressed by God?

And if the child was deaf, how wide was the territory that separated him from Arthur and Agatha, let alone from Toby, who had gone away? Arthur might stand before the boy, he might take him in his arms, look into his eyes. But he could say nothing to him.

If this was God's work, Arthur thought, it was trickery. What did he mean by it? He put the child in Arthur's path. He dangled him like a temptation, like an inducement . . . and then he stole the child's ears so that the boy could hear nothing of Arthur's explanations, his apologies, his words of love and regret, so that he could not know his mother, or his grandfather, or his father.

There was a lesson here, Arthur decided, picking up the spoons. He did not understand what it was, but he felt almost certain now that God was near. There were no plagues of locusts or serpents, no behemoths or angels, no yawning leviathans or pillars of fire or seas dividing or bushes burning without being consumed. Still, he thought, he felt it, God's quizzical consideration of him, the question in God's mind.

"If you could see him," Arthur asked Peggy, "even just once . . . would you do it?"

Peggy's hands stopped. She looked up and met Arthur's eyes. "What are you saying?"

Arthur said nothing. He looked down at his hands.

"Arthur." Peggy gripped the rag in her hands. "Arthur, what are you saying?"

And then Arthur knew he would have to make this decision alone. So here was another lie he would have to tell.

He shrugged, picked up a spoon, and began polishing. "Would it be worse, or better? I ask myself this," he said.

Peggy stared at him a moment longer. Then she dropped her eyes and sighed. After a minute she dug her rag resolutely back into the jar of silver cream. "Well, we don't have that choice, do we?" she asked. "Thank God."

THE NEXT MORNING, Saturday, Arthur backed the car out of the barn and drove back into Creston. He turned off again onto Route 6, the same route he had traveled following the bus the day before. He passed the place on the road where he had stopped to change the flat tire, reached the intersection with the signs. The day was calm, the sky a frail, chalky blue. The snowfields shone dully on either side of the road, a depthless expanse of white.

Three miles later he saw the entrance. He'd hardly even had to search for it. A long drive, recently plowed, curled away among trees whose bare branches hung heavy with snow. He turned the car onto the driveway.

He did not expect to find anyone at the school on a Saturday, and as he followed the long lane he felt comforted by this. He just wanted to see the place. If it was true, if it was true that the child, his grandson, was deaf, that he came here to this school, then Arthur wanted only to see where it was that he spent his days. He did not know what he expected. He did not know anyone who was deaf.

But almost as soon as he thought this, he released his foot from the accelerator in surprise.

There was Mr. Duvall's hand, reaching for the hearing aid in his ear, that gesture with which Arthur was so familiar, the hand cupping the ear for a moment, hesitantly, as if expecting a vague pain.

He had never thought of Mr. Duvall as deaf. But of course there was something wrong with his hearing. Arthur had learned over the years to face Mr. Duvall when he spoke to him, had learned the feel of the man's eyes on his mouth when he spoke. He heard something, Arthur was sure. He could speak on the telephone, but he didn't call often, and he kept conversations short. He made few errors of what could appear to be inattention; his eyes were working all the time, watching you. But certainly he did not hear well.

Arthur stopped the car and turned off the ignition. He stared ahead down the empty lane ahead of him. A fence ran along one side, its posts capped with snow. A bird alighted on one, scattering snow, and then lifted off again and flew away.

Arthur had always supposed that Mr. Duvall's hearing had suffered as a result of his age, that it was something that had afflicted him as he grew older. But he was not so very old even now. What was he? Nearing seventy, surely. Sixty-seven? Sixty-eight? He had turned sixty the year before the baby was born. Arthur remembered that, because Mrs. Duvall had thrown a party for him at the house. There had been bottles of vodka and fresh flowers frozen in bricks of ice on silver trays—Mrs. Duvall had seen this in *Life* magazine, in a picture from somebody's wedding. There had been caviar, and salmon mousses molded into the shapes of fish. A tent had been rented for the lawn behind the house, overlooking the lake, and a parquet dance floor laid on the grass. Colored paper lanterns in red, white, and blue—it was near the Fourth of July—had been strung from the trees and inside the tent. A series of flaming torches led down the hill toward the water, where candles floated on wax paper boats on the lake's surface. Branching silver candelabra burned on the tables. Summer flowers exploded from crystal vases. An orchestra played under the trees, their instruments dazzling.

It had been Arthur's job that night to park the cars. He and Toby and three of Toby's friends, whom Arthur had hired for the occasion—boys who had recently earned their driver's licenses and were thrilled to be driving the guests' expensive automobiles—had parked cars all night long on the field behind the barn. Arthur had devised a complicated valet system for keeping track of the keys and for remembering who drove which car, but there had been a terrible confusion over several cars late in the night when a crowd of people had begun to leave.

As he stood helplessly in the driveway, his hands full of keys, Arthur looked toward the house and saw Mr. Duvall at the front door, shaking the hands of those who were departing. Arthur saw him take note of the collection of people waiting in the driveway, a group that had grown larger as Arthur and the boys tried frantically to sort out which keys belonged to which car.

Mr. Duvall had come down the front walk and steered Arthur away from the guests, his hand on Arthur's shoulder. Arthur tried to explain.

"Why didn't you just leave them in the goddamn ignition?"

Mr. Duvall cut him off, glancing back at his guests and then out over the fields.

He had displayed in front of his guests no sign of impatience or worry. "Wendy, I've never seen you looking so lovely," he called, smiling, to a woman waiting in the driveway. "Tell me you're my birthday present."

The woman had been wearing a hairpiece that fell down her back in hard, golden waves. Mr. Duvall turned around to smile at her as he and Arthur walked past, his fingers hard under Arthur's elbow. "Charming," he murmured. Arthur thought the woman looked as hard as nails in her false hair and frozen expression.

"I'm surprised at you, Arthur," Mr. Duvall said when they had moved away from the others and reached the stone wall and the break that led up a flight of steps, the route the boys and Arthur took when they sprinted up the hill to the barn to retrieve the cars. "It's unlike you to make such an utter mess." Arthur had said nothing; he did not want to tell Mr. Duvall that Arthur himself had decided that they should not simply *ask* people which car they drove when they were ready to leave — he and the boys ought to know this, Arthur felt, or at least appear to know this. They ought to simply bring the right car down to the front door, as if by magic; and the system he'd worked out, though he saw now that it had been too complicated, too unwieldy, had been designed to do exactly that. After all, that was how the rich expected things to be done for them. They expected other people to pay attention to them, to their possessions.

Mr. Duvall stopped and bent his head to light a cigarette, his lighter snapping under his fingers. "The Van Dunns drive a Benz," he said quietly, without looking behind him. "Blue. Vanity plate VAN ONE, as if he had a squadron of them, which he doesn't. He's the short, fat one with the ugly wife in unpleasantly revealing red by the front door." He turned his back to his guests and pulled on the cigarette, releasing smoke upward into the night air as if he had all the time in the world. "Nick and Holly Morgan have a black Porsche. Brand-new. He's the tall one with the scarlet cummerbund, blotto blond wife on his arm and falling off her shoes." He had proceeded to rattle off who drove which car, his descriptions of his guests riddled with dislike and scorn and a knowledge that made Arthur feel afraid of him.

"Now," he said, exhaling smoke through his teeth, "fix it. Hurry." And then he had turned away, strolling back to his guests, who were waiting under the lamplight. And as he left, he touched his ear as if to pick up what was being said among them, whatever expressions of dislike lay behind their civility, their bonhomie, the pretense of their birthday wishes for him.

The evening had ended, for Arthur, in a shambles. They had sorted out the cars eventually, but not before Arthur had lost his temper, first at one of Toby's friends, who had been humiliated, and then at Toby himself. When the last guest had driven away, the taillights of the final car disappearing down the lane into the fragrant darkness of the summer evening, and the Duvalls' front door had been closed, the sawing of the tree frogs became audible in the sudden quiet. Arthur had climbed the hill toward his cottage and into the orchard. For a minute or two he could still hear in the silence behind him the sound of summer beetles driving into the glass shades of the lamps that lined the path up to the Duvalls' front door. In the morning the walkway would be littered with their bodies, crunching underfoot, the glass filthy with dead insects. He would have to clean the lamps. Mrs. Duvall hated it when they were dirty.

Arthur moved into the shadowy warmth of the orchard. The sweet scent of rotting windfall apples rose from the ground.

"Dad." Toby's voice came from among the trees. "We're over here."

Arthur made out Toby's form under a tree, and someone beside him.

"It's me, too." Agatha had spoken.

Aggie had been dressed for the party in a pale yellow chiffon dress that had been purchased for her at Bloomingdale's. Arthur had caught glimpses of her once or twice over the course of the evening as she made her way among the guests or was escorted onto the dance floor by her father. She had looked like a very small, fragile moth, the smooth cap of her dark hair shining, the layers of her dress stirring. In the darkness beneath the tree, Arthur could make out the folds of her dress spread around her on the grass. She was sitting close to Toby; Arthur had the sense that they had been touching, that she had been comforting Toby. He felt ashamed of himself, sick over his display of temper with the boy who had come to help Toby out of friendship. "Don't be so bloody stupid," Arthur had shouted at him. And to Toby, "You are not *helping* me. You are making it *worse*."

Arthur wanted to apologize. He wanted to go to Toby and put his arms around him. He wanted to say he was sorry, that he was ashamed of his fear of Mr. Duvall, his fear of the guests' ridicule and annoyance.

But Agatha had started to laugh. "Did you see the woman whose dress fell off on the dance floor? It fell right off one shoulder and down around her waist. She had her shoes in her hand, waving them around her head. Her husband kept trying to make her sit down."

They were quiet for a minute.

She went on. "One couple ended up in my bedroom."

Neither Toby nor Arthur said anything.

"There was a man stealing silver, too. I saw him put four spoons in his jacket pocket. And there was a lady who kept going around and emptying all the cigarette dishes into her clutch."

Arthur moved to the tree and sat down, his back against the trunk beside Toby. On Toby's other side, Aggie went on, leaning against Toby's shoulder.

"They're not all awful. I know that," she said quietly. "But they're the luckiest people in the world, aren't they? I mean, in terms of money. And they're so insincere and mean and racist and snobby and embarrassing and . . ." She searched for the word. "They're so *unforgivable,* somehow. Don't they have an obligation to be better than that?"

"That's why they call it the root of all evil," Toby said.

Arthur knew Toby was capable of bitterness against the Duvalls; they hardly acknowledged him and certainly did not acknowledge his friendship with Aggie. Yet the way he spoke now—he seemed so adult, measured rather than rash.

Aggie leaned around Toby to look at Arthur. "Was he absolutely horrible to you? About the cars?"

Arthur stared into the darkness, embarrassed. "I made a mess of it," he said quietly.

"You can say it, Dad," Toby blurted out. "You can just say it. Yes, he was horrible. He was a bastard."

"It's all right." Aggie leaned back against the tree again in the darkness. "I know he can be awful, Arthur," she said. "They both can. I'm sorry. I try not to take it personally. Maybe you shouldn't, either."

And that was right, Arthur thought. They were wiser than he—Toby and Agatha. They knew when to be angry. They knew how to forget, too. He was the only one to get it wrong.

"Let's go for a swim," Toby said.

Agatha jumped up, her dress a blur of gold in the darkness. Arthur saw she'd discarded her shoes. Her feet looked white and tender in the grass. "Come on, Arthur," she said. "Come swim with us. There's still some candles burning on the lake. They look beautiful."

Arthur had held up his hands to them. They had stepped toward him and reached down, but he had not let them pull him up. He held their hands a moment. "You are wonderful," Arthur said, looking up at them. "Both of you. Splendid."

"Splendid." Aggie had leaned down to kiss his cheek. "You sound like Dad."

Arthur realized that she was right. Her ear was perfectly tuned to the way her father spoke. Arthur had been listening to him for years. Perhaps he did sound like him.

"You mean you love us." Aggie smiled down at him.

"Yes," Arthur said. "Yes, that is what I mean to say."

"We know," Aggie said.

ARTHUR LOOKED UP, startled at the sound of a car engine. A sedan was coming down the narrow lane toward him. He started Mr. Duvall's car hurriedly and pulled off into the snow on the shoulder of the road as far as he dared, hoping he wouldn't get stuck.

There were two men bundled in coats and hats in the car that passed him. The driver raised a silent hand in greeting and touched his hat brim as the car briefly pulled even with Arthur's. At least they didn't seem surprised to see someone, Arthur thought. They did not stop to ask him what he was doing there. After their car had disappeared, he drove on.

Ahead of him the road dropped away and turned a sharp corner. Here the land was so uneven, its rock-strewn gullies, deep in snow and ice, colliding into the slopes of adjacent hills, that it was impossible to see more than a few hundred feet ahead. Stone walls began abruptly at either side of the road. Arthur caught glimpses of the snowy fields that rolled up beyond them to meet the sky; dry snow blew up from the frozen surface and hung in the air like a dust storm. The lane took another sharp bend, and Arthur slowed the car as the road broadened suddenly and emptied into a circular drive before a long, low white clapboard house, snow lying like cake sugar on its shingled roof. By the front entrance a sign trimmed with holly branches heavy with berries read ROCK HALL FARM SCHOOL.

The main building of the school, surrounded on three sides by a grove of fir trees that backed up against a steep, rocky hillside, was an old house; Arthur guessed it was perhaps a hundred years old, with ten black-shuttered windows across the second story and two chimneys of pink brick. A clapboard annex at one end looked newer to Arthur; the windows were larger, and a red door with a snow-covered porch roof gave onto a shoveled walkway that led to a small parking area and an enclosed courtyard holding children's metal playground equipment, the seats of the swings filled with snow. At the other end of the house, another new addition connected the main building to an old barn that had been renovated sometime recently. Dramatic picture windows broke up the barn's south face. Arthur could see children's artwork hanging up against the glass—construction paper snowflakes, and Christmas trees painted with bright daubs of color, and the silhouettes of red cardinals.

Arthur drove slowly around the circle and pulled into a plowed parking lot near the barn. There were only a handful of cars in the lot, all but one of them covered with snow. He turned off the engine and cracked open his window. The silence of the morning was penetrating, and Arthur felt it as if it were something physical, a compression of space that was simultaneously, mysteriously, like the wrenching open of an unseen window in the sky above. He recognized the quality of this silence from the Duvalls'; in its midst he had the same contradictory sensation of being surrounded both by infinite space and by a thudding, incorporeal nearness like a weight against his skin.

On long winter nights alone at the Duvalls' he had often put on his coat and scarf to wade out, struggling against the drifts, into the empty fields. There he stood, his heart pounding, and listened—though for what, he could not have said. How was it that such profound silence seemed to contain *something,* something he was inexplicably certain of, something of which he was not exactly afraid . . . and yet there was an element of fear in it. The blood in his ears on those nights made the only sound, a percussive fanfare for something that failed to announce itself but that he nevertheless felt indisputably in his bones and teeth and behind his eyes. The night wind played over his face. The stars burned above him in the cold black sky. Something weighed in the silence, an unseen presence in which Arthur felt himself observed.

As he sat in the car, taking in the school buildings, he suddenly noticed a line of figures proceeding down toward the house from the ridge to the west, a man leading a straggling row of a dozen children, their bundled shapes standing out against the whiteness. They came down the hillside through deep snow in a zigzagging line. Every so often, the man at the head of the line turned back in midstride as if checking on the progress of those behind him. He balanced something over his

shoulder—Arthur thought it was a folded-up artist's easel—
and in his free hand he carried a black suitcase.

Arthur ascertained that his boy, his grandson, could not be
among those making their way down the hill toward him; these
were older children, in their early teens perhaps. But surely
they were students at the school; what else would they be
doing there? Perhaps they lived at the school full-time? He
watched them, his curiosity distracting him from worrying
about their approach and his inexplicable presence there. But
then they reached the end of the parking lot and crossed
through the break in the stone wall. They would walk right past
his car.

He straightened up in the seat, his hands on the steering
wheel, but it was too late to start the car and drive away. He sat
there instead, rigid with worry, trying to compose his face into
an expression of casual innocence despite his sense of having
trespassed on a place in which he had no business, or at least
no business he could explain to anyone. The group drew even
with him, and the young man at its head, who strode along with
an energetic, bouncing gait, glanced briefly at Arthur as they
walked past. The children, too, gave quick looks in his direction, as if they might have been expecting someone. Arthur
raised his hand tentatively in silent greeting, but only a couple
of them returned his gesture.

His shoulders began to sag, releasing their tension, as the
last child, bundled up heavily against the cold and wind, moved
past him. And then a gloved hand tapped on the glass of his

window. The man who had been leading the procession had returned and was leaning over by the side of the car, looking in at him. Arthur rolled down the window. His mouth had gone dry. He tried to think of something to say, some explanation he could offer, but his mind had gone utterly blank, as if giant hands were pressing down at his temples, squeezing all memory of language from him. He took note, however, that the thing the man had been carrying was not an easel after all, but a camera tripod.

"You've come about the ad?" The young man didn't wait for an answer. He went on energetically, "Listen, if you don't mind, I've got to get the kids inside. They're freezing." His face, curly blond hair escaping from a felt cap, was boyish, cheerful. "Can you hang on? I mean, inside, of course." He indicated the house behind him with a gloved hand. "I'll meet you in the front hall. Someone'll have coffee going in there. Ten minutes, tops. OK? Do you mind? We've been taking snow pictures, and I want to get the kids started in the dark room. Then I'll be right up." He headed off at a trot after his charges, the tripod bouncing on his shoulder.

Arthur hadn't said a word. After a minute he rolled up the window and sat there. What was the man talking about? What ad? And then Arthur remembered that he had the newspaper with him. He'd stopped in Creston earlier to fill the car with gas, and he'd bought a paper at the same time at the stationer's across the street. He reached for it now on the seat beside him, leafed hurriedly through the pages until he came to the classified ads. And there it was: ROCK HALL FARM SCHOOL FOR THE

DEAF SEEKS WEEKDAY DRIVER FOR ITS MORNING BUS RUN IN CRESTON. EXPERIENCED DRIVERS ONLY. APPLY TO AARON ADLER, AT ROCK HALL FARM SCHOOL. An address and phone number were listed.

Arthur closed the paper and laid it on the seat beside him. EXPERIENCED DRIVERS ONLY. He took off his glasses and folded them in his hand.

He'd been a tailor once and was hired as a driver, when he didn't know how to drive. But now he really *was* a driver. He was a driver, and he was a man longing to know his lost grandchild, and somehow, he thought, somehow the force of his need had been aligned exactly with the force of opportunity, the two of them called forth from behind their boulders in the desert to set out and walk right into each other across the enormous field of the world's chance.

If this wasn't a sign, he didn't know what was.

He'd be a fool, wouldn't he, to turn away from this? It was true he had not come about the ad, but he'd seen it now; and what greater coincidence could one ask for? They wanted a driver, for God's sake.

And what was he, if not a driver?

He looked up at his face in the car's rearview mirror. His eyes stared back at him, but after a minute, he had to look away. With his face cut off like that, just his eyes and the bridge of his nose visible, he looked like someone Arthur didn't know at all. He looked like a perfect stranger.

SEVEN

THE CROQUET LAWN AT Breakabeen was a private place, surrounded by fir trees and reached from the house by a mossy path that ran under a long arbor overrun with vines; clusters of new grapes, tiny and hard as stones, hid among the leaves. The surface of the grass court, onto which one entered from the damp shade of the arbor, was buckled with the uneven tunnels made by moles, and on the Saturday of his third weekend visiting Aggie at Breakabeen, Arthur helped Walter muscle an old roller out of the six-car garage at the bottom of the hill. On the gravel driveway, under the cobwebbed windows of the apartment above the garages, they scrubbed off the worst of the rust on the roller, oiled it, and dragged it up the hill.

"This is a big place for you to look after." Arthur struggled up the hill alongside Walter, alternately pushing and pulling the heavy old roller along the path that wound among the beech trees. "It's a lot of work, yes? You have help?"

Arthur had noticed that though the house was in good repair, the gardens and lawns looked neglected. He'd been inside
the greenhouses with Aggie on his first weekend visiting her;
Walter had made impressive order there, at least. He had tal-
ent for the enterprise, Arthur had thought, looking around with
Aggie while Walter hovered nearby, watching them anxiously.
The glass was clean, the shelves of pebbles and trays of seedlings
were raked free of debris, and the plants were flourishing,
including several ancient agaves and bromeliads that Arthur
thought looked old enough to have been there since the war;
there were some just like them in the greenhouse at the
Duvalls', and Arthur had gone to the public library in Creston
to look up how to take care of them. A knotted clematis vine,
thick with star-shaped purple flowers, curled up the posts and
over the roof of the pergola at the front entrance to the greenhouse, and Walter had cleared the ground outside of weeds and
spread a layer of chopped leaves for mulch. Elsewhere, though,
the property had the appearance of a place long abandoned. It
looked like too much work for one man to take care of, anyway,
Arthur thought.

"I can do it," Walter had replied, breathing hard. "I don't
want help."

Arthur felt doubtful; still, one task at a time, he supposed,
and in a few years Breakabeen would be a model of cleanliness
and order, inside and out. There was something about the estate, though, that made Arthur feel as if Mrs. MacCauley was
bent on purgation rather than straightforward tidiness. There
were no borders of flowers or shrubbery; with Walter's help, she

was ridding even the outside of the house of anything unpredictable or out of place. The lawns would be smooth and free of weeds, running up like glass against stone walls and the stuccoed facade of the house. Trees would be pruned high. There would be nothing to suggest the unruly extravagance of growing things. It would be clean and still . . . and somehow bleak, Arthur thought. He liked the meadows of wildflowers that surrounded the Duvalls' house, the ivy that grew up the walls of the barn, the creeper that blazed crimson in the fall and ran over the fence lines.

They emerged with the roller onto the croquet lawn, eliciting cheers from Aggie and Loretta. Walter wanted to push the roller himself, so Arthur went to join the girls, who were sitting in the sun against a stone wall, a heap of croquet mallets and wickets and balls beside them on the grass. Aggie and Loretta were the two keenest croquet players among the girls at Breakabeen. They and Arthur had played every weekend, cursing the molehills, Loretta reaching over the massive mound of her stomach to wield the mallet in a comical fashion.

Aggie lay on her side on a rug, her head resting in one hand, fingering the wool in Loretta's knitting bag. Loretta herself leaned against the wall, a cushion at her back and her legs splayed out, her knitting—a white baby sweater—propped up on her stomach. The roll of red hair at her forehead bobbed as she counted stitches. Arthur had been to one of the knitting classes at Breakabeen; they were held on Saturday morning before lunch, in one of the parlor rooms. Mrs. Dillon—she never told them her first name—had the habit of holding up her

gloved hand like a traffic policeman in order to prevent inter-
ruptions while she was talking, even though no one ever interrupted her. She came to assist the girls with their projects,
draping the chairs in the room with ambitious samples of her
own work for the girls to inspect—intricately cabled sweaters,
checkerboard socks, knitted skirts and matching sweater sets.
Arthur had been conscripted to hold skeins of yarn that needed
winding. "Thank you for your assistance, Mr. Duvall," Mrs.
Dillon had said, passing him as she patrolled the room, inspecting the girls' progress. Later, though, he'd caught her whispering with Mrs. MacCauley in the hall outside the room, when
Mrs. MacCauley came to the door with a tray holding mugs of
milk and a plate of cookies. Arthur had turned away, worried.

Now he took a seat beside Aggie and Loretta on the grass,
resting his hand heavily on Aggie's head for a moment as he
sank down beside her. Warm sunlight fell on the crown of his
head and made Aggie's a blaze of color, as if shot through a
prism. The grass, thick with clover, smelled sweet.

Aggie had not wept again, at least not in front of Arthur,
since his first visit to Breakabeen two weeks before. Her grief
on the morning he had discovered her in the music room had
disconcerted him beyond anything that had happened yet. He
had seen Aggie cry only a few times in her life; she was a stoic,
even as a child. She had had a nasty fall one summer from one
of the apple trees in the orchard and had cut open her head on
a stone; she still had the scar from it, a little white half-moon
that showed in the part in her hair sometimes. She had not
cried once during the whole episode, though she hadn't been

much older than eight at the time. Mrs. Duvall had not been able to bear the sight of the blood, so Arthur had driven Aggie to the doctor's office, where they had taken her away from him to stitch up the wound. She had neither cried nor protested, holding up with a fortitude Arthur found heartbreaking in a child so young. Afterward, Arthur had brought her home, where Peggy and Kitty made the children ice cream sundaes in the kitchen and cosseted Aggie with a rug on her lap and ginger ale in a tall glass with a straw. Aggie had been very quiet, but she had not cried, though she had thrown up all her ice cream after Arthur had taken Toby back up to the cottage, Peggy told him later.

That morning in the music room at Breakabeen, Arthur had steered Aggie outside through the echoing front hall, afraid they would be discovered by Mrs. MacCauley. They had hurried down the front driveway, his arm around her shoulders.

At the end of the driveway Aggie had stopped, staring out into the street. A car passed by, but the driver, an old woman with both hands gripping the steering wheel up high, avoided looking in their direction.

Aggie had wiped her face and run her hands down the front of her shirt. "We need to go back," she said finally. "She'll wonder where I am. She comes looking for you if you're not where you're supposed to be." But Aggie made no move to leave.

Arthur reached into his pocket and gave her his handkerchief.

She took it and blew her nose. "Sorry," she said. "How is everyone at home?" She turned toward him, her eyes red and swollen.

"Fine. Good. Everyone is OK," Arthur said. They had not told Aggie about Kitty, who was home from the hospital at last but was clearly weak and diminished, her speech still slurred and her right arm curled uselessly at her side. Peggy fussed over her endlessly and snapped at Arthur. And Toby had terrified Arthur by telling him that he'd called the Duvalls' house in Florida, trying to reach Aggie, but that no one had answered, though he'd tried several times. Arthur knew he would have to tell Toby about Aggie soon; Toby asked about her every day, quizzing Arthur about when she'd be back, asking whether he'd heard from her.

"Just *ask* Duvall, Dad," he'd said, annoyed, when Arthur had demurred. "It's just an innocent question: When's she coming back? *Where* are they?"

Aggie's face crumpled again. She leaned against Arthur as if exhausted. He could feel his anger at the Duvalls, his anger at the boy who had done this to her, and also his own love for her, the sad pleasure of holding her.

"I want it to be over," she said. "I wish I was Loretta and only had a couple of weeks left."

Arthur closed his eyes.

"We had this class last night." She drew back a little from his shirt, turning her face to the side and leaning her cheek against his chest. "It even scared Loretta. Mrs. MacCauley says it's better for us to know what's going to happen, that we don't want to . . . abdicate our authority. We're not puppets, she said. We're women giving birth to babies, and we have to face that fact and not let anyone take that away from us. We have to understand it so we can handle it with dignity. We won't ever forget what's happened, and so when we look back on it, even if we aren't keeping our babies, we need to feel proud."

Arthur said nothing. The February day Toby had been born, a midwife and a neighbor woman had come to help Anna. He had been shooed outside, where he'd wandered the streets. Hours later, a neighbor boy had come running to find him; he was lingering in the Naschmarkt, watching the bundled-up women purchase meats and vegetables for their dinners, watching them handle the goods at the stalls and haggle with the shopkeepers. Arthur had hurried back with the boy to their rooms above Julius's shop to find the midwife dislodging the placenta from Anna's uterus, pushing down on Anna's stomach with the heel of her hand. Anna had cried out as Arthur came to the door, but she had looked radiant at the sight of Arthur standing there.

"You have a beautiful son," the midwife said, motioning to the cradle by the bed and then turning her attention back to Anna. "Like a pit from a plum," she said with satisfaction. Something slid out from between Anna's legs, and Arthur had withdrawn, reeling. The room had smelled of the birth. He had thought he would never forget that smell, nor the sight of Toby in the cradle that first day.

A wave of missing Anna, of mourning her, rose up in him. Anna had been older than he; she was thirty-five when Toby was finally born, after several miscarriages. She had thought for a long time that she would not be successful at carrying a baby fully to term. After Toby was born, by the time the laughing young girl who was the midwife's helper had drawn Arthur back into the room, the midwife had bathed Anna's face and tied a blue ribbon in her hair, a girlish touch that had wrung Arthur's heart.

Anna had beamed up at him and held out the baby. "*Nicht ist er schön, Arthur?*" Isn't he beautiful?

"I can feel it moving, Arthur," Aggie said against his chest now. "I can feel it kicking."

She pulled away from him, and he offered her the handkerchief again. She glanced up at him apologetically. "I know you don't want to hear this, Arthur. I wouldn't want to if I were you."

He wanted to take her away, he thought. They were standing just inside the gates, and the empty street ahead of them felt like a temptation. "It is not that," he said. "I have . . ." He grimaced and touched his chest, hesitating, trying to find the words for what he felt. "I have . . . *sorrow*. Here."

Aggie took another shaky breath, straightening her back. "Sometimes I think about running away," she said. "That's what Loretta is going to do if her parents won't help her. She says we could go together, help each other. She says we could go to school and become nurses."

Another car came down the street. A man drove, and two boys in the backseat crowded to the window to stare out at Arthur and Aggie. They stayed there, their faces pressed to the glass of the car's rear window, gazing back at Arthur and Aggie until the car was out of sight.

"Would you help us?" She turned back to look at him, and her eyes held him. "If we ran away, would you help us, Arthur?"

"*Aggie.*" He felt a wrenching inside him, as if something were tearing, separating muscle from bone. How could he help her? He was *responsible* for her. And she was not his child. Her parents had decided this for her; that it was not what he would have done made no difference. He had no authority here, no power.

And yet there was something else, too, the secret fantasy of an imagined life with her, raising this child as if it were his own. Aggie herself would be—what? His *wife*?

It was unthinkable. He looked at her . . . and for a moment he wavered. They would have to live in hiding if he took her away now. Anna had told him the story of how Adam and Eve had been turned out of paradise weeping, the angels pressing into their hands seeds for sustenance, and sweet-smelling spices that they could burn for offerings to God, whom they had offended. He'd hated the thought of that first night, Adam and Eve cowering in the howling wasteland east of paradise, staring out at the shape of the Garden of Eden, silhouetted under its canopy of stars against the night clouds. From far off would have come the perfume of the roses and spice trees, the scent of the rivers of milk and balsam and wine and honey.

Who would want to live like that, looking back at where you were forbidden, at what you had been denied? He *knew* what exile meant, he thought; Aggie did not know what it would be like.

"You shall be as a driven leaf," went the words of the prayer Anna had whispered as the bombs fell in London.

His thoughts were like the birds frightened up from the

marshes around the lake at the Duvalls', flocks that rose into the air in panic. There was Toby . . . what would happen to Toby if Arthur took Aggie away? Arthur's longing for Aggie, his hopeless longing for her, could not exist in the same world as his love for Toby. And how could he have what he wanted with Aggie—this foolish notion of them together in a little house somewhere, the baby between them—and still have Toby? He would have to choose. And there was no choice, of course. He could not leave the Duvalls'. He could not cast himself out willfully into the desert.

"You do not understand," he said, and his helplessness felt like sickness. "Aggie, you do not understand."

She stared at him a moment longer. "I know," she said. "I told her you wouldn't help us—that it was too much to ask."

"I would help you!" he blurted out. "My heart is . . ." He looked away. "*Mein Inneres bricht.* My heart is *breaking.*" He slapped his hand against his breast and felt it, the truth of his pain, though it was so much more complicated than he could explain to her, than he dared explain to her. "I want to help you," he said. "But this is not the way, not . . . running away."

"It's OK," she said. "It's not your fault."

Arthur felt a cold despair, a freezing in his lungs and hands and feet that made him afraid, for a moment, of losing his balance. "You will not run away. Promise me, Agatha. Promise," he said.

"I'm sure I won't," she said after a minute, looking at the ground. "I'm sure I'm not brave enough, in the end. And I don't even know if it would be the right thing, anyway."

And then she began to cry again. "How can I love it so much and hate it so much at the same time?" she said. "Tell me, Arthur."

LATER—THOUGH IT was too late by then—he understood what he should have done, especially once he'd learned that the baby was Toby's, too.

Here was another story Anna had told him. When the infant Moses' ark of pitch and clay came floating down the Nile and snagged in the thick stands of bulrushes, Thermutis, the Pharaoh's daughter, stepped toward it into the shallows from her place on the bank. But the basket was too far away for Thermutis to reach it, and she hesitated. She asked for help, but her handmaids were afraid of Pharaoh and his edict to slaughter every infant boy in the land, so they hung back, unwilling. And in that moment of Thermutis's hesitation and her friends' refusal, Anna told Arthur, God acted. As Thermutis stood there, the hem of her gown dragging in the waters of the Nile, her arm suddenly began to lengthen, extending over the waves and the bulwark of rushes until her fingers were miraculously touching the edge of the basket and she could pull it safely to shore. And as if God was enjoying this display of his wonder, the executive power of his reach, he didn't stop there. When she lifted the baby in her arms, Thermutis's leprosy was magically cured and her skin glowed with health. And then God sent the angel Gabriel flying down to earth, and Gabriel gathered the trembling handmaids in the vise of his wings and buried them in the earth, jamming them like corks into the midnight of the earth's darkest, coldest caverns.

Then, like the silence following a storm, all was quiet on that riverbank. The rushes waved, the water lapped at the shore, oxen sank their snouts into the shallows. Thermutis stood with the baby in her arms, and nearby—as if at God's instruction— waited Jochebed, the anonymous wet nurse, ready to regain her son.

But where had been God's pity when *he* needed him? Arthur thought later. Where was the arm mysteriously lengthened? How hard would it have been, really, to say to Mr. Duvall, "This baby, this baby of Agatha's, is also the baby of my son. Whatever happens between Aggie and Toby, this baby is our grandchild. He cannot be lost." He had made it so complicated for himself, so impossible, out of fear, out of selfishness, out of the foolish, selfish desire of a man for a girl who was younger than his own son. That desire had been in the way; it had stood like a boulder between him and what he might have done, so that he could not see around it.

But God could have moved that boulder, could he not? He could have given Arthur a voice when he lacked one. Just as God caused Thermutis's arm to unwind from her shoulder like a ship's rope, couldn't he have reached into Arthur's throat and plucked up his voice, fanning it with the powerful wind of God's own intention, making him heard? Couldn't God, as the baby was held in midair between the nurse at the hospital and the woman who stepped forward, her hands open and ready, couldn't he have lengthened Arthur's arm, made him snatch back what was his own?

It all had to do with wanting the right thing to begin with, Arthur thought. Thermutis knew she ought to rescue Moses. But Arthur had sacrificed the baby to his own fear, to everything he thought he had to lose—son, home, job, Aggie herself. He had been a coward, he had been jealous, and he had been angry, and he had abandoned his grandchild.

He could not blame God for that.

That was all his own doing.

SOMETIMES IN HIS DREAMS he came to the empty coffeehouse. The front windows had been blown out. Here and there, on the jagged pieces of broken glass embedded in the edge of the window frame, he could still make out the etched frieze of intertwined leaves and flowers, the little sunbursts of edelweiss. Filth from the street—rubble, broken brick, broken furniture—had banked up against the overturned marble tables like leaves against the trunks of the chestnut trees in the Prater in the smoky air of fall. The glass cases that had held the strudels and the tortes had been shattered. Broken crockery lay on the floor underfoot. Arthur stood in the door, looking over the high-ceilinged room, the tufted banquette seats with their slashed leather cushions, the ornate gas fixtures, and the long mirror, dimmed and speckled, that reflected the ruin, with a silvery bull's-eye of concentric circles cracked into one corner where it had been smashed. Sometimes, in his dream, he would step carefully over the wreckage and the fallen timbers and make his way toward an out-of-the-way table around the corner, where Dr. Ornstein sat, his back to Arthur, frowning over a chessboard, his forehead resting against his fingertips. Arthur knew not to speak to him, not to disturb him, but he watched the doctor's fingers slowly lift the pieces and replace them in a new position on the board. Arthur stood at a distance, his hat in his hand, while Dr. Ornstein muttered over the board. All around them, the empty city was completely silent; even the bells from Stephansdom had ceased to ring.

"I am putting it to rights," Dr. Ornstein said. "But it is very complicated. Do you understand?"

Arthur nodded. "I have faith in you, sir."

Sometimes in these dreams it was Arthur's job to save Dr. Ornstein. At other times, Dr. Ornstein was inventing the world, and Arthur, who knew how easily mistakes could be made, stood humbly in the background and held his breath.

ARTHUR DID NOT IGNORE the reason Aggie was at Breakabeen, why all the girls were there. Most of them, he learned, came from families like Agatha's, rich, socially prominent, fully aware of the price they would pay for having a daughter in such a position. Not only the daughters suffered under such circumstances, he understood. Fathers lost important business contracts. Mothers were ostracized from the Junior League, from the garden club, from the bridge circle.

Brothers and sisters would be spurned. Whole families could be ruined by the disgrace.

He understood that the girls were made to feel ashamed at what had happened to them, and he heard enough of their conversations to know that their fathers, almost uniformly, had been enraged, that their mothers had intervened, and that Breakabeen had been the solution. Was anyone fooled by them, Arthur wondered, these mysterious disappearances? And what would happen when the girls returned home? They would be expected to go on as before. They were never to speak a word of what had happened to them. If they thought about their lost baby, they were to keep such thoughts to themselves. If they had been taken advantage of by a boy who did not love them, they were to keep such humiliation to themselves, too. If they loved a boy and lost him, they were to remain silent and unprotesting.

"Appearances are everything," Loretta said, knitting away furiously as she sat alone with Arthur and Aggie one Saturday evening on the grass outside. "I know a girl who was told by her mother to prick her finger and smear it on the bedsheets on her wedding night. Her mother even put a needle in her daughter's suitcase, in an envelope folded up inside her new peignoir." She put down her knitting, stared out at the fading light of the evening. "You know that girl, Winnie? The one with the wall-eye? Her older sister is getting married next spring. When she found out that Winnie was pregnant, she came into her room with a knife one night and told her that if anyone found out that Winnie had gotten pregnant, she'd kill her."

"My God." Arthur was horrified. "I cannot believe such a thing."

"And you know what's even worse? She told me she was raped. She said her parents knew the boy, and knew his parents, and wouldn't do anything about it because his father is chairman of the board of the company that Winnie's uncle works for. They make fertilizer or something."

Arthur was silent for a moment. "But your parents?" he asked finally. "They will let you keep the baby?"

Loretta picked up her knitting again. "Only if I never come home again. They're trying to work out something with my aunt and uncle. They live in Ottawa. No one ever goes to Ottawa, so they figure they're safe if I'm there."

"Tell him what your mother said." Aggie reached out and picked up a ball of wool that had fallen from Loretta's knitting bag.

Loretta bent over her knitting. "It would be different for my aunt and uncle than it would be for my parents. See, if the girl isn't your daughter, but you just take her in, then you actually *want* to tell everyone what happened to her, because then you're a saint and performing an act of charity. And my aunt *will* tell everybody, too. She won't make up any story about how I'm five years older than I actually am, and how my young husband died tragically, and how we're all raising the baby together." Loretta glanced at Arthur, her needles going furiously. "My mother doesn't like my aunt—that's my father's sister. She knows it will be awful. And they'll have to pay them a lot of money to take me and the baby. If it was just my mother, she'd let me come home. But my father would be just as happy if the earth opened up and swallowed me. It would have been better for him if I'd died a tragic death. And my mother has to do whatever my father says, because he's the boss. I think my mother's hoping that I can just come home ten years from now or something, and no one will do the math."

"No," Arthur protested. "No, that is not the truth."

"Oh, yes," Loretta said. "I'm afraid so. It's the same story for all of us, isn't it?' She turned to Aggie.

Aggie turned the ball of wool over in her hands. She nodded, but she didn't say anything.

Loretta glanced at Arthur. He met Loretta's eyes and then looked at Aggie. He didn't know what to say to her.

What did you say to someone whose parents would prefer she were dead?

ARTHUR DID NOT WANT to upset Aggie. He wanted to ask her what she felt, what she wanted, if she wanted to keep her baby. He wanted desperately to know the identity of the baby's father. But when he was with Aggie, he felt only that she must know that she was loved, that he loved her, hoping that would somehow be enough. He said nothing and imagined it a kindness.

He admired Mrs. MacCauley for providing what he came to see as the necessary antidote to her charges' unhappiness—plenty of organized activity that left them too distracted to think about what was happening to them, punctuated by doled-out reminders of their burden, their responsibility, their grief, their anger.

Yet the truth of Mrs. MacCauley's circumstances, that she herself had borne Walter out of wedlock when she was only sixteen years old, that she had given him up for adoption and then returned for him five years later, only to discover that he wasn't all right in the head—all this, conveyed to him and Aggie by Loretta, who seemed to know everything about everybody at Breakabeen, troubled him.

"Just imagine it," Loretta said one afternoon when they were going for a walk. "She comes to the orphanage. She doesn't even know whether he's still there, but she's worked hard, she's saved her money, she's gotten her position here at this house, she's even gotten permission from the old gentleman to bring her baby here—and they bring out little Walter by the hand. What could she do?"

"So why does she do this?" Aggie asked. "After he died—the old man—why did she turn the house into . . . into what it is?"

"Well, she can't get over it, can she?" Loretta put the back of her hand up to her forehead, blotting perspiration on her brow. The red roll of her hair sagged in the close evening air. "It's what her whole life is about. She got pregnant—that's mistake number one. And then she gave up Walter—that's mistake number two. And then going back to get him—that's number three."

"She's just reliving it, every day, with all of us," Aggie said.

"I'd say so," Loretta said. "She can't sort it out, exactly where she went wrong."

They'd reached the top of Breakabeen's main street. The shops had closed for the evening, but the soda fountain at the drugstore stayed open until eight o'clock. "Let's go down and embarrass the people having ice cream sodas," Loretta said. "I'm thirsty."

MRS. MACCAULEY, HOWEVER her feelings about her own circumstances had failed to resolve themselves, Arthur thought, at least wanted the girls to feel capable of bearing the consequences of their pregnancy. She did not gloss over the births as they occurred or pretend that they had not happened. At meals she spoke to the girls about protein and vitamins in their diet, about the virtue of a healthy regimen and a disciplined day, not just for their baby but also for themselves. In the "afterward," she said, for life; although the way she said it, Aggie told Arthur, made it seem that life after these pregnancies, these deliveries, these babies kept or given away, was a mountain whose summit never seemed any nearer.

"Try the prunes," Mrs. MacCauley urged in her quiet way, passing the bowl down the table at the midday meal on Saturday. And though a few girls made faces, most were sufficiently under her sway to accept a spoonful on their plates and bravely get them down. Arthur had begun to detect a note of worship among them, a kind of fierce sisterhood that developed over the weeks of their stay at Breakabeen.

Mrs. MacCauley also insisted on each girl's returning to Breakabeen after her delivery and release from the hospital so that the others could say their good-byes. And every birth was announced, regardless of whether the girl was keeping her baby.

"There is no forgetting," he had heard her say. "Remember that."

ON THE DAY he helped Walter find the roller and repair the croquet lawn, Arthur had arrived while breakfast was still going on. He came to the door of the dining room and paused a minute, waiting until Aggie looked up and saw him.

"Mr. Duvall." Mrs. MacCauley rose from the table after a second's hesitation and came to shake his hand. "How nice to see you again." This was his third Saturday at Breakabeen, and Arthur worried that she was not entirely happy to see him, that she seemed to be growing suspicious of his continued presence. He tried to steer clear of her when he was there, sometimes taking Aggie and Loretta out for a drive—though there was no place to go—and hoping to avoid conversations in which he might make some misstep, might give himself away. But Mrs. MacCauley, though she looked at him carefully, a question in her eyes, was never anything but polite. "Will you join us?" She touched Walter on the shoulder. "Bring a chair for Mr. Duvall, Walter. Will you have coffee, Mr. Duvall?"

Arthur sat down beside Aggie and accepted a cup of coffee from a girl who had risen and poured it for him at the sideboard, where breakfast was laid out: a glass bowl of fruit compote, a chafing dish of oatmeal, toast in a long rack, and crystal dishes of jam and honey. Aggie nudged his shoulder with her own and smiled at him.

"You're all wondering about Nan." Mrs. MacCauley took her place again and touched her mouth with her napkin. She reached into her pocket and withdrew a slip of paper, glancing at it briefly before returning it to her pocket. She looked up at Arthur as if trying to decide something—what could she say in front of him?—but her hesitation lasted only a moment. "Nan delivered a baby girl, six pounds seven ounces," she said. "Just after midnight last night."

The sound of scattered applause came from the girls at the table. Clearly, Arthur thought, this was the response they had been coached to offer.

"Well done, Nan," Mrs. MacCauley said when the clapping had died away. She offered a quick smile and then returned her attention to her plate.

"You were there to help her, Mrs. MacCauley?" The girl beside her spoke quietly.

"She did very well. We should all be proud of her," Mrs. MacCauley said. But she had not answered the question directly, Arthur noticed.

"How is the baby?" The girl to Mrs. MacCauley's left spoke up again, her tone anxious.

"I saw her," Mrs. MacCauley said quietly. "I saw both Nan and her baby." She did not raise her eyes. Instead she got up from her chair and crossed to the sideboard, putting a spoonful of fruit compote on her plate and returning the spoon to the dish. Arthur watched the girls exchanging looks. He glanced at Aggie, whose face had grown worried.

Mrs. MacCauley returned to her seat and took a delicate mouthful. She ate, Arthur thought, like someone who had trained herself over the years to swallow what she did not like, or worse, to reject all claims of the flesh, even appetite. He watched her set down her spoon.

"We've talked about being prepared, haven't we?" She looked up finally at the girls seated at the table. They had fallen very still. Mrs. MacCauley's eyes met Arthur's for another moment and then moved away. Arthur reached tentatively for his coffee cup but did not lift it to drink, letting his fingers rest on the delicate handle.

Mrs. MacCauley went on. "We've talked about making a decision, and making our peace with that decision, and then moving on with dignity. And we've talked about how difficult it can be sometimes . . ." She hesitated. "Nan had decided, with her family, to give up the baby for adoption. She had also decided that she wanted to see the baby before it was taken away. That was her decision." She smiled a little. "You know how I feel about such things. I don't encourage you to close your eyes, girls. I encourage you to see clearly." She stopped again. Arthur felt her eyes on him, but he did not look up. He fingered the handle of his coffee cup. Mrs. MacCauley did not need to say that she believed men to be the enemy for him to feel it at that moment, to feel the heat of her gaze. Loretta had been right, he thought. Mrs. MacCauley did not like men very much.

"Nan's baby was born with a small but unfortunate defect," Mrs. MacCauley said quietly. "She has a harelip."

There was a murmur of sympathy at the table. Arthur looked up and saw that a number of the girls looked distressed. Others were staring down at their plates.

"This is one of those things that occurs," Mrs. MacCauley went on, though her tone was gentle. "One of those things for which we cannot be entirely prepared. It made it difficult for Nan, of course."

"No one will want it," said one of the girls near the end of the table, her face soft and round with baby fat and her hair set severely in a rolled style that seemed too old for her face. She was looking out at the others, her expression challenging.

Mrs. MacCauley shook her head. "You might think so at first," she said, "but I can promise you that is not the case. She may be especially beloved, in fact, because of her challenges."

The girl shook her head stubbornly, but she was staring down at her plate again and did not meet Mrs. MacCauley's eyes. A few others glanced at her as if in silent agreement, but then turned back to Mrs. MacCauley.

"It is better that you know the truth, that you understand what can happen," Mrs. MacCauley said. "As you have learned from your own circumstances, the unexpected, the unimaginable, can overtake us at any moment." She paused, looking around seriously at the girls. "But you would be mistaken if you imagined that no one will want to adopt Nan's baby. Perfection—of people, of places, of anything—is not at the heart of our attachments." She folded her napkin. She did not look at

Walter, but Arthur saw her—the girls saw her—reach over to lay a hand on his arm for a moment. "Walter, the flowers are lovely this morning."

She smiled at the group. "Nan will be here for lunch with us in a few days, before going home. I know you will all tell her how proud of her you are."

Arthur did not look at Aggie, who sat silently beside him. Was it necessary, he thought, for Mrs. MacCauley to have said all that?

When Dr. Ornstein dressed that morning so many years ago now, when he sat down on the little slipper chair in his wife's dressing room and took his striped trousers from the press and pulled them on, when he gazed at himself in the mirror, hooking a finger into his lower lip and pulling it aside in a grimace to inspect a sore tooth, when he washed his hands and dried them on a towel, he had not known how that day would end. He had sat in the coffeehouse thinking of nothing, simply savoring the taste of the cream in his coffee, or perhaps thinking of the annoyance of crumbs on his shirtfront, the inconsequential fatigue in his shoulders, a note he had forgotten to write, a surgery he would perform the next day, the hidden, secret pleasure of his wife's breasts inside her dressing gown that morning, the curiously pleasant, familiar smell of his own fingers lifted for a moment to his nose.

Sometimes, Arthur thought, it was better not to know what could happen to you.

. . .

SATURDAY MORNINGS WERE free time for the girls at Breakabeen. There were no lessons or lectures or performances, no improving presentations on sewing or cooking or personal hygiene. Most of the girls seemed to fall asleep again directly after breakfast. You came upon them all over the house, reclining in chairs with their feet on the damask-covered ottomans with their Persian fringe, or stretched out on window seats, cushions behind their heads, books fanned face-down over their chests, their bellies baking in the sunshine. Some of them returned to bed without even attempting to do anything else, dropping their shoes on the floor and collapsing on their rumpled sheets, snoring softly. Arthur and Loretta and Aggie agreed that it seemed as if a sleeping charm had been cast over them all.

"Aren't we funny prisoners, though," Loretta said that morning, yawning as she set down her knitting needles to watch Walter hurtling back and forth over the croquet lawn with the roller. "All of us with our big bellies." She yawned again. "It'll be much nicer without the molehills." Walter, red-faced with effort, passed them with the roller. "He doesn't tire out, does he?"

"He never rests," Aggie said. "He's like you, Arthur. He's always rushing from one thing to the next."

Arthur blinked in the sunshine. He did not think of himself as always rushing, but it was true that there was a lot to do at the Duvalls', and he was anxious not to make a mistake. It had become a matter of pride with him that he did not need to be told what to do anymore; he knew the place so well that he could anticipate what needed to be done, taking the cars to the garage for servicing, cleaning the gutters, sawing up a fallen tree for firewood, dividing the daffodils.

He watched Walter pushing the heavy roller, shoulders bent. Arthur very rarely watched another man work, he realized. The sight made him sleepy.

Walter finished his breakneck race across the lawn. He did not pause to inspect his work or mop his forehead, though, but set off back down the hill, the roller gaining speed ahead of him.

"Thank you, Walter," Aggie called after him, but he didn't turn around.

Loretta tossed aside her knitting. "Come on," she said. "Let's play. Help me up, you two."

Aggie and Arthur rose and took her hands. "Heave-ho," said Loretta, and they tugged her up. She staggered into Arthur, laughing.

And then Arthur became aware that they were being watched. He turned his head, Loretta in his arms, Aggie laughing at his side. Mrs. MacCauley was standing just inside the end of the arbor, looking out at them on the lawn.

The three of them fell silent.

"May I see you a moment?" Mrs. MacCauley did not raise her voice, nor did she need to say whom she meant. Arthur steadied Loretta and then let his hands drop from her waist.

Aggie started to come with him, but Mrs. MacCauley held up her hand. "Just for a moment, Agatha, please." She turned around without waiting for Arthur and started back toward the house.

Loretta looked at Arthur and Aggie. "I think she's on to you, Arthur."

"Oh, Arthur." Aggie's voice was stricken. "This is all my fault."

MRS. MACCAULEY WAS waiting for him in her office, standing behind her desk with her back to the door when Arthur followed her in a moment later. Her office was as tranquil and austere as he remembered from his visit there a few weeks before. The room faced west, and though the morning was clear, the light in the room was vague and indirect, as if filled with faint smoke. Only one closely shaded lamp at Mrs. MacCauley's desk had been turned on, dropping a circle of yellow brightness onto the blotter and some opened letters. Arthur noticed a vase holding a single lily on the corner of her desk. He wondered if Walter crept into his mother's office every day and left a fresh flower for her.

"Close the door, please," she said without turning around.

Arthur did so, and then remained standing. "Don't worry," he had said to Aggie. "Don't worry." But he had not been able to offer her any other comfort. He was about to be disgraced here, or worse. What could he have said that would have made either of them feel any better?

Mrs. MacCauley turned around to face him. "Who are you?" she said. Her face looked drained, as if she'd had to ready herself for this encounter and did not by nature enjoy a confrontation. She stood behind her chair, her long white fingers gripping the chair's back. She wore a navy blue dress with an attached collar of white lace; her face rose above it, long and pale, her large, dark eyes accusatory. For a moment he had an image of her dressing that morning in her apartment at the house, her hands carefully doing the small buttons of her collar, avoiding her own eyes in the mirror. When had she realized he was not who he claimed to be?

His shoulders, his neck, his back, were coating with sweat.

"I asked"—Mrs. MacCauley's voice was angry, but there was a touch of fear in it, too, he thought— "who *are* you?"

Arthur let his eyes travel around the room, its careful painting, its soft carpet, the magnolia leaves in the copper bowl on the hearth, the immaculate desk with the pretty figurine of a shepherdess resting atop a stack of papers. Mrs. MacCauley had worked very hard for all this, forced order in the midst of the worst sort of chaos. Loretta said she had served here as housekeeper to the man who eventually left the estate to her in his will. What attachment had existed between them? Arthur wondered. What bargain?

She is in charge of all these girls, Arthur thought. If anything happened to them, to any one of them, it would be her fault.

"It is not what you think," he said quietly. Something drained out of him at that moment—the flaring of will, the boldness that had allowed him this absurd impersonation. He realized that he did not know how to explain to Mrs. MacCauley who he was to Aggie, or why he was there at Breakabeen now. He thought of the Duvalls' for a moment, of his cottage there, of his dressmaker's dummy, the curves of her silhouette in the window when he trudged up the hill through the orchard toward his house in the early evening. Sometimes the sight of the figure there—unmoving and watchful, like a mournful prisoner—made him stop in disbelief and horror. Was this all that awaited him? Was this all he had managed to gather around him? Was this what his life amounted to?

It was not so simple to explain his life, to explain what had happened to him.

He held up his hands. He could not meet her eyes. "I am the driver," he said.

Mrs. MacCauley waited. "Forgive me," she said icily after a minute, "if that does not make things entirely clear to me."

Arthur closed his eyes for a moment.

"I can have you escorted off the property with a single phone call, sir." Mrs. MacCauley's voice had risen. "I would rather not have you leave in that fashion, for obvious reasons. But do not think for a minute that I will allow you to leave, however you take your departure, without a full explanation." The skin around her mouth and nose had gone white.

"It is not easy," Arthur said. "I am sorry."

Something about his tone must have calmed her. She pulled out her chair and sat down in it as if exhausted. After a minute she extended her hand wordlessly toward one of the armchairs on the other side of the desk.

But Arthur did not sit. He did not want to have a conversation with her in which he had to try to explain so many things that could not easily be explained, a conversation that would remind him of his foolishness—his love for Aggie in all its dimensions, his servitude to her father.

"I am her father's driver," he said finally, looking down at the floor. "He asked me to bring her here. I did not think it was right, the right thing to do. I did not want to leave her." He stopped. Mrs. MacCauley's eyes were on his face. "I have known her since"—he held up his hand some distance from the floor—"she was small. Like this. A child." He looked up finally. "I just come . . . innocently. To make sure she is OK."

"Does he know you are here? Her father? Does her mother know?"

Arthur shook his head.

She turned her face away from him, frowning at the glass-fronted bookcase near the desk.

"We did not mean . . . I did not mean to be untruthful, to tell lies. Aggie knew none of it. It only came to me while we were here, the first day. I thought you would make me leave." He stopped. "There was no plan."

"What is your relationship with Agatha now?"

She was still staring at the bookcase. Was it obvious? Arthur wondered. Was it so obvious that he loved this girl, loved this girl with her rich parents and the child growing in her belly.

What kind of joke was this, Arthur wondered now, that God should watch Arthur and Aggie walking toward each other and not snatch Arthur from Aggie's path, redirect him so that he might not suffer the rest of his days? What was God's purpose if not to protect you from disaster, to smite your enemies, to place into your hand a torch when all was dark? But of course—millions of voices had called to him once in the darkest darkness. If he had heard them, he had given no sign.

Mrs. MacCauley turned in her chair to face Arthur. She clasped her hands together. He saw her knuckles whiten.

"You are asking me . . ." Arthur began.

"I am asking you whether what you are doing is good for Agatha."

Arthur stared at her. He had not expected this question.

Mrs. MacCauley continued. "I do not like what you have done, Mr.—"

"Henning," Arthur hurried to answer. "My name is Henning. Arthur Henning."

She inclined her head. "I do not like what you have done, Mr. . . . Henning. You have made a fool of me. You have caused me to take risks that I would not, under any circumstances, have taken had I known who you were. I assume at least some of the other girls know you are not, in fact, Agatha's father? I assume I may add that to your list of offenses?"

"Only Loretta," he said. "And Irene. But she is gone now."

Mrs. MacCauley closed her eyes for a second, as if taking in the extent of her humiliation and seeing whether she could bear it.

"I am sorry—" Arthur began, but she cut him off.

"I understand—I believe—that you are acting out of affection for Agatha." She turned her head aside. "It is all over your face," she said frankly, turning back to meet his gaze.

Arthur did not know where to look. His face burned. "You do not have to call her father," he said. "Please."

She glanced up at him, then reached over the blotter and took up a letter that was lying there.

Arthur looked at it and then at her.

"He has written to me," she said, "her father. He writes that no one is to visit Agatha while she is here, that he is to be informed if anyone comes."

Arthur waited. "She will not say who is the father of the baby," he ventured finally. "That is why. And he wants to know who is it."

"They generally do."

Arthur gestured suddenly at the letter, impatient. "Why? What good will it do now? So he can take his gun and shoot him?" He came forward and sat down heavily. He put his head in his hands. "This is how you knew. Because of the letter."

"I suspected before," she said. "I am not a fool. Forgive me, but you are . . ."

Arthur winced. "I know," he said. "You don't have to say."

She made a gesture that seemed to be one of concession; she would not humiliate him further. "But I had no proof," she added, "until today."

"And now you will call him and . . ." Arthur waved his hand. "There will be so much trouble," he said hopelessly.

Mrs. MacCauley said nothing for a moment, staring down at

her desk. Then she raised her head. "You understand, Mr. Henning, that Agatha and her parents have agreed that the child will be given up for adoption."

"They would not take in the baby," he said. "I know them."

"But you? What if you were her father?"

Arthur looked at her. "How can they give it away?" He raised his hands and then let them fall again into his lap. "I could not live with myself."

Glancing down at her wrist, Mrs. MacCauley took a tissue from her sleeve and held it in her palm. Arthur remembered what Loretta had told him—that Walter had been given up, just as Aggie's baby was to be given up. When had she learned about Walter? he wondered. What had made her go look for him in the orphanage? What had made her go back into the desert, like Emtelai?

"There are circumstances," she said, "when it is for the best."

"I know," Arthur said quickly. "I know that." He did not want her to find him unsympathetic. He was not unsympathetic; in the face of all he did not know about Mrs. MacCauley and her history, in the face of Walter himself, he felt humble, in fact. Just seeing Aggie like this, he, too, could hate a man who could do such a thing to her. "Aggie is young," he said. "She has her whole life. I understand."

He waited. Mrs. MacCauley would send him away, he thought. She would call the Duvalls and she would send him away and he would . . . he could not even imagine what would happen. He would lose his place. He would lose his job. He would lose Aggie herself. And the baby? He heard Anna's voice, coming to him from the floor of the shelter on King's Road where they had knelt side by side, Toby and the baby between them, as the city above them fell into ruins. "You shall be as a driven leaf," Anna had whispered. "Be careful you do not become as a driven leaf." A woman in the shelter, a big, mannish woman with a helmet on her head, had made all the people there sing a song over and over again while she conducted them, her filthy palms keeping time on her thighs. "Roll Out the Barrel," the song was called.

> Every time they hear that oom-pa-pa,
> Everybody feels so tra-la-la,
> They want to throw their cares away,
> They all go lah-de-ah-de-ay,
> Then they hear a rumble on the floor, the floor,
> It's the big surprise they're waiting for . . .

Arthur had thought at first it was a song about a bomb dropping, but finally he understood the words. That woman had made them sing it over and over a hundred times, Arthur trying desperately to manage the nonsensical syllables, until the all clear sounded. One old man with a tremor had refused to sing, turning his face away, but the woman had berated him until his wife, frightened and embarrassed, made him join in.

"I am only the driver," he told Mrs. MacCauley now. "I know I have no say. I only come to be company for her so she is not alone. Please."

She smiled slightly, but it was a cheerless smile. "We are all alone, Mr. Henning, in the end."

Arthur felt himself react. "I do not think so." He shook his head. "No. Not alone. I do not think so. Aggie is not alone . . . because she has me. I am not alone because I have her. There is no love in that family," he went on quickly. "You do not know. There is no touching, no laughing, no sitting side by side. I do not know what is wrong with them except too much money, too much drink. Something." He gestured impatiently. "And I do not know how I can help her now . . . What can I do? I can only come and—what? Play croquet, go for a walk . . . But when the baby is born, Mr. Duvall will send me here to get her and bring her home. I know that. He will call me and say, 'Arthur, go and get Aggie tomorrow.' And I do not want to do that," he said, standing up suddenly. "I do not want to be only the driver, Mrs. MacCauley."

He looked down at her. "I will make no trouble. Please. Let me stay and take care of her. Do not send me away."

Mrs. MacCauley stared at him for a long moment. Then she made a quick dismissive motion with her hand. "I cannot have you here," she said, and when he started to protest, she held up her hand angrily. "That is *your* fault, not mine. If you had said who you were from the start . . ." She stopped, collecting herself, and then went on. "I understand what you are saying to me, Mr. Henning. I *understand*. But now that I know who you are, I cannot be expected to harbor you here, without her parents' knowledge. You cannot expect me to—"

"No. You do *not* understand," Arthur cried. "You want her, you want all of them, to be alone . . . because you are alone."

Mrs. MacCauley's face went white.

Arthur stopped. He sat down heavily again. He put his hands on the edge of the desk and leaned over until his forehead was resting on his knuckles. "Forgive me," he said. The room was utterly quiet. He could not even hear her breathing.

When she spoke, her voice was almost a whisper. "All right," she said. "All right. I will not tell them you have been here. But you must leave. Today. Now. And you must not come back."

Arthur looked up and met her eyes. "Until the baby is to be born," he said. "I want to be here then."

She hesitated, blinking at him, breathing hard. He saw that her eyes were red. "All right," she said. "We'll call you when it's time."

Arthur stood up wearily. He felt that he had just engaged in a terrible battle with her, one in which they had exposed each other in a dreadful and intimate way. He did not feel angry anymore. She was his adversary, but they understood each other in the way of adversaries whose knowledge of their enemy is perilously close to love.

She stood up, too. "Please speak to Agatha before you go. Explain to her. Then I want her to come here to me. I want her to understand. I am not cruel, Mr. Henning."

He nodded once, the conciliation due her, then stepped away from the desk. But when he reached the door, he turned back and looked at her. "I do not think you are cruel," he said. "But I am sorry for you. You are the first American, after the Duvalls, I am sorry for."

. . .

AGGIE WAS IN THE HALL, white-faced, when he came out of Mrs. MacCauley's office. "What happened?" Her face was pale.

He gestured to her to move away from the door.

"I have to go," he said when they were in the hall. They stopped, but Arthur had the sensation of being listened to in that cavernous, empty space. He drew her with him out the front door and stopped under the portico.

"She was furious," Aggie said. "She's furious at me, too."

"No, no. She knows it was me who did it all. She is not angry at you. She wants to talk to you, make sure you understand her."

"But she made you leave."

He shrugged. "She has to."

"Is she calling Dad?"

Arthur shook his head. "She will not call him."

Aggie was silent for a minute. "Arthur. I want you to know, what you did . . . it's the kindest thing anyone's ever done for me." She looked at him, and he felt for a moment that they had become equals, that the distance between their ages had dropped away. "You were very good at it," she said.

Arthur dropped his eyes. "No, I was not," he said. "You are ridiculous." He felt tired now. He reached out and touched her face. He was foolish. Of course, she thought him foolish. "You do not know . . . ," he began, but he could not go on. He took her hand and pressed it to his lips. "I remember the first night I saw you," he said. "On the stairs, in your nightgown. You ran away."

Aggie smiled. They had done this before. "How disobedient," she said.

"No. You were afraid," he said. "It was natural."

He looked at her. How could this young woman, this girl with the baby growing inside her, be the same person as that child who had sat on those steps that night so long ago, watching him?

"Your eyes," he said. "They were so big. I remember that."

"They hadn't told me about Toby," she said. "I didn't know who he was."

"He was afraid, too."

Aggie did not say anything. Arthur still held her hand. He shook it after a moment, as if chiding her. "You ran away, but then you came back. You were our first friend," he said. "If not for you, we would have been . . . so lonely."

"You were lonely anyway," she said. "It was terrible what happened to you, Arthur. I know that."

"But you made it so I could bear it. Every day, we expected you."

"Arthur," she began. She gripped his fingers. "If you hadn't liked me, you and Toby, I don't know what I would have done."

"*Liked* you?" He brought her hand up to his cheek and closed his eyes, and in the darkness Arthur raised his hand to rap on the glass of the coffeehouse window. Dr. Ornstein looked up from his newspaper, slowly allowing the pages to fall as he met Arthur's eyes. They gazed at each other across the crowded coffeehouse, through the glass of the window, in which all the reflections were shattered—the tables and chairs, the stiff, upright backs of the waiters in their short jackets forked into shards of blackness, the endlessly repeating pleats of newspapers and periodicals folded on their bamboo frames.

"I had a friend," Arthur began. "In Vienna." Dr. Ornstein's lovely daughter . . . had she worn her hair in braids? Or loose down her back? "He had a daughter, a beautiful girl. Sometimes I do not know anymore what she looked like. Sometimes I think she looked like you a little. She and her brother, they took fencing lessons near where Julius was, near the shop. Their father, Dr. Ornstein, came to meet them sometimes in the evenings." He stopped again, closed his eyes. He came to meet them, Arthur thought, and he stepped out into the street, into the convoy of trucks filled with screaming men who had gone insane. "I do not know if he ever saw them again."

He opened his eyes. "I mean to say . . . yes, that night, maybe he saw them. I cannot remember now. It is confused in my head. But after." He brought Aggie's hand to his mouth, pressed his lips to her fingers. "*Liked* you?" he said. "Liked you? Aggie, we loved you."

"That's the first time," she said. "That's the first time you've ever said that."

He gripped her hands. My heart, Anna had called him. "Love me," she had pleaded with him in London. "The world is ending, Arthur. Please love me." And he had protested, struggling out of bed onto the cold floor of Ivo's spare bedroom, going to the window and wrenching aside the blackout cloth.

"Look," he had said, desperate. "Look, Anna. There are the stars, and the moon. You see? The world is not ending. We are safe. You are safe." He had turned from the window, but she had been weeping, hunched over Toby in the bed, her cries muffled.

"I love you, Papa," Dr. Ornstein's beautiful daughter said, waltzing into the coffeehouse and surprising her father with a kiss. "Give me some of your coffee, sweet Papa." And she had picked up a spoon and licked it, sighing.

"*Liebchen,*" Arthur had whispered to Toby, over and over, holding him close in the berth on the ship from Land's End. "Toby?" he had said in his son's ear that first night at the Duvalls'. "We will go sleighing, Toby, yes?"

"Remember," he had said, kissing Toby good-bye that first day when he had to drive Mr. Duvall into the city. It had been so cold that morning, and he'd had to wake Toby early, pushing his feet into his old shoes because Arthur had no boots for him yet, and when they had come down to the kitchen in the big house, Toby's shoes were filled with snow, even though Arthur had carried him most of the way. Peggy had peeled off his socks, and Kitty, sitting by the fire, had taken Toby on her lap to rub his feet between her hands. Peggy found boots for him later, somewhere. She had taken Toby's hand that morning. "Come and see what's in this box," she had said, leading him toward the back hall, where a litter of kittens had been born two nights earlier.

Dr. Ornstein laughed at his beautiful daughter, snatching his spoon back from her, gesturing to the waiter: Come and bring my beautiful daughter anything she wishes.

"You *have* known it," Arthur cried, pulling Aggie's hands to his chest and pressing them there. "My God, Aggie, you have known that we loved you. Please."

"It was so great to have you there," Aggie said. "You have no idea. When it was just me and Peggy and Kitty, I was still afraid, somehow, because they could come get me anytime and take me away upstairs. And then you came, and Toby, and everything at the cottage was so nice, and I could go there . . . I just wanted to be with you all the time."

"It is the same," Arthur said. "It is still the same. The cottage. You are there with us."

But Aggie shook her head. "No," she said. "It's different now. It's different."

He did not understand her. He did not understand, and there was no time for her to explain because he heard footsteps in the hall and turned to see Mrs. MacCauley standing there. She was not looking at them. She was turned aside as if in discretion, but there was no one with her. There was nothing else to see there. She was waiting.

"I have to leave," Arthur said. He bent to Aggie again, put his mouth to her ear so Mrs. MacCauley would not hear him. "Call me on the telephone. When it is time. I will come then. She said I could come then. OK? I will be here."

Aggie leaned against him.

"Stop crying now," he said into her hair. "Stop crying, Aggie. I love you."

"OK," she said. "OK." And she did stop.

She put her arms up around his neck and hugged him. He hugged her back, pressing his face into her hair.

He looked back only once as he drove away. He saw Aggie enter the house again and saw Mrs. MacCauley come to meet her across the great emptiness of the hall.

EIGHT

THE DUVALLS' ORCHARD was small, a dozen trees scattered over an acre on the slope of the hill between the big house and Arthur's cottage. Harvesting the apples would take Arthur two weeks, less if Toby and a friend came to help. As the date when Aggie's baby was due to be born approached, Arthur had found it harder and harder to concentrate on anything. At least working in the orchard was pleasant: the fruit smelled sweet and the bees droned peacefully as they wove through the trees.

The summer had been hot and dull, day after long day of clotted heat that lay heavily against his skin. Gnats swarmed at his eyes and mouth when he worked outside. He missed Aggie with a longing that felt unbearable at times. At night, to escape the heat, he carried a chair to the stone stoop outside his front door and sat alone under the porch light, a book in his hand; but he did not read very much. His eyes kept traveling to the path through the orchard, to the route Aggie always took coming up the hill to see them.

When it grew late, he would go inside and lie down on his bed, his eyes closed; but he could not sleep. He tried the exercises Aggie had taught him, her fingertips on his temples: close your eyes, focus on one place ("Make it a nice place, Arthur," she had said, as if she knew the other kinds of pictures that crept into his head. "Don't let your mind go away from that place"). But his mind instead swam here and there like a drowning man clutching at rocks in order to free himself from deep water.

Sometimes, when Toby came home after being out with his friends, Arthur would get up and offer to make them sandwiches, and then they would sit together on the grass outside in the dark, looking at the stars. But Arthur became speechless on those evenings, knowing where Aggie was, knowing everything he could not say to Toby, and he sensed that Toby did not understand him—neither his apparent eagerness for company, forcing sandwiches on Toby at midnight, nor his failure to make conversation once they sat down outside. Usually Arthur just lay quietly in his room instead and listened to the noises of Toby getting ready for bed: the water running in the sink, Toby's sneakers hitting the floor beside his bed, the protest of the springs as he lay down, and then the silence.

It was as if Aggie had died.

He had done a second summer mowing by the time the apples were ready, the fine, barbed chaff suspended in the air and settling on his hair and face and painfully in his lungs. He had the same asthmatic response to mowing that he'd had to living in London during the war, when mortar dust had clogged the air; he could remember putting his finger to Anna's face and drawing a line in the dirt on her cheek as she lay in bed beside him—unwashed, unmoving, staring at the ceiling—after their return through the streets once the all clear had sounded. Now, after a long day on the tractor, he felt a constriction in his lungs that made him light-headed, a state that contributed to his sense of disorientation that summer, his sense that what was happening to Aggie was not real, not final.

The mowed hay lay in slanting rows on the fields, lines of heavy gold against the green of new shoots pushing up through the piercing stubble. A man would come with the baler while Arthur attended to the orchard, and the heavy rolls of hay would be speared and carried up to the barn. A neighboring farmer who pastured cows all over the county would use the hay in the winter.

Some of the apples—the Baldwins, the Macouns, the Gravensteins—would be wrapped in paper and packed in boxes with a fancy label to be mailed to some of Mr. Duvall's clients at the bank—a gentleman farmer's crop, Peggy said dismissively every year as she and Arthur sat side by side in the kitchen, wrapping the apples in the special paper printed with a pen-and-ink drawing of the big house that had been commissioned by Mrs. Duvall. "He wants it to look like he grew these himself," Peggy said. "Mr. Lord of the Manor."

Some of the crop Peggy would put up as applesauce, a hundred jars with an equally fancy label, also to be given away to visitors to the big house, though there were few of them that summer. Mr. Duvall came home less than a half-dozen times in June, July, and August combined—each time to entertain a handful of business associates who would play tennis on the clay court and drink quantities of alcohol—and then never for more than a night or two. It almost seemed as if he was uncomfortable at the house; and perhaps it *was* strange for him, Arthur thought, as if his small family had simply disappeared. Which in a way, he thought, it had.

But although Arthur drove Mr. Duvall in and out of the city when he called, the two men exchanged few words that summer, and Mr. Duvall never mentioned Aggie. He never asked about Toby, either, though that was not unusual. (Sometimes Arthur wondered if Mr. Duvall remembered that Toby existed.) He expressed concern about Kitty's health, though, and the strain on Peggy of looking after her. That he'd even noticed Peggy's unhappiness surprised Arthur at first; but of course Mr. Duvall didn't miss a trick, as Peggy said. Certainly he could identify suffering—or shame, or regret, or longing, Arthur thought—as skillfully as he could assess an opportunity to make money, and he seemed to be very good at that. But apparently he possessed no instinct for comforting. Arthur sensed that in fact Mr. Duvall felt it was not his responsibility to comfort other human beings. But it wasn't just that; it was more as if Mr. Duvall assumed that the gesture of any one person toward another, whether for good or evil, was necessarily borne out of self-interest, that there was no such thing as an unselfish, purely generous impulse. Expressions of concern were only a necessary form of social politeness.

How could a man so fortunate have come to believe so little in goodness? Arthur wondered. He thought of Dr. Ornstein, of the way the doctor had opened the door to the coffeehouse that evening: He had not hesitated at all, Arthur thought now, closing his eyes and trying to see it. No, there had been no hesitation. And now he thought he could remember that in fact Dr. Ornstein had left his hat on the table in his haste to hurry outside. Yes, there was his hat, a green loden, familiar and soft, slightly stained on the brim, fallen to the floor, where the sweep of Dr. Ornstein's coat had caught it as he hurried outside. And he had hurried, hadn't he?

Sometimes Arthur remembered that he himself had been inside Julius's shop that evening, peering from the window while Julius tugged at his sleeve to pull him away, pull him into the safety of darkness in the back room; he could not have seen into the coffeehouse at all. But it was easy to forget this; he could see Dr. Ornstein so clearly now, hear him speaking. Sometimes he could take Dr. Ornstein's hand in his own and turn it over, inspecting it, while the doctor discreetly turned his face aside. What a marvel, this hand that could glide over the keys of his beautiful Bosendorfer and make such music, that could touch a human body so knowingly. There was a light that shone around Dr. Ornstein as he sat in the coffeehouse in Arthur's memory. It did not come from him exactly, this light; it was more as if a flashlight were being trained down a long hallway, bouncing over objects and people: Anna as Arthur had first known her, laughing, her mouth open; Julius eating his soup; the streetcar rattling around the Ring; a leaf on the pavement beneath his foot. It was always Dr. Ornstein who waited at the end of this long hallway, sitting behind his newspaper, or bent over the chessboard, or kneeling on the street, his hands over his head.

Somewhere on the street that evening long ago, Dr. Ornstein's beautiful children had been running toward him, even as men jumped from the trucks and filled the streets with their shouting and their clubs and their curses and their hatred. But Dr. Ornstein had had no thought but for his children's safety, Arthur thought, his great love for them outweighing the fear he must surely have felt.

THIS YEAR, AS IN years past, Arthur started worrying early about what to do with the apples they couldn't even seem to give away. One year, without asking the Duvalls' permission, he had offered bushels of them to Toby's school for the children to eat with their lunches, and he had continued to do so every year since. The remaining apples, though, had to go into the basement in the big house for storage or, packed loosely in crates, to the handful of neighbors with whom Arthur had become familiar over the years, people whose wealth seemed to equal and in some cases surpass the Duvalls', with servants Arthur had met through Peggy. Arthur drove boxes of apples out to these big houses with their sweeping drives, the trunk of Mr. Duvall's long black Lincoln sagging under the weight of the boxes, and brought them to the kitchen entrance. The cook usually came to the door, wiping wet hands on a dish towel, eyed what he had to offer, and finally asked him to carry the apples down to the basement or into the cold pantry, standing aside to give him room as he came in the door, crates heaped in his arms. He'd intended the fruit for the servants, not their masters, Arthur thought, but even the servants in those houses were used to having servants.

He had not seen Aggie since he had driven away from Break-abeen that last weekend in June, but they talked on the phone. He had tried, early on, to persuade her to let him tell Toby where she was, but the conversation had gone so badly that he had not asked a second time.

"He could write letters to you," he had said, standing at the kitchen phone at the big house, watching through the window as Peggy helped settle Kitty in a chair on the grass in the sun. "He is worried, Aggie. He does not understand why you would go away from us with no word."

"I know," she said. "I know. I understand. You just have to tell him I'm traveling."

"But what traveling? No postcard? No telephone call? He knows something is not right."

Aggie said nothing. Arthur tried to imagine her on the other end of the phone, sitting on the little chair with the needlepoint seat in the hall at Breakabeen.

"Aggie?" he said.

"I'll talk to him when I get back."

"It's hard always to be lying to him." He didn't mean to sound accusatory, but he couldn't help it. "I don't like it."

"Sorry."

But she did not sound sorry. He had the sense that her attention had been diverted, that she was no longer listening to him.

"I don't understand," Arthur said abruptly. "You explain this to me."

"No." Aggie's answer was short, and he could tell that her mouth was close to the phone again, that she was hunched over it now, her voice fierce. "I don't have to explain *anything*. It's what I want."

"OK, OK." Arthur backed down. "I only thought it would be good for you. He is your *friend*."

"Everybody knows what's good for me right now."

"I know," Arthur said. "I know. I'm sorry."

"Can I talk to Kitty, please?"

Clearly, the conversation was over.

They had told Aggie about Kitty finally, trying to make her illness of earlier in the summer less frightening than it had been, the change in her since the strokes less dramatic. Still, Peggy told Arthur, Aggie called home often, worried. Kitty seemed bewildered sometimes during her conversations with Aggie over the phone. One of Arthur's worst days that summer had come when Kitty had not recognized him for a moment. Sometimes, Kitty did not seem certain who Aggie was, either.

"Yes, OK. I'll get her," he said in defeat. And that was it,

Arthur had thought—Aggie's final ruling on the subject. He wondered if she would ever tell Toby what had happened to her. And he wondered again, for the thousandth time, what boy had lain with Aggie and made her pregnant. Who, and where, and when.

TOBY STOPPED ASKING Arthur about Aggie, but not before they exchanged angry words about it. Arthur began to feel that all his relationships had taken on a strain: Peggy was absorbed with Kitty, and Arthur rarely ate down at the big house that summer. Toby would go down and play checkers with Kitty sometimes in the evening, but he complained that Peggy hovered and fussed. Toby seemed to make a point of staying away from home, visiting with friends, going out at night, working long hours at Snyder's Orchard. Yet Arthur's sense was that Toby's silence did not mean he had forgotten about Aggie; his restlessness, in fact, seemed evidence to Arthur of Toby's unhappiness over her disappearance. The fact that they did not talk about her made her absence more pronounced. And one day, after weeks of saying nothing, Toby suddenly broke the silence anyway.

"Heard from Aggie lately, Dad?" he said one morning when he came into the kitchen while Arthur was fixing breakfast. Toby took the milk out of the refrigerator and poured a glass for himself, leaning back against the counter. He had on a torn T-shirt, and his beard was nearly full, red and curly.

Toby had not mentioned Aggie for some time, and Arthur was taken off guard. Also, he didn't like Toby's tone of voice; he felt as if he were being challenged, that Toby had waited as long as he could stand it before accusing Arthur. "You know I have not heard," he said, carefully measuring tea into the pot. "You know I would tell you."

"I'm not the only one who wants to know where she is, you know." Toby set down his glass and stared at it for a moment before going on. "They took her off somewhere, didn't they? They're hiding her."

"On holiday," Arthur said stubbornly. He screwed the top on the canister of tea. "With her mother."

"On holiday," Toby repeated. He touched his glass on the countertop, pushed it with a fingertip. Then he looked up. "Dad, they'd have to tie her hands and feet and stuff a gag in her mouth to get Aggie to spend this long with her mother somewhere. Wherever they are."

"Why do you think I know about this?" Arthur said in exasperation; but it was a feigned reaction, and he knew he was a poor liar.

"Because I think you know where she is, and I think you won't tell me. And I think Peggy knows, too, and she won't tell me, either. Nobody will say anything about it."

Arthur walked across the kitchen past Toby to put the milk back in the refrigerator.

"So something has happened to her, or something has happened to Mrs. Duvall, or . . ." Toby gave up. He turned around to take a piece of bread from the breadbox and jammed it down into the toaster. And then he looked back at Arthur. "What's the matter, Dad? Don't you trust me?"

"It is nothing to do with that," Arthur said, but he softened at Toby's tone; he could hear the appeal in it. "I don't know anything," he added, wanting only to put an end to the conversation. "She is on holiday. People go on holiday."

Toby turned on Arthur, the change in his demeanor swift, as if he had been holding himself in check and had suddenly snapped. "Do you think I'm an idiot?" he shouted. His face was transformed by anger. Arthur felt a moment's shocking fear of his son.

Arthur crossed to the other side of the kitchen table, putting it between them. "I tell nothing because there is nothing to tell," he said. "Don't shout at me."

"You're lying. They've got you in some kind of knot, some kind of deal. And you're afraid of them, so you do what they tell you."

"I never!" Arthur brought his fist down on the table. The sugar bowl jumped, and the spoon fell to the tablecloth, spilling sugar. Arthur swept at it savagely with his hand. It clattered to the floor. "You do not understand this," he said, and realized he was shaking. "You should say nothing to me about it."

Toby stared at Arthur. "The Duvalls take Aggie away somewhere, for some secret purpose, and you don't even have the guts to stand up to them," he said. "You know she's not happy there with Mrs. Duvall, if they even *are* in Florida; I can't ever get the phone there to answer. But you know what it's like for her to be with her mother. It's horrible. If anyone knows that, it's you and me. But you won't step up to the plate, Dad. You won't help her. And you won't let *me* help her."

Toby's toast popped up out of the toaster, and Arthur jumped. "Why do you young people think you are always the savior?" he said suddenly, and his voice was full of scorn and anger. "You think we know nothing, that we . . . we bungle things. But you, you think you are the big heroes, that you go in and fix everything on your big white horses. But you know nothing. You know *nothing* about this. Nothing. You are a *child*." He turned away from Toby, breathing hard. He had not meant to be cruel. He was ashamed. But it was too late.

Toby did not come home that night.

By the time Arthur was ready to begin work in the orchard, a wordless truce had been reached between them, though they had exchanged no apologies. But Toby took a week off from Snyder's, bringing his friend Tim Warren with him for help when Arthur was ready, and the three of them started work together.

The weather was fine that week, as hot as it had been all summer, but a breeze blew and the air was clear and full of light. The boys were fast pickers, much faster than Arthur, and sometimes he found himself standing idly on the ladder, his head and shoulders hidden in the leaves, his hands resting on a branch. He was tired all the time that summer, sleeping in only two- or three-hour stretches, sometimes less; he slept most deeply in the chair in his living room at the end of the workday, a book propped open on his lap, his head falling forward to his chest as if drawn there by a string. Many nights he abandoned the bed altogether and sat in this chair, hoping for sleep, the window open beside him. The future, he felt, had ceased to exist, slipping quietly away. The present was a half-open door through which he passed like a sleepwalker every morning. But the past yawned behind him, a cave of darkness.

Anna had been preoccupied with death in England, terrified of Germany's advance across Europe. Many of her stories to Arthur had been about dying. He remembered the story of the death of Abraham, how, when it came his time to die, Abraham refused to go and bargained with God and the angel Michael. It was so hard for Abraham, Anna said, to die that he made God and the angel Michael carry him around the earth instead, and he even made them take him to his own house, where he saw that his wife, Sarah, had died of grief at the loss of her husband. But still he would not go. So God sent Death to Abraham, as Abraham would not come willingly to him, but he made Death sweet-faced and sweet-smelling, to woo Abraham. And still Abraham would not go; he made Death reveal himself for what he was—two-headed, with one face like a serpent's and one like the blade of a sword, Anna had said, making Arthur shudder. But Abraham's soul was too tenacious.

"So how did it go for him, in the end?" Arthur had whispered, lying facing Anna in the bed in London, their hands clasped together between them.

And Anna had brought her face close to his, her breath on his eyelids. "God took Abraham's soul from him in a dream."

Standing in the apple tree, his face hidden from Toby and Tim, who called cheerfully to each other and talked as they worked, Arthur looked up through the leaves to the blue sky, the birds crossing overhead, the lazy white clouds high above. You had to be a fighter to earn losing your soul in that painless way, he thought, God's hand passing with a sigh into your breast as if into water, catching the bird that was your soul and carrying it safely away. Everyone who had died in the camps in Europe—did God see flocks of birds rising from those places? Did he, like a surgeon, give those people sleep at the last moment, before performing his last amazing act on their behalf, the execution of their death? Did he gather those rising souls to him and call them all home? The bird in Dr. Ornstein's heart—for Dr. Ornstein was a fighter, surely, in God's eyes— did that bird beat its wings and soar straight up to heaven? Or did it circle the world one last time, turning its eye upon the rolling face of the earth, letting the wind pass through its feathers, Dr. Ornstein's sensitive surgeon's fingers, splayed out to catch the currents of the air, play them like music? Did Dr. Ornstein see Arthur there, searching the sky, looking for him?

The soul of a fighter was a bird, released from life by God's finger pressing your eyelids closed; but if you did not fight, Arthur thought, if you did not love what had been given to you to love, then Death came without disguise, turning the blade of his face against you, and cut you down where you stood.

Arthur moved his hands from the ladder, ran his palms lightly along the branch of the tree.

And then he heard his name being called. Peggy was coming up the hill, holding her kitchen smock above her knees, the wind flattening the stiff brush of her hair.

Arthur backed down the ladder and came out from the trees to meet her. She hurried across the orchard toward him. Over the summer she had grown heavier, and she struggled up the hill now. "They called," she said, breathing hard as she came up to him.

Arthur stopped.

"From that place. About Aggie. They just called."

Arthur unhooked the canvas sack from around his neck. "She is all right? What did they say?"

"They just said she was going to the hospital."

Arthur tried to think what to do next. He had been waiting for this. It should not have felt like such a shock.

Toby had stopped at the foot of a ladder propped against a tree some distance away across the orchard. He was looking at Peggy and Arthur.

Peggy glanced in his direction. "What are you going to tell him?"

"I don't know." Arthur stooped to pick up the sack. "You can tell him something?" He began to turn away. "They didn't say anything else? She is OK?"

Peggy stepped back. "I don't know what to say to him, Arthur. You need to talk to him."

"I have to go," he said. "I can't talk to him now."

But Toby had already approached them. "What's up?" He stopped beside Peggy, looking between her and Arthur. "What's going on?"

Peggy shook her head and wound her hands under her apron. "I left Mother alone. I'm going back down. You call me, Arthur." She turned and hurried back down the path.

Arthur took off his gloves and hoisted the canvas sack over his shoulder. "I have to go someplace, Toby. You can finish here, please?" He had begun walking away.

"Where are you going?" Toby came after him. "Wait a minute! What's happened?"

Arthur did not stop. "I have no time to talk now," he said. "I will be back—couple of days."

But Toby caught his arm. "Dad!"

Arthur paused. "I have to pack some things, Toby. I have to go."

"Tim," Toby called, "I'll be back in a minute."

They saw Tim's arm wave at them out of the branches of a tree. For a moment Arthur registered the strangeness of the sight, a human arm extending from the boughs as if boy and tree had been grafted together. But he had to hurry.

In his bedroom Arthur took two shirts and clean trousers from the closet. He got his good shoes out from under the bureau.

Toby sat down on the bed watching him. "You have to tell me," he said finally, as Arthur rifled through drawers. "I know it's about Aggie."

Arthur turned to his bureau. In the mirror was the little photograph of Toby in the apple tree, the childish curve of Aggie's cheek under the hood of her jacket. He stopped for a minute, looking at it, and then opened another drawer, hunting for a clean handkerchief.

"Dad."

Arthur glanced at him. Toby looked very young suddenly, his beard like a child's foolish disguise. His forehead and ears were pink from the sun. He put up the back of his hand to rub his nose and across his mouth.

Arthur sat down on the bed. He hoisted his suitcase onto his lap, opened the clasps. He did not look at Toby.

"What's the matter with her?" Toby said. "Is she sick? Is she going to die?"

And then he put his arm up in front of his face.

Toby had wept easily as a child—every time Arthur had to leave him with Peggy and Kitty, every morning for weeks after he started school in America, at any slight, real or imagined, every tumble, every fall, every bump and bruise, often at night, for no reason that Arthur could discover other than the sadness of what lay behind them: the months of bombing, Ivo's death, Anna's death, the baby's death. He had been frightened of everything—birds in the sky, the sound of snow sliding from the roof, the rusty clatter of the alarm clock Arthur used to wake himself in the morning for Mr. Duvall's early trips into the city. Arthur could remember the sight of Toby's face, mouth open, eyes shut, wailing. "Look at what he's been through," Peggy had said. "He'll grow out of it." And he had, eventually.

Arthur leaned over and put his arm around Toby. How unfamiliar he felt; it was hard to reconcile this grown boy with the vulnerable child that had been Toby when they moved to America so many years before. "It is not like that, Toby . . . She will be all right," he said. "Don't worry." This had been unfair to him, Arthur thought, closing his eyes for a minute. It was time to tell him the truth. He could settle things with Aggie later.

And then he thought: But women do die in childbirth.

Of course they do.

He pulled Toby close to him for a moment and then released him. He had to go. He could not talk about all this now.

But Toby doubled over, his face in his hands. "I'm sorry," he said. "Dad, I'm sorry."

Arthur stopped. He stood up abruptly and looked down at Toby. The hair on Toby's arms, as he wrapped them around himself, lay in little whorls, pink and gold. A flicker of unease ran over Arthur's skin. He stood perfectly still.

Toby rocked on the bed, his face hidden from Arthur.

Arthur took a step closer to the bed, stood over him. And then he looked away. "I have to go," he said, and he kept his voice neutral. "Peggy is here. You and Tim . . . you finish with the apples. Please."

And then he picked up his bag and walked out of the room.

They had been awful, all those times when he'd had to leave Toby crying as a child. Arthur had hated leaving Toby at school, tears running down his little face, one hand held firmly by the principal, the other hand reaching after Arthur, begging. Returning to the Duvalls' from the city, Arthur had fought panic every time—the absurd certainty that something had happened to Toby while he'd been gone, that Toby had died. When the boy had woken at night, crying, Arthur had stumbled across the hall and knelt beside his bed, gathering Toby into his arms. His own heart, he'd thought, would break at the sound of Toby's cries of terror and grief.

He could hear him crying now—a grown man crying like a baby—as he walked down the stairs. He could hear him, but he wouldn't turn back.

Dr. Ornstein sat in the coffeehouse, folding and refolding his newspaper impatiently, checking his watch, adjusting the silver ribbon on the prettily wrapped parcel of chocolates he had bought for his children. He was a man who liked to give gifts, pressing a little package into his wife's hands for no particular occasion, standing by, pleased, his hands linked behind his back, as she opened it and exclaimed over . . . what was it? A pin shaped like a bird, a ruby in its eye, diamond-studded feathers on its back. Dr. Ornstein shrugged, demurred. It's nothing, a trinket, he said. And to his son? He gave books, always books, Arthur thought, wrapped in paper, inscribed "From your loving father" on the flyleaf. For his daughter there would be a shawl, an enamel bracelet, a ribbon. There was no weeping in Dr. Ornstein's apartment on the Türkenschanz- platz. Dr. Ornstein gathered his children into his arms; he forgave them, every time.

Life was short.

As Arthur backed Mr. Duvall's car out of the barn, Tim Warren, standing under a tree in the orchard, raised his hand uncertainly. But Arthur did not wave back. He did not trust himself to make any gesture. Maybe Tim was the one, he thought wildly. It might have been any one of them, any one of the boys Peggy could not tell apart.

MERCY HOSPITAL IN Euphrates, fifteen miles west of Breakabeen, was an old whitewashed brick building surrounded by towering oak trees. Newer wings were connected to the main building by elbows of glassed-in walkways that glowed with light in the soft dusk of the September evening. By the time Arthur arrived and found his way through the town to the hospital, the sky overhead had melted into a grave and beautiful blue darkness in which a few stars appeared faintly. A yellow light was on over the front porch at the building's main entrance. Two white benches on the porch on either side of the front door were empty except for one man, who sat quietly, all alone, a hat on his head, his face turned away.

Arthur parked Mr. Duvall's car on the street and ran his hands through his hair. He had played the radio the entire way in the car, trying not to think, and now his ears rang in the silence. The long-limbed oak trees in late summer leaf loomed against the sky, the air beneath their branches soft and close. A lawn swept down to the street, where a few cars were parked under the streetlights. Arthur got out of the car and walked toward the main entrance. As he approached, the man sitting on the bench glanced in his direction and then stood up and let himself into the building. It was too dark to make out anything other than the shape of his hat; Arthur could not tell if he was young or old.

Inside, he gave his name to a nurse in a white uniform who sat alone at a wooden desk, a small lamp illuminating some files and papers on the desk's surface before her. The blades of a ceiling fan turned overhead. Behind her ran a long, poorly lit parlor filled with scattered groups of furniture, shabby wing chairs and couches, tables strewed with magazines and books. Here and there a yellow-shaded lamp had been turned on, but the room was empty; only the faces in the portraits looked out from the shadows.

"You're a relative, sir?" The nurse was writing his name in a book on her desk. Arthur watched her hand move across the paper.

"Yes. Relative." Arthur held his hat. When she glanced up, he added, "Uncle."

The nurse looked back down at the logbook on the desk. "Maternity is on the second floor, the east wing," she said. She checked at a little watch on her wrist. "Visiting hours are over in twenty minutes, though. The elevators are down the hall to your left."

Arthur turned away. There was no sign of the man who had been on the porch when he approached the building. The hall was empty and utterly quiet. The elevator, though, arrived with a noisy clanking; the elevator operator, an old man in a green jacket and white shoes, his face deeply lined, opened the metal accordion doors and Arthur stepped inside.

The second-floor hallway was as quiet and dim as the main floor, and Arthur hesitated after the elevator doors closed behind him. A brighter light shone from around a corner far away down the green tiles of the corridor, so Arthur went in that direction. He passed a little darkened alcove on his left, with a small crucifix on the wall and a window that looked out over the front lawn. Someone was sitting in a chair in the alcove facing the window, but the gentleman shifted a little, turning his face away as Arthur passed. A black hat lay on the seat of the chair beside him.

"Excuse me," Arthur said in a low voice when the nurse behind the window at the station around the corner did not notice him immediately. She reached forward and slid the window aside a little.

"I am looking for Miss Duvall's room, please."

The nurse looked down, consulting the clipboard on the desk. "Miss Duvall is in labor and delivery," she said. "Are you a relative?"

"She is all right?" The news that Aggie was there, perhaps delivering her baby at that moment, made Arthur feel faint.

The nurse gave a little sigh, a tiny noise in the silence of the hall. "Are you a relative, sir?"

Arthur clutched his hat tightly. "Yes. A relative. She is all right?"

"Visiting hours are over in a few minutes. She won't be out by then." The nurse bent down and wrote something on a piece of paper and handed it to him through the opening in the window. "You can call here later."

Arthur stared at the piece of paper. "Something is wrong," he said.

"Nothing is wrong, sir," the woman said in a weary tone. "Miss Duvall is in labor. You'll have to call later."

"I cannot call," Arthur said. "I have to stay here. Where is she? I have to see her."

The nurse closed the window a little and leaned back. Arthur heard her call something through an open door to someone in the room behind her. After a moment, another nurse in a stiff white hat appeared. She approached the window and slid it open briskly. "You'll have to wait somewhere else, sir. Visiting hours are over. Miss Duvall will be some time still. There's no need for you to worry."

"But I have nowhere to wait! Where should I go?"

"The lobby downstairs stays open all night," the nurse said. "We can call down there when Miss Duvall is back in her room, if you like."

Arthur nodded.

The nurse slid the window closed again and turned away.

ARTHUR SAT ALONE in the dark lobby downstairs, his hat on his knees. On the wall in front of him, between two lamps with sinewy, branching arms, the eyes of the man in the portrait gazed into the distance past Arthur's head. Arthur's thumb ran back and forth over the soft brim of his hat. He had no idea how long he would have to wait. He'd brought nothing to read. He had not imagined having nothing to do.

After a few minutes he stood up and went to the window that looked out over the hospital's lawn and the street beyond. As he stood there, headlights swept around the corner, and a car pulled onto the street in front of the hospital, stopping under one of the streetlights. Arthur recognized it as the old sedan from Breakabeen. He retrieved his hat from the chair and hurried outside past the nurse, who was speaking quietly into the telephone.

Outside, he stopped on the porch. Mrs. MacCauley had gotten out of the car and then stooped to say something to whoever was behind the wheel—Walter, presumably. She stood upright again as the car pulled away, and Arthur began to descend the steps of the porch to go and meet her, but she stopped again suddenly at another car parked nearby, as if she'd been called by someone who sat inside in the darkness of the backseat. She bent down, her hand resting on the open window.

Arthur stopped abruptly at the bottom of the steps.

Were these the people who had come to take the baby away? Was that how it happened? Were they waiting to carry it off in the dark of night, the baby still warm from Aggie's body? Arthur would not even be allowed to see the baby, this child of Agatha's. Was he never even to lay eyes on the child or hold it, even for a moment?

After another minute or two, Mrs. MacCauley turned away from the car and began walking up the long path that slanted across the lawn toward the front entrance of the hospital. Arthur put on his hat, but he did not move to meet her.

She had her head down as she came, putting something away in her purse. She wore a gray cardigan over her dress, and a small black hat, gloves on her hands. She looked, Arthur thought, as though she were dressed for a funeral.

But why had she not been here from the first? Why had she left Aggie alone?

She looked up as she approached the drive that passed before the porch, and when she saw Arthur, she hesitated, her surprise evident on her face. Arthur enjoyed a moment's unpleasant satisfaction that his presence there had unnerved her. Perhaps she had not expected him to come, after all.

She crossed the driveway and came to stand before him. In only a moment, she had managed to compose herself. "Good evening, Mr. Henning."

"You are not inside with her." Arthur knew he was being rude, but suddenly he had no desire to be polite with her.

"I brought her here, Mr. Henning. I saw her settled in. We are not allowed to accompany the girls during delivery."

But Arthur's anger was mulish. "You have left her alone."

"It can take many hours to bring a baby into the world, Mr. Henning—" she began, but he cut her off.

"I know how many hours it takes. I know about it. I have a son," he said harshly, moving to block her progress. "I had a daughter." He realized he was breathing hard. But he did not want to tell her about Anna and the baby. It was none of her concern, none of her business, as they said in America. "I thought you would be with her."

"She is perfectly well cared for." Mrs. MacCauley switched

her purse to her other arm. Under the light from the porch, her face looked pale.

Arthur stepped in front of her. "Who is in that car, the one parked there? Are they the ones who will take the baby?"

Mrs. MacCauley looked startled. She glanced toward the hospital's front door as if looking for help. "The adoptions don't take place immediately," she said. "There is a process."

"But it is all arranged. You have arranged it."

"It has been arranged through me, by Agatha and her parents."

"Yes. Quick and be done with it," he said, looking away from her. "Send it away." He struggled to keep his composure. The prospect of the loss of the baby—the now certain loss of the baby, though of course it had never been anything but certain—was washing up against him with such force that he felt unsteady.

"I want to see the baby. Aggie's baby," he said.

"There is no need for that."

"It is not if there is need. I *want* to see it." His English was stumbling, but he didn't care.

"You have no rights to that baby, Mr. Henning. Not to see it, not to touch it, nothing. Do you understand me?" She looked angry. He wondered that he had ever thought her kind, that he had ever admired her.

Arthur watched her. His chest rose and fell with emotion. "Still," he said. "Still. I want to see it." He regretted how dramatic he sounded; he did not want her to know anything of what he felt.

How could he have been so stupid as not to recognize that this moment was coming, had been coming from the beginning? What had he thought? he wondered. What had he been thinking? But he knew what he had been thinking: he had thought that it would be sad, yes, and that Aggie would need him to comfort her; he had thought he was equal to that. He had not reckoned on this, though—his own sadness, the purely irrelevant and shocking force of a longing for which there would be no answer, no comfort, no redress. He had no claim here. No power at all.

Mrs. MacCauley pulled her purse up close before her chest. "I have seen a great many girls deliver babies they did not intend to have, Mr. Henning, and I have seen them give up those babies to families who have wished for a child they could not have on their own. Agatha will be no different from any of them. Her—"

"No. No, she *is* different," Arthur broke in. "It is not Aggie who would give it away, this baby. It is the Duvalls. They have made her to do this thing—they have forced her."

"She has given her absolute consent to this. No one has forced Agatha's hand here." She paused. And then she looked directly at him. "You must ask yourself, Mr. Henning, why your own feelings here matter so much. This is not your child. It is no relation to you. I understand that you consider yourself Agatha's friend, but it is hardly an appropriate—"

"What? What is not appropriate? I *am* her friend. Of course I am! And now her baby will be taken away from us. It is . . . it is horrible." Arthur turned aside, too upset to continue. He was suddenly so angry that he was afraid of himself.

She began to try to edge past him, but Arthur moved swiftly, aware, as he came close to her, of the ugly, thrilling sense of power that came with such a physical display. He would not touch her—he was not brutal enough to catch her arm—but he knew he was threatening. "Who is in the car, the one there?" He gestured roughly toward the street.

"That is not your concern." Her eyes were wide. He saw he had frightened her.

"That is not my concern? I ask you a question!"

But she moved quickly, slipping past him, and he fell back. That was as much as he would ever be able to do, he thought. The world was full of men who would be different, who would be different with even less provocation, men who would have caught her by the arm, their fingers pressing hard, men who might have shaken her. But he was not one of them.

"I want to see the baby, Mrs. MacCauley," he called after her. "Please."

But she did not stop, hurrying up the steps of the hospital and away from him.

He turned back. The car parked at the street was still there, its occupants sitting in the dark. He began to move slowly toward the street, but he had not taken ten steps when he heard the car's engine start and saw the headlights blaze. And by the time he had reached the edge of the lawn, it had pulled away from the curb, and in a moment the taillights disappeared around the corner. Arthur stood alone on the grass in the soft night air, the leaves of the trees stirring above his head, his hat in his hand.

ARTHUR SAT BESIDE the bed. He'd had to extricate Aggie's limp arm from the bedclothes to take her hand in his own, and now he held it gently, his thumb reflexively stroking her fingers. She had been asleep since being brought up, motionless and pale on the gurney, to her room three hours before, just as the sun had risen.

He had seen the baby. The young nurse in the nursery had smiled at him when he waved at her through the window, summoning onto his face with enormous effort an expression of innocent happiness that he hoped was believable; she had held the baby up to the window for him when he'd pointed to the bassinet with Agatha's name on the card at the baby's feet. Arthur had stood there, his fingertips against the window, and the nurse had smiled at him and then down at the baby, tucking in a little corner of the blanket more securely.

"Boy?" Arthur had mouthed, guessing, trying to smile again.

She had nodded and held the baby up closer to the window so Arthur could look down into his face.

He'd had to turn away. He had not been able to look at him for more than a minute. The nurse, mistaking Arthur's emotion, had smiled kindly and put the baby back in his little bassinet.

Arthur had walked around the corner, fumbling for his handkerchief; coming toward him down the hall, a young man, his arm hooked tenderly through his wife's, raised his glowing face to Arthur. The woman, taking slow and careful steps, was dressed in a pretty flowered robe and slippers; her face, like her husband's, shone with happiness.

Mrs. MacCauley had been nowhere in sight. It had been so easy, after all.

It was almost noon now, and the sun blazed outside the window. Arthur stood up from beside Aggie's bed and went to the window to adjust the curtain so that the light did not fall on her face. A warm breeze blew outside, and the heavy bouquets of leaves on the oak trees stirred. Arthur leaned his forehead against the glass, feeling the sun's heat on his face.

"Arthur?"

He turned around quickly.

But before she could say anything else, Aggie doubled up and retched convulsively onto the sheet beside her head, her hands fluttering helplessly over her stomach. She cried out in pain.

"I want to go home," she said finally, lying back against the pillow. Her face was white, her eyes ringed with exhaustion. "I want to go home."

AGGIE STAYED AT the hospital for five days, a week in which so much changed in Arthur's life that when he finally returned to bring Aggie home, he did not know her, did not know his son, did not know himself.

He had called Peggy from the hospital that first afternoon, intending to tell her that Aggie would have to stay for several days and that he would wait there until she was ready to leave the hospital, but Peggy had interrupted him.

"He wants you to come home, Arthur. He says he has to go somewhere."

"What?" Arthur stood inside the narrow telephone booth on the main floor outside the hospital's coffee shop. "What?" he said again.

"Mr. Duvall. He says you're to come home. He knows you're there."

Arthur stiffened. A little flicker of fear ran through him. He'd had no orders from Mr. Duvall to come for Aggie; he'd never said to Mr. Duvall that he intended to be there when the baby was born. He was there because her own father and mother would offer her no comfort. He was there because he loved her. He had stepped over a line, he knew, though he could not say where that line lay, nor at what moment he had crossed it. It had happened long ago, he thought. It had happened without his realizing it.

"Maybe they called him and said you were there. I don't know how he knows. But you're to come back."

"I can't leave her." Two doctors in white coats stood talking in the corridor outside the open door to the coffee shop; one of them held a sandwich wrapped in wax paper. From inside the coffee shop, Arthur could hear the sounds of conversation, the clatter of dishes, the ring of a cash register's bell.

"He says he has to go somewhere, Arthur," Peggy said. "You'd better come back."

Arthur arrived home sometime just before dawn. He put the car in the garage and came back outside, his suitcase in his hand, into the penetrating blackness of the soft night air. The familiar smell of the fields, always more pungent at night, rose up from the ground. Wallace Mountain loomed thick and silent against the horizon, dark against dark. Arthur walked across the grass instead of following the path to the cottage. It must have rained at some point while he'd been gone; the earth gave a little under his shoes, offering a gentle, forgiving resistance. Mist hovered just above the grass.

He'd had no sleep in two nights except for an hour on the trip home, when he'd pulled the car over onto the side of the road and had lain down on the front seat, his head crushing his hat on the seat beside him.

There were no lights on in the cottage. Arthur crossed the grass and let himself in through the kitchen. He set his case down quietly by the table. He filled a glass of water from the tap and began to feel his way into the living room.

Toby spoke from out of the darkness. He was sitting in Arthur's chair.

Arthur jumped. The water in his glass splattered onto the floor.

"I couldn't sleep. Sorry." Toby shifted in the chair. "Peggy said you'd be back tonight."

Arthur set the glass on the table. He put the backs of his

hands up to his eyes. "I have to drive Mr. Duvall somewhere tomorrow. I don't know where. I need to sleep a little bit."

"Where's Aggie?" Toby's voice was quiet.

Arthur could not make out Toby's face clearly in the darkness of the room. He felt ill with fatigue and sadness. Aggie had cried when he left, clinging to him in a way so uncharacteristic that he had been worried. Arthur had gone past the nursery on his way out of the hospital, but the bassinets had been moved and he couldn't tell which baby was Aggie's anymore. They had all looked the same, little bundles wrapped tight in blankets. "I am tired, Toby," he said. "We will talk later, OK?"

"She's pregnant, isn't she?" But there was no question in Toby's voice. "Did she have the baby?"

Arthur put his hand on the table to steady himself. He pulled out a chair and sat down. He closed his eyes for a minute and then opened them again. The room was still dark, but he could see Toby hunched in the chair across the room now, and the pale color of his shirt. "She would not let me say anything, Toby," he said. "She is coming home in a few days now. She will tell you then."

Toby said nothing.

"I have to go to sleep," Arthur began. He wanted to get away, get upstairs, get away from Toby. He did not want Toby to speak.

Toby moved suddenly in his chair. "Where's the baby?"

Arthur brushed at something under his palm on the surface of the table. He heard the sound of a pin hitting the floor. He bent over as if to search for it, but the room was too dark for him to see anything so small. "The baby is in the hospital," he said. The air in the room seemed very close. "Why can't you open the window?" Arthur said suddenly, starting to get up, but Toby spoke.

"Is she bringing the baby home?"

Arthur crossed the room in the dark, knocking painfully into the corner of the table. He stumbled, swore. At the window he pulled aside the curtain to struggle with the sash. "Why are you sitting here with the windows closed shut?" he said irritably. "It is too hot in here."

"There was a thunderstorm. Sorry. I closed the windows when it started to rain."

Arthur turned back. The room was a degree lighter. He could see Toby more clearly now. "The baby will be given up. Adopted," he said. "It is a little boy."

Toby leaned forward in the chair, his head in his hands. He said something indistinct.

Arthur turned back to the window. There was no sound of the birds outside yet, but when the sun creased the horizon, they would begin to call to one another, Arthur thought; it was such a sweet noise, the sound of birds waking. In Vienna he had never been aware of it. He stared out the window. The shadows of the trees fell across the grass in the moonlight. There was a pulsing sound in his ears. "I want to go to bed," Arthur said, but his voice sounded far away to him. "I am very tired now."

"It was a mistake," Toby said into the darkness. "It just . . . happened. We made a mistake."

Arthur shook his head. "I have to drive Mr. Duvall someplace tomorrow," he said. "No. No, it is today already." He brushed at his head, confused, then strained to see out into the darkness; the buzzing had grown louder in his ears. The porch light on the leaves threw shadows that wavered over the grass like spilled ink.

"We didn't think," Toby said. "We . . . it was just something that happened." He was quiet for a minute. "Dad," he said when Arthur said nothing. "Dad. I'm sorry. I'm so sorry, I . . ."

Arthur put both hands on the windowsill and leaned over, struggling to get his head outside into the air. Before Christmas, he thought. During the school holidays. There had been a snowstorm. Arthur had driven Mr. Duvall to Hartford, had ended up having to stay in the YMCA near the train station because the roads were too bad to drive home. And then it had been two days before the snow ended and the roads were clear, except by then there had been no point in driving home, as Mr. Duvall would be done with his business meetings the next morning, so Arthur had called the cottage to say he would just wait, after all. Aggie had answered the phone.

"We're playing Monopoly," she had said, and her voice had been bright. She had sounded happy to hear from him, happy to speak to him. "I'm losing, as usual. He's got Boardwalk *and* Park Place."

Toby had called out something and Aggie had laughed, but Arthur had not been able to make out what Toby said.

"Poor Arthur," Aggie had said. "Stuck in a YMCA all by your-

self. Do you have a book or something? Can you get a paper?"
She knew how he liked to read the newspaper. He liked everything about the newspaper, in fact, and read all of it indiscrim-
inately: the girl Friday ads, the ship crossings, the fur auctions,
the stamp and coin columns, the bankruptcy proceedings, the
real estate listings. He looked at the car ads; he thought he'd
like to have a car of his own one day, a white T-Bird—those
were just out. He circled ads for small farms—$21,000 for five
acres with two wells and a stone farmhouse in Danbury. He
tore out the radio program schedule, underlining performances
by the Berlin Philharmonic, and the programs *The Secrets of
Scotland Yard* and *X Minus One,* though he never remembered
to listen to them. He never failed to look at the piano advertisements. Someone always wanted to sell a piano, it seemed;
nearly every day, one could buy a Steinway grand for about
$750. He never saw a Bosendorfer for sale; he thought he might
have bought one, no matter how much it cost, if he'd ever seen
one advertised. The newspaper, he thought, was proof of America's success, its limitless possibility. One could buy anything in
America: mink hats, skating rinks, boats, cigarette lighters that
played music when you opened them, shares in companies that
made everything from pipe fittings to chicken feed to vaccines
against polio.

Yes, yes, he had a newspaper, he told Aggie. There was a
Howard Johnson around the corner from the Y that had stayed
open despite the storm. He'd been able to eat there, and they
even had peach ice cream, a favorite of his and Aggie's. There

was a box for the *Hartford Courant* on the sidewalk outside the HoJo, but a waitress had kindly given him the restaurant's copy because the coin slot was frozen over.

They had talked for only a few minutes. He had never spoken to Toby.

"Everything's fine here. It's plenty warm," Aggie had said. "Toby brought wood in for Peggy. I think she's glad Dad's not here. She didn't even get dressed today."

And then they had hung up, and Arthur had lain in bed that night in his room at the YMCA, carefully folding over the pages of the *Hartford Courant*, his glasses on his nose, with the warm sound of Aggie's voice still in his ear.

It had been then, he thought now, in the embrace of a snowstorm, with a fire burning in the hearth, and no adult anywhere nearby. Of course.

Of course.

He hung his head desperately out the window.

"I know it was wrong," Toby said. He had gotten to his feet. Arthur could hear how his voice came from somewhere else now. He was coming nearer to Arthur.

The baby, Arthur thought. His heart knocked wildly against the wall of his chest.

"Dad," Toby was saying to him. "Dad?"

When he felt Toby's hand on his shoulder, Arthur's body gave a long and involuntary shudder. He turned around and stepped away from Toby, wiping his mouth with his hand.

"That is your child," he said. "That is your child who is being given away."

Toby's face was devastated.

"You don't love her. You want to fuck her only, because she is the daughter of your enemy." Arthur shuddered again. "You would fuck her here on the floor of this house, and you do not understand *anything*." His voice had risen. He heard himself shouting. "Now you will make me lose everything, everything. Everything I have worked to give you. . ."

Toby began to speak, but Arthur cut him off. "They find this out and we will be gone from here. They will cut me off with *nothing*." He was panting. "They will send me away, and the baby—*your* baby, *Aggie's* baby—will go away to strangers . . ." He had to stop, speechless at the dimensions of what yawned in front of him, the English words suddenly so unfamiliar, so crude and stumbling and insufficient. "We will have *nothing*," he shouted suddenly, his voice returning to him. "We will have nowhere to go. You have ruined her. You have ruined me. Nothing," he shouted incoherently. "Nothing."

Toby began to speak again. He was crying, but Arthur put his hands over his ears, backed away. "No," he said. "Don't tell me."

Toby came toward him, his hands outstretched, but Arthur struck out into the air between them, struck out repeatedly into the darkness, until he was sure Toby was gone.

LATER, HE REMEMBERED the clean sweep of air as his hand sliced through it again and again as if he were fending off an attack, how just then the world had seemed to divide, the continent of his past shearing off from the present.

At least he had not struck him, he thought. He tried to remember Anna's prayer for forgiveness, but no words would come, only the image of her lips moving, the clean part in her hair under the lamplight. They had found Anna's remains in the rubble of the Anderson shelter. They had found the baby's remains, one arm only, still in its little white woolen sleeve.

In the days after Toby disappeared, Arthur sat for hours alone in the orchard.

Had God been there in the room that night? he wondered. Had God blown a mighty breath between him and Toby, a wall of breath between father and son, trying to prevent the final harm?

I raised my hand against my son, Arthur thought, and put his head down on his arms. I raised my hand.

THE TRIP FOR WHICH Mr. Duvall had supposedly called Arthur back from the hospital never materialized. It was four days before he called the cottage, four days in which Toby had disappeared without a trace. Arthur had called all of Toby's friends, desperate and humiliated; only Tim Warren had been gentle, and Arthur thought he knew something about where Toby had gone. "Please, Tim," he said. "Please, tell him to call me."

Mr. Duvall's words, when Arthur answered the phone, were exactly as Arthur had predicted to Mrs. MacCauley so many weeks before.

"You can get Agatha tomorrow, Arthur," he said. "They're expecting you."

Arthur said nothing. He noted the way Mr. Duvall had phrased it, though, as if he knew Arthur had been waiting for permission.

"Arthur?"

"Yes," Arthur said. "OK."

"I'm coming home on Friday. You can pick me up at six. And Mrs. Duvall will be coming in Friday morning. Peggy has the flight information."

Again, Arthur said nothing. They're circling the wagons, he thought. It was a phrase Aggie had explained to him once, about American cowboys and Indians. They will shut me out, he thought.

"Arthur?" Mr. Duvall broke the silence. "Speak up. I can't hear you."

You're not coming home unless I come and get you, Arthur thought. "OK. Yes," he said at last. He did not trust himself to say anything more.

THERE HAD BEEN a mistake, and Arthur arrived at the hospital to get Aggie only to discover that she had been taken back to Breakabeen already and was waiting for him there. It was that error—the worst kind of error Mrs. MacCauley could have imagined, he thought—that put Arthur at the hospital on the same day that the couple who was adopting the baby arrived to take him home. Mrs. MacCauley's presence at the hospital early that afternoon as she walked with the couple to their car, Arthur's stumbling upon them as he left the hospital to drive to Breakabeen—all of it, he thought later, was like a joke. Had she seen him, had she known he was there, Mrs. MacCauley surely would have imagined that he would do something desperate—snatch the baby, accost the young couple. But that suspicion would only have suggested how little she knew him, Arthur thought, how little she understood about what had happened. He already understood that he had lost. He had no rights. No claim. Everything had been taken away from him. He knew, now, that it had been inevitable.

He followed the couple to their house in Wappingers Falls; he watched the man help his young wife from the car, leaning down to take her elbow, the baby a bundle in her arms. The setting sun struck the side mirror of Mr. Duvall's car and sent a blade of light into Arthur's eyes as he sat in the front seat, his mouth dry. The cool shadows of early evening had begun to lengthen over the little handkerchiefs of dusty lawn before the houses. Here and there a curtain had blown free of a window sash and lay limply over a sill. An ice cream truck pulled up at the far end of the block in the falling twilight under the rippling leaves of the street trees, its bell tinkling. When Arthur blinked, the man and woman were at their door.

When he took his hands away from his eyes, they were gone.

He had to turn around and drive back to Breakabeen then. He was late for Aggie, who had been expecting him for some hours. It was well past dinnertime by the time he drove up to the house, and Aggie was sitting alone on the steps under the portico. She looked so much like her old self that Arthur felt the disorientation that had plagued him all summer descend over him again.

Arthur embraced her, kissed her, helped carry her bag to the car. He did not meet her eyes. She ran inside once to tell Mrs. MacCauley she was leaving, but Mrs. MacCauley, who Arthur was sure had no desire to see him again, did not accompany her back outside.

When Aggie was settled in the seat beside him, Arthur drove away from the house. Neither he nor Aggie looked back. In a fairy tale, Arthur thought, the house would have vanished behind them like smoke.

"We'll be very late getting back," Aggie said finally into the silence of the car.

"Yes. It will be late." Arthur stared ahead through the windshield. The branches of the trees hung close over the road, which wound around sharp curves. The road seemed to have been cut out of the rock. In another month, Arthur thought, fall would begin and the woods to either side of them would be filled with golden light.

He reached over to turn on the radio. "You want some music?" A buzzing static filled the car. Arthur punched the buttons fruitlessly for a minute, but nothing came in clearly. He turned off the radio. Aggie sat silently beside him.

Arthur tried to push away the image of Toby and Aggie together, snow piling up on the windowsills, the fire dying. He tried to push away the image of Toby's face, the baby in the woman's arms, her husband helping her from the car, the ribbons on the porch railing of the house in Wappingers Falls. He wanted to go somewhere, he thought. Anywhere. The thing he'd always liked about driving was the way it seemed so easy just to go wherever you wanted, to drive all the way to California, if that was where you decided you wanted to go, your arm hanging out the window, your fingers tapping the steering wheel, until your tires ground into the sand at the edge of the Pacific Ocean. The whole country, the whole world, opened up to him sometimes when he was driving. Now, as darkness fell over the road, filling the woods beside them, engulfing the horizon, the Duvalls' house pulled him with an inevitable force, his route home narrowing like a pass through a chasm. He could drop his hands from the wheel, he thought, and the car would take them back there just the same.

He did not know what to say to Aggie, or how to break the news of Toby's disappearance, though even he did not then know how permanent, how final, that disappearance would be. Did she love Toby? he wondered. She had made her decision about the baby without his consent or his knowledge; but of course she had not made that decision alone, he remembered. The Duvalls had done that for her. What had she wanted, really, for herself?

He did not want to punish her. Surely there had been enough punishment for her already, hers the most painful punishment of all. That she had chosen to give herself to his son, that she had allowed the baby, the baby that was part of them all, to be taken from her—none of this, in the end, touched his own love for her, and though it lay now in his hands like a broken thing, he understood that it was only some version of his love that he looked at now, a skin that had been shed by something infinitely finer and more brilliant, something that would be revealed again when the time was right. The mystery of the thing was that it could not be seen.

They did not speak for most of the drive home, but when he turned onto the lane, Aggie said, "It's all right, Arthur. Take the car up to the barn. I'll walk down. I'd like to walk down." And so he turned off at the branch in the lane and headed up the hill toward his cottage and the barn.

He carried her bag for her, and they crossed the grass toward the cottage in the darkness. Arthur could not stop himself from looking for a light, hoping that Toby would have returned. It would be a long time before he would stop hoping for that.

She stopped at the door of the cottage. Her awkwardness as she hesitated, his sense that she understood that something had now changed between them, that she would no longer enter his home as if it were her own, broke through the wall of his bewilderment, his sorrow, his humiliation.

"He's not here, Aggie," he said gently. "He has gone away."

Aggie looked up at him. He saw her hand move reflexively over her belly and then fall away.

"What do you mean?"

And so he told her then. He drew her down to sit on the step beside him and he took her hand; and when she pulled her hand away to put her palms up over her face, turning away from Arthur, he didn't move. He just sat there, in case she needed him.

. . .

OVER THE NEXT few weeks and months they talked together sometimes about what had happened, until finally one day there seemed nothing left to say, and mention of Toby and the baby gradually fell away from their conversation like stones dropped into a deep pool, the ripples of their disappearance vanishing finally on the surface of the water. Arthur never told Aggie that he knew where the baby had been taken; he understood the darkness of those visits, their hold over him, and he wanted to protect himself from what Aggie would think of him if she knew.

And then one day, of course, the baby was gone, the family was gone, the house in Wappingers Falls was closed up, the window shades drawn.

There seemed nothing left to tell.

NINE

ON SATURDAY NIGHT, several hours after his interview with Aaron Adler, the young teacher at Rock Hall School, Arthur let himself into his cottage just as the sun was setting behind Wallace Mountain. The house was cold and dark. Arthur sat down on the bench by the back door in the kitchen to unlace his boots. For a long time after Toby went away, Arthur had found it hard to come into the house, where Toby's absence resided so powerfully. He had lingered outside, taking his meals on the stoop, reading until late at night under the porch light, going for walks, all stratagems of delay and avoidance.

He tugged off one boot now and sat back to rub his hands, which were thawing painfully after the walk up from the big house in the cold. By habit, his eyes avoided the dark sitting room, his dressmaker's dummy standing in the corner, and the dark stairwell that led upstairs into more darkness.

He didn't know how he would stand it when Aggie left.

Arthur had not lied to Aaron Adler: he told him he was the driver for a family in Creston, that his regular driving duties had lessened over the years, that he found himself now with time on his hands. All that, Arthur thought, was true.

Aaron had nodded enthusiastically. "Great. That's great. Hey, is there someone we can call for a reference?" Arthur gave him Peggy's name and the kitchen telephone at the big house. He'd have to explain something to her, he thought.

"How do I . . . how do I talk to them?" Arthur had ventured as he rose to leave the interview.

"You shouldn't need to say anything, really, but they all read lips pretty well," Aaron said. "They're not a rowdy bunch. They'll be all right. We can teach you some sign language if you're interested."

Aggie had been in New York the night before for dinner with her father; she'd left a note for Arthur on his kitchen table at some point during the day on Saturday, probably while he'd been at Rock Hall. "Let's go out for pizza," she'd written. "I'm at Tivoli. I'll come up when I get home."

Arthur had spent the afternoon helping Peggy, who was readying the house for the meeting Mr. Duvall planned to hold there Friday night. It had been a long time since he'd had people to the house. Pushing the vacuum over the rugs, Arthur thought that despite all his attentions, and Peggy's, the house had the air of a place that had stood vacant for a long time and had become, in the intervening years, slightly shabby and out of date. Mice had chewed at the fringe of the Oriental carpet in the living room. The silk drapes in the library were faded. Paint flaked from the plaster walls of the little sitting room Mr. Duvall used as his office when he was home. Arthur had pushed a chair over the tattered fringe of the carpet to hide the damage.

He sat for a moment now in his dark kitchen, his thoughts turning reflexively toward the little boy. What was he doing now, at six o'clock on a Saturday night? Having his bath, perhaps . . . a bath would be good, Arthur thought. He got up with effort. All these years of sleeplessness—they were catching up with him. A tiredness ran through him, a profound lack of desire. In the wake of Aggie's leaving, nothing would matter very much, he thought. But he would have to fight against that, like fighting against the tug of deep water. And there was still the boy—still the prospect of bringing the boy into the light, turning Aggie to face him. There was still the prospect that she might stay. What else if not that, he thought, might make her stay?

He ran the water in the tub very hot, so hot that he had to hold his breath when he sank down into it. His belly looked slack as he lay under the steaming water, his legs thin. He rubbed at his knuckles and fingernails with a brush.

He was dressed and combing his still-damp hair, frowning at himself in the mirror in his bedroom, when he heard Aggie's voice from downstairs.

"Yes. Up here," he called back to her.

From downstairs he heard music begin. Aggie had put a record on the phonograph. It was Mario Lanza, singing "Dein ist mein ganzes Herz," from *The Land of Smiles*. Aggie had given him the record, the tenor arias of Mario Lanza. The phonograph had been a birthday present for Toby when he turned sixteen. Arthur had never thrown away Toby's record albums. He'd never thrown away anything of Toby's; his jacket still hung in the narrow hall closet below the stairs, his room was just as he had left it eight years before, his architectural models lay on the shelves above his bed gathering dust. Occasionally Arthur put on one of the classical records Aggie had given him over the years, Mozart or Strauss or Franz Lehár, composers Aggie chose because they had lived in Vienna. She had always wanted to know more than he had felt able to tell her about his life before he came to America; he could never think of anything but the most irrelevant things, the faded flowers in the blue vase in the window of the *Konditoreien* near Julius's shop, the gray-green floes striated with white in the canal of the Danube in December, the enormous hunched shadow of the statue of Maria Theresa creeping over the grass in the gardens outside the Imperial Library one day shortly before he left Vienna forever. Everything he remembered seemed melancholy—Dr. Ornstein's long, sad face, the curiously white and clean half-moons at the base of each of his fingernails, the tiny hole made by a moth in the ankle of one of Dr. Ornstein's black stockings.

How much there was to remember; it surprised Arthur sometimes. But what was the point of it?

"Do you think you'd ever want to go back?" Aggie asked him once.

"I don't know anybody there," Arthur had said. "Anyway, it is not a good place for Jews."

AGGIE WAS SITTING on the footstool in front of the fire, her chin in her hand, when Arthur came downstairs. He sat down in his chair beside her. "So. How are the old people?" He touched the footstool with the toe of his shoe. His ankle in his old gray sock struck him as thin and repulsive; he withdrew his foot.

"A new guy moved in yesterday. He thinks he's Fred Astaire, dancing all over the place." Aggie lifted her arms and swayed. "He calls all the nurses Ginger. The others think he's crazy."

Arthur shrugged; the assessment made sense to him. He had been upset by some of the people he'd seen at Tivoli, the ones laced into wheelchairs with twisted sheets, the woman he'd glimpsed once, lying in a bed—she'd had no nose, only a black opening on her face where her nose had been. Last Christmas, at Aggie's request, he had brought in a tree cut from the woods down near the lake, and he had stayed that evening for the party to decorate it, moving awkwardly around the room carrying a tray of cups filled with spiced cider. The people who didn't seem to understand anything, who looked at him vacantly when he offered them cider, had made him embarrassed. He'd been sweating with anxiety, but Aggie hadn't seemed to notice. "Go talk to Mrs. Petty, Arthur," she'd whispered at one point, hugging his arm. "She's interesting. Just go along with whatever she says. Use your imagination."

But he had no imagination, Arthur thought. He watched Aggie as she stared into the fire. His mind was in a kind of arrested state, not daring to move out beyond the tether of the present. He did not dare think about Toby. He had not dared think, until the child's reappearance, about the grandson he had lost. Julius, and Ivo, and Anna, and the baby—what was the point of thinking about them, imagining what they might have become, what they might have meant to him as the years had gone by? Even Dr. Ornstein had drifted away from him as the years had passed, appearing less and less often in his dreams and thoughts, as if Arthur had failed to grasp some essential message Dr. Ornstein had tried to impart to him and had driven Dr. Ornstein away with his stupidity. He grew weaker every year, fainter, until now he was wraithlike in Arthur's dreams, a shimmering substance into which Arthur could plunge his hand, trying and failing to catch at his coat sleeve. He had discovered that he minded Dr. Ornstein's disappearance from his life more than God's. Of God he had never been certain, anyway, but at least he knew Dr. Ornstein had been real, had lived once, had known what it meant to have a man's heart, to play his fingers over the keys of his beautiful piano, to touch the mysterious wounds of his patients. Occasionally in his dreams, in a disquieting transposition, Arthur became Dr. Ornstein himself, sitting in the coffeehouse, and Aggie was Dr. Ornstein's slim, lovely daughter in her white lamé fencing foil, her face hidden behind the mask; this kind of confusion was worth nothing, Arthur thought. It was not imagination, at least. It was as good as senility.

Aggie pulled up her knees and wrapped her arms around her legs. At twenty-four, she had turned into a lovely woman, much more lovely, even, than he might once have predicted, Arthur thought, with a clarity of skin and eye and feature that made it a pleasure to gaze at her. He watched her, the firelight on her face. He cleared his throat. "They will miss you there, at Tivoli."

"I'll miss them." Aggie looked up at him and then back to the fire. "But it's time, Arthur. It's time for me to go."

Arthur looked away from her. On Monday morning, he thought, he would see the boy; perhaps he would even take his hand to help him up the steps of the little white bus Aaron had shown him.

"I've made a deal with Dad, Arthur," Aggie said then.

Arthur shifted in his chair. He did not know whether he wanted to hear about this deal or not.

"He wants me to stay until this weekend, until the party."

With some effort, Arthur made himself speak. "Yes?"

"I said OK. I guess it matters to him in some strange way that I'm here." She paused.

Arthur said nothing.

"I know you don't want to talk about it," she said. "I'm sorry."

Arthur held up his hand. She was wrong, he wanted the gesture to suggest; she overstated his feelings. He would be fine. But the fact of the boy's reappearance—his presence, so near to them at that very moment—lay between them. He did not want to talk to her in the way she wanted. He did not want to give her his blessing, much as he understood her desire to go away, much as he sympathized. He had found her child. And yet he still could not decide if it was a kindness or a cruelty to bring that child before her. If she knew he was there, she might stay, and there was the possibility that Arthur's world might be refashioned, he thought, that the places where pieces of it had been torn away might be healed. Or she might blame him forever and ever for showing her what she could not possess, showing her what she had lost. The difficulty of it, the sadness of it, the prospect of his aloneness—it was too much. He had to turn his face aside.

"Oh, *Arthur*." Aggie reached up and put her hand on his knee. "Arthur, don't make this so awful for me. Please."

He waved at her again, a gesture of what he hoped she would interpret as nonchalance. "OK," he said, getting to his feet. He would not cry in front of her like a child. He was pathetic. "Let us go and have pizza."

AARON ADLER RODE along with Arthur on Monday morning in order to introduce him to the children and show him the route. He sat in the seat behind Arthur's right shoulder, his elbows cocked over the bar, his young, beautiful face glowing with health and enthusiasm and innocence; beside him, Arthur suffered the truth that he had grown withered, old, full of a sickness that was the sickness of a world Aaron had missed through a fortunate accident of birth—though another war loomed now, too, darkening the horizon. It was 1964, almost twenty years since the war Arthur had lived through had ended, since the plains of the Ukraine and the forests of Poland had filled with the ghosts of the Jews, but Arthur thought it would never end, not really. They would always be there, wandering lost in the wilderness.

There were only six children on the bus route; most of Rock

Hall's students were boarders. That there were even six deaf children in Creston and its outskirts, a relatively rural area, was unusual, Aaron told Arthur. Two of the families had moved to the area because of Rock Hall, Aaron said, but the others? Aaron shrugged. They were just unlucky.

Arthur thought of God, folding his arms, turning his face away the day the baby was born. But what if it had been worse than that? What if God himself had marked the boy as a kind of punishment for his parents? What if he had reached down and touched the child's ears with his fiery fingertip, the world stunned into freakish silence inside the child's head? What was an accident? What was luck, good or bad? Did anything at all happen without God's intervention? Anna had liked to thank God for whatever fortunes befell them—a big commission for Julius, a tasty soup, Toby's birth. But the misfortunes? The murders? The deaths? How had she accounted for those? Arthur could not remember.

When Arthur turned the bus onto the boy's street, he felt his stomach tense. Aaron, who had turned around in his seat to sign something to the child behind him—a lumpen boy with pale skin and dark circles beneath his eyes—didn't seem to notice that Arthur stopped the bus in front of the boy's house, that he had known which house was the right one.

Arthur stared ahead through the windshield, paralyzed with fear. It had not occurred to him that the boy's mother might recognize him. What would she do now? Would she hurry down the walk to the street, pushing the boy ahead of her, and then recoil as she saw Arthur?

"There they are," Aaron said.

She was coming down the walk, a short gray coat thrown over her shoulders, her hand in her hair. The little boy ran ahead of her, his red scarf flying. Aaron stood up to speak to her. Arthur, his view of the child suddenly eclipsed, had to crane around Aaron to find the boy again . . . and there was Toby, running down the street in London beside the black iron fence, holding a stick that he clattered against the bars. "Stop it," Arthur had said, reaching down to take the stick. "People will be angry at your noise." A small funeral procession had crept past them, the cars filthy.

The boy leaped up the steps of the bus. His coat, unzipped, swept Arthur's shoulder as he ran past, heading for the back of the bus. The touch of it rippled through Arthur like the cracks that had spread across the ice when Toby and Aggie threw stones at the pond in winter, jagged lines running crazily over the ice.

The woman stood at the bottom of the steps.

"New driver," Aaron said, leaning over to speak to her. "I'm just showing him the route."

Arthur registered how attractive she was, the silken fall of her red hair, the gray, thickly lashed eyes, the round chin. He felt his lips move away from his teeth in a wretched smile. She looked at him for a moment, and he thought he saw hesitation in her gaze. Her smile faltered. Or did it? But then he reached out for the handle that pulled the doors closed, and in a moment they had shut her out.

His eyes swept the rearview mirror. The boy had clambered

into a seat toward the back of the bus. He knelt there, his hand raised to the glass, looking for his mother. She had stepped back, pulling the coat closed over her chest with one hand, raising the other toward the window. She backed away from the street as Arthur pulled the bus forward, the boy kneeling in the seat behind him, waving and waving at his mother.

"Well, that's all of them," Aaron said. "Think you can manage?"

Arthur found it difficult to speak. "Their names," he said. "I will forget their names."

"That's Jonathan who just got on," Aaron said. He turned around. "Dan, with the glasses. Lizzie, Frank, Sam . . ."

Arthur glanced in the rearview mirror as Aaron ran through the children's names again. The little boy had sat down finally. Arthur could see only a fraction of his head. Jonathan. It was strange to have him named after so long.

Aaron folded his arms over the bar again and watched the road ahead with Arthur. "Some families are better than others about having a deaf kid. Jonathan's mother, Mrs. Daniel, she's great."

Arthur tried to compose his face. "Yes?"

"Isn't he a beautiful kid? Did you ever see hair that color?" Aaron leaned back in the seat. "His father's just left for Virginia, a military contract at Langley. He's an electrician, does something with fighter jets. She's worried he's going to end up in Vietnam. He's been gone a lot."

Arthur turned the bus onto Route 6. A plow had been through, and the road was scraped down to a hard layer of gray, shoulder-high walls of snow to either side. The light from the fields of perfect white snow was too bright, aching with brightness.

Aaron hooked his arms over the bar again. "Well, so that's the drill. You're OK?"

Arthur didn't answer for a moment. He was looking into the rearview mirror, his gaze lingering on Jonathan, the narrow chin, the small shoulders, one little hand holding the bar of the seat in front of him. He sat quietly, his face turned toward the window. An ugly gathering of crows suddenly wrenched away from the white fire of the field near the gritty edge of the road, swerved into the air, and headed toward the snow-laden firs ahead, flapping slowly and heavily as if weighted down.

"Arthur?"

"Yes. OK." Arthur dragged his eyes back to the road and took a breath. "OK."

"Can you stand, sir?" Julius had said to Dr. Ornstein in the street after the troopers had left. They had all been speaking in whispers. The street had been empty except for a figure or two hurrying from doorway to doorway in the quivering darkness, trying to get home. "You can stand? Yes? Come with me, sir. It's all right now." Julius had blanched as Dr. Ornstein mutely held out his bloody hands, his mouth trembling, his skin gray. Together, Julius and Arthur had grasped the doctor under his arms and lifted him. Arthur's hands could remember the feel of the little man, how weightless he had been. His color had been sickening, his trousers filthy from the street. Arthur had been afraid Dr. Ornstein might have a heart attack as he leaned into them, his chest heaving. "My God," Julius had said under his breath. "My God. What is the sense of it?" There had been vile-smelling stains on Dr. Ornstein's trousers, blood on his shirt-front and running from his nose.

They nearly dropped him when a horse and carriage clattered past, careening wildly over the stones, disappearing through an archway. An old waiter from the coffeehouse, ancient and splayfooted, a bottle of brandy clasped beneath one elbow, had hurried out to help them. He held open the door of the coffeehouse, then bolted it behind them once they were safely inside—an absurd gesture, Arthur remembered, for the front window had been smashed. The waiter kept repeating Dr. Ornstein's name, calling him "good doctor," "good sir." There was spittle gathered in the corners of his mouth; the four glasses he held in his hand rattled and chinked from his trembling. "Let me help you," they had all said, again and again, bending over Dr. Ornstein while he held his hand to his heart and closed his eyes. "Here. Let us help you."

Arthur glanced back in the mirror of the bus again. Dr. Ornstein sat beside Jonathan, the two of them watching together out the window. Dr. Ornstein stooped his shoulders a little so that he could peer out through the glass over the boy's head. He put a hand on Jonathan's head, stroked his shining hair, letting his old hand linger there.

Arthur closed his eyes briefly, opened them again to the glare of the road. When he glanced into the mirror again, Jonathan was alone.

When the children left the bus, filing down the aisle

and—every one of them—jumping the last step, Arthur had seen his own hand go out toward the boy, toward Jonathan's head, as he filed past. But Arthur had missed him, his hand caressing the air. Arthur had leaned forward, wanting to slip his arms into the child's wake, wanting to wear it, the shape of the child billowing, his little footsteps thudding on the snow-covered ground as he ran away.

It was like that every day, all week long. Arthur could hardly steer for looking at Jonathan in the rearview mirror of the little bus.

Dr. Ornstein never appeared again.

Where are you? Arthur asked the empty bus. Speak to me. But the doctor never answered, any more than God had ever answered. Dr. Ornstein just sat slumped in the chair in the coffeehouse, his eyes closed, his face gray and sweating, one mangled hand crossed over his chest.

FRIDAY NIGHT, THE NIGHT of Mr. Duvall's dinner party, Arthur came down to the big house to help Peggy in the kitchen. He sat at the table, a flowered apron tied around his waist, his glasses on his nose, spooning mashed potato into the baked, hollowed-out skins. At six, Aggie came into the kitchen, her shoes in her hand. She was wearing a red dress that Arthur had made for her a few years before, the bodice tight, the skirt full. The narrow belt had rhinestones on it. She put her shoes on a chair and sat down across from Arthur.

She had spent every evening that week up at the cottage with him. They had played games on the trunk that Arthur used as a table in front of the sofa: Parcheesi, checkers, chess, gin rummy. His eyes had kept filling up with tears. She had held his head between her hands as he sat across from her, their knees almost touching.

"Oh, Arthur," she had said. "Don't."

Once or twice he had thought she would relent, that there was something in her expression that spoke of her indecision, her uncertainty, and his heart had thrilled in an ugly way: she would not leave him.

But she never said she would stay. And he could not decide what to do about the boy.

They walked sometimes after dark, he and Aggie, out into the fields in the moonlight and down toward the lake through the whispering grove, where little clouds of snow here and there drifted silently to the ground. She took his arm and held it tightly and they said hardly anything between them. But the enormous strength of her kindness, their kindness toward each other, the losses they carried between them, were present all the time. "You don't have to stay here, Arthur," she said once, when they sat on the stoop outside his front door, staring out into the moonlight that illuminated the fields almost like day, the strangeness of the light magical and sad. "Dad can get someone else to drive him. You're not *worried* about him, are you?"

He had not known how to tell her that he was afraid to leave because he hoped Toby would come back one day. What would happen if he came back and there was a stranger in the cottage? How would he ever find Arthur again?

Aggie pulled one leg up beneath her and leaned over the kitchen table, watching Arthur fill the potato skins.

Arthur glanced up at her over his glasses.

She frowned, looked away from his eyes.

Peggy came over with a platter of smoked salmon. "You want to take this in to them?"

"Do I *want* to? No, I don't want to." Aggie took the tray from Peggy and set it down on the table. Peggy had dressed for the evening in her black uniform, over which she wore her old apron now. There were seven men at the house that night for dinner, including Mr. Duvall, and five women. Aggie said one of wives was not a wife at all but someone's mistress, and that her father had been angry that she'd been brought along. "What a hypocrite," she said. She ran her fingers restlessly through her hair. "He's taking his pound of flesh." She closed her eyes.

"It is an expression?" Arthur said.

"Yes. It is. It means—"

"These have got to go in," Peggy said stubbornly.

"OK." Aggie got up and took the platter. "I'm sorry."

She left the room. Peggy returned to the stove. "You're making it hard for her," she said.

Arthur put down the spoon he'd been using to mound the potatoes.

"Don't make it so hard for her," Peggy repeated. "She needs to go, Arthur."

"You think I don't know it? I know it." Arthur brought the tray of filled potatoes over to her. She opened the oven door for him, and he pushed the tray inside.

"You're not making it hard?" He was angry, though he knew he had no right to be angry at her. "You make it so easy for her?"

"Take those bottles in there. Put them on the sideboard." Peggy didn't look at him.

Arthur grabbed the wine bottles and pushed through the swinging door into the pantry that led into the dining room. Only the wall sconces over the sideboard had been turned on, and the table stretched out into the dusk of the room, where the white linen cloth, the crystal glassware, and the silver bowls of white roses laid down the table's center glowed in a ghostly way. Arthur walked around the table and went to stand by the window, staring out into the snow and the darkness.

All week he had watched Jonathan through the rearview mirror on the bus in a fever of longing. The little boy never made any sign of recognition or greeting. That morning, though, he had dropped a red mitten in the snow by the bus; Arthur, staring at it for an instant, had suddenly heaved himself from his seat to snatch it up in his hand and hurry after the child.

"Jonathan," he called. "Jonathan." And then he remembered. When he caught up to the child at the door, he put a hand on his shoulder and the boy turned, startled, to look up at him. Arthur held out the mitten, and their fingers met for an instant. And when the boy leaned forward quickly to hug him, his head butting the front of Arthur's coat before the school door opened and he ran inside, Arthur's breath left him for a moment.

Sometimes in his dreams of Dr. Ornstein, Arthur had been a pursuer weighted down as if by deep water, unable to move quickly enough, or at all sometimes, as Dr. Ornstein fell under the blows of the men who leaped from the truck, heavy-booted, arms and legs cocked unnaturally like the swastikas they wore on their sleeves, their clubs whirling. Sometimes Dr. Ornstein was a skater who sped away down the frozen surface of the canal, his hands laced nonchalantly behind his back, the tails of his white doctor's coat flapping. Arthur had felt his mouth frozen when he tried to call out, his tongue foolish and clumsy. Sometimes he had just stood in the archway of Dr. Ornstein's apartment and watched the doctor's hands running over the keys of the piano, tears running down his face.

As Arthur stared out the window, a small herd of deer, twelve, thirteen of them, moved out from under the trees and across the lawn toward the shrubs by the house, their legs stiff like the limbs of marionettes, their movements hesitant, wary.

He turned when he heard the door to the dining room open. Mr. Duvall stood against the light. Arthur turned back to the window.

After a moment Mr. Duvall came into the room. "The house looks very nice," he said. "Peggy says you've been helping her, Arthur. Thank you."

Arthur looked back at him. Mr. Duvall moved away. He leaned his stick up against the table and withdrew a matchbook from a drawer in the sideboard, striking a match and raising the hurricane globe over the tall white candle on the sideboard. He lit the candles at both ends of the sideboard, soundlessly replacing the glass chimneys, and then he reached for the light switch to turn off the lights. Arthur watched him for a moment and then turned away to look out the window again. He felt Mr. Duvall cross the carpet and come to stand near him at the next window, looking out over the snow. Together they watched the deer progress slowly over the hillside, heads raised, alert. Arthur was aware of the silence in the room.

"You have nothing to say to me?" Mr. Duvall had not moved from the window.

Arthur waited. His mouth had gone dry. Your grandson, he wanted to say. My grandson. They have called him Jonathan.

"What was his name?" Arthur turned abruptly to face him. "Mr. Duvall, what was my son's name?"

Mr. Duvall made a noise of what sounded to Arthur like disgust. "You think I'm a fool," he said.

"His name was Toby," Arthur said.

Mr. Duvall's hand moved irresolutely toward his ear, fell away. "I know his name, Arthur. You should be careful now."

Tomorrow, Aggie would leave, Arthur thought. He had already been told by Mr. Duvall that he was to drive Aggie to the airport.

"You don't have to," Aggie had said. "Arthur, look at me. You don't have to. I'll be back. Or you can come visit. Please."

How he loved her, Arthur thought. He loved her in a way he had never loved Anna, whose presence had never held for him this threat of loss; though he had to wince at the irony of how absolute her loss had been, in the end. But he had loved Aggie with an operatic love, a fawning, hysterical, agonized, moaning love, a love in which he had to reckon with his body and its demands, the urge to touch her cheek, her neck, her breasts, to pull her to him. Everything with Anna had been allowed; with Aggie, none of it. When he had touched her as a child, fastening her coat under her chin, forcing her feet into her skates, holding her hand, he had not known what he held.

"He is deaf," Arthur said. "The boy is deaf."

Mr. Duvall turned toward him.

"It was you," Arthur went on. "Now I know it. At the hospital. The night he was born. You were in the car. You signed the papers. You gave away our grandchild. Our deaf grandchild. Someone drove you there."

Now he knew he had surprised him, and he felt the satisfaction of it. It was something, to take Lee Duvall by surprise, a kind of wretched triumph. "You think *I* am the fool. Well, you are right." He gave a little laugh. "I *am* the fool. We are both fools."

Mr. Duvall was silent beside him, but Arthur glanced at him long enough to see that he had delivered a blow. Mr. Duvall was thinking fast, trying to take in what Arthur had said. So now Arthur *did* know something that Mr. Duvall didn't know, hadn't guessed, hadn't been able to ferret out.

"Toby?" Mr. Duvall said. "It was Toby?"

"He looks exactly like him," Arthur said. He moved close to Mr. Duvall and stood before him. "Only there is this." He touched his own ear, then reached into the air by Mr. Duvall's temple, and he felt a tremendous, surprising sorrow as he did it. He remembered his first night in the Duvalls' house, remembered how cold the sheets had been when he slipped in beside Toby that night and gathered his little boy's body to him, the snow's light held trembling in the window, the Lehmans in their cold twin beds under the eaves. "Nothing," he said finally, quietly. He snapped his fingers. "He hears nothing."

Mr. Duvall stared back at Arthur in the flickering candlelight.

"I miss my son," Arthur said. "I sent him away because of you, because I was afraid of you, of what you would do to us." He put his hand to his chest. "But you could have kept him here, with us," he said, "—the baby. Why didn't you want to keep him?"

He realized as he said it that the question was genuine, that it arose now not out of rancor, or spite, or even hatred. He could not *understand* it, how Mr. Duvall could have given away the baby. It did not matter anymore if Mr. Duvall knew the truth, Arthur thought, or that he knew what had happened between Aggie and Toby. They should all know the truth now.

Why had Mr. Duvall given the baby away?

"Toby?" Mr. Duvall's face looked drawn, a pugilist's deflated features.

Arthur shrugged, the gesture conveying his disgust, the waste of it all. "Now she will go away to California. And you and I will be left here."

"The boy . . ." Mr. Duvall searched Arthur's face.

How old he looked, Arthur thought. Arthur turned away, frowning. So they were both old now. That is what happened. But he did not want to give Jonathan to Mr. Duvall.

"You *know* the child? Arthur?"

Arthur backed away. "I heard it," he said. "I heard about it."

"You're lying." Mr. Duvall reached for his stick. "You've kept enough secrets, Arthur. You tell me this. You tell me!"

"I will tell you nothing! Nothing!" Arthur stepped up close to Mr. Duvall's face. It was as close as he had ever come to him. Once, years before, Mr. Duvall had shaken his hand. Arthur could not remember the occasion at first, and then he realized that it had been at Mrs. Duvall's funeral, after the funeral. Mr. Duvall had passed him at the cemetery and had shaken his hand. He had shaken the hands of many people that day, and Arthur had thought it was a strange custom, as though the survivor were being congratulated for some solemn, even regrettable, stroke of good fortune.

Arthur had not driven Mr. Duvall to the cemetery that day; Aggie and her father had ridden in a limousine from the funeral home, so Arthur had driven himself, in Mr. Duvall's car. He did not know whether Mr. Duvall had distinguished Arthur, standing there that morning with his hat in his hand, from all the other people there, the people who had come even though they did not like Mrs. Duvall, even though they knew she was a drunk, even though they did not like Lee Duvall or were afraid of him. Mr. Duvall had passed down the chain of hands, Arthur's hand just one of many. None of them had meant anything to him.

"You tell *me* something," Arthur said now. "Who will mourn your daughter when she goes away to California tomorrow on the airplane? I will take her there, I will carry her suitcases, I will wave good-bye to her. *I* will mourn her. I will mourn her as I mourn my own son, as I mourn the baby we gave away. Between us, you and me. Between us we gave it away."

Mr. Duvall's hands fluttered over his stick.

"Go there, Arthur. Come here, Arthur. Wait for me here, Arthur. Don't be late, Arthur. Do not notice my mistress, Arthur, do not have any opinion about how I spend my money, Arthur, how I treat my child, how I treat my wife, how I live my life." Arthur stopped, breathing hard. "I had a son who was waiting for me," he said. He stared at Mr. Duvall. "You gave away the boy once. You do not get him back now. I will not give him to you. I will keep this." He hit his chest once, hard, and then again, as if Mr. Duvall had missed it, and then he backed away and left the room.

Aggie was in the library, standing in her red dress in front of the fire, her hands behind her back, open to the warmth of the flames. Arthur stopped in the doorway. The conversation in the room came to a halt.

"Excuse me." Agatha slipped through the crowd, came toward him. He turned away into the hall. In the closet he found an old coat of Mrs. Duvall's, a fur. He turned around and held it out to her. She looked at him for a long moment. And then she came and turned her back to him, and he helped her into the coat, letting it fall over her shoulders. He turned her to face him, did up the clasp at the neck.

They went out the front door together, Arthur's hand under her elbow.

"Your coat," she murmured. "You have no coat."

But the car was at the end of the path at the front door, and Arthur turned on the engine and the heater; a blast of cold air shot out at their feet. Aggie burrowed down into the coat, but she said nothing. Arthur turned the car around and drove down the lane. Behind him, in the mirror, he watched the lights of the house recede into the snowy wilderness.

He drove carefully. "Are you all right? You are cold?" he asked at one point.

"I'm fine," she said.

A little later, as they drew near Creston, she said, "Where are we going?"

The little boy, little Jonathan, would be asleep, his head on his pillow, Arthur thought. He wanted to take her there, to the street outside Jonathan's house, to have her know what he knew at last: that the child she had given away was within reach, that she could lay her eyes upon him if she wanted, that he was well, safe, unharmed. She had said to him once, "Maybe it's better like this, Arthur. We didn't love each other in that way, Toby and I. I mean, that's what I think now—that we didn't love each other, really. I didn't think it then. But you know that."

It gave him the worst kind of comfort, he thought, to know that in the end Aggie had not loved his son in the enduring way of true lovers.

HE HAD STAYED by her all that first fall after Toby left, after the baby had been given away. In the long years afterward, they had kept each other busy with crossword puzzles and walks and a new dog and, in the spring, endless games of chess played on a card table they set up in the orchard. He'd become a good chess player, careful, wily, almost prescient. She had gone away to college the next fall, to Barnard, in the city, and she had come home on the weekends and shown him her books, explained her studies. Boredom had troubled them sometimes, boredom with their separate lives, with each other even, but they had waited it out with the faith of the long married. He had wanted to kiss her a thousand times, wanted to take her into his bed and make love to her with a passion he knew himself capable of only in her presence; but he had been content— he had been happy even—with her hand in his sometimes, her arm linked inside his own when they went out to walk. She'd dated various men in college; she told him about them. He'd discovered the ways in which he could manage disinterest or at least fatherly concern. Sometimes she fell asleep in his cottage, and those were the worst moments, when he sat in his chair across from her and watched her sleeping on the sofa in the firelight, his hands pressed together between his knees, his hands over his mouth, his hands over his eyes, his head in his hands.

Aggie sleeping. Those were his moments of greatest temptation, when he could look at her without restraint. But of course sleep itself was elusive, too. No wonder he longed for it with her, longed to lie down beside her and take her into his arms and sleep the blissful sleep of the dreamless, of the unafraid, of the lucky.

She might stay. She might stay if she saw the boy, he thought.

"Arthur," she said, "I have to tell you something."

He had turned onto the street. He glanced at her.

"Just pull over, please?" She moved inside her mother's fur coat, gathering her legs up beneath her, and he caught the smell of Nina Duvall, her perfume, something troubling, disturbing in the air. This was Aggie, he thought, disconcerted.

"I want you to look at me," she said.

They stopped in front of the house. Arthur gave a deep sigh. There were no lights on, though in the house across the street there was the sound of music, voices, the smell of smoke issuing from the chimney. Cars crowded the curb. The people who lived there were having a party. He remembered that Aaron had said that Jonathan's father had gone away, and he felt fear, another war looming.

He turned his face away from the bright lights of the busy house across the street, looked again at the little boy's house, Jonathan's house. He would grow up to be brilliant, he thought. A scholar. A mathematician. You did not need to hear to understand science, did you? There was always reading. He could be a doctor.

The car had warmed up, but his feet still felt cold.

"I have something to tell you, too," he said.

They fell silent, though, and he wondered what she was thinking, what she wanted to say to him now.

After a moment, she spoke into the darkness. "When I was little," she said, "I used to pray that my parents would die and that you'd adopt me. I wanted to live with you and Toby forever. I thought I could move out of the big house and come to live in the cottage with you."

Arthur said nothing. Here is your son, Aggie, he thought. Here is your son, sleeping.

"I would be like Wendy in *Peter Pan*. Remember Wendy?"

Arthur had read the book to Aggie and Toby one winter. He'd found it a terrifying story.

Aggie went on. "I would cook for you, and keep house. It was all I wanted. I used to lie in bed at night and fantasize about it." She shifted again in the seat beside him. "And then I grew up. And I had the baby, and Toby went away, and my mother died."

Don't leave, Arthur thought. Please don't leave me.

He would show her the boy. He could have everything back; through Jonathan, he could have Toby back, and Aggie would stay with him . . .

Aggie looked away, made a restless movement, as if she would get out of the car, and Arthur tensed.

"Whatever might have happened," she said then, "—I don't know. But I know what I *did* have. And I know what you were to me then. What you are now. In another lifetime, Arthur —" She stopped and laughed a little. "Don't I sound old? In another lifetime, as if this one were over?" She turned to him. "Don't do this to me, Arthur. I can feel it, what we know and don't say. We've felt it all this time. It's partly because of this that I want to go now."

He opened his mouth, but she put up her hand. "Don't say it," she said. "Don't say it. Just let me go. The way you've loved me all these years—now just let me go and then we'll always have it."

"I have nothing," he said.

But that was wrong, he thought, because she reached over to him then and they collided clumsily in the front seat, her forehead bumping against his mouth, her mouth against his collar, all the old stratagems of avoidance and carefulness and awareness of risk and danger still between them. And yet there was something else, as well, that had been there all along: their desire and their sorrow and what they had managed, some-how—with the grace of God, Arthur thought, suddenly hum-ble, struck by the infinitely graceful and merciful action of everything he did not understand—to keep alive between them.

PUT IT IN YOUR POCKET, Dr. Ornstein said to him the next morning, and Arthur put Aggie's letter, left for him on his kitchen table, into the pocket of his coat. She had taken a cab to the airport. "Don't worry," she had written.

I will ride with you, Dr. Ornstein said graciously, and Arthur drove down the lane from the Duvalls', back the way he had come the night before, back to the boy's house.

No need to speak, Dr. Ornstein said, holding up his hand. I am with you.

The morning was cold, overcast, snow in the forecast. Arthur had listened to the radio in the kitchen while he made coffee, strong, black, thick coffee into which he spooned whipped cream, the exercise like the movement of limbs that had lain asleep, a giant under the continent, for years and years.

Arthur checked his watch. It was early, but maybe not too early to call on a stranger.

He could learn sign language, he thought. He could teach Jonathan to ice-skate, to play chess, to steer a sled down the long, thrilling hill from the barn. A dog, he thought. Maybe the boy would like a dog.

He got out of the car in front of the boy's house.

I wait here, Dr. Ornstein said. Go on.

Arthur hesitated at the curb. He had shaved that morning, his hands trembling as he watched himself in the mirror. By the time he awakened, Aggie would be gone already, she'd told him.

You'll be here when I get back? Arthur wanted to lean down and look at Dr. Ornstein full in the face, but the early morning sunlight filled the car's window. His own face looked back at him when he stooped down.

You're the driver, Dr. Ornstein said.

The telephone number was in Canada, Aggie's letter said, an exchange at the Université du Québec. Toby had a roommate, her letter said, so either one of them might answer the phone. That was like her, Arthur thought, to have prepared him for a stranger's answering the phone.

How much had she known? Everything, he supposed. Or at least she had guessed everything. And he? He had known nothing. He had never imagined that Toby had been in touch with her, that he would have left the end to be played out by Aggie's hand alone. And indeed it had been hers to decide, Arthur acknowledged, hers the first and greatest loss, all the justice hers to imagine, the final mercy hers to bequeath.

What are you waiting for?

He put his feet into the fresh snow, hesitated, stared down at his footprints as they appeared behind him.

"You'll know what to do," Aggie had written in her letter.

Somehow, he thought, when the woman opened the door, her face grave but not unwelcoming, the little boy at her skirts, smiling up at him in recognition, Aggie had been right.

He would find the words to say. He would find the words to say who he was, why he was there, and what he imagined, everything he could ever have imagined.

ACKNOWLEDGMENTS

Many friends and colleagues were generous with their time and knowledge over the course of my work on this novel, and their contributions, small and large, were all significant. Thanks go to my husband, John Gregory Brown, and to my editor, Shannon Ravenel, and also to Lisa Johnston, Scott and Phoebe Hyman, Jonathan Green, Allen Huszti, Ed Schwartzschild, Stella Suberman, Tiffany Cummings, and lastly, especially, Jennifer Brice, for long and fruitful conversations about storytelling, for her friendship, and for getting me out to walk and talk, rain or shine, come hell or high water and sometimes both.

READERS GUIDE

Discussion Questions

1. When Arthur and Toby arrive at the estate, Arthur is terrified of making any kind of mistake that will jeopardize his position. How does Arthur's experience in Austria and London define the way he behaves in America and at the Duvalls'? Does his code of conduct evolve?

2. Secrecy—what information should be shared, when, and how—is a major theme in *Confinement*, and each character bears the burden of truth differently. What do the ways in which Arthur, Mr. and Mrs. Duvall, Aggie, Toby, and Mrs. MacCauley handle the truth say about them? Is it always better to know the truth?

3. Arthur poses many hypothetical questions about the existence of God, and is basically uncomfortable with his Jewish identity, yet he often reflects on Anna's biblical stories, and the memory of Dr. Ornstein emerges at key points throughout Arthur's life. How does Arthur's uniquely personal spirituality shape his decisions? What does Dr. Ornstein seem to represent?

4. Explore the various forms of prejudice the characters in *Confinement* encounter. To what extent do these societal,

interpersonal, and intergenerational power struggles each play a role in defining alliances? How do certain characters subvert stereotypes, and to what end?

5. Within the first hundred pages of *Confinement*, the identity of the father of Aggie's child is revealed. Did knowing this crucial fact early on alter your expectations? Why do you think the author arranges the sequence of events the way she does?

6. Arthur makes a startling accusation when he confronts Toby about his physical relationship with Aggie. Do you agree or disagree with Arthur's interpretation of Toby's actions? Why?

7. Aggie and her friend Loretta decide that the reason Mrs. MacCauley maintains the house for unwed mothers is because she herself never recovered from her own experience. In your opinion, what are Mrs. MacCauley's motivations? When all is said and done, do you think she deserves Arthur's pity?

8. It could be argued that Mr. and Mrs. Duvall are products of their era and social class and that Aggie was a victim of circumstance. Arthur strongly believes that the Duvalls could have—and should have—taken an alternative course of action. Do you?

9. Knowing how much pain he has endured as a result of being in love with someone who can never know his true feelings, why does Arthur choose to place himself in temptation's path again by interviewing for the bus driver position? What does love mean for Arthur?

10. Toby has a loving but complicated relationship with his father. As you read the scenes in which he criticizes Arthur for not being more assertive, did you find yourself agreeing with Toby or wanting to defend Arthur?

11. Discuss the significance of the book's title—and how the author's use of imagery reinforces the theme of confinement.

12. In her departing letter, Aggie gives Toby's contact information to Arthur and writes, "You'll know what to do." How does Arthur interpret her message? What do you think Arthur will do with all of the information now in his possession?